MASTER
of
SWORDS

ANGELA KNIGHT

BERKLEY SENSATION, NEW YORK

THE BERKLEY PUBLISHING GROUP
Published by the Penguin Group
Penguin Group (USA) Inc.
375 Hudson Street, New York, New York 10014, USA
Penguin Group (Canada), 90 Eglinton Avenue East, Suite 700, Toronto, Ontario M4P 2Y3, Canada
(a division of Pearson Penguin Canada Inc.)
Penguin Books Ltd., 80 Strand, London WC2R 0RL, England
Penguin Group Ireland, 25 St. Stephen's Green, Dublin 2, Ireland (a division of Penguin Books Ltd.)
Penguin Group (Australia), 250 Camberwell Road, Camberwell, Victoria 3124, Australia
(a division of Pearson Australia Group Pty. Ltd.)
Penguin Books India Pvt. Ltd., 11 Community Centre, Panchsheel Park, New Delhi—110 017, India
Penguin Group (NZ), Cnr. Airborne and Rosedale Roads, Albany, Auckland 1310, New Zealand
(a division of Pearson New Zealand Ltd.)
Penguin Books (South Africa) (Pty.) Ltd., 24 Sturdee Avenue, Rosebank, Johannesburg 2196,
South Africa

Penguin Books Ltd., Registered Offices: 80 Strand, London WC2R 0RL, England

This is a work of fiction. Names, characters, places, and incidents either are the product of the author's imagination or are used fictitiously, and any resemblance to actual persons, living or dead, business establishments, events, or locales is entirely coincidental. The publisher does not have any control over and does not assume any responsibility for author or third-party websites or their content.

MASTER OF SWORDS

A Berkley Sensation Book / published by arrangement with the author

ISBN: 978-0-7394-7368-9

BERKLEY SENSATION®
Berkley Sensation Books are published by The Berkley Publishing Group,
a division of Penguin Group (USA) Inc.,
375 Hudson Street, New York, New York 10014.
BERKLEY SENSATION is a registered trademark of Penguin Group (USA) Inc.
The "B" design is a trademark belonging to Penguin Group (USA) Inc.

PRINTED IN THE UNITED STATES OF AMERICA

This book is dedicated to my grandmother, Naomi Williams. All her life, Grandmother has been a gracious southern lady whose kindness and purity of spirit has been an example to her daughter, grandchildren, and great-grandchildren.

Master of Swords is also dedicated to my mother, Gayle Lee, who has cared for my grandmother with such unstinting love; and for my father, Paul Lee, who has been so generous in seeing to his mother-in-law's care. You both have provided a beautiful example of love, patience, and faithfulness in the most difficult circumstances imaginable.

I would like to also dedicate this book to all the families struggling with Alzheimer's disease. I wish there really was a Sanctuary where those suffering from the disease could regain themselves. It's my most sincere prayer that one day there will be.

AUTHOR'S NOTE

The Black Grail destroyed in chapter two of this book is the same as the one seen destroyed at the end of the previous book, *Master of Wolves*. The incident is related from another point of view.

MASTER
of
SWORDS

PROLOGUE

Camelot
402 A.D.

Through a haze of red exhaustion, Gawain watched his rival reel and fall from his sword stroke. The last of his five opponents.

Thank Jesu.

He turned, his broken ribs screaming, and blinked hard, trying to free his eyelashes from the blood that tacked them together. Taking a step forward, he almost fell over one of the knights he'd defeated. Agony shafted up his thigh as he fought to regain his footing. His leather leggings hung heavy and wet, and he knew the wound in his thigh was responsible.

Cold. It was June, but he felt like the depths of winter. He'd lost too much blood.

A blurred ring of faces surrounded him. As he crossed the combat circle, their applause and cheers came to him as if from a great distance. A robed woman hurried past—one of Merlin's newly created witches, intent on healing the men he'd bested.

No, not a witch, a Maja. They were called Majae now. He had to remember that.

Just as he was about to become a Magus. *If* the boy wizard found him worthy. Merlin had refused three other winners so far, though no one knew why.

He looked across the combat grounds to the two slender figures standing next to Arthur. Merlin and his lover, Nimue. To look at him, you'd think the wizard too young to shave, what with that narrow, thin face and stripling's body. At least until you looked into his eyes.

Something powerful and ancient looked out of Merlin's eyes, something far more god than boy.

Gawain took a step toward the wizard, but the world revolved around him, forcing him to stop in his tracks and grit his teeth. *I will not fall in front of him.* He'd endured too much to ruin it with weakness now.

Locking his gaze on the boy who was no boy, he dragged his right leg forward another step. And then his left.

Plop. Plop. Plop. The crowd had gone silent as they watched his struggle. Gawain could hear the slow, steady drip of his own blood hitting the sand.

Another step. And another. He seemed to be looking at Merlin through a long gray tunnel.

At last, thank Jesu, he reached his destination. From the corner of one eye, he saw King Arthur gravely watching. Arthur, whose dark hair had once been shot through with gray, yet who now looked younger than Gawain.

But it was Merlin whose gaze held him. He thought he saw stars shoot across those black irises.

I should kneel, Gawain thought distantly. He tried to bend his knee, only to sway, almost pitching onto his face. *Perhaps not.*

For lack of a better alternative, he braced his legs apart like a horse run until it was all but dead. Next to Merlin's elegant delicacy, he felt like a horse in truth, all towering dumb muscle. "My King," he rasped to Arthur. Then, in a careful bow of the head to Merlin, "My lord."

"You fought well," Merlin said in that surprisingly lilting voice. "You showed courage, yes, but then, all of Arthur's knights are courageous. But you also fought with intelligence, and most importantly, with honor. You have won the right to my Gift." He extended a hand, and Gawain looked down. For a moment, those long, pale fingers were empty.

Then light flashed, and the Grail filled them.

Gawain caught his breath. It resembled no other cup he'd ever seen with its elegant, impossible lines. Within it, sparks danced on the surface of a glowing blue liquid. Alien as it looked, the potion smelled delicious, like honey and sunlight and a woman's kiss, impossibly seductive.

Yet gazing down into those sparkling blue depths, he felt a sudden shaft of fear.

"The final test is this," Merlin said softly. "If you drink of my cup, you will become immortal, but you will also watch your mother and your father and your brothers die, and then your brother's children, and their children, and theirs, and so on through time. Your life will be a thing of blood and struggle as you fight to save your fellow humans from themselves. You may eventually guide them to freedom, but you will never know it yourself."

Gawain stared at him. The combat ground suddenly dipped and revolved around him, and he hastily stiffened his legs again.

"There will be no peaceful fireside for you, no circle of grandchildren around your knees," Merlin continued in that soft, implacable voice. "Instead of good meat and a goblet of mead, you will drink blood to live. And your children, when you sire them, will be born mortal, though with the potential to become what you are. If they are too weak or too greedy or too mad, you must stand by and watch them die, one by one. But if they're found worthy, they will inherit the same yoke you'll wear. And they, too, will know no peace. So choose well, my young friend. And choose knowing there is no going back."

Gawain swallowed against the great cold knot that had

grown in his chest with every word the wizard had spoken. Such a choice. He'd fought for the chance to drink from Merlin's Grail, had bled for it, and yet—it wasn't until this moment that he'd realized just what winning would mean.

Unable to hold Merlin's infinite, pitiless gaze, he looked away.

Into the warm, dark eyes of Arthur Pendragon. Arthur, who'd accepted him into his court, who'd made him a knight, who'd gotten drunk with him and told him bawdy jokes, who'd led him into battle against the Saxon invaders.

Arthur, who'd drunk from Merlin's Grail.

Gawain turned to Merlin. "I would follow Arthur Pendragon through the yawning gates of hell. I will not leave him to this battle alone."

And he took the cup, aware of Arthur's grim smile.

It felt far heavier than it should have, but he didn't let himself think of that. Instead, he turned the goblet up and drank it down in one hard slug, like a man taking some noxious potion.

At first, it tasted like springtime—light and foaming on the tongue. Gawain started to smile as it rolled down his throat in a sweet stream. . . .

Then it hit his gut, and the world exploded. He reeled, distantly aware of Arthur catching him with strong hands. Fire engulfed his belly and raced into his veins in a savage blaze of heat. Gritting his teeth, he fought not to scream as he writhed in the king's arms, clutching at Arthur's embroidered robes with desperate hands. It seemed his very eyeballs were afire in his skull, his tongue blazing, as if he were burning from the inside out. His muscles knotted and twisted under his flaming skin, his bones shifting and crackling like kindling.

And then the fire just . . . vanished. Winked out, leaving him cold and hollow.

Panting, Gawain clung weakly to Arthur, who supported his weight with no effort at all. Finally, he pulled away and forced himself to stand on his own feet. Licking his dry lips, he felt the twin sharp edges of fangs against his tongue.

A Magus. He was a Magus now.

Dazed, he looked around into Arthur's face.

The king gave him a slight smile. "Thank you."

Avalon
510 A.D.

Gawain rode the great warhorse up the grassy hillside, enjoying the whip of wind in his face and the thundering beat of his stallion's hooves. Reaching the top, he drew rein, bringing his mount to a dancing halt.

Overhead, the moon rode the cloudless sky, serene as a goddess against the stars. Behind him, Avalon lay sprawled like a woman sleeping in the dark, the pale marble of its villas gleaming and graceful.

For a moment, Gawain allowed himself to think about the century since Merlin had left them. Just as the alien wizard had warned, he'd spent decades at war, first against the invading barbarians, then fighting the traitor Modred and his rebels. He'd come to crave the frenzy of battle, the knife-edged elation of defeating death.

Then Queen Guinevere's vision had told her it was time to leave. They'd been among the humans for a century, after all, and their failure to age was beginning to raise questions they had no intention of answering. They needed a haven where they'd be safe from their mortal charges.

So as Merlin had taught them, the Majae created magical doorways and brought the Magekind here. Here, to this twin Earth.

He'd been told it was located in something called the Mageverse—the home of Merlin, and the source of the Magekind's power. One could draw magic here as easily as drawing breath.

And the Magekind weren't the only ones doing so, either. Though this version of Earth was oddly empty of humans, there were plenty of magical creatures here—unicorns, dragons, even pointy-eared immortals called the Sidhe, humanity's cousins.

Unfortunately, there were also the beasts the knights had christened Hellhounds. Long-legged and reptilian, with a mouthful of huge teeth and entirely too much cunning, they resembled a cross between a wolf and a crocodile, with the personality to match. Packs of them roamed the forests, killing unicorns, griffins, and even Sidhe, if they could take one unawares. Gawain, like the rest of the knights, had come to view killing them as a service to the rest of the planet's magical inhabitants.

He was almost bored enough to go Hellhound hunting now. But he'd have to be suicidal as well to take on a pack alone, so he paused, trying to decide whether to return to Avalon. Mayhap he'd hunt some comely Maja instead . . .

Rooooarrrrrr!

The sound rolled over the trees, deep and throaty, ringing with rage. It was answered by a dozen high-pitched barks Gawain knew all too well.

A pack of Hellhounds had cornered something.

Frowning, he set his heels to his horse's ribs and sent the beast thundering down the hill toward the source of the combat. It wasn't hard to follow. Between those furious roars and the Hellhounds' shrill baying, the noise was deafening. He rounded a stand of trees and drew rein in surprise.

As he'd thought, a pack of the vicious reptiles had cornered a victim, but it was not one Gawain would ever have expected.

It was a dragon.

Blue scales shimmering in the moonlight, the great beast breathed a plume of glowing magic at the nearest of the Hellhounds. The monster fell back, yelping as it burned in magical fire. The dragon tried to move in for the kill, but two more of the Hellhounds darted forward to sink their crocodile teeth in its haunches. With a roar, the dragon reared, swiped at them, and tried to throw itself skyward. A ripped and bleeding left wing flopped, broken, and the dragon fell back to earth.

Gawain winced in involuntary pity. Powerful as the dragon was, it wouldn't have a chance against a pack of Hellhounds, especially maimed.

The Hellhounds—hunched, massive, covered in great armored plates—surged forward, howling. Blood flew as their teeth scored the dragon's gleaming hide.

Before he had time to think better of it, Gawain drew his sword and dug his blunted spurs into his warhorse's side. Screaming its challenge, the well-trained stallion bounded into a full charge.

One of the Hellhounds saw them coming and tried to leap away, but Gawain swung his blade in a furious overhand chop. The creature's head went flying.

Another Hellhound snapped at Gawain's warhorse, but he twisted in his saddle and drove the bloody sword into its chest. The monster choked and tumbled backward, twitching in death.

The dragon's long tail caught another Hellhound in the ribs and batted it off into the dark like a child's ball. As the dragon struck at a forth with flashing teeth, Gawain hacked a fifth in two.

Apparently that was too much for the surviving Hellhounds. With a mass yowl, the survivors broke in all directions and fled.

Leaving Gawain alone with the dragon.

Panting, bloody, the creature turned and looked down at him, plainly puzzled. Its head was the size of his entire body, and its handlike forepaws were tipped with claws the length of his belt knife.

It could swallow him in one bite.

Well, that was stupid, Gawain realized. Like an idiot, he'd gone and saved something that could eat him.

Spurring his stallion, he tried to rein aside as the dragon opened its great jaws.

Too late.

A tide of shimmering magic rolled over him. The horse reared with a scream of equine terror, and Gawain cursed as magic burned across his skin.

The dragon hissed. Halfway through, the hiss became words. ". . . spell should translate our words for each other."

Gawain's fear drained away into astonishment. His jaw gaped as he stared up at the great beast studying him with such interest. Nobody had told him dragons were intelligent.

He retained just enough wit not to say so, however. Clearing his throat, he managed, "Your spell worked."

"Good," the dragon said, examining him with lively interest. "My name is Kel. And it seems you just saved my life."

A year later

"*Come, Kel,*" *Gawain* muttered under his breath. "Where are you? I want to fly."

As if hearing his complaint, a point of light flashed like a star in the heart of Avalon's central square. An eye-blink later, the light expanded into a vertical shimmer the height of a man. Gawain grinned in anticipation.

He and the dragon had become fast friends over the past months, hunting Hellhounds together or exploring the Magekind's new world. Since learning to assume human form, the dragon loved seducing Majae almost as much as Gawain did. Tonight, however, Kel had promised him a flight. If the dragon would ever show up . . .

A huge, blue-scaled head thrust through the glowing opening, which rippled around it like water. Horns topped the massive skull, and crimson eyes gleamed with intelligence from below bony brow ridges. Knife-length teeth flashed as the creature spoke. "What are you waiting for?" Kel demanded in a voice so deep, Gawain felt it in his bones. "Step on through. I have a few friends I'd like you to meet." His head withdrew through the magical gate, which rippled and bounced in reaction.

"What friends?" Frowning, Gawain strode over to cross through the gate himself. Magic slid across his skin with his passage, tingling and foaming, but he'd grown used to the sensation by now. "Kel, I thought we were going to fly . . ."

Reaching the other side, Gawain broke off in blank astonishment. He'd been to Kel's cavernous stone home in Dragon Lands before, so he was no stranger to its curved, alien walls and strange green lighting.

But during the previous visit, he hadn't been surrounded by dragons.

Four of them filled Kel's echoing cavern with their powerful bodies and restless tails. They were massive, brawny creatures, like animated hillsides covered in shimmering scales of gold, blue, red, or white. Great wings rustled as they shifted from foot to clawed foot, and their tails flicked, long as chariot teams.

Vampire or not, Gawain felt his mouth go dry in instinctive fear. "Jesu." He had to clear his throat as he turned to give his blue-scaled friend a tight smile. "Well met, Kel." *What the hell are* they *doing here?*

"Welcome, Gawain!" Kel gave him a grin so full of teeth, Gawain would have been terrified if he wasn't already used to his friend's idea of good humor.

"This is the human?" a white-scaled dragon asked. Green eyes the size of dinner plates blinked and narrowed as the creature examined him. "Why, it's small. It can't be very smart, with such a tiny head."

In this company, Gawain had to admit he felt tiny. He was also beginning to wonder if the creature had a point about his intelligence. What *was* he doing here? "Kel . . ." he began through a fixed smile.

"Don't be deceived." Kel edged protectively closer, forcing the white dragon to step back. "Gawain and his people may be smaller than we are, but they're just as intelligent and equally courageous. As my friend proved when he saved me from those Hellhounds." Lowering his huge head, he muttered, "Please, Gawain—patience. I'm trying to overcome my people's fear of you."

What about my fear of them? Gawain thought. He contented himself with a nod and stepped closer to his friend's towering shoulder. Kel would protect him. He hoped.

A golden head swooped down, huge nostrils flaring. Gawain managed not to jump. "It smells odd," the dragon said. "Like blood. And it looks rather disgustingly soft. And . . . hairy."

"On the other hand, they have a certain quick grace," Kel told him evenly. "As for their looks, I've found you get used to that."

"You flatter me," Gawain said dryly.

"Well, I don't like it," the red dragon announced, stepping back with what looked like revulsion curling its lips. "Nothing good can come from associating with such . . . creatures. The Dragon Lords won't like this at all."

"Soren is a Dragon Lord, and he has no problem with it."

"Soren is an ambassador," the red retorted. "He has to associate with the disgusting things. And at least he has the grace not to *enjoy* it."

Kel laughed darkly. "I could tell you a thing or two about what Soren enjoys." As the others looked scandalized, he added smoothly, "He, too, realizes the humans have much to offer us, if we but put aside our fear long enough to learn from them."

"Fear?" Now offended smoke rolled from the red dragon's nostrils. "I certainly feel no fear of that revolting little beast. Nor do I believe it has anything to teach me I wish to know."

"You would be surprised, Rawiri," Kel said. "I have made several visits to their city, Avalon, and, like Soren, I find their ways intriguingly different from ours. For example, their males and females mate for life instead of a single season, and . . ."

Rawiri snorted, his breath ruffling Gawain's hair. "I have

flown over that *city*, as you call it, and I fail to see how I could even fit inside one of those tiny stone hovels."

"Hovels?" Gawain muttered.

"To begin with," Kel said, ignoring his irritation, "you assume their form." Magic flashed in the dragon's crimson eyes. Knowing what was coming, Gawain straightened hastily away.

The next instant, the huge beast was gone, replaced by a muscular man his own height, dressed in a doublet and breeches. His skin held a faint blue sheen, while his hair fell to his shoulders in a fall of indigo. His eyes, however, were the same red they'd been in dragon form. Kel flashed a smile. "As you can see, the transformation is not even difficult, once you learn the trick of it."

"Perversion!" Rawiri hissed, his spined crest fanning in agitation. "Consorting with those creatures is bad enough, but to assume their revolting shape—you are as mad as they say!"

"Revolting?" Gawain drawled, his sense of humor suddenly reasserting itself. "You wound me."

The dragon glared at him with hatred. "I would eat you, but I do not care to pollute my belly."

Kel went still. "Or face my rage."

Fear flickered in the dragon's eyes and turned to defiance. "This will not be allowed. They will stop you." He turned and lumbered to the front of the cavern, then flung himself out through its mouth and fell like a stone. An instant later he reappeared, wings beating furiously as he flew upward.

"That can't be good," Gawain murmured to Kel.

The gold dragon flicked its tail. "He's off to tattle to the Dragon Lords, Kel. You'd best take your new pet and fly before he brings their outrage down on your head."

Kel glowered and returned to his true form. "Am I some new-hatched fledgling supposed to cower every time one of the Dragon Lords huffs? Not likely."

"Why must you try to change everything?" the white

dragon demanded suddenly, frustration growing in its voice. "Why can't you simply let things be?"

"Because it's boring, Ngalo," Kel snapped back. "We're so locked in our own ways of thought, one day we'll merge with the stone of our own caves. And nobody will even notice."

Ngalo spread massive wings, then refolded them with a flick. "There's nothing wrong with a little boredom."

"Actually, I begin to agree with you," Gawain murmured.

The dragons ignored him. "If nothing else, you should consider what your actions are doing to your uncle," the gold dragon told Kel. "People begin to talk. Tegid could lose his position as a Dragon Lord if they decide he's unable to control you."

"He doesn't control me." Kel's tail whipped once. "He is merely a hidebound bully who has tormented my mother since they were hatched. I hope he does lose his seat. In fact, perhaps *I'll* challenge him . . ."

"I would not advise it, nephew."

Kel and Gawain turned. A red dragon even bigger than Rawiri filled the mouth of the cave, a muscular green dragon standing a bit behind it.

Without taking his gaze away from the newcomers, Kel extended a forearm to Gawain and lowered his voice. "Climb on. I may need to get you to safety."

Gawain did not have to be asked twice. He grabbed his friend's clawed hand and quickly scrambled up to straddle his neck. They moved toward the entrance, but the two newcomers blocked the way.

"So, Kel, you plot against me." The red dragon's tone was chillingly pleasant. "I'd reconsider, were I you. The bones of my past challengers ring our cliffs."

Kel displayed impressive teeth. "I'm faster than they were." Around them, the others went very still.

Gawain winced. Sitting on the back of a dragon during a duel suddenly struck him as a very bad place to be.

Uncle and nephew glared at each other, spiked tails lashing with clicking sounds on the stone. Then the green dragon spoke, his voice deliberately loud.

"When Rawiri told me you'd brought one of these . . . creatures to our lands, I did not believe him," the green dragon said, cold yellow eyes focusing on Gawain. "Yet it seems there are no depths to which you will not sink."

"Evar, befriending humans is not a perversion." Kel growled, without taking his eyes from his uncle. "Learning new things keeps one quick of mind."

"And more importantly, it embarrasses me." The red dragon fanned his spiked crest, eyes narrowing. "Which is the whole point, is it not? To create doubt in my leadership?"

"Doing exactly the same thing in exactly the same way for centuries is not leadership, Tegid. It's laziness."

"You accuse *me* of laziness?"

"Kel . . ." Gawain murmured, wishing for his sword. If the dragons began to fight, he could end up crushed between those huge bodies. And there wasn't a damned thing he could do about it.

Kel ignored him in favor of glaring at his rival. "Have we become so weak, Uncle, that any new idea can throw us into a panic? Do we have so little strength—or so much cowardice?"

"Cowardice!" Evar turned to Kel's uncle. "Are you going to let that stand, Tegid?"

Tegid's eyes narrowed. "Kel, I order you to stop consorting with these disgusting apes. I—"

"You're in no position to order me to do anything." He stalked closer. "Now, my friend and I are going flying." A taunt in his voice, he added, "Don't look for me to return anytime soon. Magekind females are soft and eager."

Both dragons recoiled, and Kel swept past, forcing Gawain to grab one of his spines to keep his seat. Reaching the cavern opening, the dragon flung himself out over empty air.

Gawain's belly rose into his throat as they plummeted downward. Kel's wings grabbed the air and they leveled out, soaring. The earth flashed below, far too close, before falling away with dazzling speed. Kel's heavy wings beat hard in the climb, carrying them out over the Dragon Lands, whose peaks shone silver in the moonlight.

"What's going on, Kel?" Gawain shouted over the wind, when he judged his friend's temper had begun to cool.

"My uncle has been a Dragon Lord too long," Kel shouted back. "And our people need to grow and learn."

"That may be, but you can't force them." Gawain's hands tightened around the spines he held as he hunkered against the wind. "Kel, are we really friends, or am I an excuse to fight your uncle?"

Kel snorted. "If all I wanted was to call Tegid out, I don't need an excuse. It's my right as a male of the Bloodstone clan. I believe what I told them back there, Gawain—we need contact with your people. It's been generations since Dragonkind produced so much as a poet. All the creativity that flourishes among you is all but dead in us. We grow slow and complacent."

"Do you really think killing Tegid is going to change that?"

"No, but it's a—"

BOOM! The spell blasted out of nowhere, a raging explosion of energy that tore Gawain from the dragon's back. Kel roared, writhing in midair, huge wings contorting in agony . . .

Gawain plummeted through the night like a brick dropped into a well. As the ground sped toward his face, he wrapped his arms around his head and prayed. It took a lot to kill one of Merlin's immortal vampires, but a fall like this just might do the job.

He hit the ground in a white-hot blast of pain. In an instant, everything went black.

* * *

The world was on fire. Gawain managed an agonized wheeze and instinctively shifted form. His skull elongated, hands becoming paws, golden fur racing over his twisting, changing body.

Until he was left lying in the grass, panting like a bellows. At least the pain was gone. As it always did, the transformation to wolf had healed his injuries.

Whole again, he rolled to all four legs, shook himself, and growled, scanning for the enemy that had attacked him and Kel.

He'd landed on a grassy hilltop. There was no sign of the dragon at all, not on the ground or in the sky. There was nothing, in fact, except Avalon in the distance, shining pale and ghostly as a dream.

Then, from the corner of one lupine eye, he spotted the glint of moonlight on silver. With a wary growl, he trotted over to investigate.

It was a sword, lying in the high grass. That was strange. Moving closer, he lowered his wolf muzzle to investigate.

The weapon smelled of magic so strongly, his hackles rose. It was beautifully made, with a four-foot blade. A small silver dragon curled around its long hilt, spiked tail extending down the tang.

To his amazement, the dragon's tiny head lifted and looked at him with dazed ruby eyes. "Gawain?" it croaked.

Astonished, Gawain returned to human form. "Kel?" Gingerly, he reached down and lifted the sword with both hands. Rotating it so the dragon was upright, he asked, "What happened?"

Fear twisted his friend's face as the tiny dragon clung to the hilt like a drowning man. "Gawain, I can't change back. The egg-sucking bastard has trapped me!"

"Who? Tegid? Or that green one? *Jesu!*" His mind raced. Avalon was full of witches. Surely one of them could cure the dragon. "Don't panic. The Majae will be able to help you, and if they can't, your mother will."

Ruby eyes blinked hard. "It's not going to work."

"What do you mean?"

"There's only one way to break this spell." The dragon curled a silver lip. "My attacker was kind enough to plant the knowledge in my mind."

He blew out a breath in relief. "Then whatever it is, let's do it and get you out of there. Then we'll find . . ."

"No." The dragon looked him in the eyes. "The only way to break the spell is to kill you, Gawain. And that I'll never do."

"What?" Back in his own cavern again, Tegid stared into an enchanted pool, the tip of his tail lashing. As he watched, the ape knight began to walk back toward Avalon, carrying the sword that held Kel prisoner. "You always were a stubborn fool," he growled under his breath. "We'll see how long your pride lasts."

Actually, this might be for the best. The longer Kel refused to do the obvious, the longer he was out of the way.

"You saved my life," Kel said to the ape with all his usual unshakable sanctimony. "The cowardly egg-sucker doesn't know me very well if he thinks I'll repay you with death."

"I'm relieved to hear it," the ape replied. "But who do you think did this to you?"

"I don't know." His reflection wavering in the scrying pool, Kel frowned. "It could be any of them."

"Tegid?"

"Possibly, but I doubt it."

"He certainly hates you enough."

The small figure lifted its wings in a shrug. "But if he were caught, it would be politically ruinous. Everyone knows I was about to challenge him. It's highly dishonorable to use a spell like this on a challenger—and what's more, it's an admission of weakness. Tegid would find himself swamped with Bloodstone rivals eager to topple him. No, it was more likely Evar, that big green dragon. Or perhaps one of the other Dragon Lords, since none of them is exactly happy with me at the moment."

Which was exactly what Tegid had intended him to think. With any luck, the others would believe the same.

Either way, he had avoided a duel with Kel he might not be able to win. The dragon was young, powerful, and skilled in battle, more so than any of Tegid's previous challengers. And Tegid had no intentions of joining the bones at the base of the Dragon Cliffs.

Of course, he could have used a spell to kill Kel outright, but that kind of death magic was much easier to detect. The other Dragon Lords might be willing to turn a blind eye to trapping the young rebel in a sword, but killing a challenger through death magic . . . they'd execute Tegid for that.

Even if the Dragon Lords chose not to move against him, Kel was right. His clan would swamp him with challengers, and one of them might get lucky.

No, imprisoning the little egg-sucker was the best choice. Given his stubbornness, it could be years before Kel finally yielded to the inevitable and killed his ape friend. That would, of course, anger the other apes, who'd want nothing to do with Kel or the Dragonkind after that.

Even better, a long imprisonment would weaken Kel. By the time he escaped the sword, he'd be easy prey, assuming he was foolish enough to challenge Tegid at all.

It was all working out exactly as he'd hoped.

ONE

The present

The low-slung black sports car shot through the night with a rumble of power that vibrated all the way to Lark McGuin's bones. She shifted in the expensive upholstery, breathing in the scent of leather blended with the lush masculinity of the driver's cologne.

From the corner of one eye, Lark watched him. The profile painted in the dashboard's blue light was starkly elegant—regal cheekbones, a strong blade of a nose, an equally aggressive chin. He'd rolled down the driver's side window, allowing the wind of the car's passage to whip his blond hair around his impressive shoulders. He looked, at most, no more than a year or two older than she was.

He was her great-grandfather.

"Thanks for coming with me tonight," Lark said finally. They were the first words she'd spoken since casting the dimensional gate that had transported them and the car to Brentwood, California. "It'll mean a lot to him."

He glanced at her. "It's my pleasure." His voice was deep, resonant. "I was always fond of John."

"He worshipped you. I grew up listening to the adventures of Sir Tristan, vampire knight of the Round Table."

"I did enjoy telling that boy war stories."

Unable to resist the urge to tease, Lark grinned. "How much of it did you make up?"

He didn't bat an eye. "About half. I've lived a very boring life."

"Yeah, I'll bet that King Arthur guy is a drag. Not to mention all those women . . ."

John's mother had been one of them, having been Tristan's mistress through the roaring twenties and well into the thirties. Lark had often wondered how her mortal great-grandmother kept the knight's attention so long. She gathered Isolde had left Tristan permanently gun-shy.

During those years, Tristan had played a walk-on role in his son's life, dropping in for bedtime stories or evening swordplay practice on the lawn.

Most Latents knew nothing of their Magekind ancestors, but thanks to his father, John grew up far more knowledgeable. He was also incapable of talking about it to anyone other than his immediate family, a limitation some Maja friend of Tristan's had magically imposed.

Lark often wondered if he'd become a war hero and later a fireman out of some desire to be worthy of his father.

"How's John doing now?" Tristan asked, downshifting for a turn.

"Much better. He's the man who raised me again." She smiled at him. "Thanks to you."

Six months before

Lark walked through the door of her tiny house feeling as if she'd been beaten. All day long, she'd fought to get food and water into her grandfather, who hadn't eaten in days. He'd met her attempts to feed him with a kind of sullen paranoia that told her more clearly than words that he had no idea who she was.

When Lark had tried to cajole one too many times, he'd lifted one big hand. He hadn't actually swung—at least he hadn't fallen that far—but she'd had no choice except to back off.

Though eighty, her grandfather was six inches taller than she was, and he still outweighed her, if only barely. She'd taken care of him at home since he'd been diagnosed five years ago, but his growing belligerence had finally forced her to put him in a nursing home.

Now she collapsed on the sagging living room couch in a haze of exhaustion and worry. Long moments passed as she sat staring blankly at the fire chief's helmet that still held a place of honor on the coffee table. It was all she could do not to cry.

John McGuin had never once raised a hand to her growing up. If he'd been in his right mind, he'd be horrified at the idea of hitting any woman, especially his granddaughter. Alzheimer's had eaten away so much of his mind. It wouldn't be long before it finally killed his body, too.

Lark knew she needed to make herself a sandwich, knew she needed to keep her own strength up, but she didn't feel like eating.

Her heart ached. She missed her grandfather, and she was coming to hate the dying stranger in the nursing home. And she hated herself even more for wishing it was over.

Lark rose from the couch and headed for the stairs. In her weariness, it felt as if her running shoes had turned to cement blocks. She kept going anyway. She had to do something, anything, no matter how insane.

She climbed up to the pitch-black attic and groped for the lightbulb chain. A dull yellow glow clicked on, illuminating boxes of old records, clothing, and a pair of dusty stuffed poodles John had won her at the fair.

It took her five minutes of searching to find the battered green footlocker. When she spotted it under a box of ancient Christmas decorations, she felt, against all reason, a spurt of hope.

This was nuts. She knew it was nuts. And yet . . . it was the only thing left to try.

Kneeling on the dirty floor, Lark lifted the stiff, half-rusted lid and looked down into its sixty-year-old contents. Gently, she lifted out the folded Army uniform with its bloodstained cuffs, then pushed aside the Nazi flag her grandfather had captured somewhere in Normandy after D-Day. There, under a battered helmet, she found a long brown box and flipped it open. Stained white silk cradled two sharpshooter's medals, a colorful collection of combat ribbons, a Purple Heart, and a Bronze Star.

And a small, sword-shaped charm.

Lark took the charm out and returned the box to its spot in the locker. Closing a shaking fist tight around the charm, she closed her eyes and began the chant her grandfather had made her say so many times when she was a little girl. The Gaelic words were difficult to pronounce, and she had no idea what they meant or if they'd do any good, but she said them anyway.

It was the only thing left to do.

When she was finished, she waited. The attic lay still and silent around her, filled with dust and the ghosts of childhood happiness.

Nothing happened. She hadn't really thought it would, and yet . . .

"Dammit, Granddad." Lark dropped her head on her fist and began to cry, first silent tears, then tearing sobs of grief.

Light flashed, so bright she saw it even through closed eyes. Her tears choked off as her head jerked up.

A shimmering hole had opened in the air. As Lark sat frozen in shock and dawning hope, a man stepped through it.

For some reason, she'd thought he'd be dressed in armor, not perfectly ordinary chinos and a blue knit shirt that matched his eyes. He cocked his handsome head as he looked down at her. "Hello."

Her mouth worked, but nothing emerged from her shocked vocal chords.

The man leaned down and . . . *sniffed.* "Definitely my lineage." He smiled as he straightened. "Are you John's daughter? I remember giving him that charm."

"G-Granddaughter." She stuttered it. Taking a deep breath, she blurted, "He needs your help."

Tristan smiled. "He has it."

He'd been as good as his word.

"We're here."

Tristan's words brought Lark out of her reverie about the past. Big hands confident on the wheel—who'd taught him to drive?—Tristan whipped into the parking lot of a sprawling stucco building. Lark escaped the car's luxurious cockpit with a feeling of relief. Painfully conscious of her great-grandfather striding at her heels, she led the way to the facility's gleaming front doors, past the massive stone sign engraved with the words ELYSIUM SANCTUARY.

Their footsteps rang on marble as they entered a soaring lobby that would have looked at home in a five-star hotel. The only thing that revealed the place's real nature were the huge elevators, each long enough to admit a stretcher and ambulance team. When Lark hit the elevator call button, one promptly slid open.

As the elevator hummed its way upward, she broke the silence. "This elevator smells a lot better than the one back at Granddad's previous nursing home. There were times I had to hold my breath all the way up and down. Thought I'd pass out before I ever hit the ground floor."

"Yes, I visited one of my children at such a place once, years ago. That's why I suggested we build Sanctuary to begin with." Tristan gave her a slight smile. "The Maja healer on staff here keeps the residents in much better health."

Lark nodded. "She certainly did wonders with Granddad."

The elevator chimed, announcing their arrival on the tenth floor, and the doors slid open. They stepped out to the sounds of laughter and cheerful groans.

Again, Lark found herself comparing it with John's previous nursing home. There, the sitting area had hosted only a single television that seemed to show nothing but reruns of seventies game shows. Dispirited residents sat slumped on a stained couch, watching without much interest.

Here, a brisk game of pool was in progress, while residents at other tables played everything from poker to Scrabble. Voices were bright and lively, and there was no scent of sickness in the air.

Lark and Tristan found John McGuin presiding over a pile of poker chips while watching his opponents across his cards. There was such merry cunning in his gaze, tears stung Lark's eyes.

When she'd first contacted Tristan, she'd doubted her grandfather would survive the week. Thanks to Sanctuary's Maja healer, he could probably look forward to living another two decades.

John looked up and saw them. His face lit with a brilliant grin. "Lark! Tristan!" He threw down his hand and rose, aiming the grin at his opponents. "Looks like you boys get to keep your quarters after all. My family's here!"

As his poker buddies watched with naked envy, he stepped around the table to pump his father's hand and accept Lark's kiss. Lark was abruptly struck by how alike the two looked—they had the same broad-shouldered build and angular features, though age had blurred the resemblance. She wondered if John felt the same sense of mental whiplash she did. Anyone looking at them would have thought he was Tristan's grandfather rather than son.

"Want to go back to my apartment where we can talk?" he suggested.

"I'd love to," Tristan said, genuine affection in his smile.

"So," John said as he led the way down the hall, "how's

the war going?" He turned a proud smile on Lark and dropped his voice. "And how do you like being a Maja?"

Lark felt her smile go tight. "It's great, Granddad. I'm learning more every day." *It's that or die.*

"As for the war, it goes much better, John," Tristan told him. "In fact, we believe we've found the means to win."

"Yeah? That's fantastic!" He unlocked the door to his neat three-room apartment and gestured them inside.

As they entered the small living room, evidence of John's proud career was everywhere. His old fire chief's helmet now rested on a bookcase, while the walls were hung with photos of his family and his firefighter buddies. An antique toy fire truck stood on the coffee table, while a framed photo of firefighters raising the flag at Ground Zero held a place of honor over the couch.

"Have a seat," John said. "Want anything, Dad? Lark?"

"I'm fine." Lark sank down on the comfortable old couch John had owned longer than she'd been alive.

Her grandfather turned his attention on Tristan again. "I've got a nice bottle of wine. Or I could make coffee."

He sounded so damn normal, gratitude swelled in a warm ball in Lark's chest.

Joining her, Tristan made an elegant gesture of refusal. "Nothing for me, thanks."

"If you change your mind, let me know." John dropped into his favorite easy chair and fixed them with an eager stare. "So tell me about the war."

For the past six months, the Magekind had been locked in a deadly conflict with the followers of a Mageverse alien named Geirolf. They'd killed the alien, but before he died, he'd managed to change his psychotic human worshippers into vampires. And in an obvious parody of the rite Merlin had used, he'd used three so-called black grails to do it.

"There's been a major breakthrough." Tristan sat forward and braced his elbows on his knees. "We've learned if you destroy one of the black grails, the magical backlash kills every vampire that was created by drinking from it."

Understanding lit John's bright eyes. "So instead of be-ing forced to hunt down five or six thousand evil vampires, all you've gotta do is find the grails."

"Exactly."

The old man blinked, sitting back in his chair. "That's a hell of an improvement."

"That's putting it mildly," Lark told him. "Galahad and his wife already destroyed one of the grails. We just need to get rid of the other two, and we're done."

John studied Lark, his gaze proud. "And you're partici-pating in this hunt now, right?"

She nodded. "We all are."

"Maybe you'll be the one to find it." He turned to Tris-tan and beamed. "She always was smart as a whip. I'm so proud of her."

"As am I." Tristan patted his gnarled hand. "You did well with her, John. She has a very strong sense of duty."

Lark gave them both a smile that felt a little tight. "Well, you two have me pegged, don't you?"

Tristan certainly did. Not long after getting John into Sanctuary, he'd reappeared in Lark's living room. "We're in a war," he'd told her, then went on to describe the battle with Geirolf and his sorcerers. "I petitioned the Majae's Council to grant you Merlin's Gift, and they've agreed you're a fit candidate. Will you help us?"

She'd stared at him in stunned shock.

It had never even occurred to Lark that she'd be consid-ered as a Maja candidate. After all, the Council had refused to make her grandfather a Magus sixty years before, de-spite his wartime heroism. Apparently somebody had con-cluded it wasn't a good idea.

They'd also refused her mother thirty years later, though that was more understandable. Glenda McGuin, a hard-partying seventies wild child, hadn't been the most stable candidate around. Witness the way she'd ended up hitting a tree at sixty-five miles an hour, leaving her daughter to be raised by her parents, since nobody had known who Lark's father was.

Lark considered herself just as unlikely a candidate for Maja as her mother had been, but evidently the Magekind felt differently.

Not that it mattered. Tristan had gotten Granddad into Sanctuary. If that meant Lark had to embrace her inner cannon fodder in return, she was willing.

The next night, another dazzlingly handsome Magus had shown up at Lark's apartment. His name was Dominic Bonnhome, and he was a Court Seducer.

It had been uncomfortable as hell at first; she hadn't known him, after all. But Dominic did know his business, and his kind, professional skill had helped get her through the worst of her shyness. On their fourth try, his climax had triggered Merlin's Gift, the spell in her genetic code she'd inherited from Tristan.

It had been like being struck by lightning. One minute she was an ordinary mortal woman. The next, her body had jolted in the grip of the spell, and the power of the Mageverse had flooded her with its hot savagery, transforming her into an immortal witch.

Actually, "immortal" was a misnomer. Lark would never age, but she was immortal only as long as no one killed her. And these days, there were far too many people in line to do that job.

But at least John was no longer dying.

Lark, Tristan, and John chatted easily for another half hour before the elderly mortal could no longer suppress his yawns.

Tristan stood. "Well, we had best return to the Mageverse." We have a great deal to do."

"I'm sure." John gave him a longing smile. "You'll come back, though?"

"Of course."

Lark kissed her grandfather good night, waited through another handshake, and led the way back to the elevator.

As it descended, Tristan suddenly spoke. "Was it worth it?"

She flashed back to her last mission, to the bodies and the blood. Not even her years growing up around the smoke and risk of a firehouse had prepared her for anything like that.

Then Lark remembered the reborn intelligence in her grandfather's eyes. "Hell, yes," she said.

Jonesville, Tennessee

"Make a left," the dragon sword shouted over the roar of the wind.

Gawain leaned into the turn, steering the big Harley Davidson Electra Glide down Henry Street with absent skill. Normally you couldn't sneak up on a deaf man on an Electra Glide, since the massive bike's Twin Cam 88 engine roared like all the hounds of hell. Tonight, however, the motorcycle sped along as silently as a ghost, Kel's magic having rendered it utterly silent. Even its headlights were off. With his vampire night vision, Gawain didn't really need them anyway.

Those he was hunting might sense his approach magically, but there was no reason to give them any extra warning.

This is it, the dragon told him in their mental link, evidently tired of shouting. *Up ahead on the right.*

There was only one building on the right, a massive structure with curving walls of cream brick and stained glass. A towering spire thrust from the building's roof, topped by a cross. Gawain frowned up at it as he brought the big hog to a halt. Human legends notwithstanding, crosses didn't bother him—or, unfortunately, those he hunted—but he still didn't care for the implications. *Kel, this is a church,* he told the sword.

And it's also where the trail leads.

They're planning to sacrifice that girl in a church? Most of Geirolf's crowd builds underground temples for this kind of sick crap.

Maybe they didn't want to spend the magic on it.

Or maybe they're the kind of assholes who like to desecrate churches. He swung off the bike and drew the four-foot blade from the diagonal scabbard across his back.

Gawain, they kidnapped a sixteen-year-old virgin to murder in an act of death magic. Kel's voice held a faint metallic ring under its deep mental rumble. *I'd say the asshole thing is pretty much a given.*

Good point. Gawain grinned, slowly and viciously. *Guess we'll kill 'em slow, then.*

His friend laughed in his mind. *Nothing like a little artistic butchery of the thoroughly deserving.*

Gawain started up the sidewalk toward the double glass doors that looked as though they'd lead to the sanctuary. His black motorcycle leathers creaked faintly as he walked. He was acutely aware of the sound, every sense alert and singing with the rise of adrenaline. *I think it's time for a wardrobe change. I'm going to need something a little more substantial than cowhide.*

Well, there are *three of them and one of you.*

Enough to work up a good sweat, anyway.

Kel snorted. *We really do need to work on your pitiful lack of self-confidence.*

Gawain laughed softly as the faceplate of his motorcycle helmet began to glow, transforming into the Dragon Helm he'd worn into combat for centuries. At the same time, his leathers shimmered with their own magical change, becoming armor that was lighter and more flexible than fabric.

Though most Magi wore enchanted plate into combat, the armor Kel created lay over Gawain's body in thousands of tiny scales of shimmering blue. Every time he moved, silver highlights rippled across the scales like the moon dancing on water. Despite their seeming delicacy, the armor could have stopped a tank blast.

Considering what he was going up against, Gawain needed all the protection he could get. Being a Magus, he couldn't cast spells. The vamps he was hunting, however, were sorcerers who drew power from the life force of those they murdered.

Gawain had been tracking this particular trio since last week. Half an hour ago, Kel had seen a vision of the three snatching sixteen-year-old Theresa Davis from the parking lot of the local mall. Luckily, the sword had been able to follow the sorcerers' magical trail.

Gawain only hoped he'd be in time to save her.

He paused at the church entrance, gathering himself, enjoying the furious thump of his own heart, the power that surged through his body. A feral grin spread across his face.

The grin disappeared when he heard a faint sound through the glass doors—a muffled female cry of pain. Over it rang an ugly shout of male laughter.

"Doors," Gawain snarled. Normally he'd kick them in, but the breaking glass would make hell's own racket. A shimmer of magic flung them wide, and he strode in, sword in hand.

Crossing the church foyer, he shoved open the sanctuary's double doors. The three sorcerers at the other end of the room looked up with a chorus of snarls. Gawain snarled back, taking in the scene with one blazing glare.

Dressed in elaborate crimson robes, the vampires crouched around a slim, blond girl who lay on the carpeted floor in front of the altar.

Theresa Davis.

They'd stripped her naked and bound her spread-eagle with a spell. She stared across the sanctuary at him, her tearful eyes wide and hopeless. Her mouth opened, but the spell magically garbled whatever she was trying to say into a strangled bleat.

"What are you doing here, Magus?" One of vampires laughed and flourished his knife. "Looking for a piece?"

Gawain's temples began to pound. A wordless roar of rage tore from his mouth as he charged down the aisle, armored boots thundering on the floor as he swung Kel up for his first blow.

Leers turned to startled fear. "What the fu . . ."

The one with the knife leaped to his feet, but he didn't have time to use it. Gawain sent his head flying with one swing of the dragon sword.

The other two dove in opposite directions, cursing. Magical armor shimmered into being around them as swords filled their hands.

The vamp on the right barely got his weapon up before Gawain hit him. Steel clashed on steel with force enough to vibrate bone. Gawain didn't care. All he wanted was the bastard's head.

Light exploded in his eyes as the vampire sorcerer shot a magical blast into his face. The Dragon Helm protected him, sending the spell splashing harmlessly away. Gawain ignored it, hammering the sword against the vampire's guard, trying to break through.

Gawain, behind . . .

He spun before Kel finished the warning, first parrying the third vamp's attack, then kicking him in the gut and sending him crashing into the pews.

Gawain whirled back in time to block the blade slashing at his head. Another stinging blast of magic. Kel countered it with his own mystical assault, sending the sorcerer stumbling away. Gawain saw his moment and swung his blade with all his strength. The other tried to block it, but he was too late. The sword took off his head at the jaw.

Whooom! A spell blast sent Gawain flying. He hit the ground hard and rolled, gritting his teeth against the wave of cold as the death spell tried to take hold. Kel smothered it the instant before he slid to a stop, panting, sprawled on his back.

"Geiroooooolf!"

Looking up, he saw the last sorcerer leaping for him, howling a battle cry as he brought his sword down like an axe. Gawain flipped aside. The vampire's blade missed his head and crunched into the floor, sinking deep into the carpeted wood.

Where it stuck.

Gawain rolled to his feet as his opponent hauled desperately at his weapon. In his panic, the vampire had obviously forgotten he could simply conjure the blade loose.

Baring his teeth, Gawain swung. His enemy's decapitated body crashed to its knees beside its rolling head.

He turned to scan the church. "Anybody else?"

"Evidently not," Kel said.

Relaxing, Gawain glanced toward the altar, expecting to see the Davis girl waiting to be rescued. "Oh, shit."

Once her captors had died, the spell that had held her had collapsed. Theresa was gone.

But she wasn't far. Gawain's vampire hearing detected the frantic pound of her heart coming from behind the priest's wooden podium.

Remembering she was naked, he thought, *Give her something to wear, Kel, would you? She'll feel a little less vulnerable.*

Magic flashed around the podium in an explosion of tiny sparks. Theresa gasped and jumped to her feet, staring down at the jeans and T-shirt that had suddenly materialized over her body. Realizing she'd given herself away, she froze, her gaze flying to Gawain.

He slid Kel back into his scabbard with a knight's automatic ease, but she didn't look comforted.

It was probably the helm. With its snarling muzzle and dragon wings spreading wide on either side of his head, it made Gawain look even more intimidating than he normally did. Quickly, he pulled it off and tucked it under one arm.

Raising his free hand in an "I'm unarmed" gesture, he

started talking, keeping his tone low and soothing as he edged toward her. "It's okay, sweetheart. It's okay. I'm not going to hurt you. I'm here to help. You're safe."

Theresa stared at him helplessly, looking like the child she was, her blue eyes huge, her mouth trembling. A gamine cap of honey blond hair accentuated her youth. "Please, please, just leave me alone!"

It's no good, Gawain, Kel told him. *She's too scared. It'd be kinder to put her out.*

Do it then.

Gawain sensed the spell roll out and engulf her. The child's eyes rolled back. She would have fallen, had it not been for Kel's magic holding her upright.

With a sigh, the knight crossed the sanctuary and picked her up.

"She won't remember anything," the sword told him as he swept her into his arms. "The police will think she was knocked cold for most of it."

Gawain frowned as he looked around the sanctuary, where his foes' bodies lay messily dead. "How are we going to explain what happened to the bad guys? A dozen witnesses saw her snatched."

"Good point." Kel contemplated the problem. "A violent argument between killers? Murder-suicide?"

"Kel, I *beheaded* them."

"You'd be surprised what a little magic can fix."

Gawain snorted. "Not really."

"No, I suppose not." The dragon's tiny eyes flared. Suddenly all the corpses were in one piece again, though spectacularly bullet-riddled. Their magical robes and armor had vanished, destroyed by their deaths, but Kel's magic had dressed them again in suitably modern garb. Automatic weapons lay in limp hands, and the pools of blood that surrounded them were consistent with their wounds.

Gawain nodded approvingly. "The local cops will take one look at the bodies and conclude they conveniently blew one another away."

"Now all you've got to do is find a phone and call nine-one-one."

Gawain settled the girl more comfortably in his arms. "Better yet, let's get her out of here and let her do it. I don't want her to wake up to this particular view."

"Good point."

Five minutes later, Gawain strode down the hall toward the building's exit. Behind him, he heard Theresa, awake again, pick up the office phone for a tearful call to the police.

Well, he thought, *that's one we managed to save.*

TWO

Lark threw up a desperate block a fraction too late. Her opponent's sword smashed into her armored ribs. With a yelp of pain, she crashed to the sawdust floor and lay still, dazed.

"You were too slow on that parry," Tristan told her, impatience in his voice. "Get up and try it again."

Panting, Lark didn't move. Her every muscle and bone ached, and her body streamed sweat under her enchanted armor. They'd been practicing for two hours, and he'd battered her black and blue. "My grandmother taught me ladies don't fight," she announced, mostly just to piss him off.

"Your grandmother was right." As Lark looked up in surprise, Tristan leaned over her and flipped up his helmet visor to reveal his implacable face. "You, however, are not a lady. You're a Maja, which means not only do you fight, you sleep with vampires you barely know and kill people before they kill you. Get up."

Lark gave him her best poisonous glare and struggled to her feet. "Does my grandfather know you're a son of a bitch?"

He lifted a blond brow. "Does your grandfather know you're lazy?"

Her sword flashed out and rapped hard against the side of his helm. He merely looked pleased. "Much better. Let's try that again."

An hour later, Lark limped through the streets of Avalon, headed for the little brownstone she'd built with her magic. All she wanted now was a hot, soothing bath and maybe a nice glass of white Zin.

For the past several months, she'd been alternating Tristan's lessons in swordplay with magical combat instruction from her Maja trainer. Between them, Diera and the knight had taught her to hold her own.

But Lark had never learned to like it. She hated fighting, hated the blood and pain and fear of it. She'd wanted to be a paramedic, dammit. She'd wanted to save lives, not take them.

Apparently, fate had other ideas . . . .

Booooom!

Lark stopped in her tracks, frowning in the direction of the noise. It had sounded almost like a magical blast, but it was a little loud for combat practice. What . . . ?

A distant voice howled, "We live in Geirolf! Geirolf lives in us!" Another boom followed.

Oh, sweet Jesus.

Armored feet rushed up behind her. As she jerked around, Tristan pelted past. "Move your ass!" he roared. "We're under attack!"

Instantly forgetting her battered body, Lark conjured armor and sword and raced after him.

They found the central square packed with battling warriors. The light from magical blasts glinted off armor and clashing swords as the constant rolling booms rattled windows.

Impossible as it seemed, Avalon had been invaded.

But how the hell had Geirolf's sorcerers figured out how to create a dimensional gate to Mageverse Earth?

A blur of red plunged at Lark from her left. Instinctively, she whirled and threw up a shield spell barely in time to block a wave of death magic. A vampire in the scarlet armor of Geirolf's worshippers charged her, following up his magical assault with a vicious swing of his sword. She parried, bracing under the brutal impact, then blasted him back as she'd been taught. The spell sent him stumbling.

Lark followed, hacking at him with her conjured blade and raining spells against his shields. Sensing something give in his magical defenses, she poured another blast into the weakness. His shield collapsed. With a yell of relief and victory, Lark plunged her sword into his chest. He reeled, tripping and falling on his back. Lark followed him down and twisted her sword in his heart, destroying her adversary without mercy. Her gorge heaved in revulsion, but she ignored it.

Decapitation and cutting up the heart were the only sure ways to kill a vampire. They tended to heal anything less than that.

Her opponent dead, Lark glanced around for somebody else to fight. The square was packed with armored warriors—Majae, Magi, and sorcerers, all grimly intent on battle. Mercy was out of the question. The Geirolfians were incapable of it, and the Magekind didn't dare let any of them live.

Lark wanted to throw up.

Spotting another sorcerer, she went after him, ignoring her own fear. Fortunately, the sorcerers were all twenty-first century people as uncomfortable with swordsmanship as she was. Good thing, too. If they'd had anything like Tristan's skill, Lark wouldn't have had a prayer.

Trying not to think, fighting not to feel, she hacked and blasted at her foes. All that mattered was keeping them from overrunning Avalon.

Boom!

The magical explosion slammed into the side of her head, powering past her shields and sending her flying. She tumbled, her body rattling in her armor like a pea in a tin cup before skidding to a halt. Something heavy landed on her chest, knocking the breath out of her with a strangled *whoosh.*

Dazed, she looked up to see a sorcerer straddling her, one fist lifted. She tried to bring up her sword, but he slapped the blade out of the way so hard, it spun from her hand.

Before she could summon a fireball to defend herself, his fingers closed over her visor and sent a spell burning into her helm.

It melted. Just vanished right off her head like evaporating dew.

Horrified and bare-headed, she looked up at the sorcerer. He raised his own visor, revealing a beefy face, sweat-slicked red hair, and razored fangs in a grinning mouth. "Hello there, pretty."

Shit! Terrified, she threw up a hand and blasted a spell into his face, but it splashed off his magical shields. Then a big hand slammed across her head in a slap that made her see stars.

Everything else went gray.

When her thoughts focused again, something heavy was crushing her chest. Her throat blazed with agony. Opening her dazed eyes, Lark realized the vampire lay on top of her, his hand fisted in her hair, his fangs buried in her neck.

And it hurt.

He's feeding on me! With a cry of disgust and horror, she lifted shaking hands and tried to call her magic for a spell. But the power answered in a thin trickle he didn't even seem to notice. Between the concussion and the blood loss, she was too weak.

He was killing her.

No! Not like this! John had lost too many people

already—his wife, his daughter. It would kill him if Lark died, too.

She tried to struggle, but her arms and legs barely moved. He'd taken too much blood. Dizzy and frantic, she tried to draw on the power of the Mageverse. Far above her head, sparks flared. For a moment, Lark thought it was her magic, answering at last.

The sorcerer jerked off her with a spray of blood. Dazed, she registered his gory mouth as he looked skyward. "The grail!" he yelled, terror in his voice. "Fuck, someone's destroying our grail!"

Overhead, light filled the sky in a silent detonation. The vampire astride her chest screamed as the blast hit him. All around her, the sorcerers shrieked. Burning magic rolled over Lark's skin, blinding her. She threw up her hands to shield her face. . . .

The vampire's weight simply vanished.

For a moment, it was as if she'd been struck deaf and blind. There was no sound, no light, no sensation.

At last she heard someone groan. Someone else cursed. Lark blinked as the stars overhead slid into focus. Her attacker had disappeared, but the pain in her throat remained. Lifting a shaking hand, she probed the wound fearfully. Her fingers could feel nothing through the mailed gloves she still wore.

"Lark?" A familiar face loomed over her, framed by his open visor. Fear widened his eyes as he snatched her into his arms. "Merlin's beard!" Throwing back his head, Tristan bellowed, "Healer! I need a healer!"

The word seemed to spin around her, and Lark let her eyes close as darkness swept over her.

"Lark?" A cool, slender hand cupped her cheek.

She opened her eyes, disoriented. She knew that voice. "Diera?"

Her mentor smiled in pleasure and relief as she crouched

by her side. A delicate, petite blonde, Diera looked like a fairy princess even in full armor. "Feeling better, dear?"

Blinking, Lark realized she was lying on her back in the city square. Belatedly, she remembered the feeling of fangs sinking into her throat, the stench of death magic. She jerked and grabbed at her throat. The flesh under her fingers was reassuringly whole. It was as if she'd dreamed it.

Diera patted her shoulder comfortingly. "It's all right, love. I healed you."

"Just in time, too."

She twisted her head around to find Tristan crouching at her head. He reached down and ran mailed fingers through her tangled, bloody hair. "You scared me, wench."

Lark sighed and let her eyes close, suddenly exhausted. "I scared me, too."

There wasn't a single bruise on Lark's face as she stared into her bedroom mirror the next night, and her throat showed no sign that it had ever been ripped by the vampire's fangs. Diera had healed her completely. At least physically.

The nightmares she'd endured all day were brutal evidence that the psychological damage was going to be a little tougher to overcome.

But if it hadn't been for Guinevere and the knights of the Round Table . . .

Even as the invasion began, Gwen, Arthur, and several of the knights had gated off, following a location spell to the second of Geirolf's grails. When Gwen destroyed it, the resulting magical blast had killed all but a handful of the invaders. Apparently, the survivors had drunk from the third grail, so the spell hadn't affected them.

They'd died anyway. The Magekind had fallen on them and wiped them out to the last fighter.

Unfortunately, Avalon had lost warriors of its own. Three Magi and a Maja had been killed in the fighting.

Thus, tonight's ritual.

Frowning into her mirror, Lark summoned the magic. It came easily this time, pouring from the Mageverse around her, transforming her cotton sleep shirt into a floor-length black gown, vaguely medieval in design. Rich velvet skirts spilled to the floor, while the gown's tightly corseted bodice was heavily worked with metallic silver thread. Eyeing its V neckline, she added a heavy necklace of silver and jet.

Lark smoothed her hands over her hair. The spell had coiled it into a complicated arrangement on top of her head, braided with silver cords in a style she'd copied from one of the other Majae.

She hated funerals even more than she hated combat.

She stepped from her brownstone to find a procession of Magekind winding past the house. Like Lark, all of them were dressed in black velvet or silk, the dark fabric heavily embroidered in silver or a scattering of jet beads. Picking up her skirts, she walked across her tiny lawn to join them.

"Hey, Lark! Wait up!"

She turned to see a tall, athletic brunette hurrying toward her despite heavy velvet skirts, accompanied by Diera and a handsome bearded man.

Caroline Du Lac dragged her into a fierce hug. "Dammit, how many times do I have to tell you—ya gotta watch the teeth!" Her voice dropped. "You could have been killed . . ."

Touched, Lark hugged her back. "Hey, some overgrown tick is not going to keep Lark McGuin down for long." She gave Diera a grateful smile. "Especially not while I've got friends like you two." She stepped back and studied her friend. "How about you? Come through all right?"

Caroline snorted. "Hey, I'm married to Ginsu Galahad over there." She jerked a thumb at her husband, who watched with an indulgent smile. "He slices, he dices, he makes evil sorcerers cry like little girls. Nobody even got close enough to muss my hair."

"That's an outright lie, darling," the knight drawled. "You made one or two cry yourself."

Diera moved up beside Lark and hooked an arm around her waist. "My children, I hate to interrupt the hyperbole, but we'd better get moving. We're holding up the procession."

They walked two miles, picking up more mourners as they passed castles, villas, and mansions, until at last they reached Avalon's central square. Four flower-decked biers occupied its center.

If things had gone differently, Lark herself might be occupying one of them.

It probably wasn't a good idea to think about that.

Wiping her suddenly damp palms on her skirt, she followed the others as they trooped around the biers to form concentric circles.

The ceremony that followed had become all too familiar over the past months. First came prayers from representatives of the faiths the fallen Magekind had practiced, then the eulogies from friends and lovers.

Finally Arthur Pendragon and his sister Morgana Le Fay stepped from their places at opposite sides of the square. An elegant figure in his black tunic and hose, the former High King lifted his bearded chin and scanned the crowd. "Centuries ago, we Magekind took a vow to Merlin to use our abilities to protect humankind from its own worst impulses, even if it meant laying down our immortal lives." Normally, he prided himself on his use of modern slang, but for solemn occasions like this, Arthur fell back into more formal cadences.

He spread his brawny arms wide. "These four kept that vow last night in battle against the worst threat we've known in all our long history. I honor their memory and their courage, but what's more, I make a vow on their biers: they will be avenged!"

Around Lark, the Magekind roared their approval as she lifted her own voice in a shout of agreement.

Arthur turned in a slow circle, scanning the crowd, letting them see his fury. "Geirolf meant to mock Merlin when he used those black grails of his to make his followers vampires. We killed him for his crimes, just as we've killed two thirds of his followers. But another third remains. As long as they exist, they can use the final grail to create more vampires. We dare not rest until we find the cup and destroy it—and with it, the last of Geirolf's spawn." Arthur lifted his chin. "But make no mistake—we will succeed, just as we've succeeded against the forces of ignorance, rage, and bigotry for centuries. And these heroes will rest in the peace they deserve."

The Liege of the Magi raised his voice in a parade ground bark as he reached for the sword hanging at his side. "Magi, present arms!" Drawing Excalibur from its scabbard, he lifted the great blade skyward. Next to Lark, Galahad drew his sword as the other Magi did the same.

"Majae!" Morgana shouted, raising her ringed hands. "Join with me in sending our lost heroes home!"

Lark sent a wave of magic at the biers, her spell blending with those the other women fired. The biers began to glow under the building enchantment, shining brighter and brighter until they merged into a white-hot ball of light. Abruptly the ball shot upward like a rocket to detonate far overhead in an explosion of dancing sparks.

Lark watched the magic fade with aching eyes. Beside her, Caroline sniffed loudly.

"Now, put aside your grief and listen," Arthur said as he stepped into the vacant space where the biers had stood, broad-shouldered and grim in his embroidered black doublet and hose. His black boots rang on the stone as he slid Excalibur back into its scabbard. The other vampires followed suit, swords rattling.

Lifting his dark head, Arthur scanned the silent crowd. "Each of those we lost had been members of the Magekind less than ten years. Heed me well—I will lose no more of my children!"

He paused, letting the silence build. No one in the crowd so much as coughed. Satisfied that they were taking him seriously, Arthur continued, "The councils have met, and it is decided. The most experienced Magekind will be paired with our newest recruits. The veterans' responsibility is to assist them in combat and ensure they have the skills needed to survive while we all hunt the last grail. And lest there is any doubt—these assignments are not a topic for debate." He looked at his half sister. "Morgana."

"Yes, Arthur." She threw her arms skyward and closed her eyes. Light burst from her fingertips. Far above the square, glowing slips of paper began to float downward like leaves.

By instinct, Lark put a hand out. One of the sheets landed in her palm, and she curled her fingers around it.

"Good luck," Caroline said in her ear, as the spell took her by the hand and began gently to tug. Lark followed the magical pull as, around her, other Magekind began to mill around doing the same.

Arms folded, Gawain watched as young members of the Magekind sought out their new guardians. "Great," he said to Bors, who was also one of the original Round Table knights. "We're both going to end up baby-sitting grass-green rookies who don't know hilt from blade. Dammit, Arthur . . ."

"Yes, well, I'd advise you not to give him a hard time about it," Bors drawled. "I don't think he's in the mood."

"I noticed." Gawain recognized the warning signs in his liege's clipped speech as well as anyone. Sometimes Arthur was open to suggestion, and sometimes you damn well took orders and kept your mouth shut. Otherwise, you caught the flaming edge of that Pendragon temper—if you were lucky. If you weren't, he carried a grudge. And Arthur could carry a grudge for a long, long time. He'd only recently forgiven Lancelot for his one night with Gwen sixteen hundred years before.

"Either way, we're going to have our work cut out for us with this lot." Gawain's gaze lingered on a young Magus who walked through the crowd with a particularly bewildered expression. "The last couple of generations have gotten soft. Too much television and riding in cars."

"Not all of them." Pain tightened Bors's face.

Gawain winced, silently cursing himself for his unthinking comment. "Anything new from Richard?"

Richard Edge was Bors's son with Meredith Edge, a Maja who'd been the knight's lover. Despite the brief relationship, Bors had helped raise Richard in Avalon until the boy's growing violent streak had forced his banishment to mortal Earth.

Bors shook his dark head. "I haven't spoken to my son in twenty-six years. His mother and I were afraid he'd start killing people, but as far as I can tell, he's done nothing but study magic."

"On mortal Earth?" Kel asked from his scabbard. "He's not going to have much luck with it there." Magic did not work well on humanity's home, and mortals had not evolved to use it. It took intervention by someone like Merlin or Geirolf to give a human the ability to work magic.

"Maybe," Bors said grimly. "The problem is, he disappeared a year ago. Meredith was unable to track him. After she died fighting Geirolf's cult, I had Morgana search for him, but she had no luck either. It was as if he'd vanished right off the planet."

Gawain frowned. "He could be dead."

"Maybe." Bors expression was grim. "But I don't like it at all."

As his friend brooded, Gawain rocked back on his heels

to watch the new Magekind wander around with their enchanted slips of paper.

A slim brunette attracted his attention. She was petite, nearly a foot shorter than he was, but her body was lushly curved. Her dark hair slid to the small of her back in a fall of silk, and her eyes were huge and brown.

"Look, somebody's gone and recruited a Playboy bunny," he joked, hoping to distract Bors from painful memories. He slipped into a mocking singsong. " 'Hi, my name is Bambi, and I'm barely legal. I love puppies and kitties and throwing flaming balls of death at my enemies.' "

Bors chuckled.

Kel spoke from his scabbard. "She's also Tristan's great-granddaughter." He always knew those things.

"Yeah? Wonder if he's protective?" Gawain eyed her, still tempted. She might be worth getting on Tristan's bad side . . .

Bors snorted. "We're talking about Tristan here. He thinks women are only good for one thing, and since she's his lineage, this one wouldn't even be good for that." He looked skyward, attention caught by the slip of paper whirling toward them as if laser-guided. "Hell. I knew this was coming."

Sure enough, the slip disappeared right into the center of Bors's chest. He grimaced. "Ah, shit. I was hoping for some pretty Maja."

Sure enough, a tattooed young male stepped out of the crowd with a noticeable swagger. "Sir Bors?"

"That's me, kid," Bors looked him over. "Come on. I don't suppose you know how to fight?"

"Well, yeah. Like, you bet your ass."

"Uh huh." The knight sounded resigned. "Let's go."

Poor Bors, Kel said in their link. *Not only does he not get free pussy, he has to ride herd on a cocky little schmuck.* Like Arthur, the dragon loved using mortal slang.

Gawain chuckled as the two men walked off. His attention returned to the pretty brunette. She paused a few feet away, apparently too focused on her task to realize she was being watched. He inhaled, trying to sample her scent without being too obvious about it. She smelled richly sexy to his vampire senses, but there was no male scent lingering on her skin. Probably unattached then.

Just the way he liked them.

As he'd known it would, the Desire woke, sending a wave of hunger through his blood. His fangs began to ache, and an urgent heat spun into his balls. He wasn't surprised. He hadn't fed in a couple of days—he'd been busy helping Gwen and Arthur find the second grail last night, and he'd spent the night before that rescuing the girl. Between them, he and Kel had used a great deal of magic. His body needed a woman, needed her blood and the sweet, erotic burn of her climax pumping magic back into him. Now.

Unfortunately, the one he had his eye on now would probably end up with whoever her assignment was.

As if on cue, her dark eyes widened, startled, as the piece of paper suddenly flew from her hand. Before Gawain could react, it zipped toward him and disappeared right into the center of his chest.

This one's yours, Gawain, Morgana's voice said clearly in his mind. *Don't get her killed, and try not to inflict more psychological damage than you can help.*

The girl blinked those doe eyes up at him.

"Umm. Hello." She paused and cleared her throat. "I'm Lark McGuin." Her voice held a hint of a sexy drawl, rich and smoky and as southern as Kentucky bourbon. She offered her hand for a handshake, and he took it. Her long fingers felt fragile and warm in his. "I guess you'll be my . . . mentor?"

"Apparently. I'm Gawain." She looked startled—at least she'd heard of him. He reached up to tap the hilt of the dragon sword sheathed across his back. "This is my partner, Kel."

The dragon extended his long neck and cocked his head, studying Lark with jeweled eyes. "My pleasure."

"It's an honor." To her credit, she spoke directly to Kel. New Maja tended to ignore him as if he were nothing but the sword he appeared to be. "Lord Tristan is my great-grandfather, and my grandfather loved telling stories about the Round Table." Turning her attention to Gawain again, she cleared her throat, visibly uncomfortable. "So what do we do now?"

Gawain suspected his smile was more than a little suggestive. "What would you like to do?"

Unease flickered in that chocolate gaze, and she shrugged. "Whatever you think best."

He frowned. Was there a hint of fear in her scent? No, he must be mistaken. Why would she fear him?

THREE

Lark followed Gawain's broad back through the crowd. He was almost as outrageously handsome as Tristan, though his face was a bit more rough-hewn and angular. Blond brows matched the neat Van Dyke beard framing his mouth and the thick blond hair that lay around his broad shoulders. An embroidered tunic covered the kind of muscular chest that was only built by swinging a broadsword, and his dark hose clung to a pair of powerful horseman's thighs. Gleaming black boots sheathed his legs to the shin, adorned by a pair of golden spurs—the symbol of knighthood.

Lark would have thoroughly enjoyed the view, if not for the sensual hunger glinting in Gawain's green eyes. After her run-in with Fangface the Sorcerer, she wanted to avoid vampires for a while.

That, however, wasn't really possible. Thanks to Merlin, Magi and Majae enjoyed a symbiotic relationship—the vampires needed to drink the witches' blood, and the witches needed to donate it. Otherwise, a Magus would starve, while a Maja's blood pressure could spike so high, she'd suffer a stroke.

Fortunately, you could bottle your donations, which is

what Lark had been doing. She hadn't had time to look for a lover since becoming a Maja, since she'd either been out on missions or training with Diera and Tristan.

Come to think of it, Fangface had been only the second vampire who'd ever bitten her.

Lark's hands curled into fists. Presumably Gawain wouldn't tear into her with Fangface's viciousness—she'd actually enjoyed Dominic Bonnhome's vampire lovemaking, after all. Still, just the thought of it made her break out in a cold sweat.

I'm so not ready for this.

But if she admitted she was afraid, Gawain would think her a coward. She'd grown up listening to firefighters joke about gutless rookies. She was damned if she was going to become the butt of that kind of joke.

John would be mortified.

Daytona Beach, Florida

Richard Edge had a hard-on. Cloaked in an invisibility spell, he leaned against the cream break face of the Breakers Shopping Mall and watched a slender, dark-haired woman walk through the automatic doors. It was late, after eleven. She must have caught the late movie at the mall cinema.

She was pretty enough, he decided, with big dark eyes and a full mouth, but she was older than he liked them. Richard's taste ran to coeds, preferably blondes or redheads.

Apparently, though, she was perfect for Jimmy Jones.

He could smell Jimmy's arousal, could sense the vicious anticipation radiating from the sorcerer as he waited a few feet away, cloaked in an invisibility spell of his own. Unlike Richard, he hadn't attempted to conceal himself from magical senses.

But then, he hadn't known anyone with magical senses was on his trail.

As the woman started across the parking lot toward her car, Richard felt Jimmy trail after her. Inhaling, he detected the metallic tang of a weapon on the wind. No scent of gunpowder, though. Probably a knife.

Jimmy liked to do his killing the old-fashioned way.

Richard licked his lips and felt his erection stiffen even more as he watched her walk away. The mall doors opened again, releasing a trio of teenager boys whooping about the movie they'd just seen, but he ignored them, completely focused on the woman and her invisible stalker.

For a moment, he imagined what his father would do if he were here. Bors would take the little fuck's head before he even knew what hit him. Personally, Richard favored cutting out the heart. Slowly. Gave him more time to enjoy it.

Smiling darkly, he started after the two. As the woman reached her Windstar, he broke into a run, his spell-silenced feet making no sound on the parking lot blacktop.

The woman walked around the van to the passenger door, one hand dipping into her purse for her keys. Apparently unable to find them, she paused to dig around, her attention on the handbag's contents.

Just as she looked down, Jimmy dropped the invisibility spell. He was a skinny little bastard, dressed in the gaudy crimson robes Geirolf's followers favored. The knife he held in one fist gleamed almost as cold as his soulless blue eyes. A lunatic grin of anticipation curved his narrow mouth.

The woman looked up from her purse, saw him, and screamed, the sound so pure and piercing with terror, Richard's cock twitched against the fly of his jeans.

Jimmy lunged for her, wrapping one wiry arm around her throat as he pressed the knife between her ribs. "Shut up, bitch!"

As she froze in terror, Jimmy lifted his head and chanted a quick spell. A dimensional gate popped into existence, and he began dragging the woman toward it. At that, she screamed again and tried to pull back, but he lifted her right off her feet and stepped through.

The instant before the gate vanished, Richard sent a spell of his own into it. As his magic showed him the killer's destination, he smiled in pleasure. They wouldn't be hard to follow at all.

Running footsteps snapped his head around. The three teenage boys who raced up, their eyes wide and white in dark faces. "Where'd she go, man?" the taller of the trio asked the others. The van had apparently blocked their view of the abduction.

"He must have dragged her off. I'm calling nine-one-one." The heavyset one pulled his cell phone from his pocket.

Waste of time, boys, Richard thought, as he turned away, still comfortably invisible.

Spotting a bar across the street, he strolled toward it. He figured he had a couple of hours to kill before Jimmy would be ready for him.

By the time they arrived at Gawain's home, Lark was pretty sure she was going to have her hands full.

He was, without question, the most seductive man she'd ever met. Even her vampire lover Dominic hadn't projected raw sex the way Gawain did.

He wasn't overt about it. No oily winks or leers or "You know you want it, baby" double-entendres. He just . . . looked at her. Not lecherously, as if picturing her naked, but with a steady, focused interest in those leaf-green eyes.

He asked her about her life and how she'd become a Maja, and he listened to the answers as if he actually cared what she had to say. Too many of the men she'd dated had made conversation as if just killing time until they could get her into bed.

Then again, they hadn't spent the past sixteen hundred years seducing women for a living.

Even the man's house was sensual. Three stories of elegant white stone, with high, curving walls and wrought-iron balconies, it was somehow medieval and modern at once. An interior courtyard hosted a tinkling fountain surrounded by a lush jungle of flowers, ornamental bushes, and cherry trees. Roses and orchids bloomed side by side—a neat bit of magic, that—scenting the air with their lush perfume.

The house's decor was just as striking. The furniture was starkly masculine, running toward big, sturdy pieces in cherry or walnut. No fussy French antiques for Gawain; he was definitely a massive leather couch kind of guy. Tapestries and paintings with medieval themes kept the place from looking too grim, providing splashes of bright color, while suits of ornate armor gleamed in corners.

Two of the three stories hosted fieldstone fireplaces big enough to barbecue an ox. The ground floor was a single huge room obviously designed for combat practice, while the second floor held a living room, a library, and a well-equipped kitchen. Four bedrooms and a modern office complete with computer occupied the third floor.

By the time they'd finished the tour, Lark was feeling completely out of her depth. She kept picturing her grandparents' home, with its kitschy firefighter figurines.

She was definitely not in Georgia anymore.

"Hey," Gawain said, interrupting her attack of insecurity, "you hungry?"

As if responding to the suggestion, her stomach growled.

Gawain gave her a cheerful grin. "I'll take that as a yes."

"*You put too* much garlic in that." Kel had partially uncurled himself from the sword in order to brace his forelegs on Gawain's shoulder. Tiny head cocked, he watched his partner minister to the pot of spaghetti sauce that bubbled on the gleaming stainless-steel stove.

"I did not. Emeril called for a teaspoon and a half of garlic, and that's exactly how much I added." He gave the pot a stir, tendons shifting in his brawny forearm.

Kel had transformed Gawain's court mourning outfit into a navy blue T-shirt that clung to his powerful chest, and a pair of well-worn jeans that hugged his butt each time he shifted his weight.

Fangface was becoming a distant memory.

"I'm telling you, it's got too much garlic."

"How the hell would you know?" Gawain stopped stirring to glare down at his tiny partner. "You don't eat."

"No, but I can smell just fine. And it needs more oregano."

"It does *not* need any more oregano."

"Ask Lark. She's the one who has to eat it."

"You're a pain in the ass, you know that?" Shaking his head, he turned to Lark and presented the spoon to her lips. "Tell Geico here he's nuts."

Battling a giggle, she leaned forward, blew on the spoon, and took a bite. Her eyes widened as the taste exploded on her tongue. "Damn, that's good! Rich, meaty . . ." She broke off, abruptly conscious of the heated green eyes staring down into hers.

"Let me see." Gawain lowered his head and gently took her mouth.

For an ambush kiss, it was astonishingly sweet. His tongue slid between her lips just once in a slow, seductive stroke. He tasted like wintergreen toothpaste and masculinity.

Lark gasped, forgetting her unease as she let herself lean into him. He felt as delicious as he tasted, all intriguing muscle and delightful vampire warmth.

Seconds spun dizzily by before he lifted his head. His gaze on her mouth, he licked his lips and gave her a slow smile. "Needs oregano."

"Told you!" the dragon crowed as Gawain turned back to the pot.

Lark leaned a hip against the counter and tried to catch her breath. "Damn," she muttered, "you're good."

He looked over his shoulder at her. There it was again—that flashing, breathtaking male smile. "I've had a very long time to practice."

And you can practice on me anytime, purred her libido. Her new vampire phobia squeaked a protest.

She tried to ignore it.

* * *

At Gawain's urging, Lark carried her plate into the living room. He followed with a pair of wineglasses and a bottle of a very fine red wine. Blood, apparently, was not all vampires drank.

As she sat down, he shrugged off Kel's scabbard and laid it across the stone coffee table before settling down next to her. Close, but not too much so.

Yep, this was definitely the setup for a seduction, she thought, eyeing the leaping fire. Which would be just fine—if she hadn't known he intended to bite her.

Fangface's ghost was back again, bloody canines and all.

Restlessly, Lark scooped up the roll he'd made and bit into it. It was crusty on the outside and soft on the inside, buttery, flavored with just enough garlic.

And she damned near didn't get it down.

Everything about this scene is perfect. Grimly, she forced another mouthful. *Except me.* She made herself take a bite of the spaghetti—again, delicious, if only she could swallow past the knot in her throat—and chased it with the wine.

"I told you, you put too much garlic," Kel announced from the table. "She's just playing with it."

"Maybe I did at that." Gawain studied her, a faint frown between his blond brows.

"No, really, it's wonderful," Lark protested. "I'm just . . . not that hungry."

His eyes shuttered. "Ah."

Bloody hell. Suddenly she remembered her grandfather tossing her into the deep end of the pool when she was thirteen. *Kid, you think too much*, he'd told her. *Sometimes it's better if you just jump in.*

Suddenly determined, Lark put the glass down on the table with a clink. "But now that you mention it, there's something else I am hungry for."

* * *

One minute, Gawain was watching his new apprentice pick at her dinner. The next, he had a lapful of warm woman sitting right on top of his erection. His cock, though frustrated by a zipper and two layers of denim, took this as a good sign. He'd been hard since he'd kissed her.

Lark's mouth swooped down over his for a kiss that made his toes curl in his cowboy boots.

And we have liftoff! Kel made the hissing sound Gawain had come to translate as a Draconian snicker. *And on that note, I'm going to bed. Looks like you've got it all well in hand.*

The sizzle of background magic that was Kel's consciousness went silent. The dragon never liked sharing minds while Gawain made love; it reminded him of how much he'd lost.

Lark, meanwhile, seemed intent on probing Gawain's mouth with her clever little tongue. Her lips moved over his, sweet and soft and demanding. Every nerve ending he had hummed approval.

Somewhere in the back of his mind, a little voice asked, *Where the hell did this come from?*

He told it to shut up. This was one gift horse he had no intention of looking in the mouth.

His hands discovered her little backside and found it perfect in those snug black jeans. Rounded cheeks just wide enough to comfortably fill his grip, long legs gripping his thighs with promising enthusiasm.

And Merlin's balls, that mouth. Tasting faintly of Emeril's spaghetti sauce, soft and teasing and just skilled enough. His cock throbbed longingly behind his zipper. His fangs twinged.

Her stroking tongue discovered one of the sharp points, hesitated, then thrust past it. Gawain groaned into her mouth.

The Desire roared to full force, demanding he sink himself into her and drive her to a white-hot orgasm. He slid a hand under the hem of her silky top, touched warm skin, and groaned in need.

"You feel so good," he whispered against her mouth. "You make my hands shake."

She drew back a little, her mouth damp, her eyes slumberous. His hand—and yes, it was trembling—found her breast and cupped her through her bra. Exploring, he discovered the lacy confection had a front closure. He promptly flicked it open and claimed bare flesh.

To his delight, her nipple rose against his palm, a hard, ripe little berry. Her breath caught. Taking the point between his fingers, he tugged it. She rewarded him with a soft moan.

Gawain was so hard now, his jeans dug into his erection. Saliva pooled in his mouth. She tilted her head back, panting, and he pressed his mouth to the slender arch of her throat. He could almost taste the blood pulsing against his lips. Enjoying the rich, heated roll of desire, he pressed the points of his fangs to her throat. Just teasing himself.

She froze. An acrid scent stung his nose.

Fear.

He drew back, frowning in puzzlement. Where had *that* come from? "Lark?"

She wouldn't look at him, instead cupping one hand over his as he held her breast. "That feels good. Do it some more." But her heart hammered against his palm, and somehow he knew it wasn't from desire.

"What's going on, Lark?"

Now she did meet his gaze. And lied right to his face. "Nothing."

"My ass." He examined her face grimly. "You're afraid of me."

"No. Of course not."

"Never lie to a vampire, darling. Even if I couldn't smell your fear, your heart is hammering like a rabbit's. What makes you think I'd hurt you? I know you've been with Magi be . . ." His eyes widened as, belatedly, he put two and two together. "It wasn't a Magus that hurt you."

She slumped and looked away. "No." There was such shame and misery on her pretty face that he winced in sympathy.

"You got into trouble during last night's invasion." Her fear was too new, too raw, for anything but a very recent cause. He pushed a strand of her dark hair away from her eyes and tucked it behind her ear. "What happened, Lark?"

She swallowed and looked away. He was beginning to think she wasn't going to answer when she finally admitted it. "When the attack started, I did okay. At first. I killed one of them." Her gaze flicked back to his with a touch of defiant pride.

Gawain nodded. "Good."

Lark blew out a breath. "But then another one hit me. He was . . . strong. They're all strong, but not like that. He knocked my sword out of my hand. I kept trying to blast him, but I couldn't get through his shields. He hit me, and I . . ."

Gawain worked to keep the rage off his face. The idea of one of those vicious bastards getting his hands on delicate little Lark McGuin . . . He cleared his throat. "The thing about the sorcerers is their death magic makes them really nasty on a battlefield. They get stronger the longer combat goes on because they draw power from the deaths around them."

"Oh." Her shoulders rounded. She still wouldn't meet his gaze. "That would explain it."

"What happened then?"

"He took me down and bit me." Lark swallowed. "Tore my throat. I tried to fight, but I couldn't get him off me. If Guinevere's spell hadn't wiped them all out, I'd be dead."

"It wasn't your fault, Lark."

"Obviously. But I couldn't stop it either. And now . . ." The girl rolled her shoulders in a jerky gesture. "Now I'm wondering what's going to happen the next time I'm in a fight." She met his gaze again. "But I won't run."

"Of course not."

"I just want you to be clear on that. You don't have to worry about me cutting and running. I won't do that." Despite the brave words, self-doubt shadowed her eyes. "I'm not a coward."

Every instinct Gawain had clamored to tell her she'd never have to face danger again, that he'd protect her with his last breath. But not only was such an offer unrealistic, it was insulting. She was a Maja, and she had her own power, her own pride. And her own responsibilities to the Magekind.

"Lark, it's natural to feel fear after what happened to you," Gawain said gently. " 'It's not the lack of fear that defines bravery . . . ' "

" '. . . It's doing the job.' Yeah, I've heard Arthur give that speech, too."

"It's not just a speech."

"I know that." Lark squared her fragile shoulders and met his gaze. "There's something else you need to know. You're probably expecting me to give you . . ." Her voice trailed off, then strengthened. ". . . blood. You've got a right to that. I'm a Maja. I've got a duty to feed Magi, especially a Magus who's my partner. But . . ."

"The idea of letting a vampire touch you makes you break out in a cold sweat." He could taste it in the air.

Her eyes narrowed with sudden determination. "I'm not going to let that stop me. I'll do it. I know you'll smell the fear—you're probably smelling it now—but that doesn't mean you have to stop."

He looked her in the eye. "I appreciate that, love, but there's no way in hell I'd ever drink from a woman who's as frightened as you are right now."

"This is not about chivalry. This is about not letting myself be crippled by one of those vampire bastards." She spoke through her teeth. *"He's not going to win this."*

Gawain shook his head. "It's not a question of winning . . ."

"Yes, it is. Gawain, he *beat* me. I'd be dead now if

Guinevere had been thirty seconds later destroying that grail. I lost. And if I don't overcome this . . ." She broke off, dragging in a deep, painful breath. "If I can't get past this, I'm no good to the Magekind."

To her horror, Lark felt tears sting her eyes. The words began to spill, faster and faster, choking her. "We've lost so many fighters, and those bastards are killing innocents. I can't just decide it's too tough and walk away."

Tristan would have given her a biting buck-up speech. Gawain merely studied her with sympathy. "I never thought you would."

Lark swiped a hand across her eyes. "Do *you* ever want to? Just hang it up, forget duty. Walk away?" She'd intended the question to sound challenging, but instead it held a note of longing.

"Everybody feels that way sometimes, especially in the middle of a war." He shrugged those strong shoulders. "But we're Magekind, and you don't get to run away from that."

"No. You've got to fight. You've got to beat the fear." And he was right. Despite the copper taste of it in her mouth, despite her pounding heart, it was obvious what she had to do.

Lark grabbed the hem of her T-shirt and pulled it off over her head. The bra he'd opened parted, revealing her bare breasts. She could have made her clothes disappear with a blink, but somehow she needed to remove them this way. "So that's what I'm going to do. Make love to me, Gawain. Please."

Blond brows flew upward. His gaze dipped to her nipples with a hint of longing before he dragged them back up to her face. "Believe me, there's nothing I want to do more. But . . ."

"No buts. Just . . . do it."

He squeezed his eyes shut and sighed. "You're killing me here, McGuin. I haven't fed in three days."

"That's what I'm saying. Feed. Take me." *Let me get it over with.*

Strong hands closed around her waist and lifted her off
his lap. She grabbed for him, but he put her on the couch,
then rose to his feet to pace restlessly. Sighing, he raked a
hand through his blond hair. "I know you haven't been a
Maja very long, but this is not the way it works."

"I'm not exactly a virgin, Gawain. I know what's going
on." Frustrated anger rose. Why was he making this so difficult? She just wanted to get it over with before her nerve
broke.

Gawain's gaze flashed to hers. "I'm not just a guy, Lark.
If I were, then maybe I could just concentrate on my own
pleasure and not care whether you got yours. If, that is, I
was also an asshole." He sighed. "But I'm a Magus. I don't
just drink blood—I need your pleasure, too, because it's
the energy of your climax that feeds my magic. Otherwise,
there's a whole magical wine cellar of bottled blood waiting for me at the Lords' Club."

"So you need me to come. I can do that."

"That's not the point." He scrubbed his hands over his
face and visibly reined in his own rising frustration. "I've
been at this sixteen hundred years. I probably could bring
you to orgasm, even as frightened as you are." He dropped
his hands and looked her in the eye. "And make no mistake, the Desire would love to take you up on your offer.
But taking you when you're this afraid would be way too
close to rape."

"Gawain . . ."

He dropped to his knees in front of her and took her
hands. "Sleep with me."

Lark blinked. "But I thought you just said . . ."

"I did. And I meant it. Tonight I just want to sleep beside
you. Tomorrow night, we'll see. But tonight I want to teach
your body that you're safe with me."

Deep in her chest, a small, cold knot seemed to untie itself. "But the Desire . . ."

"Can wait another night, Lark. It looks like we're going
to be partners for a while, so there'll be other opportunities

to make love." His warm thumbs stroked the backs of her hands. "What do you say?"

She blew out a breath and tried not to feel guilty at her relief. "All right."

Gawain picked up Kel's scabbard and looped it over his shoulder as he led the way to the stairs. With every step he took, his randy body growled at him. He tried to ignore it as he showed her to his bedroom.

Lark stopped just inside, lovely brown eyes going wide. "Wow."

Resting a hand on the small of her back, he glanced past her shoulder. A full suit of sixteenth-century German plate armor stood shining in the light cast by the stone fireplace, while his favorite jousting saddle stood at the foot of the immense canopied bed. Tapestries, rich with color and skillful needlework, depicted battles or scenes of castle life. One entire wall was occupied by a mural depicting the Round Table with all the original knights, including those, like Bedivere, who'd died in combat.

"That bed . . ." Lark moved toward it, her pretty backside swaying, unconsciously seductive. "You could sleep five in that thing."

And he had, though he had no intention of mentioning that to her.

She gazed up at the red silk canopy which fell around the bed like a knight's campaign tent. One delicate hand came to rest on a gleaming oak bedpost carved in the shape of a javelin. "Damn, Gawain, you could get women with this bed alone."

He laughed. "Well, I'd like to think looks and skill have something to do with it, too."

"If you ask me," Kel said, "it's a bit over the top."

Gawain looked down at his sword. "I thought you were asleep."

Your body woke me. It says to tell you it's pissed.

Tell it I heard it the first time. Aloud, he said, "Maybe you should consider another nap." He hung Kel's scabbard over the bedpost.

Why aren't you seducing her? You need to feed, Gawain. You've gone too long without a woman. You're going to get weak. What if . . .

She's afraid of me, Kel.

The dragon went silent, shocked. *But . . .*

I'll explain later. Sleep.

As he watched, the dragon stiffened, his body seeming to solidify as though it were the steel it resembled. Again, the sizzle of Kel's magical consciousness faded to silence.

"What happened to him?" Lark asked, staring at the sword with an uneasy frown. "It's like he just . . . turned inanimate."

"He shuts himself down when I go to sleep or need some privacy." Gawain turned to flip down the heavily embroidered coverlet for her. "It's the only way we can keep from driving each other craz . . ." He looked over his shoulder at her and broke off.

While he'd been busy with the bed, she'd transformed her jeans and top into a cotton sleep shirt. The points of her nipples were visible through the soft pink fabric. As he gaped, she moved past him and crawled into bed, her rounded backside unconsciously teasing his growling libido. He swallowed and blurted, "You know, you've got the most delicious ass I've ever seen."

Lark gave him a wicked look. "Yours isn't so bad either."

Gawain stared at her, wrestling with the impulse to pounce. Regaining control, he blew out a breath. "Glad to hear it." He took off his T-shirt, decided his self-control wasn't sturdy enough to risk losing the jeans, and slid in next to her.

"Are you sure you don't want to . . . ?"

"I'm sure," he lied.

FOUR

Lying next to Gawain's big body, Lark realized, was con-
ducive to anything but relaxation. "How long before the
sun comes up?" The Daysleep would put him out like a
light. Then, maybe, she could sleep.

"Another hour yet." He rolled over on his side and
braced his head on his arm. Biceps shifted temptingly in
the light of the fire. "I thought we could just lie here
and . . . talk."

"What about?"

"You."

She snorted. "I'm not that interesting."

"What was it like growing up in the twentieth century?
With television and computers and all those techno toys?"

"What techno toys? You know what a firefighter makes?
We were doing good to afford McDonald's on Saturday
night. Any extra cash we had usually ended up going to
people who'd just been burned out of their homes."

"Your father was a fireman?"

"Grandfather, and he was a paid fire chief. Little southern town. My grandmother was the president of the Ladies'
Auxiliary. We used to follow Granddad to fire calls and

serve lemonade to the firemen." She folded her arms under her head and stared up into the folds of the canopy bed, remembering. "One of my earliest memories was sitting next to a little girl whose kitten had died in a fire. I felt so sorry for her, I gave her my doll."

"Sounds grim."

"Actually, it made me feel pretty good. I did something to help someone in an awful situation. You can get addicted to that kind of thing."

The conversation settled into a comforting rhythm after that, as she told him about her grandmother's fatal stroke, her mother, and her endless childhood speculations over just who her father had been. "My favorite theoretical candidate was Mick Jagger."

Without cracking a smile, he said, "I'm happy to say you don't look a bit like your daddy."

She laughed. "How about you? What were your folks like?"

His expression went oddly distant. "It's . . . hard to recall them now. I remember my father's great boom of a laugh, and I remember the long red fall of my mother's hair. Horseplay with my brothers. But when I try to see their faces . . ." He broke off.

"I've often wondered what it would be like to have lived all those centuries. My God, you were there when the Magna Carta was signed."

"Actually, I think I had a dentist appointment . . ."

She picked up her pillow and hit him. Laughing, he fended it off before continuing more seriously, "After a while, you learn not to think of how long it's been." His voice had acquired an odd cadence, a hint of an accent she couldn't identify, almost Irish, yet not. "You come to live in a bubble of now, because if you think too much about the past, the sheer weight of it will crush you. You have to focus on the present. The music, the books, television programs, the video games. All those things anchor us. Keeps us . . . human."

"Arthur and his Elvis obsession."

"There you go. Personally, I love television. Especially cop shows."

"You actually admit to watching television? Most people swear they watch nothing but CNN."

"Most people say they don't masturbate either, but they lie."

She laughed. "So what else do you like to watch?"

He didn't answer.

"Gawain?"

Deep, even breathing.

The sun must have risen, she realized. He'd fallen into the Daysleep between one breath and the next.

With a sigh, Lark rolled over and curled against Gawain's muscular ribs. In moments, she, too, was asleep.

Lark woke to her body's purr of desire. She was enveloped in the scent of warm male, and a hard body spooned the length of her back as she lay on her side. One brawny arm lay possessively around her waist. Her eyes widened as she felt a thick ridge pressing against her panties-clad butt. Even through his blue jeans, it was obvious her bed partner had one heck of an erection.

She lifted her head and looked back over her shoulder at him. The enchanted fire had put itself out, and the room was too dark to make out anything. Either it was night— and Gawain would be awake if it were—or there was a spell shield on the windows. Vampires didn't actually burst into flame in the sunlight, but they did get really nasty burns, so magical shielding was required.

For a moment, she wished for a flashlight, then remembered her magic. A quick spell, and a tiny globe of light floated on the tips of her fingers.

Lark sat up, easing regretfully from Gawain's loose hold. He was in the Daysleep anyway. He wouldn't wake up until the sun set.

So she turned around and looked at him. And caught her breath as her body's hum of need grew louder.

Even asleep, with all that thick blond hair tumbled around his face, he looked tough and competent. And his body—she'd never seen a chest like that outside of a hunk-of-the-month calendar. Unlike the hunks, though, he was dusted with blond body hair that somehow made him look more real than their shaved and airbrushed perfection.

In the light of her spell, she suddenly noticed a thin raised line running across his biceps. Looking closer, she saw more of them snaking over his pecs, abdomen, even across his shoulders and down his back. They looked as straight as if someone had laid them out with a ruler. She puzzled over them several minutes before realizing they were scars from old sword wounds that must have predated his becoming a vampire. Anything afterward would have healed whenever he turned into a wolf.

Damn, he'd led a hard life even before he drank from Merlin's Grail.

Who'd have thought a man who'd been a warrior so many centuries could be so . . . sweet. She smiled slightly, realizing Gawain would probably hate hearing himself referred to in those terms.

Her gaze drifted down to his groin, where that erection of his still pressed hopefully against his fly. Not even the Daysleep had been able to discourage it. Yet all he'd done was hold her.

She let herself imagine making love to him, feeling that strong body move against hers, that luscious cock sliding deep. His mouth on her throat . . . Unease rose, but it was paler this morning. As if somehow he'd taught her body to trust him during the night.

"Enjoying the view?" His voice sounded deep and drowsy. Lark looked up at him, surprised, and he gave her a smile. "The sun just set."

Gawain rolled over onto his back and stretched out his powerful arms as he arched his spine. His washboard belly rippled, and his chest expanded as he gave vent to a jaw-cracking yawn. Lark stared. He seemed to completely fill his aircraft carrier of a bed.

She was still drooling helplessly when he rolled to his bare feet to tower over her. She blinked at his naked torso and listened to her heart pound.

"Hungry?" he asked.

"God, yes." Lark licked her lips and reached for him.

"Great. How does an omelet sound?" He turned just before her fingers touched him, sauntered to the headboard and scooped up Kel's scabbard.

"That was not exactly the breakfast I had in mind," she told him dryly.

"You need to keep up your strength, darling." Wicked white fangs flashed in his grin. "You're going to need it."

After a breakfast that was just as tasty as her abandoned dinner—the man really was a great cook—Lark discovered what he'd meant by that "you're going to need it" crack. And it wasn't going to be nearly as much fun as she'd hoped.

"Kel, armor me up please," Gawain said, as he led the way to the huge round practice chamber that occupied the bottom floor of the house. "Lark, you, too. And blunt your blade."

Obediently, she conjured a practice weapon, making sure the point was rounded off and the edge nonexistent. Kel grimaced as he morphed the Dragon Sword to match.

Automatically, she looked around, assessing their surroundings as Tristan had taught her. The stone walls threw back ringing echoes that could potentially be deceptive; she made a mental note to watch out for them. Overhead, massive wooden ceiling beams added to the medieval effect of all that rock, while the floor was covered in a thick, soft layer of sawdust they kicked up with each step.

At least it wouldn't hurt when she fell on her ass.

Despite a jittery suspicion she wasn't ready for this,

Lark called her magic and conjured her armor. She felt it shimmer in around her body, first light as foam, then solidifying until it covered her in sturdy magical plate.

The weight of it instantly brought back the last time she'd worn it. She saw the fireball, felt the sorcerer's body crushing down on her chest, the pain of fangs ripping into her throat. . . .

"She's having a flashback," Kel warned.

"Hey, Lark!" Gawain snapped, dragging her out of her sick preoccupation.

She sucked in a breath and flipped up her visor to see him watching her with concern. Her brows flew upward as she registered what he was wearing.

The knight's armor was constructed of thousands of tiny interlocking scales that seemed to flow around his big body like water. Intricately designed plate armor covered points of particular vulnerability—his chest, knees, elbows, shins, and forearms. Each solid section was engraved with dragons, soaring or rampant in the attack, wings spread wide, long necks snaking. Protective runes were worked in around the dragons in a language she didn't recognize. Probably Draconian.

Good God, Lark thought, staring up at him in uneasy awe, *he's bigger than Fangface the Sorcerer. Hell, he's bigger than a space shuttle.* Her unease spiraled in on itself, building into panic. *He's going to kick my ass. He'll ask Morgana to assign him somebody who isn't a gutless spastic. And Tristan will disown me.*

"Snap out of it," Gawain said sharply.

"What?" Jolted, she glowered at him, feeling defensive and embarrassed.

"You're getting worked up again. I can smell it from here." He raised his own visor and gentled his tone. "Look, this is only a training session, just like the ones you've been having with Tristan for the past six months. No big deal."

Lark gave him a smile that felt a little sickly even to her. "Wouldn't you rather just have sex?"

"Yeah, actually, now that you mention it. But we could get sent out on a mission any minute, and I don't want actual combat to be your first time using a sword again. We need to get you over the hump now."

"You're right." She sighed and flipped her visor closed. "I really hate that in a guy."

"He does that being right thing a lot," Kel agreed. "Except when he's wrong, and then he's even more annoying."

Despite her anxiety, she found herself grinning. "What's so annoying about that?"

"He still thinks he's right." The tiny dragon grinned back.

Gawain lifted an eyebrow. "Whenever you two are done with the comedy routine, we can get started."

"If you insist." But the teasing had relaxed her a little, and she was able to fall into guard as Tristan had taught her, only a light film of sweat dampening her palms.

Instead of charging her as she'd half feared he would, Gawain glided sideways, starting a spiraling pattern she recognized from her practice sessions. Automatically, she slid into a counter circle. For such a tank of a man, he moved with grace, as light on his big feet as a dancer.

In any real fight, he'd eat her alive.

Abruptly, sparks began to gather around Kel, surprising her. That's right—the dragon could work magic, though for a practice like this, a spell would be more light than force. Even as the energy ball shot toward her, Lark tossed up a shield and ducked aside, letting it splash harmlessly away. Then—what the hell—she moved in to engage her opponent.

Gawain met her with a sword swing she figured was about half speed. Lark parried and hit back, aiming for his right arm. He blocked—again not nearly as hard as she suspected he could. Instead of dancing apart again, they settled into an exchange of sword work that was almost slow enough to qualify as lazy.

Lark caught the flash of his smile through his visor. "Good. You're getting the rhythm."

He's right. This isn't so bad, she realized, relieved. *I can do this . . .*

Steel flashed out of nowhere. Lark jerked up a parry a little too slow. The flat of Gawain's blade landed against her helm with a sharp *thwack!*

"Pay attention."

"Ass," she muttered inside her ringing helm. Temper steaming just a bit, she sent a blast of light rolling off her left hand and right into his face.

Kel blocked the spell, but in the instant Gawain was dazzled, she came up inside his guard and landed a solid thump alongside his ribs.

Pleased, he nodded. "Good one."

She didn't even see the return swing that picked her up and dumped her on her backside hard enough to jar her teeth.

The nerves she'd been so worried about disappeared in a flash of temper. Unhurt thanks to her armor, she rolled to her feet and charged in. He parried, pivoted smoothly aside from her charge, and caught her right on the ass with the flat of his blade. She hit the sawdust on her face.

Growling, she jerked onto all fours and spun to glare at him.

Gawain just watched her calmly. "You know better than that. You get pissed off, you get dead."

Lark curled her lip, barely even noticing that she wasn't afraid anymore. She really, really wanted to put him on his butt. Just once. Her left hand fisted in the sawdust . . .

And gave her an idea.

"Up and at 'em, Lark," Gawain told her, moving closer.

"Give me a second," she rasped, dropping her head as if winded.

Just as she'd known he would, he frowned and took another step forward. "Hey, are you . . ."

Lark shot a spell into her handful of sawdust and flung it at him like a fastball.

Kel didn't quite shield fast enough. It hit his visor with a wet plop and promptly exploded into goo. Before the dragon could burn it off, Lark surged upward and swung.

This time it was Gawain's helm that rang like a bell. He hit the ground on his back.

"Yes!" Lark did an impromptu end-zone boogie around his astonished, prostrate body.

He promptly hooked her ankle with his foot and jerked. She tumbled and he pounced, flattening her under his weight.

Flipping up his gooey visor, he growled, "Peanut butter? You took me down with a ball of *peanut butter?*"

She couldn't breathe. *Weight crushing down on her chest, a fanged face looming over her . . .* Terror jerked her heart into a ball of ice.

"Gawain!" Kel snapped.

"Shit!" He jerked off his helm and threw it aside, then rolled away, lifting his free hand in an I-mean-no-harm gesture. "Lark, baby, it's me. You're okay!"

The sight of those worried green eyes thawed the knot, and she caught her breath with a gasp. She doubled over, panting and sickened. "Oh, man."

"Hey, I'm sorry about that." He eased back to her side. "I wasn't even thinking. Screwed that up, didn't I? And you were doing so well."

"The peanut butter thing was clever," Kel put in. "I wasn't expecting that at all."

Her thundering heartbeat had begun to slow. "Yeah, Tristan always told me the only way to beat a guy like you was to cheat."

Kel snorted. "Lark, when it comes to battle, there's no such thing as cheating."

She sat back on her heels with a sigh. "Just what Tristan always says."

"You okay?" Gawain studied her, his gaze anxious.

Lark looked up at him, taking in that rough-hewn face and armored Humvee of a body. Suddenly his worry for her struck her as unbearably sweet.

She leaned forward and kissed him.

It was an impulse kiss, more fast smack than anything else. But as she started to draw away, the taste of him registered, male and sexy and unbearably tempting.

She found herself leaning in again for another taste. And this time, he kissed her back.

Heat rolled through her like molten honey, and Lark moaned softly. She slipped her tongue into his mouth, tasting him. He responded with a lazy tongue swirl of his own, and the kiss heated.

When they finally came up for air, Lark drew back a little. Green eyes searched hers, hooded.

She cleared her throat and tried to calm her ragged breathing with a change of subject. "I did okay, though. At least at first."

The Desire heated his eyes again. "You did great—until I scared you."

"It wasn't your fault." She sighed. "I'm just going to have to work on it."

He stroked a gentle armored hand through her hair. "You'll get better."

"Yeah." And she would. He'd shown her that much. "I think I'm going to be all right with the magic and the sword stuff. Maybe we should try some hand-to-hand now." She met his gaze and tried to pretend the very idea didn't make her heart pound.

Gawain studied her face, his eyes softening. "Yeah, I think I can show you a thing or two."

Her lips twitched. "Oh, I'm sure of it."

He laughed. "We probably need to drop the armor. Hard to practice these kinds of techniques in full plate."

"Would a *gi* do?" Reading his lifted brow, she explained, "I took martial arts for a while. My granddad wanted to make sure I could fend off pushy dates."

Gawain gave her a teasing smile. "I'll keep that in mind."

Lark closed her eyes and started to transform her armor

into a loose cotton *gi*. At the last moment, though, her feminine ego rebelled, and the *gi* became silk instead.

When she opened her eyes again, Gawain was looking at her with heated approval. Since he himself wore nothing but loose, low-slung cotton pants, her view wasn't bad either. "God, I love that chest."

"Funny," he drawled, giving her *gi* jacket a longing glance, "I was thinking the same thing."

Lark laughed. "Charmer."

"I do try." He crouched to lay Kel in the sawdust, then straightened and moved toward her. "Okay, let me show you what to do the next time one of those bastards gets you on your back."

She smiled at him, unable to resist the urge to tease. "Does that mean you want to be on top?"

"One of my favorite positions," he agreed, straight-faced.

Lark lay down, then braced herself up on her elbows as he dropped to his knees beside her. "Now, if you start feeling panicky, let me know."

"Sure. Though actually, I feel a bit better now that neither of us is in armor. You're a big guy anyway, but suited up, you look like a tank."

"That's the idea," Kel said from the sawdust. "If you can intimidate the hell out of your opponent, you've got an instant advantage."

She grimaced. "Whereas bad guys look at me and think, *Happy Meal!*"

"Sweetheart, it's all in the attitude. A Maja with a couple of flaming balls of death around her hands is plenty intimidating." Gawain crawled over her on all fours, careful not to actually touch her. His long hair hung in his face, and he tossed his head to throw it out of the way so he could meet her eyes. "Is this okay?"

Lark eyed the luscious expanse of his tanned shoulders and cleared her throat. "It's fine."

"Good." For once, his expression was intent, serious.

"First off, if a sorcerer's got you down like this, your objective is to get him the hell off as fast as possible. Don't bother struggling—just fry his ass. Pour as much magic into him as you can. That's your best weapon."

His mouth looked deliciously kissable. *Concentrate, Lark.* "Magic. Best weapon. I know that. But that guy the other night—he'd stunned me with a blast. Next thing I knew, he had me pinned."

"Like this?" He caught her wrists and pressed them into the sawdust, then lowered his body over hers until their bellies touched.

Lark swallowed. His fingers felt strong and warm without the cold metal of his gauntlets covering them. "Yeah. I couldn't move my hands."

"You know, the magic doesn't have to come from your fingertips," Kel said from his nest of sawdust. "Dragons breathe their spells. Hell, you could beam it from your eyes like Superman if you wanted. Body parts are just a focal point. The magic comes from inside."

Lark looked up at Gawain and promptly yielded to temptation. "You mean like this?" Puckering her lips as if blowing a kiss, she breathed a spell into his face.

"Whoa!" His eyes widened at the blatantly sexual buzz she'd sent him. He blinked, and a flush climbed his cheeks as he hardened against her belly in a delightful rush. "Ummm. Probably best not to use that particular spell on the bad guys."

Lark gave him a deliberately heavy-lidded glance. "Tell you what—I'll save it for you."

He cleared his throat. "You do that."

Damn, but he liked her, Gawain thought. Yes, she was woefully inexperienced, but then, so were Geirolf's sorcerers, at least compared to him. As long as he kept an eye on her, she'd be okay.

Merlin knew keeping an eye on her would be no

hardship. That lush little body was driving him crazy. With every breath, heat pooled in his balls and spun into his rapidly lengthening erection.

And she wanted him, too. He could smell the intoxicating scent of arousal rising from her half-clad skin.

Unfortunately, there was a hint of fear mixed in with her need. Which was no surprise either, really. She was a full foot shorter than he, no taller than five-four or so, with a slender build that intensified the impression of fragility.

Her features were equally delicate in her heart-shaped face. Her slim nose was just a touch long, and her mouth was full-lipped, sweetly sensual. Her hair fell around her shoulders in a cascade of dark silk that seemed to invite his fingers.

He couldn't help noticing there was nothing small about those full, pretty breasts. Most of what little height she had seemed to be leg. Add that long swan's neck, and she looked like a vampire's wet dream.

And she kept staring at his mouth.

Oh, hell. If he didn't call this off, he was going to lose it and really scare her.

"I think that's enough for today." Gawain released her slim shoulders and rolled away from her.

Distance. He needed distance.

Right now.

Lark watched as Gawain rose to his feet and turned away from her, his entire body stiff. And she knew exactly why.

He wanted her.

But after spending the past couple of hours in mock combat, Lark found the idea of his hunger a lot less intimidating than it had been. He'd proven he wouldn't hurt her, no matter what the provocation.

And she wanted him. Really wanted him, not just to work through her fear or to prove a point to both of them. She wanted to make love, something she hadn't done in far too long. Even her encounters with Dominic had been purely about triggering her Gift.

With Gawain, she knew she'd feel real passion. She'd feel alive for the first time in months, without the weight of guilt or grief or fear.

And God, she needed that.

"Gawain," she said softly, rising to her feet.

He didn't turn around. "What?"

"You're not the only one who's hungry." She untied her *gi* belt.

Gawain glanced over his shoulder at her just as she let the jacket slide off her shoulders. He turned completely as she pulled off the loose shirt that lay under it, then dropped the silken trousers. The way his eyes blazed as he watched made her feel like the hottest thing since Carmen Electra. He swallowed. "Are you sure you're ready for this?"

Lark smiled slightly, knowing her arousal must be perfuming her scent. "Take a deep breath," she suggested, "and you tell me."

He inhaled, and his eyes widened. "Oh, you're sure."

"I always did like mammal females," Kel said from the sawdust. "You're all so soft and warm." He sighed gustily. "Ah, well. I suppose this is my cue to sleep."

"That might be best," Gawain agreed without looking away from Lark's nudity. His voice sounded gratifyingly hoarse.

With a last longing look at her, Kel dropped his muzzle and closed his ruby eyes the instant before his body stiffened.

Even as Kel went to sleep, Gawain was stripping off his pants.

If anything, the knight was even more impressive without the armor. She blinked, taking in the sculpted beauty of his broad torso, the long powerful legs, the brawny arms. His skin retained a tan that must date back sixteen centuries, when he'd first drunk from Merlin's Grail and become immortal. The brown tone contrasted with the pale gold of the chest hair that formed a tree-of-life pattern over his muscular pecs. The pattern narrowed as it flowed down to his groin, as if mapping the way to treasure.

He was fully, deliciously erect, his staff thick and jutting over a pair of full, taut balls.

And she was just as ready for him.

FIVE

Lark ached to touch that luscious erection, but she didn't want to rush the moment. Instead, she reached out and brushed her fingertips across his ruff of chest hair. It felt intriguingly springy, yet surprisingly soft.

As she moved her hand, her thumb brushed a tiny dark nipple. The little point tightened, and Gawain made a low, sensual sound in his throat.

Lark looked up at him, enjoying the slow, sweet burn of arousal. After teasing each other for so many hours, touching him was such a sweet relief.

"That was nice," he told her. His lids lowered, shielding the bright green of his gaze even as his lips parted, revealing the points of his fangs.

An image of the sorcerer's bloody mouth flashed through her mind. She froze.

Gawain's gentle hand caught hers. "Don't think about that bastard. He's dead. And if he wasn't, I'd kill him for you." His gaze searched hers, demanding her belief. "I'm not going to do anything you don't want me to do."

"That's fine," she told him steadily. "Because I want you to do everything."

Intent on proving just that, Lark rose on her toes, threaded her fingers through his long hair, and drew his head down. His mouth opened under hers, lips like damp satin, flavored with masculinity, rough and wild.

She put everything she had into the kiss, with gentle bites of his lips and slow, swirling thrusts of her tongue. He kissed her back, his big hands sliding down to cup her bare backside and lift her against his muscular belly. She caught his brawny shoulders to steady herself, leaning into him, enjoying the hard strength of his body. His cock pressed along the length of her belly, hungry and thick with his need.

Gawain lifted his head just a moment, meeting her gaze. His lips were damp, his green eyes hot. Then his mouth swooped down again.

This time he didn't let her take the lead. The kiss was all feral male demand, so hot and seductive, Lark melted against him with a low moan.

With an answering growl, he bent her backward over one bare arm so he could reach her breasts. She gasped as he drew one nipple into his mouth, raking it gently with his teeth, then suckling hard enough to send her head into a pleasurable spin.

Lark dropped her hands to the sculpted muscle of his shoulders. Running her fingertips over the heated satin topography of his skin, she gently explored the strong ridges and hollows, combed her nails through his chest hair, thumbed his small nipples.

With a low groan of pleasure, Gawain pulled her upright and released her nipple. "Merlin's beard, that feels good."

Tracing the fine trail of hair down his belly, she paused just over the flushed head of his cock. "I'll bet I can make it feel even better."

He laughed. "I'll bet you can, too."

"Mmm." Lark wrapped her fingers around the hard shaft. Its flushed head was already beaded with a drop of precome. She stroked her thumb over it and enjoyed Gawain's growl.

Inspired, she pulled away from his arms and dropped to her knees before those brawny horseman's thighs. His cock jutted at her, flushed and delightfully thick surrounded by its nest of golden curls. Hers. All hers.

Lark cupped him possessively, rolling his balls between the fingers of one hand as she stroked the other down his veined shaft. "Well, hello there," she said to the fat dewed crown. "Would you like to play?"

"Definitely." The laughing heat in Gawain's voice made all kinds of things draw tight low in her belly.

She grinned up at him and leaned closer, taking the velvet thrust of him into her mouth. He tasted delightfully salty, and the head of the big organ felt silken against her lips. She swirled her tongue over it and listened to him groan.

Her anxiety had drained away. *Nothing like a guy with a big dick to put everything else into perspective.* She caught his shaft by the base and angled it upward, licking along its sensitive underside as if enjoying a candy cane. He groaned, one big hand coming to rest on her head, tangling in her hair. For a moment, she stiffened, remembering Fangface's vicious grip. Then she shrugged the memory off and took Gawain's balls in her mouth, suckling gently.

"Oh, Merlin's beard, you're good at that . . ." he whispered, his voice choked.

Before she could try out the next erotic torment on her list, he dropped to his knees in front of her. "Want to see what *I'm* good at?" His mouth covered hers in another of those deliciously tempting kisses.

When he let her up for air, she gasped, "I've got a pretty good idea already."

Gawain laughed darkly. "Now, that's what I like to hear." He paused for a moment, staring at her bare breasts with hungry intensity. When he finally reached out to cup her, she let her head fall back with a sigh.

"You're beautiful," he murmured, and tugged her nipples gently, milking them into hardening even more.

Lark lifted her head to contemplate him through

shuttered lids and waves of pleasure. "You're not so bad yourself."

Gawain grinned and slid an arm around her waist, lifting her as he leaned forward to take a nipple into his mouth again. Pleasure furled through her like a silken ribbon as he swirled his tongue around the peak.

She was all but writhing by the time he pressed her back onto the thick sawdust and went to work on her breasts in earnest. Caressing and teasing, he suckled until she fisted both hands in his hair, maddened by the sweet pleasure.

Just when she'd thought she'd explode from that alone, he began working his way down her torso in a string of teasing nibbles that let her feel the tips of his fangs. Panting, she tossed her head against the sawdust. "You're driving me insane!"

His laughter gusted against her belly button. "Good."

"Sadist."

"Watch how you talk to the vampire, Lark." Settling down between her thighs, he spread them wide and lowered his head. "Or he'll have to punish you."

"Oooh, God," she groaned. "Be my guest!"

The first molten swipe of his tongue made her arch off the floor with a gasp. He circled her clit next, teasing it, then sucking the tight pearl into his mouth. The intensity of the pleasure made her thighs quiver.

Then he found her sex with a forefinger and slid slowly inside, and she made a helpless, high-pitched sound of pure need.

"Very nice," Gawain murmured. "All slick and tight." A second finger joined the first in a lazy pump. She rolled her hips pleadingly. He looked up her body into her face, anticipation hot in his eyes, and gave her another delicious pass of his tongue.

Panting, Lark hooked a bare heel over his shoulder, urging him on as he stoked her closer to orgasm with every hot move he made.

As delicious as all that felt, though, she was dying to

experience that thick cock. "Any time you want to replace those fingers with something else . . . AH! . . . go right ahead."

Green eyes met hers over the arch of her body. He smiled and thrust two fingers deep. "So I have your permission?" Another breath-stealing thrust.

"Oh! Yes, oh, God!" She squeezed her eyes closed, gasping at the ferocious pleasure.

"Don't mind if I do." Big hands caught her by the ankles and spread her wide.

Lark's eyes flew open just in time to watch him rise over her and aim himself for her slick channel. For a moment he paused, kneeling there, his body a delicious sculpture in brawn and lust, green eyes hot. His parted lips showed the tips of his fangs.

Then he leaned down, braced a powerful forearm beside her head, and began stuffing her one slow inch at a time, working his cock in with short, delicious digs. His grin was feral and very male. "You're tight," he purred.

"You're huge!" Lark panted and let her head fall back to the sawdust.

"Keep it up, and you'll give me a swelled head." He pushed deeper, putting his weight behind it. "Among other things."

Even Dominic hadn't felt anything like this. He stretched her hard, balancing her on the knife edge between pleasure and pain, until he was all the way inside.

Muscled torso pressed against her soft belly, he braced himself above her. His handsome face was intent, hungry, as he stared down into her eyes, visibly enjoying her reaction to his entry.

"Like that?" Gawain rumbled.

She lifted one leg and wrapped it around his sweat-damp waist. "Oh, God, that's an understatement."

"Mmmmmm." His lips curled. "It does feel like you like it." He started withdrawing, a slick satin slide. "All wet and snug."

She hummed, a wordless purr of approval, and rolled her hips, enjoying the stroke of his delicious cock.

The muscles of Gawain's broad chest flexed under her gaze as he began to pump, slow and lazy, a man who clearly loved making love for its own sake.

Pleasure bloomed with each long stroke, glowing brighter and brighter. Lark wrapped both legs around his waist and hooked her ankles together so she could grind up at him, chasing the orgasm that hovered just out of reach like a glowing balloon. As her need grew, she dug her nails into his shoulders, unconsciously spurring him on.

Responding to her demand, Gawain increased the force of his thrusts until he was grinding against her clit, driving that big cock to her depths in short, tormenting digs.

The orgasm she'd been chasing burst wide in a hot white explosion. She threw back her head and yowled at the delicious pulsing burn.

With a hungry growl, Gawain rolled with her so that he was on the bottom, driving his cock up into her depths. Writhing astride him, she didn't notice his hand tangling in her hair, pulling her head up.

His mouth covered the pulse beating in her throat, and she felt the sharp sting of his fangs. Shocked, she jerked, the motion driving his cock even deeper. A spurt of fear rose and she tried to pull away.

This time Gawain didn't back off, his big cock working in her depths, spilling pleasure with every thrust as he fed. Her fear died, drowned in blazing pleasure and the trust he'd worked to build. Stretched wide as his cock impaled her and his mouth suckled her throat, she could only come again, screaming hoarsely. He stiffened, his cry muffled against her neck, and came, pumping endlessly deep.

Panting, dazed, Lark lay spread across Gawain's big body, listening to his thundering heartbeat slow. He arched his back, withdrawing his softening cock with a groan. She echoed it and clung to him.

Her throat ached, but like the burn in her sex, it was a good pain. "You bit me," she murmured sleepily.

"I'm a vampire. We do that." Then he lifted his head and examined her face, worry in his eyes. "Did I frighten you?" When she didn't answer at once, he cursed himself. "I'm sorry, I just . . ."

"No, it was wonderful." She smiled at him, pleased by his concern. "I just . . . wasn't expecting it. I thought you were going to warn me."

He dropped his head and stroked her hair. "If I'd warned you, you'd have convinced yourself to panic again. As it was, you were too turned on."

Lark eyed him. "That was high-handed of you."

He sighed. "Yes, it was. Do you mind?"

"Well," Lark drawled, "I could turn you into a frog, but since you just gave me a mind-blowing multiple orgasm, I'll let you off with a warning."

"Gee, thanks."

With a silent huff of laughter, she settled back onto his chest to enjoy the sheer, sensual pleasure of lying across him. A companionable silence ticked by before he said, "Are you hungry? I feel the need to feed you again."

Lark lifted her head and smiled at him. "You know, I think I could get used to this."

Lark and Gawain adjourned to the kitchen while she ate a lazy midnight lunch—a sandwich this time, chased by ripe strawberries he fed her one by one. They were both feeling replete when Kel interrupted.

"Gawain, we've got company at the door."

He looked at his friend, who rode his shoulder scabbard as usual. "And they didn't call first? Who?"

"Tristan and his new apprentice."

Lark looked up in surprise. "Wonder what he wants?"

Gawain rose from the table. "Let's find out, shall we?"

Somehow he had a feeling this wasn't a casual visit, though he and Tristan were good friends. They'd fought side by side for centuries, saved one another's lives, gotten drunk together, even shared a woman or two. As Bors had said, Tristan didn't have a high opinion of women in general; his failed romance with Isolde had left scars that had never really healed.

Something told Gawain, however, that Tristan was going to be protective of Lark. Hell, he felt protective of Lark, and he'd known her less than a day.

So he wasn't surprised when he opened the door to find his friend on the other side looking tense and uncomfortable. Beside him stood one of the most gorgeous women Gawain had ever seen in his very long life. Well over six feet tall, she had the blond Nordic beauty of a particularly lush Valkyrie. She was also icily pissed off. Those sapphire eyes were snapping.

A round of introductions revealed her name was Helen Satterwhite. She and Lark were apparently acquainted, judging from the commiserating look they exchanged.

"May I have a word?" Tristan asked, after what he apparently judged was a decent interval.

Gawain nodded, mentally bracing himself. "Of course. Tour of the garden?"

"Sounds good," said Tristan, despite the fact he'd helped Gawain plant it.

Lark looked at Helen. "Want some coffee?"

"Love some," the blonde said crisply. "Somehow I have the feeling this is going to be a long night."

The two women headed for the kitchen as the Magi stepped outside. Gawain walked over to the fountain and sat down on its stone lip. After a pause, the knight joined him, looking, if anything, even more uncomfortable.

They sat listening to the falling water until Tristan finally broke the silence. "I heard you'd been assigned to mentor my great-granddaughter."

Gawain raised his brows at the pointed mention of the familial relationship. "She's a good kid. Recovering from a nasty trauma during the invasion the other night, but she's dealing with it well. She has some decent combat skills, too. I gather you've been working with her."

"Yes, for the past six months. We've built a good rapport." Tristan looked him in the eye. "My apprentice has some very strong skills, too."

Gawain went still.

Somehow I don't think he's talking about combat, Kel said in their psychic link.

Probably not.

Tristan didn't drop his gaze, though Gawain suspected his own was going cool. "I was wondering if you'd like to switch students. I'm comfortable with Lark, and Helen, well, she's very beautiful."

"Tristan, Morgana made those assignments. I don't think we're supposed to swap."

Tristan shrugged his broad shoulders. "Why should she care?"

"If she worked a spell to determine who should work with whom, she'd care."

"*If* she worked such a spell. Would you object to my asking her?"

As a matter of fact, he would. A great deal. He didn't want Helen the Ice Goddess. He wanted brave, clever Lark.

But Gawain had also fought alongside Tristan for sixteen hundred years, and that was not a bond he was willing to sacrifice. Besides, he suspected he already knew Morgana's answer. "Go ahead." Somehow he managed to say the words pleasantly.

"I'll establish a connection for you," Kel told Tristan. He murmured a chant.

After a pause, an image shimmered into the air. Morgana lay curled like a sated cat in a bed scarcely smaller than Gawain's, dressed in a cream silk gown that revealed a great deal of spectacular cleavage. Soren, in human form, lay next to her, barefoot and lazy-eyed, his pale skin shimmering with a faint blue tint suggestive of his true form's scales. He and Kel exchanged a sibilant Draconian greeting.

Morgana, however, did not look pleased at the interruption. She barely waited through Tristan's exquisitely polite request before she snapped, "Those assignments were not capricious, Lord Tristan. I cast that spell specifically to determine who should best serve with whom, because I knew someone would come whining up asking them to be changed. I just never thought it would be you."

"Morgana, she's my great-granddaughter . . ."

"And if family ties were that important to you, you would have known her longer than six months."

Gawain winced on his friend's behalf.

Tristan stiffened. "You're correct, of course. If I'd remained involved in John's life as I should have, he wouldn't have gotten so sick, and I could have trained Lark from the beginning."

"Tris . . ." Gawain murmured.

But his friend continued with that icy dignity. "Still, I—"

"I thought Arthur made himself clear on this subject at the funeral," Morgana interrupted. "Was I mistaken?"

A muscle flexed in Tristan's jaw. He opened his mouth, then closed it again. "No. He was quite clear."

"Good. Now, gentlemen, your respective apprentices are waiting. I suggest you take care of them." The image winked out.

Gawain spoke in the ringing silence. "Tris, I'm not going to hurt her."

"You won't intend to, no." The knight rose from the fountain lip and walked into the house.

Gawain remained where he was and scrubbed his hand over his face. "That was ugly. I think I'd better sit out here while he talks to her."

"That would probably be wise," Kel agreed.

"Do all my friends think I'm an asshole?"

"You're not an asshole," Kel replied. "But you're not exactly a father's dream date for his daughter, either."

". . . *the minute he* heard Gawain had been assigned as your mentor, he charged over here. I had to run to keep up," Helen told Lark, adding another shot of whiskey to her coffee. "I get the distinct impression I'm about to get kicked to the curb."

Lark winced. "I can't believe Tristan would do that."

The blonde shrugged. "You know what they say. Men are pigs. And Magi are pigs with fangs."

"Lark?" Tristan said from the doorway, "would you walk with me, please?"

Lark shot her fellow Maja a look and rose from the table. "Sure."

Helen lifted her cup in a toast as Lark started into the living room with her great-grandfather.

"What's going on, Tristan?" Her tone was cool, reflecting her growing annoyance with the whole situation. Where the hell did he get off, sticking his nose into her life?

He moved to the couch and sat down, motioning for Lark to join him. "I wanted to talk to you about your new . . . partnership with Gawain."

Don't tell him off. John wouldn't like that. "What about it?"

Tristan hesitated, a frown on his handsome face. "Gawain is a very brave, skilled knight. You could learn a great deal from him."

Lark eyed him. "Somehow I get the feeling there's a *but* attached to this."

Tristan sighed. "He is also very good with women. But he's not very good *for* women. I don't want you getting hurt."

"I appreciate your concern, but I'm a big girl and . . ."

The knight leaned forward and met her gaze earnestly.

"Gawain has romanced some of the most beautiful, most powerful Majae in the Mageverse. Many of them fell in love with him. But he always walks away."

"Tristan . . ."

He held up a hand to stop her words. "I know you, Lark. You see us in romanticized terms to begin with. You'll fall for him if you're not careful. And he's going to hurt you, because he always does."

She spoke between her teeth. "I can take care of myself."

"Morgana was one of his lovers, Lark. If she couldn't keep him . . ."

Now humiliation replaced her anger. Her cheeks burned. "I'll keep that in mind."

Tristan studied her with sympathy. "Another man will love you. But it won't be him."

"You've made your point, Tristan."

He hesitated, distress in his eyes. "I'm sorry, Lark. But I had to say something."

"I realize you're trying to help. Thank you." She just wanted him to leave.

The knight started to speak, then sighed, and rose. "Good luck." Lifting his voice, he called, "Helen? Let's go."

The blonde walked out of the kitchen, her mouth tight. "Yes, master."

He stopped and stared at her. She stalked past him toward the door. Tristan's jaw firmed as he strode after her. "We'll talk again later, Lark."

"Sure. 'Bye."

Lark listened to the front door close behind them with a soft click. For a long moment, she sat on the couch without moving, trying to sort through the tangle of emotion she felt.

"Well, that was uncomfortable." Gawain walked into the living room, took off Kel's scabbard, and lay it down on the coffee table. Sitting down beside her, he studied her. "You okay?"

She shrugged. "Well, at least he cared enough to say something. But it wasn't terribly flattering to either of us."

"It was also slightly hypocritical," Kel growled. "Tristan's not exactly a poster boy for sweet romance, centuries of poetry notwithstanding." The dragon's ruby eyes were narrow with indignation.

Lark found herself smiling. "So you're saying I *can* trust Gawain?"

"Weeelllll," Kel drawled with a sly smile, "I wouldn't go *that* far."

Gawain rolled his eyes. "Thanks a lot."

SIX

Gawain woke from the Daysleep as he always did—abruptly, catapulting into full wakefulness without any drowsiness in between. It was as if his warrior's body hated being trapped in sleep and came alert the instant it could.

Immediately, images from the night before cascaded through his mind—Lark's sweet bare breasts and long legs, the wicked humor in her face as she'd teased him, the hot taste of her blood. He grinned in anticipation and rolled over, expecting to take up where they'd left off.

But the bed was empty.

Frowning, he sat up and listened hard with his vampire hearing. The house was just as empty as his bed.

Bloody hell, she'd jaunted off somewhere. And if the sorcerers attacked again before Gawain could get to her . . . He remembered the helpless terror in her eyes as she described the sorcerer's attack. "Dammit, Lark," he growled, then raised his voice to a bellow. "Kel!"

There was a metallic ring from beside the bed, as if the sword blade had rapped against a bedpost. "What?" the dragon yelped.

"Where's Lark?"

"How should I know? She's not in bed?" The sword paused as if extending magical senses. "Oh, hell, she's not even in the house! And she didn't check in with me before she left."

"Find her." He reached for the scabbard and drew the sword.

The dragon glared at him from within his loose hold. "Watch the tone, mammal. I'm not your slave. She's . . ." Kel broke off. "Damn. Morgana's calling."

A stab of fear surprised him. "Has there been an attack?" *Lark, her delicate face pale with terror . . .*

Kel frowned. "I'm not sensing anything."

He relaxed fractionally. "Good. Put her on." Though Morgana wasn't going to be happy when she found out Lark had vanished.

An image of the Maja formed in midair, her expression cool with disapproval. "Nice of you to answer my call, Lord Gawain."

"Just woke up. Is Lark all right?"

Dark brows winged upward. "She's not with you?"

"No."

Her dark gaze chilled even more. "You haven't even had her forty-eight hours, and you've already lost her?"

"She's at the Ladies' Club," Kel put in. Meeting Gawain's gaze, he added, "I just located her. She's having a meal with her friends."

"Well, when she can tear herself away," Morgana said coolly, "tell her I've got a murder I want you two to investigate."

As they often did, Lark, Caroline, and Diera met at the Ladies' Club, a sprawling Mediterranean-style villa that occupied the central square. In stark contrast to the masculine decor of the Lords' Club, it was decorated with a jungle of plants, statues of Roman and Greek goddesses, and clusters of wrought-iron furniture. The best cooks among the Majae rotated duties in its kitchens, and its evening buffet was to die for.

"He fed on you without warning you?" Caroline demanded, her expression scandalized over her salad.

Diera gave an uncharacteristic snort and sipped her wine. "Yes, that sounds like Gawain."

Lark swallowed a bite of her BLT. "The really disgusting thing about it is, he was right. I probably would have freaked if he'd asked my permission first. Instead, he seems to have gotten me over the hump."

Caroline grinned. "So to speak."

"Actually, not quite," Diera said. "Gawain's little . . . efforts did help . . ."

"I wouldn't call them *little*." Lark smiled and sipped her tea.

Diera went right on as if she hadn't spoken. ". . . But you've still got a psychic wound in your aura big enough to drive a Toyota through." Magical sparks flared in her gaze like tiny fireworks. "I can see it."

Lark put down her glass and stared at her mentor in dismay. "So what you're saying is, this is still going to be a problem."

"Yes." Diera searched her gaze and offered delicately, "I could heal it for you, the same way I fixed that bite. Blunt your memories a bit. We do this kind of psychic surgery all the time with mortals."

Caroline nodded. "You have to. Otherwise they'd either have major psychological scars or sell us out to the *National Enquirer*. Or both. It doesn't hurt them if you know what you're doing."

"And I certainly do." Diera examined Lark's frozen expression and gave her a slight smile. "But you're still not comfortable with the idea."

"It's not that I don't trust you . . ."

The Maja made a dismissive gesture. "Don't worry about it, dear. Letting someone muck around in your head isn't a pleasant prospect."

Caroline smirked. "Yeah, she might discover all your secret fantasies about naked cops in shiny motorcycle boots."

Lark blinked. "I don't have any fantasies about naked cops in shiny motorcycle boots."

"Oh. That must be me, then." She threw her head back in mock ecstacy. "Bust me, officer! Ticket me again!"

Lark shook her head at her friend's antics. "Why would you fantasize about cops when you're married to Galahad, stud of the Round Table?"

Caroline grinned salaciously. "You should see him in motorcycle boots."

"Pervert." Diera sniffed.

"Goody Two-Shoes."

Caroline's eyes narrowed at their friend. "Come to think of it, didn't I see you strolling in the park last night with a vampire boy toy of your very own?"

"That was Antonio, and he's my apprentice, not a boy toy." But her attempt at an aloof tone was spoiled by a small, secret smile.

"Apprentice. Yeah, right." Caroline cut her eyes at Lark and intoned. " 'The Force is strong in this one. You should see his light saber.' " She held her index fingers apart in the universal symbol for Big Dick.

Lark snickered, then stopped as her eyes went wide. "Are you talking about the same Antonio that's been training with us?" Antonio Calendri had joined in on their practice sessions several times, engaging Lark in swordplay while Diera critiqued her magical attacks. Muscular and handsome, he'd been a Magus for just over a year.

Diera nodded. "That's him."

Caroline's eyes widened in delight. "The one with the crush on you?"

A flush stained Diera's delicate cheekbones. "Antonio does *not* have a crush on me."

"Yeah, right." Lark turned to Caroline. "That poor man is so far gone, and she just pretends not to notice."

"But getting back to Lark's problem . . ." Diera said, just a little desperately.

Lark grinned and propped her chin on her fist as she studied the Maja wickedly. "I'd rather talk about Antonio. So, is it a two-handed light saber, or just a hand and a half?"

"This is serious, Lark," Diera snapped. "It's not just your life at stake now. It's Gawain's."

The humor drained from her. "Dirty pool, Diera."

Her mentor didn't flinch. "I'm sorry, darling, but this is vital, particularly after what happened the other day. You have a lot more power than you think you do. You *must* stop hamstringing yourself and use it."

"Believe me, when Fangface latched onto my jugular, I used all the power I had."

Diera leaned forward and met her gaze earnestly. "At that point, yes, but by then, he'd taken too much of your blood. You need to start drawing the full load *before* you're down and bleeding out."

Frustrated, Lark glowered. "What makes you think I'm not doing that now?"

"Because I've watched you fight Antonio. You're holding back. You don't trust what you are. Deep down, you don't really believe you've got these abilities, so you're not drawing on the Mageverse the way you could." To Caroline she added, "You see this kind of thing all the time with new Majae."

"I gave Fangface everything I had! He was just too damn strong."

Her mentor sighed. "Lark, the death magic the sorcerers use is powerful, but it's also finite. Once the psychic energy from their last murder is gone, it's gone. But the power of the Mageverse has no limit. You just have to learn how to draw on it."

Sometimes she really hated this mumbo-jumbo crap. "Is that your way of saying, 'Use the Force, Luke'?"

"Something like that. The next time you confront one of

the sorcerers, just remember the power is there. You simply have to let yourself use it."

"But what if I can't?"

"The time will come when you've got to. And the way things are going lately, it will be sooner rather than later."

Lark snorted in disgust at her friend's warning. "Thanks a lot, Diera."

The Maja smiled dryly. "What else are friends for?" She hesitated. "And as long as I'm giving out sage wisdom . . ."

"Oh, God, now what?"

"Your assignment with Gawain concerns me."

"Not you, too!"

Caroline propped her chin on her fist. "You mean somebody else has been sticking her nose in your private life?"

"Yeah, only it's a him. Tristan." She told them about her great-grandfather's warning.

"He's got a point, Lark," Diera said. "Don't read too much into whatever you and Gawain have going on. Yes, he's handsome and charming, and Merlin knows he's skilled, but he's not interested in more than a night or two. You definitely won't be getting a Truebond out of him."

The bitterness in her voice made Lark's brows climb. Caroline gasped exactly what she was thinking. "Ohmigod. You and Gawain had a thing!"

Diera shot her an exasperated look. "When you've been around as long as we have, everybody has had a *thing* with everybody else. And everybody knows it."

Caroline rolled her eyes. "Avalon—the biggest small town in either universe."

Ignoring her, Diera turned an intense gaze on Lark. "Have you ever wondered how Kel stays alive? Obviously, he can't eat, he's a sword."

Lark blinked, taken aback by the abrupt conversational detour. "Well, I assumed he absorbs energy from the Mageverse."

Diera shook her blond head. "He and Gawain have a symbiotic relationship. He draws on the knight's life force."

Caroline whistled soundlessly. "In other words, Gawain is eating for two."

"Exactly. Which means that unlike most of the other Magi, he can't subsist on bottled blood. He needs the psychic charge from taking it directly from a woman during sex. And he's never had a problem getting it."

Caroline grinned. "So you're saying if he were mortal, he'd have, like, six thousand STDs. Talk about a Magic Johnson."

Lark groaned at the pun. "You should be ashamed."

The grin only broadened. "It's a gift."

"Stop it," Diera snapped, out of patience. "This is serious."

The humor fled Caroline's gaze. "No, actually, it's not. Lark is a big girl. She can protect herself. And not all relationships with knights of the Round Table end in broken hearts. There's a good chance Gawain will see what the rest of us do, that she has a lot to offer."

Lark was so absurdly touched, she had to turn it into a joke. "Awww, I didn't know you cared."

"Ignore her, she's a newlywed," Diera growled. "Not all of us get happy endings. And I don't want you to end up miserable."

Her friend meant well—she might even have a point—but Lark was getting tired of the conversation. "Speaking of those who haven't had a happy ending, do you know how to break the spell on Kel?"

Diera gave her a long look before she evidently decided to allow the shift of subject. "If I did, it would already be broken." She curled her lip. "We all know the method the original spell-caster had in mind, but obviously nobody's going to do *that*."

"Wait. Whoever turned Kel into the sword told him how to break the spell? Why the heck hasn't he done it already?"

"Because he'd have to kill Gawain."

Lark stared at her, appalled. "I thought you said they have a symbiotic relationship?"

She nodded. "As long as Kel's a sword. If he slays Gawain, the spell breaks and he's free again."

"Wait a minute, how could he do that?" Caroline demanded. "He doesn't have a body."

"Death spell," Lark realized. "If they're linked, Gawain would have no way to block it."

"That, or someone could use Kel to run him through. Either way, Gawain's dead." Diera shrugged. "On the other hand, if Gawain dies from some other cause before Kel is freed from the sword . . ."

". . . Kel will die," Lark finished.

"Deprived of Gawain's magical sustenance, his consciousness would begin to fade. Eventually, there would be nothing left but the steel of the sword."

Sickened, Lark pictured it: the tiny dragon, slowly freezing into metal. . . . She shuddered.

It was almost as appalling as the thought of Gawain himself dead, all that seductive power gone, the green eyes lifeless.

"Diera?" The voice was rich, deep, and familiar. The three women turned to see a tall, dark-haired vampire moving through the Ladies' Club as the other diners watched him with tolerant amusement. Generally, men were encouraged to stick to the Lords' Club, but all of them recognized a lovesick Magus when they saw one.

Reaching their table, he looked down at Diera with heat in his dark eyes. "I woke from the Daysleep and you were gone."

Antonio Calendri had a long, lean swimmer's build, a gorgeous mouth, and a lusciously slurred Italian accent that seemed to breathe sex into every syllable he spoke.

Caroline and Lark threw each other a knowing glance. Caroline, irrepressible as always, rose and extended her hand. "You must be Antonio. I've heard so much about you. I'm Caroline Du Lac."

Antonio shook her hand, white teeth flashing against his olive face in a charming smile. "Ahh, Galahad's wife! I've heard much about you, too." Sweeping the table with a glance, he asked politely, "May I join you?"

"Go right ahead!"

"Please do," Lark agreed. *It'll distract Diera from her obsession with my love life.*

He slid into a chair next to his mentor, all dark, catlike masculine grace, the perfect foil for Diera's fairy princess beauty. As his gaze went to her face, intent with longing, a blush climbed Diera's cheeks. She glanced away, clearing her throat.

Caroline cut her eyes at Lark, who fought a smile.

Antonio leaned toward Diera. Before he could purr whatever bit of seduction he had in mind, a rising, scandalized murmur rose, very different from the reception he'd reccived.

Someone called, "Gawain, what the hell are you doing in the Ladies' Club?"

"Looking for a lady," the knight's deep voice shot back. "Haven't found one yet."

Someone catcalled a friendly insult in return.

"Damn," Caroline breathed, saying exactly what she was thinking. "He came into the club after you! He must be pissed."

Lark craned her neck and spotted him scanning the restaurant. His eyes narrowed as he saw her, and he started in their direction, his strides long and determined.

From the corner of her eye, she saw Diera tense. Antonio frowned.

Reaching their table, Gawain loomed over Lark's chair. "I'm sorry, were Morgana's instructions not clear enough for you?" His deceptively pleasant tone provided a sharp contrast to the angry snap of his eyes. "You're my responsibility. If you gallivant off somewhere and get yourself killed, I can assure you Arthur Pendragon is *not* going to accept, 'I was asleep,' as an excuse!" His voice climbed perilously close to a shout.

Lark stared up at him, astonished.

"You'll have to excuse him, dear," Diera said into the ringing silence. "He's not used to waking up alone. Usually he's the one who sneaks out in the middle of the night."

Lark's jaw dropped as she turned to stare at her friend. Where the hell had that come from?

"Diera . . ." Antonio said in a warning voice, his narrowed dark eyes snapping.

Gawain studied him, then lifted a brow at Diera. "This must be your apprentice. Shouldn't you be off training him?"

Diera merely smiled, catlike and taunting. "Actually, he needs very little training. He may not be as experienced as some, but he makes up for it with enthusiasm."

Gawain's smile was downright icy as he looked down at the stunned young Magus. "Do *you* think you've had enough, Antonio?"

A muscle flexed in his jaw as he stared at Diera with angry eyes. "At the moment, yes." He rose from his seat and strode toward the door.

Diera stared after his broad back, her face stricken.

Caroline gave her a pitying look and leaned in close to whisper, "Go after him, dumb ass."

The Maja rose, threw down her napkin, and hurried in her apprentice's wake.

Gawain turned his attention on Caroline with a coolly lifted brow. "I imagine you're Galahad's assignment. Does *he* know where you are?"

"We're Truebonded, Gawain," Caroline snapped, referring to the deep psychic link married couples formed. "Of course he knows where I am. And he says he's known you since Jesus was a little boy, and you've never been this big a jerk. What's eating you?"

"Morgana called me this morning with a mission, and I had to tell her I'd already lost my new apprentice. She wasn't exactly thrilled."

Lark winced. "Sorry." *Way to go, McGuin—you haven't*

*been partners with the man two days, and you've already
managed to embarrass him.* "What mission are we talking
about?"

"There's been a murder Morgana believes was the work
of one of our sorcerer friends. She wants us to check it out
and see if we can track down the bastard."

Lark nodded and tossed her own napkin aside. "All
right, let's go."

As she rose from her seat, her gaze met Kel's over
Gawain's shoulder. The little dragon shrugged its metallic
wings in an I-don't-know-what's-gotten-into-him-either
gesture.

Diera hurried from the Ladies' Club, following her apprentice. "Antonio! Wait. Please."

He finally stopped in the club's courtyard, shoulders
squared as he stared out over the wrought-iron fence at the
moon just rising over Avalon's gleaming skyline. He did
not look around.

She stopped there, suddenly at a loss. Remembering the
things she'd said, shame stung her so hard, she winced.
Taking a deep breath, she stepped beside her lover and
stared up into his profile. He looked as handsome and
stony as a Roman statue.

"I suppose I owe you an apology." Diera forced a laugh.
"Gawain has always had a talent for turning me into a little
witch."

Antonio turned to look down at her. For a man with
such warm eyes, his gaze could go remarkably icy. "Considering your extensive experience, I'd think you'd be beyond blaming others for your behavior."

She winced again. "You're right, of course. It's just . . .
I did love Gawain once, very deeply. When he left me, I
wanted to die."

"Do you still love him?" Vulnerability and pain flashed

across Antonio's face, sending a stab of regret through her.

"No." Diera blinked in surprise, realizing that she meant it. *When had that happened?*

"Then why are you letting such old resentments poison your life?" He searched her expression, then shook his dark head. "You're the most beautiful and giving woman I've ever met. There's nothing I love more than touching you, being with you. But unless you can let go of the past, there will never be anything between us except stolen kisses in the dark." Catching her chin in one strong, warm hand, he lifted it until she met his eyes. "Is that enough for you?" His beautiful mouth firmed. "Because it's not enough for me."

Releasing her, he turned and walked through the wrought-iron gate.

Blinking, Diera watched his broad back move rapidly off into the moonlit night. Suddenly she realized if she let him go, she'd lose something precious.

"Antonio?" she breathed. "Antonio!" He didn't stop. Diera broke into a run. "Wait!"

Wheeling, he reached for her even as she threw himself into his arms. His mouth crashed down on hers, hot and possessive with relief and hunger.

Diera closed her eyes and kissed him back.

Gawain silently gritted his teeth as he stalked from the Ladies' Club, acutely aware of the amused stares that followed him. Caroline was right—he'd acted like an idiot.

Finding Lark with Diera had put the finishing touches on a rotten start to the night. Like Tristan, his former lover had probably spent the afternoon regaling Lark with tales of his recklessness, faithlessness, and general lack of morality. Never mind that Diera herself hadn't exactly been blameless in their romantic debacle.

"Is there a reason you acted like a jerk?" Lark asked, her tone almost matter-of-fact despite the temper he could hear simmering in her voice.

"As I'm sure Diera told you, I don't need a reason."

"Actually, he's always got reasons," Kel put in. "Sometimes he acts like a jerk because he's pissed, sometimes because he's scared, and sometimes just for the sheer orgasmic joy of pissing off everyone he knows."

"Shut up, lizard." Reaching into a pocket of his jeans, he pulled out the folded front page Morgana had sent him. He handed it to Lark. "Take a look. Grim thinks there's a high probability this is death magic." Merlin's Grimorie was a sentient book, and the repository of the wizard's magical knowledge. Among other things, Grim could display every newspaper on the planet within his pages. That ability had come in particularly handy during the Magekind's sorcerer hunt.

Gawain watched as Lark unfolded the paper and read over it before looking up at him. "So where do we go from here?"

"There's a good chance our vampire friend's magic has left a trail," Kel explained. "I should be able to cast a spell on the body and track him."

She frowned. "But you're going to need the body first."

The dragon nodded his small head. "Yes, but that won't be a problem. Watch . . ."

Through their link, Gawain felt Kel call the magic. It rose in a glittering psychic tide and spilled into the paper Lark held.

An image floated off the page, a ghostly photograph of a smiling, dark-haired woman who looked about thirty-five. According to the newspaper article, Candice Sanders had been a wife, teacher, and mother of three who had been kidnapped from a mall parking lot in Daytona Beach, Florida, two nights before. She'd been found nude and butchered in a vacant lot yesterday, thrown away like so much garbage.

Looking at the floating photo, Gawain felt his fury increase. "I hate these bastards," he growled. "We've fought a lot of assholes over the centuries, but these guys . . ."

"Concentrating here," Kel interrupted. Gawain fell

silent, simmering. The image floated away. He and Lark hurried after it.

Just ahead, Kel conjured a dimensional gate that grew from a tiny glowing point to a magical doorway in the space of a blink. The photo flew through the opening, and they followed.

The three emerged in utter darkness that smelled of formaldehyde, disinfectant, and an underlying reek of death. "Lights!" Lark snapped.

Overhead fluorescents switched on, obeying her spell.

They stood at one end of a small room with walls and floors covered with green ceramic tile. In the center stood a metal table with grooves around the edges and a set of big lights overhead. The opposite wall held ten metal doors, each about three feet square.

"Is this a morgue?" Lark whispered, looking around uneasily.

"Looks like it." Gawain watched the photograph float toward one of the metal doors and disappear. A surge of Kel's magic opened the door. Tiny wheels squeaked as a sliding metal table rolled out.

What was left of Candice Sanders lay on it. Lark gasped, the blood draining from her face. Gawain didn't blame her. He'd fought on more battlefields than he could count, seen men chopped up like cord wood or blown apart by explosives, but this kind of blatantly sexual butchery was different. "You okay?"

She straightened her slim shoulders and nodded curtly. "I saw some nasty stuff when I was a firefighter, but this . . . These guys really are monsters."

"Yes, well, they'll shortly be dead monsters," Kel said. "At least, as soon as we track them down. This kind of magical viciousness leaves a trail."

"If they didn't erase it," Lark pointed out.

"This lot usually doesn't have that much skill or power," Kel told her. "Certainly not enough to cover up something like this."

Again, the dragon's magic spilled toward the body. The spell hit the corpse and began to glow in a storm of furiously swirling crimson sparks. It shot upward . . . and splashed, as if hitting some kind of magical barrier.

"Huh," Kel said, craning his neck past Gawain's ear. "Somebody has power." He started to chant in Draconian, the words sibilant. The sparks of his spell spun faster, beating frantically against the shield, which began to glow, as if it were heating under the bombardment. But it didn't crack.

"Oh, no, you don't, you bastard," Kel growled. "You're not beating me." More power, a hot river of it, so much Gawain felt his knees buckle. The dragon was drawing from the very essence of his life, but Gawain didn't protest. They had to find whoever did this and make sure he never did it again.

Suddenly a delicate hand reached up and closed around Kel's hilt. Lark lifted her voice, adding her chant to his as she poured her magic into him. Gawain grunted in relief and straightened as the pressure eased.

With a soundless psychic explosion, the shield burst. Quickly, the Maja summoned a gate, and the spell hit it, redirecting it toward the killer's location.

"Armor up," Gawain ordered, drawing Kel as they started toward the gate. He wasn't surprised when the armor took longer to form than it normally did—that spell had taken a hell of a lot of magic.

Which might come back to bite them on the ass when they actually had to fight the bastard who had cast it. Unfortunately, they didn't have a choice. The killer had probably spotted their gateway by now. They had to strike before he could escape.

They had to make sure Candice Sanders was his last victim.

SEVEN

Lark, Gawain, and Kel stepped through the gate into a small, astonishingly dirty living room. Clothes lay on the floor, and beer cans and empty boxes of Chinese takeout lay on a cheap pressboard coffee table, but there was no one in sight.

"I'm not sensing anyone home," Kel said, a frown on his tiny muzzle. "I don't understand. The spell should have taken us to the killer's current location."

"I don't think this is it," Lark said. "Don't sorcerers live better than this?"

"Usually." Gawain frowned as he studied the chaos.

"But that spell worked," Kel growled. "I felt it work."

"One thing's for sure. Whoever lives here is a pig." She toed a pair of dirty skivvies away from her foot. "This place literally smells like shit."

Gawain's eyes widened. "And blood." He started across the room to an open doorway where he stopped, startled.

A man lay sprawled spread-eagle on the unmade bed, gutted, his vacant eyes staring at the ceiling. He was dressed in familiar crimson robes.

"Well," Kel drawled, "Looks like somebody beat us to the punch."

Steeling herself against the smell and horror of death, Lark followed Gawain to the bedside.

If anything, the sorcerer's corpse looked even worse than his victim's. He was covered in blood, dark and coagulating. More of it soaked the bed and splashed the walls, flecked here and there with stomach-churning chunks of meat.

"This isn't Magekind work," Gawain said, frowning. "None of us would have left the body like this."

"If nothing else, we'd have cleaned up," Lark agreed, stepping closer and dropping the magical shields she'd learned to maintain at scenes of violent death.

Suddenly she could see patterns of energy—not bright and glowing, like that used by Magekind, but the dark, pulsing forces of death magic. The traces seemed concentrated over the bloodied, hacked chest. Which she realized, was empty. "His heart was cut out."

"Well, given that he's dead and his head is still attached, that does stand to reason," Gawain pointed out.

"No, I mean that it was cut out as part of a ritual. I saw something like this before on another mission. Somebody worked death magic on him."

Gawain frowned. "A sorcerer?"

She shot him a look. "Well, it certainly wasn't a Maja."

"Are we sure he's the one that killed Candice?"

"Yes," Kel said promptly. "The spell wouldn't have led us to him otherwise."

"Besides, this guy's native magic is the same as the magic around Candice." Lark frowned, studying the patterns of energy swirling around the corpse. One set of mystical fingerprints were dim, fading—the sorcerer's innate power, which had been largely drained away. The other . . . "Kel, doesn't his killer's magic have the same pattern as the shield we destroyed?"

The dragon's head cocked, considering the suggestion. "I think you're right. That's odd."

Lark frowned, working it through. "Whoever killed the sorcerer put up that blocking spell around her."

". . . before coming here and executing Candice's killer." Gawain moved closer to the bed, examining the corpse. "He must have a hell of a lot of power. It's virtually impossible for one of us to catch another asleep. For this guy to be in bed, spread-eagle like this, suggests his killer put him there. And since our boy had just committed mystical murder, he would have had more than enough power to fight back."

"What if it was a woman?" Lark pointed out. "Maybe she seduced him, and then. . . ."

He considered the idea. "Possibly. But why?"

"Why do lovers ever kill each other?"

"I don't think so," Kel said. "For a woman to kill a man she's just banged, she has to be pretty pissed off. Look at the body—that's not a rage killing."

Lark lifted her brows. "Sure looks pissed to me."

"Not as much as you'd think." The dragon pointed at the body with his muzzle. "The edges of the wound are too clean, too deliberate. His hand was steady."

"His?"

Kel shrugged. "Or hers."

"Or theirs," Lark suggested. "If there was more than one of them, that would explain a lot, too."

"No," Kel said. "The magic here is too uniform, too solid. If there was a group of sorcerers doing this, there'd be more than one magical signature."

"Either way, why would one sorcerer kill another?" Gawain asked.

"Power," Kel replied promptly. "There's more power to be had from sacrificing a being of magic than in killing a mortal. They're just harder to kill, so most of Geirolf's lot don't attempt it."

"Which implies that this particular bastard is one we

need to stop *now* before he gets any stronger," Gawain said. "I think it's time for another tracking spell."

He drew the sword and held it out over the body. Lark wrapped both hands around his and closed her eyes.

Again, she felt the hot, alien rise of the dragon's magic, flavored with Gawain's life force. She sent her own to join it, pouring herself into the spell, letting Kel use the power she gave him.

The spell poured outward with a psychic roar. Hastily, she opened a gate and watched it slam through, warping the doorway toward a new destination as it went. For a moment, she felt resistance—a set of magical wards on the other side. Kel snarled another chant, and she gave him more power without being asked. The barrier exploded under their combined strength, and the gate popped through.

Gawain pulled away from her and leaped into the opening. Taking a deep breath, she followed.

The little blonde had quit struggling and started dying. Richard Edge purred in pleasure against her torn throat as he fed on her blood and life force simultaneously. Compared to the sorcerer he'd killed two hours ago, she was barely a magical appetizer. Still, sacrifices always made him horny, so he'd stopped at a bar on the way home to grab a girl. He'd snatched her from the parking lot and gated back to his sanctuary before she even had time to scream.

She'd done plenty of screaming since then, though . . .

Boom!

Richard jerked his head up, ignoring the blood that flew from the girl's throat as he tore his fangs free. Something had just hit his wards. Something powerful and pissed.

Knowing he had seconds at most, he rolled off his victim, grabbed a knife from the bedside table, and buried it in her heart. She jerked and died, and he syphoned off the last of her life.

He was going to need all the power he could get.

Calling his armor, he sprinted for the library. Gate spells tended to head for the largest uncluttered space, and in his sanctuary, that was it. Considering that his home was buried a good two hundred feet down in solid bedrock, they certainly didn't want to chance gating anywhere else.

Richard charged into the room just in time to see an armored figure leap through the dimensional gate. Instantly, he recognized the distinctive snarling dragon of the knight's helm.

Tilting up his visor, Richard gave his visitor his best chilling grin. "Why, hello there, Uncle Gawain."

He had the pleasure of seeing the knight's eyes widen before he charged. With a roar, Richard swung his sword in a blow intended to take off Gawain's head.

Automatically, Gawain parried the sorcerer's attack, though the impact reverberated in his bones. He knew that face.

Merlin's balls, it was Richard Edge!

Edge had been only a teenager when Gawain had last seen him, and he was in his forties now. Still, there was no doubt at all he was Bors's son. He had the same dark hair, the same large brown eyes and angular looks paired with a broad-shouldered, almost bullish build.

But the vicious light in those eyes was nothing Gawain had ever seen in Bors's.

He struck out in a vicious return blow that forced Edge to leap away with a vampire's speed.

"How the hell did you fall in with Geirolf?" Narrow-eyed, Gawain fell into a combat crouch and began to stalk the sorcerer. From the corner of one eye, he saw Lark hanging back, assessing the situation, looking for an opening to strike.

Good girl. Use your head.

Edge curled his lip, hate blazing in his eyes. "After Daddy banished me from Avalon, I had to do something to occupy my time." Wheeling, he swung his sword in a deadly arc right at Lark's head. She jumped back with a yelp of alarm, barely avoiding a beheading.

Growling in rage, Gawain jolted forward, but Edge was as fast and agile as his father. The sorcerer spun aside, parrying his thrust and sending a blast of magic into his face. Even through the Dragon Helm, Gawain felt the burn.

Damn, Kel said in their mental link, *the little prick has power.*

Let's see if he has the control to go with it. He gave the sorcerer a taunting grin. "I always did have a bad feeling about you. Even Bors said you were a budding sociopath."

Edge smirked, spreading his arms wide. Behind him, Lark gathered herself for an attack, magic building around her hands. "And now here I am, in full flower."

Trying to keep the bastard's attention focused on him, Gawain sneered. "Well, I'm about to rip you out by the roots."

"I think not. I've found another way to immortality than Merlin's Gift, and I've got more power now than you or dear ol' Dad ever dreamed of." He lifted one blazing hand . . .

And Lark fired, blasting him with a roiling blaze of magic.

Which promptly struck Edge's shield and splashed harmlessly away. With an offhand gesture, he turned and blasted Lark full in the chest, slamming her into the bookshelves behind her.

Shit! Heart in his throat, Gawain started toward her, just as the books exploded into flame and rained down on her head. Before he could take another step, a glowing shield formed over her, and she knocked them away.

As she struggled clear of the burning wreckage, Edge lunged at Gawain again, taking advantage of his distraction. His sword rang against Gawain's helm in a shower of sparks.

Cursing, Gawain knocked it away with his own blade, the two weapons clashing together, magic roiling around them like opposing magnetic fields.

"Mmmm." Edge made a purring sound in his throat. "Once I've killed you, I'll drain Kel like a cheap battery. Doing you two will keep me in magic for months."

"The only one who's going to die here is you," Kel spat.

Edge gave them a smug smile. "We'll see, won't we?"

But as he lifted his sword, a flaming book struck him squarely in the helm.

Edge whirled with a growl of fury as Lark prepared to lob another book at him. "You little *bitch*! You're going to die for that."

A huge fireball began to grow around his left hand.

Lark barely reinforced her magical shields in time to absorb Edge's blast.

Jesus, he had more power than Fangface! Fear dug icy fingers into her heart, but she fought it down and sent another burning tome rocketing toward him.

Edge ducked away, then started to lunge at her, but Gawain headed him off. As the two men hacked at each other, Lark gathered the blazing books with a spell and sent them orbiting around the room. If nothing else, she could pelt Edge with them until Gawain had a chance to take his head.

Her hands were sweating inside her gauntlets, and the smell of burning paper hung acrid in the air. Even stronger than that was the stench of death magic. Edge had more power than any sorcerer she'd encountered before. Lark could almost taste it—roiling, oily, burning her skin like some toxic sludge. Even Fangface hadn't had that much raw magical voltage.

When Edge had hit her with that first blast, she'd thought the spell was going to eat right through her shields and kill her on the spot. Ironically, when she'd hit the bookcases, the raining books had absorbed some of that lethal magic and saved her life.

Watching the two men fight only added to her sense of

being totally out of her depth. Edge moved like a cobra, lashing out with his sword in blurring attacks she could scarcely see. Gawain parried every blow and retaliated with his own breathtaking speed, weaving around his opponent and powering ringing blows against his defenses.

Edge is damn near as good with a blade as Gawain, Lark thought grimly.

And it was past time she jerked her thumb out of her ass and did something to help.

Pouring more magic into one of her flaming missiles, Lark slung it at the sorcerer, but he deflected it with an off-hand swat and launched another attack at Gawain.

She had the unhappy suspicion Edge was better with a blade than most of the younger Magi she'd seen. You had to train since childhood to attain that level of skill.

Spotting an opening, Lark sent another pair of flaming books shooting toward Edge. Again he spun aside. Gawain lunged after him, swinging Kel like a scythe. Edge parried and hacked back at him, forcing the knight to retreat.

Lark edged closer, waiting for an opportunity with her heart in her throat, hovering just out of reach of the flashing weapons.

As if in slow motion, she watched Gawain's booted foot come down on one of the half-burned books. His ankle turned. He started to go down . . .

Edge will gut him. Forgetting her fear, Lark threw herself between the two men and sent all her power blasting into the sorcerer's face. He bellowed in pain, jerking back. She had time to feel a moment's satisfaction . . .

Edge's fist hit the side of her head with all the power of a vampire's arm. She saw stars as her body slammed painfully into the edge of a table, which toppled and threw her to the floor. Her head smashed into the inside of her helm with another stunning burst of agony.

For a moment, Lark could only lie struggling to draw a breath, distantly aware of Gawain's roar of rage and Kel's higher metallic screech. Power blasts volleyed across the room. Something exploded, raining heat over her armored body. Instinctively, she sucked in a breath and tried to roll to her feet, but her legs gave under her before she was fully erect. Reeling, Lark collided with the wall and caught herself. The room spun around her, darkening at the edges. . . .

Hard arms closed around her. Panicking, she tried to beat them off, only to hear Gawain snap, "Calm down! It's me!"

Lifting her, he leaped. Lark sensed the familiar magical rush of a dimensional gate passing over her body. Then they were through, and she sucked in a hard breath, inhaling cool, clean air untainted with magic and smoke. Helplessly, she began to cough.

"Well," Gawain growled, "That was a complete goatfuck."

The world went out.

Breathing hard, Edge watched the gate vanish with a soundless magical pop. Savage exultation rolled over him in a heady wave.

He'd fought one of the knights of the Round Table and won.

Killing the bastard would have been better, of course, but forcing him to retreat was almost as good.

Damn, but they weren't kidding when they said revenge was a dish best served cold. His had been cooling for two decades, ever since Bors had told him he wasn't fit to be a Magus.

Well, tonight he'd come one step closer to ramming that particular bit of arrogance down dear old Dad's throat.

He glanced around, taking in the wreck of his sanctuary. Many of his precious volumes of mystical lore were in flames, but even that wasn't enough to dim his euphoria. So what if he'd collected those books for two decades? He had no need of them now.

Still, he was going to have to move his lair somewhere

else. It wouldn't take Gawain long to come back with reinforcements.

Edge was almost tempted to hang around anyway—one of the attacking party was sure to be Bors—but he knew that would be a mistake. The fight with Gawain had drained his reserves too far, and the little bitch's last blast had actually hurt. He'd need to build his strength again before he could risk another confrontation.

He'd come so far since Geirolf's death.

Months spent stalking, killing, and draining his fellow cultists had begun to pay off. Yet one fight with Gawain, Kel, and the bitch had eaten deeply into those precious reserves. Battered as he was, he'd have to hunt again tonight.

It was too bad he hadn't managed to kill Gawain. An astonishing amount of raw magic was bound up in one of the knights of the Round Table. An immortal, with over a thousand years of magical life spent both absorbing the energy of the Mageverse and feeding from magic-using women . . .

What's more, Gawain had drunk directly from Merlin's own Grail, then passed on the wizard's power to generations of offspring. The stored mystical energy from that alone would carry quite a kick.

Add to that the raw, alien magic bound up in the dragon sword—God, what a meal those two would make!

But perhaps he'd be wise to set his sights a little lower than Gawain and Kel. An ordinary Magus—even a knight of the Round Table like Bors—wouldn't have the Dragon Sword's magic to back him up.

It was certainly something to think about.

His hands shaking, Gawain held the Dragon Sword over Lark's unconscious body as she lay in his bed. "Is she going to be all right?"

"We need to get her helm off. I'll . . ." Ruby eyes widened. "Cachamwri's eggs, it's dented like a Coke can!"

"What? Where?" Laying the sword down beside her, he

gently turned her head. "Shit." There was a fist-sized hollow on the left side of her enchanted helm. And if the helm looked like that . . . "We need a healer. Now."

"Calm down, I can take care of her." Gawain felt Kel's magic call to his, then sweep across Lark's still body. The helm vanished, revealing an icily pale face marred by a constellation of bruises. Most sinister of all, blood matted her dark hair, and the shape of her head looked . . . wrong.

Gawain stared at the wound, appalled and sickened. "If she'd been mortal . . ."

"She'd be dead, but she's not mortal and I can heal her. Now shut up."

Gawain sank down on the bed next to her and gave himself up to whatever magic Kel needed. "We almost lost her. I almost lost her."

"But you didn't. Watch it, my reserves are low from the fight. I'm going to have to draw on yours."

Gawain gritted his teeth as he felt Kel's magic start sapping his strength. His body seemed to grow heavier. Suddenly he felt every ache and bruise from the battle. Swallowing, he lay back against the headboard, silently cursing himself.

The dragon's magic flowed over her body, glowing fiercely.

Lark drew in a sudden, sharp breath.

"There we go!" Kel said triumphantly, allowing the power field to fade. "Just a little bit more."

Another surge of power, the drain so fierce Gawain thought for a moment he was going to throw up. Then, blessedly, Lark stirred and moaned.

"God, my head hurts," she husked, without opening her eyes. "I feel like crap."

"No surprise," Kel said. "What were you thinking, stepping between us and that psychopath?"

"Not so loud," she pleaded. "And I was thinking you were about to get whacked."

Gawain sensed her drawing on her own magic to

complete the healing Kel had begun. Dragging himself upright, he examined her anxiously.

Lark looked up to meet his gaze, frowning. He was relieved to see that she looked alert and clear-eyed. Even the bruises had vanished, though blood lingered in her hair. "Tell me you killed him."

Gawain shook his head. "I had to get you out of there. You were badly hurt."

Her frown deepened. "You should have finished it, Gawain. Now we've got to worry about catching that nut job again."

Exhausted, he let himself sag back against the headboard as his eyes drifted close. He ached in every muscle, and he felt dangerously weak. "You were hurt. Look, I have to . . ." He never managed to finish the sentence.

Alarmed, Lark jerked upright as Gawain's head lolled. He looked pale, almost bloodless. "He's passed out!"

"Healing Sleep," Kel told her. "Between fueling my magic during all those powerful spells and fighting Edge, he's done for the night. He'll need to recharge from the Mageverse and feed when he wakes."

Lark frowned. Magi drew much of their sustaining magic from the Mageverse itself; that was the reason for the Daysleep. They drew the rest from their partners during sex and blood drinking. "Is he going to be all right?"

The dragon's small head nodded. He looked almost as haggard as his partner. "Just let him have a pint or two from that lovely throat, and he'll be right as rain."

She snorted and rolled off the bed, feeling suddenly full of energy. Her stomach growled, but she ignored it in favor of their immediate problem. "What's this about Edge and Lord Bors?"

"Edge is Bors's son," Kel explained.

Lark frowned. "That's not Mageverse magic he's using."

"Cachamwri's breath, no. Edge's application to become a Magus was refused decades ago. Somehow he must have hooked up with Geirolf in the meantime."

The descendants of those who'd drunk from Merlin's Grail were called Latents because they carried the genetic potential to become Magekind. But unless repeated sexual contact with a Maja or Magus triggered the Gift in their DNA, they remained mortal.

The Majae's Council decided which Latents received Merlin's Gift after checking to ensure they were morally and mentally capable of dealing with such power. It wasn't a decision anyone made lightly, since it wasn't uncommon for new Majae to go insane. And an insane Maja was a Very Bad Thing. Lark imagined a psychopathic Magus would be even worse.

Because qualified applicants were so rare, most Magi were in the habit of fathering large numbers of illegitimate children. The theory was that the more of them there were, the more likely one or two of them would make viable Magekind. Most of them had no idea what they were; John had been an exception.

"How did Edge find out he was a Latent?"

Kel furled his wings back and settled down, looking more like a tiny silver swan than a dragon. "His mother was a Maja. She raised him in the Mageverse."

Lark's eyes widened. "He's a Latent on both sides?" And one of them a knight of the Round Table. Boy, that was a prescription for the Bad Guy From Hell.

For a moment, she imagined what it would have been like to grow up in the Mageverse, knowing you had the potential for immortality and incredible power. Believing it would be yours, only to be denied. "No wonder Edge is pissed. But how did he end up serving Geirolf?"

"I have no idea." Kel yawned delicately, his long forked tongue curling like a cat's. With a sigh, he settled his tiny head down on his partner's forearm. "I've got to go to sleep, or Gawain won't be able to rest as deeply as he must. Try to stay out of trouble, child." Jeweled eyes slid closed.

"I'll do my best," she told him dryly.

An instant later, he froze in place. It looked as if

someone had cast the sword's hilt in just that pose, with its triangular head resting on Gawain's armored arm. Then the armor covering Gawain's muscled body melted away, leaving his big body naked and lax in sleep.

Visibly exhausted though he was, his body was still breathtaking enough to make her own purr in approval. She remembered the instant when he'd stepped on that book and started to go down. She hadn't even thought twice about stepping between him and Edge.

Which would have been fine, if it had only been duty that motivated her. Unfortunately, she knew her act of self-sacrifice had more to do with the tender heat she'd seen in Gawain's eyes when they'd made love.

"Oh," she muttered, "that's so not a good sign."

Particularly considering that Tristan and Diera were united in the belief that he'd never see her as anything but a tasty little side dish. And they had a point. After all, this was the same man who'd broken Diera's heart—Diera, who was so much more powerful, experienced, and lovely than Lark.

If Gawain could walk away from a Maja like that, what chance did she have?

EIGHT

Lark's first impulse was to head for the Ladies' Club. Unfortunately, it was still nightfall, and she didn't want to leave Gawain alone in the Healing Sleep.

As she debated what to do next, her stomach rumbled a demand for dinner. She made a quick trip to the kitchen downstairs, assembled a sandwich in Gawain's well-stocked kitchen, and returned to the living room to eat it in front of the fire.

As she munched, Lark's mind kept returning to the battle. She'd been so far out of her weight class, there hadn't been much she could do but sling books and take a blast for Gawain. It was humiliating.

What would Tristan do in this situation?

She could almost hear that deep, rich voice. *Know your enemy, Lark.*

In other words, find out more about this Edge character and determine a way to bring him down.

Ordinarily, Lark would turn to Diera for help with a question like this. Though not quite as old as Tristan and Gawain, her friend had been around for almost a thousand years. Tristan knew Bors, too, of course, but somehow she suspected this kind of thing would strike him as gossip. Diera, on the other hand, knew where most of Avalon's metaphorical bodies were buried—heck, she'd probably held the torch for the grave diggers.

Unfortunately, she and Gawain also had a history, one Diera was uncharacteristically bitter about. Lark wasn't sure she wanted to poke that particular wound.

Still, if anybody knew anything about Edge, Diera would be the one. The sorcerer had to be dealt with, period, so her friend was just going to have to suck it up.

Decision made, Lark pulled out her cell phone. The device had no business working in the Mageverse at all—not only were there no cell towers here, its battery was dead. Luckily, like almost everything else in Avalon, it was enchanted. "Diera," she told it.

A moment later her friend's voice answered. "Lark?"

"Yep, it's me. Listen, I've run into a situation, and I was wondering if you could help." Better to avoid mentioning Gawain if she could avoid it.

"Certainly, darling. Why don't you come to the house and we'll discuss it over tea." She sounded pleased with herself. "I have a great deal to tell you, too."

"I . . . can't just now. Gawain's in a healing sleep, and I don't want to—"

Alarm rang in her voice. "What's wrong?"

A bit surprised at her friend's obvious concern, Lark filled her in on the fight with Edge, then sketched in its aftermath.

"I agree, you definitely shouldn't leave him alone under those circumstances," Diera said when she finished. "Wait a moment, and Antonio and I will be right over."

The phone went dead.

Oh, this should be interesting.

She looked up to see a dimensional gate forming next to the fireplace. An instant later, Diera stepped out of it, followed by the tall, muscular dark-haired Magus.

Apparently they'd kissed and made up after their earlier

fight. As Lark greeted them, Antonio watched Diera's every move as if utterly smitten, a fact that obviously flustered the Maja.

Delighted, Lark disposed of the remains of her dinner and conjured tea for the three of them. Diera and Antonio seated themselves on the couch so close together their knees bumped.

"First, I'd like to apologize for my abysmal behavior earlier tonight," Diera announced, giving her tea a subtle zap to adjust its sugar content to her liking.

Lark made a dismissive gesture. "Don't worry about it, Diera. We're friends. God knows you've put up with a lot worse than that from me."

"That may be," Antonio said in his deep, accented voice, "but even an immortal cannot afford to waste her life in such bitterness." His gaze slid to Diera's face and lingered hungrily. "A woman of such beauty and intelligence has so much more to offer."

And from the sound of it, Antonio was dying to sample Diera's offerings. Lark lifted her tea and took a sip to hide her threatening grin.

Diera colored prettily and patted the hand he'd rested on his muscled thigh. "After I calmed down, I realized what a little bitch I'd been. Actually, I think losing my temper like that did me some good. It showed me exactly what my bitterness has done to me. It's been two years since Gawain and I broke up. I need to forgive him, ask his forgiveness in return, and move on."

Directly to Antonio, it would seem.

A surprising burst of jealousy shot through Lark. *Forgive him for what?* She fought down the impulse to ask and sat back in her armchair. "Sounds like a positive step."

Diera turned earnest blue eyes to hers. "When Gawain wakes from the Healing Sleep, please call me. I want a clean slate between us."

"I'd be happy to."

Her friend nodded briskly. "Good. Now, about Richard Edge . . ."

Relieved at the change of subject, Lark studied her friend. "What can you tell me?"

Diera hesitated. "Actually, I think it would be wise to bring Bors in at this point. He deserves to hear what you've told me, and he may be able to throw some light on where to look for his son. It's obvious Edge will move elsewhere, now that you've found his temple, or his lair, or whatever it was."

Lark grimaced. "Diera, I don't know Bors. I'm not comfortable giving him news like this. Shouldn't we wait for Gawain?"

"And lose hours we could use to investigate this? I don't think that would be wise."

She stifled a curse. "I suppose not."

Diera nodded briskly and produced her own cell. "Bors? Diera . . . I'm well, thanks. Listen, a friend of mine and I need to talk to you. It's about Richard."

She fell silent a moment, then nodded briskly. "I'll create a gate for you."

Like Diera, Bors arrived with his assignment, a rangy young man named George Rivers. The kid immediately moved to prop a tattooed shoulder against the fireplace mantle and regard them all with an air of acute boredom. Lark had the impression he wished he were off killing something.

But it was Bors that held her interest. Dark and brawny, his resemblance to his son was uncanny. Ironically, he appeared younger than Edge, since he'd drunk from Merlin's Grail in his early twenties. Then there was the animation and warmth in his gaze, so different from the reptilian chill in his son's.

It was painful to watch that warmth drain into horror as Lark related the events of the night.

"Oh, Merlin's beard. Richard—one of Geirolf's cultists?" Bors stared at her, his expression stricken. "And he tried to kill you and Gawain?"

"I'm sorry," Lark said awkwardly, mentally cursing herself for not waiting to stir up this particular hornet's nest until Gawain was awake.

Bors sat forward in his chair, broad shoulders hunched. "I loved that boy," he whispered. "And his mother doted on him." Suddenly he stood restlessly and began to pace. "Maybe that's the problem. Maybe we loved him too much."

"You and his mother were Truebonded?" Lark asked.

Bors looked around at her, jolted from his guilt. "Meredith and I? No. Lovers for a time, nothing more. But when she became pregnant with Richard, I was determined to play a part in his life." He stopped his pacing to stand with his dark head down, lost in thought. "In retrospect, that was yet another mistake. She should never have tried to raise him in the Mageverse. We should have known better." Blowing out a breath, he admitted, "And I should have stayed out of his life. If nothing else, he wouldn't have been able to give Gawain such a run."

"Why not?" His apprentice asked from the fireplace, dropping the disinterested pose.

Bors shrugged. "I taught him how to use a sword from a young age, just as we knights were taught centuries ago."

"What's wrong with raising children in the Mageverse?" Lark asked, puzzled. "You both wanted to be with him. Seems to me that was just what you should have done." John would have loved to grow up with Tristan's full-time attention.

"The problem is that children are mortals." He started pacing again, his strides long and restless. "They need to be raised among mortals, not by people who can realize every whim with a thought."

"What's more, it doesn't take a child long to realize he changes when everyone else here does not," Diera added.

"Since there are so few children in Avalon, the child comes to feel isolated, unable to connect with those around him."

"And with Richard, it was even worse. By the time he became a teenager, it was obvious something had gone badly wrong." Bors's face was tight with remembered pain and guilt. "He was callous. He . . . one of the neighboring Maja had a dog, a toy poodle. Yappy little beast, but harmless, and she adored that animal." He stopped pacing to run an agitated hand through his hair. "Richard killed it. Ran it through with his sword and left it to bleed to death. Said it had annoyed him. He was all of twelve."

"Oh." Lark winced. Killing and tormenting animals was one of the signs of developing sociopathy in teens.

Bors nodded. "And then there was what happened with Diera."

"Diera?" Lark raised her brows and looked at her friend. "What'd he do to you?"

Antonio frowned, tensing protectively.

Diera glanced at him and took his hand. "Nothing that dramatic. He had a little crush on me, but he was a child. I tried to let him down gently . . ."

"And he threatened to kill her," Bors gritted.

"He didn't mean it. He was a child, simply speaking out of frustration and rage."

"He may have been a child then," Antonio told her, looking even more upset, "but he's certainly not one any longer. You could be in danger."

"I doubt it. We reinforced Avalon's wards after the invasion." She gave him a comforting smile. "There's no way he could get through."

The young Magus did not appear comforted.

Lark turned to Bors. "What happened after he threatened Diera?"

"Meredith finally moved to mortal Earth with him. We'd hoped he would form a sense of empathy among his own kind, but it didn't work."

"No," Lark said softly. "He'd been raised among

Magekind, so he wouldn't have fit in back on Earth either."
Suddenly Tristan's distance from John was much more understandable.

"Exactly." Bors stood with his head down, his expression troubled. "He was constantly in trouble, with his
teachers and other children. He was expelled from school,
stole a car, got in trouble with the law. I think he would
have sold our secret to the first reporter he found, but his
mother put a spell on him to make sure he couldn't talk."

"God." Lark rubbed a hand over her face, wincing. "The
teenage years are normally hard, but . . ."

"Yes." Bors sighed. "I moved in with them early on, trying to help Meredith control him, but my attempts at disci-
pline only made him angrier."

"That must have been tough," Lark said softly.

"And it got tougher when Richard turned eighteen, because he fully expected me to submit his name to the Majae's Council to become a Magus."

"And you said the only thing you could say," Diera said.

"Which was, of course, no." He blew out a breath.
"Richard was furious. He swore he'd make me regret ruin-
ing his chances at immortality. He never spoke to me again."

Lark stared at Bors. "What chance at immortality? The
council would never have approved him, not with that track
record."

"Exactly. I actually considered submitting his name just
to keep the family peace, knowing he'd be denied. But I
hoped that my refusal would make him see he couldn't
continue to follow this path."

"But it didn't work."

Bors sighed. "No."

"What about his mother?"

"She continued to try to help him for several more years
before she finally gave up and washed her hands of him. To
my knowledge, she hadn't seen or spoken to him in fifteen
years. The irony is that she died in that final battle with
Geirolf's army three months ago." He turned and walked to

an armchair, then dropped into it heavily. "In a way, it's a blessing. She doesn't have to see what he became."

"I'm sorry," Lark said softly.

"I never dreamed he was capable of anything like this. It wouldn't have surprised me to discover he'd become a petty thief or been shot in a barroom brawl, but this . . ." His voice trailed off. "My worst nightmares never included anything like this."

Antonio spoke softly. "What are you going to do now?"

Bors looked over at him, his gaze flat. "The only thing I can do—kill him."

His apprentice straightened away from the fireplace in alarm. "Dude, I don't think that's a good idea. He's your kid. Yeah, sounds like he needs killing, but you shouldn't have to do it."

"There are others who can fulfill that duty," Antonio said quietly.

Bors shot him a glittering look. "Maybe I deserve to suffer."

"I think you've already suffered more than enough," Lark said.

"It's pointless," Diera agreed. "And not particularly safe. You can't afford to go into combat like this. He'll eat you alive."

"*I don't care.*" The knight slammed his palm against the coffee table, making the cups rattle and jump. "I did this! I am responsible for making him what he is!"

Diera rose from her seat and went to kneel beside Bors's seat so she could meet his eyes. "Perhaps when he was eight, but Richard is in his forties now. He's responsible for making himself what he is."

"And what he is, is a monster." Bors gritted his teeth. "I kill monsters."

He rose from his chair and started for the door.

"You're not going after him now?" Lark demanded, shooting to her feet in alarm. "Without reinforcements?"

Bors gave her a glittering look over his shoulder. "Of

course not. First, because I'm not a fool, but more importantly, my primary responsibility is to Arthur. He must be informed my son has turned traitor." Pain flashed across his face. "Arthur will probably dispatch the Round Table." Straightening his shoulders, he strode from the room like a proud man walking to his execution.

His apprentice threw them a look of such helpless, worried frustration, Lark found herself feeling for him. He strode after his mentor. "Hey, dude, wait up."

Antonio and Diera rose to their feet. "We'd better follow them. I fear what he'll do in this mood."

They, too, hurried after the two men.

Feeling helpless, Lark watched them all go. Her instinct was to follow them, but she knew she didn't dare leave Gawain.

"Well, that was about as pleasant as gutting a man with a dull spoon," she muttered. "And it didn't tell me a damn thing that would help find Edge."

The sun was up when Lark picked up her enchanted cell and made the call she'd been craving.

She needed to talk to her grandfather. Needed his wisdom, his common sense, but most of all, she needed to remember there was at least one thing she'd done right.

He answered the phone on the first ring. He was probably carrying his own cell around in his pocket. "Lark? Hi, baby! How's it going?"

Her throat thickened at the sound of his dear, familiar voice. "It's been a rough night, Grandpa."

Quickly, she filled him in on the fight with Edge and her conversation with Bors. "I spent the rest of the night searching Kel's library for a good locator spell, but nothing I tried worked. I have no idea where Edge is. But I'm pretty sure he's either killing somebody or planning to kill somebody. And there's not a damn thing I can do about it."

"Sounds like you've done everything you can do, honey.

Besides, by now your friend Diera's probably got all the other Majae working on it. They'll find him."

Lark sighed, feeling tired and defeated. "God, I hope so."

He paused. "So they paired you up with Lord Gawain, huh? How's that going?" His attempt at a casual tone failed completely.

"Granddad, if you're hoping for a budding romance, don't. Tristan says Gawain's a great guy, but he goes through Majae like you go through your sock drawer."

"Hey, you're not just any Maja, kid. And you're sure not anybody's sock. Unless Gawain's a dummy—and he couldn't be if the stories I've heard are true—he's going to realize that. Don't sell yourself short."

"I won't."

"Good. Hey, it's nine o'clock in the morning, which makes it—what? Almost noon there. Shouldn't you be in bed? Sounds like you're going to need your sleep."

"You're probably right." Judging, at least, from the gritty condition of her eyes. "Hey, you have fun today, you hear? Go find yourself some more poker victims to fleece, you card shark. I love you."

"I love you, too. 'Bye, honey."

Gently, she turned off her cell and tucked it away.

Feeling battered, Lark walked back into Gawain's bedroom and closed the door. With the windows heavily shielded against daylight, it was dark as a coal shaft. She conjured a dim light and made her way toward the bed.

She paused at its massive footboard and studied Gawain's sleeping form. Wide as the mattress was, he seemed to take up most of it as he sprawled there in all his tanned, muscular glory. His color was better than it had been after last night's battle, and the lines of exhaustion had smoothed. His blond hair was disordered in sleep, tousled over his forehead, giving him a deceptively boyish look. Kel lay on his right side, tiny head still resting on his arm.

She looked at him a long moment, admiring his raw

masculine beauty. Then, taking a deep breath, she climbed into bed next to his big, warm body and curled up against his side.

After a moment, she lay her head on his chest and listened to the slow, comforting beat of his heart. A smile spreading across her face, she fell asleep.

A low, masculine growl jolted Lark awake as a heavy male body rolled on top of her like a hot blanket. Lark jerked, her heart leaping into her throat as powerful arms slid around her from behind. For a moment she froze in panic, remembering Fangface's attack. Magic roared through her, filling her hands with force. The instant before she blasted her attacker through the nearest wall, she heard Gawain's deep groan. "Lark . . ."

Swearing, she banished the spell she'd been gathering. "Gawain, dammit, I almost fried you!"

"Shush." He pressed his mouth to her pulse and inhaled, breathing her scent. His cock hardened against her in a breathtaking rush. "You smell so good." A big hand came to rest on her breast, carefully cupped and squeezed. Her nipple hardened against his palm.

Her sense of humor surfaced. "And good morning to you, too."

"I need you, Lark." His voice was low, hoarse—and unmistakably pleading. "Please."

She frowned, thinking he sounded a little out of it. Belatedly, she remembered Kel had told her he'd had to drain Gawain's magical reserves dangerously low. *Just let him have a pint or two from that lovely throat, and he'll be right as rain.*

"Lark? Do you want me to go?"

"No." She turned her head and met his mouth with her own. "God, no."

He groaned in relief and kissed her, his tongue delving deep as his fingers plucked and teased her tight nipples.

His mouth wasn't quite as sweet as usual, but then, she knew her own wasn't either. A quick spell took care of that, and she pressed closer.

He kissed better than any man she'd ever met, slow and seductive even as hungry as he was.

At last he pulled away from her lips and transferred his ravenous attention to the breast he'd been toying with. Lark shuttered her eyes in pleasure as his tongue swirled and his lips suckled.

Then, abruptly, he caught her shoulders and rolled her over onto her belly.

"Gawain?" She licked dry lips.

He only growled as he slid a knee between hers. A second knee joined it, and he spread her thighs wide. His hands slid up, cupping both breasts to tease her aching nipples again. Lark caught her breath as pleasure began to roll through her, slow and rich as a wave of heated honey.

She squirmed. His thick cock rested against her butt like a seductive threat. Lark panted as her arousal spiraled at the sensation. "God, I want you."

"Good." Gawain nuzzled her ear, then caught the lobe between his teeth for a gentle bite. It felt so delicious, she angled her head over, letting him nibble as he pleased. With a rumble of approval, he traced his tongue down over her throat, licking at her banging pulse.

His right hand was just as busy, stroking and tugging one nipple into sweet little jolts of delight.

His left hand slid down her body, finding the juncture of her thighs. Lark caught her breath as he delved between her vaginal lips and slid one strong finger into her. Pumped. Once, twice, as he tormented her nipple skillfully, magnifying the rough pleasure. "Your breasts are so beautiful," he rasped. "All of you is so beautiful."

She rolled her face against the tangled curtain of his hair and grinned. "You have such a way with words."

As if in retaliation for her quip, the points of his fangs scraped gently across her skin. Lark moaned, loving the sensation. Gawain growled a deliciously predatory reply against her throat.

Suddenly he slid his knees under them both, braced a hand, and raised off her, then drew her into his arms until she was sitting astride his thighs, her back against his chest. With a flash of hunger, she realized the pose made her completely available to anything he wanted to do to her.

Despite the lust she could feel thrumming through his big body, he patiently returned to his stroking, teasing nipples and sex until she found herself hunching against his hand. His cock lay between her labia, not entering, just tantalizing her with its hard, erotic promise. Lark panted, maddened.

She couldn't see a damned thing. All she could do was feel—the heat and muscled contours of his body, the hands that tormented and aroused, the rigid cock that jerked between her thighs.

At the same time, he teased her throat in preparation for his bite. Delicate little licks and taunting scrapes of his fangs sent her arousal spiraling. She rolled her hips harder, deliberately forcing his cock against her clit, feeling the first building pulses of her climax.

"You're wet," he growled in her ear, his fingers making liquid sounds as he stroked her.

"And you're hard," she panted, wanting all that ravenous hunger inside her.

"Yeah. I'm going to fuck you."

She gasped at the stark, carnal phrase, the anticipation in his voice, the dark note of triumph. Somehow it all turned her on even more. Then he circled her clit with a forefinger, jerking her need another notch tighter. Lark moaned and rolled back at him, shivering. He made a purring sound in his throat and went on teasing her.

Just when she thought she'd go insane, he pushed her off his lap and onto her belly, then lifted her hips until her backside thrust into the air.

Ready to be mounted.

The round, smooth head of his cock brushed her slick labia. Then, slowly, he began to enter her, working his width inside. Lark groaned at the fierce pleasure and tossed her head back, loving the way he felt.

With a growl, he came down over her, pushing more and more of that big cock deeper and deeper. Until, finally, he was seated to the balls.

To her shock, he reached up under her body, found her wrists, and wrapped one hand around them, shackling them with his long fingers. As she gasped, he reached up with the other hand and swept her hair aside to bare her neck. Readying her for his bite.

"Now," Gawain breathed. "Now we fuck."

His hips began to roll against her ass, pushing his big cock in and out with such power, each thrust ground against her clit. He started out slow and almost brutally deep, so much so that she twisted in his grip, instinctively trying to pull away. But though his hold on her wrists didn't hurt, it was also unbreakable. He controlled her halfhearted struggles without effort and went right on with those deep, inexorable thrusts.

"Gawain . . ." She shuttered her eyes, on the edge of pain from the feel of that big cock probing so deep, yet at the same time teased by the wicked climax hovering just beyond her grip. "Please, it's too much. . . ."

"Not yet." He leaned down and pressed his open mouth to her pulse, the tips of his fangs resting against the throb, almost biting. They scraped her skin as he whispered, "But it's about to be."

Lark gasped. She felt overwhelmed, helpless, twisting on the end of that massive cock, surrounded by his powerful arms and big, brawny body, the cool points of his fangs pressing her skin. Arousal shivered through her in a river of heat.

Gawain picked up the pace, grinding his hips a little

faster, fucking her a little harder. The pleasure grew, hot and dark, spurring her with wicked little pinpricks of heat. Lark rolled her hips back at him, wanting more. Craving it.

He growled like a hungry cat and bit, sinking his fangs into her throat. She cried out in pleasure-pain, arching. His hips slapped hard against her backside, driving his cock to the hilt.

Then he began to feed in long, hungry swallows. Holding her like this, he couldn't manage long strokes, so he ground his cock in tight circles until it seemed to corkscrew her creamy flesh.

All the while, he fed, drinking from her throat, his fangs burning her skin, that one hand holding her wrists pinned. Helpless, moaning, she could only writhe.

Lark's climax surged out of nowhere like a glowing tsunami, swamping her with blinding pleasure. She cried out as it raced through her body, each ripple of pleasure stronger than the last, jerking against his grinding hips.

He pulled free of her throat and roared, shoving his cock to its full length as he came. Lark screamed in echo, twisting against him like a woman in torment, completely overwhelmed.

And loving every moment of it.

NINE

Breathing hard, Gawain bent over Lark, listening to the galloping thunder of her heart. His own was beating pretty hard, too. She lay limp under him, panting into her pillow. Carefully, he tugged his softened cock from her sex, released her wrists, and rolled over onto his back with a groan.

Her muffled voice emerged from the depths of the pillow. "I think you killed me."

He lifted his head sharply. "Lights!" As the bedside lamp came on, he examined her in its illumination. She looked sleepy and sated, but he asked anyway. "Did I hurt you?"

She snorted. "I was kidding. I'm just kind of pleasantly sore and wrung out."

Gawain relaxed. "You need a hot bath. Hey, Kel . . ."

"What?" the dragon asked from his scabbard.

"Mind filling the tub for us?"

Water began to bubble in the adjoining bathroom. *You're in a good mood,* the dragon observed in their link. *A hell of a lot more chipper than you were last night.*

Good sex does that.

Lark lifted her head from the pillow and eyed the sword. "How'd you get there? You were lying next to Gawain."

"I sheathed him before I woke you," Gawain explained, rolling over to stretch. "Being in bed with an enchanted sword on a bouncing mattress is a really bad idea."

"Good point."

The dragon grinned. "Sharp, too."

With a groan, she picked up the pillow and slung it in the sword's direction. "No puns that bad this early."

"Hey!" Kel protested. He caught it with a spell and levitated it threateningly. "If it's a pillow fight you want, wench . . ."

Before the dragon could hurl the pillow back, Gawain rolled out of bed and snatched her into his arms. "We have other plans, dragon."

As he headed into the bathroom, the pillow popped him in the back of the head. "Coward."

He kicked the door closed behind him. Lark laughed and curled a slender arm around his neck. "I could have taken him."

"He'd have inundated you in so many feathers, you'd have thought you were in a remake of *The Birds*," Gawain told her, carrying her to the huge bath, full and bubbling like a Jacuzzi thanks to the dragon's magic. Throwing a leg over the marble lip, Gawain added, "He hates to . . . dammit, Kel!" He jerked his foot out of the water and glowered down into the tub's depths. "It's ice cold!"

Through the door, he heard the dragon's wicked chuckle.

"Laugh it up, gecko!" Gawain called back. "I'm going to line your scabbard with sandpaper."

Clinging to his neck with one hand, Lark made a hasty gesture with the other. He sensed the buzz of magic. "Look, it's hot now. No violence required."

Gawain gave her a deliberately toothy grin. "But violence is my best thing."

"Well," she drawled. "Not your *best* thing . . ."

Laughing, he stepped into the tub to find it the perfect

temperature. He put her on her feet and settled down with her into the foaming water.

Lark groaned in pleasure as she sank to her shoulders and leaned back against the tub's smooth wall. "Oh, man, you were right. I needed this."

"Yeah," Gawain agreed, settling back. "You can get clean with magic, but there's nothing like a good soak." Eyeing the nipples peeking over the bubbling water, he grinned. "Plus, you can't beat the view."

Cuddling Lark in the tub, Gawain listened as she described breaking the news to Bors and her subsequent efforts to find Edge.

"I tried a dozen spells," she finished, "but none of them worked."

"Don't worry about it," he told her. "By now, Arthur has Morgana, Guinevere, and another dozen witches looking for him. Somebody'll turn him up."

"I hope so. We need to find the son of a bitch." She sat up and conjured a bottle of shampoo.

"I agree with you, but when it comes right down to it, he's no match for the Magekind. Now that he's on the radar, it's not going to take us long to get rid of him." Gawain reached for the bottle. "Let me do that."

She handed it over, a frown on her pretty face. "I feel sorry for Bors, though. He looked so haunted."

"This has been his worst fear for years." Gawain poured a thick dollop of shampoo into his palm. "For one thing, he saw what Arthur went through when Modred led that rebellion against him. Arthur ended up killing his son, and it almost destroyed him. I thought he and Guinevere would never have another child. . . . Wet your hair and scoot over here so I can shampoo you."

Lark obeyed and rested her shoulders against him. "Arthur and Guinevere have a child?"

"Yes, he's thirty or so. Unlike Edge, though, the Majae's Council has cleared him to become a Magus, but his mortal career is going well and he doesn't want to give it up. Nobody's pushed the point."

Lark titled her head back as he started rubbing the shampoo into her hair. "Considering our manpower problems and the Sorcerers' War, I'm surprised they haven't just drafted the poor guy."

"I don't think Arthur wants to go there. And who can blame him? Though I suspect if somebody told Logan the situation, he might just volunteer."

The lather felt cool as it foamed over his hands, and he stroked it through her long, dark mane, enjoying the silken feel of the strands.

"That feels good," she told him with a sigh as she relaxed against him.

"I was just thinking the same thing. Your hair is beautiful—so thick and soft."

She turned her head against his shoulder and opened one eye to look up at him. "Why, Gawain, that sounded suspiciously like a compliment."

"Hey, I've complimented you before."

" 'I love your tits' doesn't exactly qualify, especially when you're sucking on them at the time."

"But I do." He reached across and cupped one in soapy fingers. "They're perfect. Just full enough, with such deliciously sensitive nipples. I also love your waist and your long legs and those big, dark eyes." She was watching him, a wry quirk to her lips, as if she didn't believe him. "And I especially love that mouth." He lowered his head and kissed her, slowly, taking his time, savoring the taste of her, chasing her tongue with his.

She relaxed into him with a sigh, and he curled his soapy arms around her. He was struck again by how delicate she was, how fragile. The top of her head didn't even come up to his shoulders.

An image flashed through his mind: looking down into her pale face after Kel had removed her helm the night before. The blood matting her hair, the horrific head injury.

His arms tightened convulsively. "Why did you step between Edge and me? He could have killed you."

"What?" She shook her head and frowned as if confused by the sudden shift of topic. "Whoa. Psychic whiplash. Where did that come from?"

He closed his eyes and rested his face against hers. "You scared me last night. You took a very big risk, and it almost killed you."

Eyes narrowed, Lark turned to look at him. "Edge was about to take your head, Gawain. What the heck was I supposed to do?"

He drew back and pushed a lock of hair back from her face. "To start with, let me take care of myself. I'm the one with the enchanted sword, remember?"

She quirked a brow at him. "And I'm the Maja—remember? It's my job to fight bad guys, too. And despite occasional panic attacks, I don't turn my back on my duty."

"I realize that, and I respect it. But Edge is even more dangerous than the other sorcerers we've encountered. And considering what happened to you during the attack on Avalon . . ." He broke off at the anger kindling in her eyes. It belatedly dawned on him that he was treading on dangerous ground.

"Yes, I got hurt. Yes, I almost died. And yes, I've been struggling with the consequences of that. But that doesn't mean I'm going to stand around twiddling my thumbs while my partner gets killed." She rose from the tub in a cascade of water, all wet, gleaming curves and snapping eyes. "And I am your partner. It's my duty to protect you, too, and I'm going to do my duty whether you like it or not."

With a splash and a thump of bare feet, she stepped out of the tub and stalked from the bathroom, wrapped in a cloak of icy dignity he could almost see.

Hastily, Gawain climbed out and followed her into the bedroom. "Courage and duty aren't the point, Lark. You need to be realistic. I'm bigger than you are, I'm stronger than you are, and Kel's magic is far more powerful than yours."

"Oh," Kel moaned from the headboard, "you are such a dumb ass."

Gawain ignored him. "We could have handled Edge without you putting your life in danger. I—"

"But thank you for making the effort on our behalf," Kel interrupted loudly. "I really appreciate it. Life as a paper-weight does not appeal to me."

"You're welcome, Kel," Lark told him, staring at Gawain with narrowed eyes. "But I think you should know, I'm getting ready to turn your partner into a frog."

"Go ahead. It'd do him good to sit on a lily pad for a couple of days and think about what an asshole he is."

Gawain met Lark's stare with one just as hot. "If not wanting to see Lark get killed makes me an asshole, that's fine with me. Look, I've fought these guys before, and I know what I'm talking about. Edge isn't just another sorcerer. He—"

"I thought you said he'd be easy pickings now that we know about him."

"Against the combined weight of the Magekind, no, he doesn't have a prayer. But against you, one-on-one . . . that wouldn't end well."

With a jerk of her hands, Lark clothed herself in jeans and a shirt. She was completely dry, even her hair falling in perfect dark waves. "Thanks for the vote of confidence."

Frustrated, he glowered at her. "You're not an idiot. This is not news to you. You know the situation as well as I do."

"And thank you for grinding my face in it!" She stalked out, slamming the door.

"When she turns you into a frog, don't come croaking to me," Kel said as Gawain lunged for the door.

But when he tried to open it, the knob wouldn't turn. He whirled on his partner with a snarl. "Open it, or I'm kicking it down!"

"Not if I put a shield around it. You two need a minute to cool off, Gawain. You might want to actually *think* . . ."

"Open. The. Door."

". . . or you could just run in there and pour gasoline on the forest fire you've managed to start until you both say a lot of shit you don't mean."

Gawain spun and lifted a foot, ready to send the door crashing open. . . .

He stopped in mid-motion. Kel, as usual, was right. He lowered his foot and turned, his shoulders slumping. "Have I ever told you you're a high-handed pain in the ass?"

"Three to four times a week, as a matter of fact."

"Well, you're hearing it again." With a sigh, Gawain moved to sit down on the bed. A drop fell off his nose, and he belatedly realized he was still naked and dripping wet.

Magic tingled over his skin as Kel read his mind. An instant later, he was warm and dry and dressed in a green knit shirt and chinos. Reaching over, he picked up the scabbard and slung it over one shoulder. "Thanks."

"You're welcome." He felt the dragon's wings brush the back of his neck as his friend settled himself. "Actually, I'm rather encouraged by all this drama."

Gawain twisted his head to eye him. "Oh?"

"You cared enough to actually argue with her. If you hadn't, you'd just order her not to interfere in your next fight. Then you'd give her ice-cold arrogance until she caved from sheer intimidation."

Gawain frowned. "Am I that big an asshole?"

The dragon tilted his head, considering the question. "It's not really being an asshole, it's more the way a military leader deals with a subordinate. But you've stopped treating her like a subordinate."

"But she is. Technically."

"Technically. But there's a lot more going on between you than that."

Restless, Gawain rose and moved toward the window to stare out at the moonlit streets of Avalon. "Maybe that's where I'm making the mistake. I don't want her putting herself in danger for me."

"Gawain, she'd do that whether you two were sleeping together or not. She knows her duty as well as you do. What's more, if she were another knight, it wouldn't even occur to you to ask her to stay out of a fight. Hell, if she were Morgana, it wouldn't occur to you."

Gawain snorted. "That's because Morgana would barbecue my balls like pulled pork. Besides, Morgana has a lot more power than Lark."

"Not that much more. Lark just hasn't learned how to bring it all to bear yet." The dragon flicked his silver wings, his expression brooding. "But somehow I have the feeling that she's going to have to figure it out. And soon."

Lark stomped down the stairs toward the kitchen. She almost wished Gawain would come roaring out of his room so they could have all this out once and for all. Unfortunately, judging by what she'd heard through the door, Kel had basically locked him in to give them both time to cool off.

Which might have been wise, but wasn't as satisfying as a good screaming fight.

She stalked into the kitchen and headed to the refrigerator. This situation definitely called for a plate of scrambled eggs. She needed protein if she was going to continue having frequent sex with Gawain.

Of course, the real question was whether it was just sex or something more. She was pretty damn sure it was becoming more from her end, but she wasn't so sure about Gawain's.

Considered from that angle, his humiliating little lecture was actually encouraging. He cared enough to be afraid for her. Which was nice, except she wasn't sure it meant anything. Chivalry was programmed into the man's DNA; of course he'd want the helpless little female to hang back out of the fight.

Thing was, she was getting sick of being the helpless little female.

Lark got a carton of eggs and a stick of butter out of the refrigerator, then nudged the door closed with a hip. After retrieving a mixing bowl from a cabinet, she cracked a couple of eggs, her movements short and sharp with controlled anger.

She hated this. Hated feeling as if she couldn't hold her own against the monsters. Hated being told she wasn't strong enough, smart enough, ruthless enough.

Most of all, she hated that she really wasn't strong enough, smart enough, or ruthless enough. Just once, she'd like to set some asshole back on his heels and prove everybody wrong.

She wanted to look into Gawain's eyes and see something a little warmer than lust and a shade of condescension.

Crouching, she reached into a cabinet and pulled out the cast iron frying pan she'd brought from home. Banging it onto the stove, she turned on the heat and went to get a glass of orange juice while she waited for it to heat.

Dumb ass. Craving the respect of a man who'd fought beside Arthur and the knights of the Round Table. A guy whose idea of a really talented Maja was Morgana Le Fay. How the hell could she hope to compete with that?

The answer was obvious: she couldn't. He was never going to see her as anything other than one of his little fuck buddies. Which meant she should either embrace her inner Happy Meal or cut her losses.

Both pride and logic voted for cutting her losses. She should keep her distance—and her sanity. Surely they could manage a little cool, civilized professionalism. They didn't have to fall on one another in a frenzy of jungle sex every time the opportunity presented itself.

So what if he was tall, breathtakingly handsome, and built like God's gift to everything with estrogen? Lark didn't have to be an idiot about this.

She didn't.

Really.

A little self-control. How hard could it be?

Richard Edge surveyed his new sanctuary with satisfaction. He'd reconstructed the entire thing thousands of miles from its original location, and buried it deep inside the Rocky Mountains. The Magekind might eventually find him, but it wouldn't be anytime soon. He'd made sure of it, having spent the past hours finding and slaying a nest of former cultists to gain the magic to strengthen his wards.

None too soon, either. He'd felt someone ping him earlier in the night—probably that little Maja of Gawain's, since it hadn't felt strong enough to be Kel. It wouldn't be long before they'd start making more serious attempts, though.

His shields had better damn well hold.

Edge frowned uneasily. If enough of them joined forces, they'd eventually punch through and he'd be finished.

The conclusion was obvious: he needed a little more juice than he was going to get from killing cultists. A knight, maybe, or one of the really old Majae.

And he needed that sacrifice fast.

A trap might do the trick, but it had to be the right kind. If the bait was too good, he might end up with the entire Round Table breathing down his neck. They'd slice him up like a hog at a redneck barbecue.

No, what he needed was something that appeared insignificant but showy, something the Magekind would want to put a stop to. Like that wretched Jimmy Jones, the sorcerer cum serial killer who had inadvertently attracted Gawain and his little friend to begin with.

Frowning thoughtfully, Edge walked into his lab. Or at least, that was what he called it, though there were no microscopes or Bunsen burners. Instead, the room was bare and windowless, its ceiling and walls of black slate, giving the impression being enclosed in a stone box.

An inverted pentagram was inscribed in the center of the floor surrounded by protective runes, all glowing a nice, bright red. Powering the pentagram continuously was depleting his reserves, but he had no choice. If some Maja got so much as a whiff of what he had, they'd be all over him.

As Edge walked through the design, magic crawled over his skin like thousands of invisible ants. Crouching at the star's center, he reached down. The stone parted like water for his hand. His fingers touched cool metal—and a sense of intense, alien magic. Edge withdrew the object, and the floor solidified again.

The cup was heavy, made of solid gold, its surface worked into shapes every bit as violent and profane as Edge's more interesting fantasies. Just touching it, he felt Geirolf's magic breathing over his skin like a cold wind.

Edge smiled in the satisfaction he'd always felt, holding his very own black grail.

The silver figure flexed its wings, lifting its tiny dragon head in a roar of rage. It began to grow larger and larger even as the blade it was bound to shrunk in proportion to its body. Its color changed, shifting from silver to blue, from metallic to gleaming scales that rippled over powerful muscle. The blade became a long tail that lashed in fury, tipped with a cluster of spikes.

The dragon's massive head whipped upward, fanged jaws gaping as his wings spread wide and beat furiously. Kel took to the air, soaring skyward, breathing gouts of fire.

No longer a sword, but a dragon in truth, roaring for rage and vengeance.

Tegid's eyes snapped open, and he jolted to his clawed feet, wings beating in agitation. Disoriented, he stared around at his cave, looking for the attacker he knew was coming.

But there was no infuriated nephew out for revenge and blood. Around him lay only the familiar curving lines of his cave, bathed in the soothing green glow of his magic. Breathing deep, he scented the waters of his scrying pool, lying peaceful on the main level below his sleeping ledge.

No rage. No blood. No Kel.

Slowly, his fear began to fade. It had been a dream.

No. Realization penetrated his relief with bone-deep certainty. It had been a vision of a potential future. One he must not allow to become reality.

If Kel ever broke the spell, the comfortable life Tegid had built would come crashing down around his ears. Once free, his nephew would stop at nothing to discover who had trapped him for sixteen centuries. He'd follow the broken spell right back to Tegid and challenge his uncle on the spot.

Tegid was not that worried about dueling Kel—how much of a threat could he be, after all those centuries as a chunk of metal? Unfortunately, the political implications would be catastrophic.

Though many might have found it more comfortable to forget Kel existed, his mother hadn't allowed it. Aegid had been determined to free her son, and she'd sought tirelessly to discover who'd cast the spell that had trapped him. Her fierce maternal loyalty had won her the sympathy and respect of many dragon females. And since it was the females who elected the Dragon Lords, Tegid had been forced to give the appearance of supporting her efforts.

Ironically, his apparent inability to find the spell-caster had ended up damaging Tegid's standing. Evar had used the weakness to build up his own power base, and so had Soren.

A century ago, Tegid had realized he had to do something radical to stabilize the situation. Something had to be done about Aegid. Luckily, she'd always suspected Evar was behind Kel's imprisonment, so Tegid made use of that belief. He'd goaded her, carefully, subtly, until she'd challenged the Dragon Lord.

It had been a mad act; she'd been no match for Evar. He'd killed her just as Tegid knew he would. What's more the females of Evar's clan had been outraged—again, just as Tegid had intended—and they'd turned on him, electing a male champion who'd killed Evar in turn.

Tegid was seen as a martyr who'd lost his sister to a dragon who had used magic to trap his nephew. The resulting wave of sympathy had enabled him to assume leadership of the Dragon Lords.

Only Soren opposed him now. Soren, who was just as perverted and unnatural as Kel when it came to his fondness for the apes.

But if it was discovered it was Tegid who'd imprisoned Kel in the sword, the clans would realize he'd deliberately thrown suspicion on Evar and manipulated them all. Soren would gleefully destroy him, assuming Kel didn't kill Tegid in combat to avenge his mother and himself.

Tegid had to make sure Kel never broke that spell.

It was time to look in on the little egg-sucker, find out what he was doing, and put a stop to any aspirations of freedom.

Steadier now, he moved to one of the great stalagmites that supported the roof of his cave and climbed down its rough stone face. Reaching the main level, he moved through the cavernous central chamber all the way to the rear. There, a narrow opening led to the chamber that held the scrying pool, along with the bulk of his treasure. Glittering piles of gems and golden objects surrounded the pool, reaching to the ceiling of the chamber—booty from his raids on the Sidhe kingdoms centuries ago. Like all dragons, Tegid had a taste for the shining and beautiful.

But all his attention was on the pool now. Three dragon-lengths across, it lay deep and still, fed by an ancient spring. When he moved to its side, its calm surface reflected his scaled red muzzle like a mirror. He opened his jaws and breathed a spell over it. A glowing plume of magic rolled across the water, which instantly began to luminesce a brilliant blue.

A moment later, an image formed on the shimmering

surface. Kel and Gawain, apparently arguing over a female named Lark. Shuddering in disgust, Tegid settled down to watch.

The grail cradled carefully in his hands, Richard Edge knelt in the center of the pentagram. Sweat rolled down the small of his back, and he licked his lips. If the Magekind ever sensed he had it, he'd be the centerpiece of that Round Table luau he was afraid of, roasted and diced before he knew what hit him. No revenge then—hot, cold, or à la mode.

That was the reason for the pentagram. Richard usually didn't bother with the physical trappings of spell work, but he wanted to make damn sure his wards around the grail stayed up and running no matter what.

Now, kneeling on the cold, black stone, he stared at the grail, admiring the intricate shapes of men and demons fornicating and killing and dying. Steadying his breathing, Richard opened his consciousness to the cup's power and let his mind drift.

Somewhere in Washington, D.C., ten of Geirolf's former cultists sat in a hotel room arguing over how best to locate the last grail.

Last grail? Looking deeper into the leader's thoughts, Richard saw the man had woken with a vision that both the other grails had been destroyed, taking with them two thirds of Geirolf's followers. Gary Myers was desperate to find the grail that had created him before the Magekind destroyed it, too. He and his followers were considering going to the nearest mall and shooting twenty or so shoppers in order to power a locator spell.

You won't get through my wards even if you do, asshole, Richard thought, and sent his mind off to find a more practical sacrifice. That group was too large for him to take out by himself.

It was a good thing Geirolf had been so paranoid he

hadn't trusted even his worshipers. The spell the alien had designed to transform them all into vampires had also ensured he could use the grails to locate any sorcerer who had drunk from them. What's more, he could kill them all by the simple expedient of destroying the cups.

Knowing Geirolf, he'd probably intended to use that threat to keep them all in line.

Unfortunately for Geirolf, however, Arthur and the Magekind were a lot smarter than he'd expected.

One minute Richard had been standing with the other priests, waiting for the moment Geirolf's death spell would destroy the Magekind. The next, the alien was dead, and everything had gone to hell in a handbasket. Thousands of Magekind warriors had streamed into Geirolf's temple, ready to kill everything that moved.

Richard had instantly realized that the better part of valor was to find the grail he'd drunk from and get the hell out. Leading two other priests, he'd fought his way to Geirolf's sanctuary where the three cups waited.

It wasn't hard to tell which was which; Richard felt a kind of mystic connection to his cup that was unmistakable. He'd grabbed it as the others snatched their own.

Before they could decide what to do next, Geirolf's lieutenant, Steven Parker, had cast the spell that had distributed Geirolf's dying life force to his followers. Even as Edge felt the sudden surge of power, Parker had used the last of it to scatter the sorcerers across Mortal Earth.

Richard found himself standing in the center of an empty city street with the grail in his hand. He'd lost no time using his share of Geirolf's powers to create a safe house for himself and wards around his grail.

Good thing, too, because the cultists all promptly went to war over the grails. Every sorcerer and his brother wanted to use the cups to create more vampire followers.

Except Richard. As far as he was concerned, other vampires were more likely to be rivals or liabilities than loyal assets. He'd far rather kill them and absorb their share of

Geirolf's magic than worry about what they might be up to behind his back.

Now he scanned with the grail, looking for the perfect victim. He needed someone just powerful enough to make good bait, without being strong enough to turn the tables on him. Not that one, definitely not that bunch. That group was too large, and that . . .

Wait. There. Edge opened his consciousness to the other sorcerer's mind, probing it with care to avoid being detected by his rival.

Oh, yes. This one would do nicely.

Clayton Roth was a vile little fuck even by Edge's standards. He liked his meals young—so young he attended Disney movies to spot them. At the moment, he was standing outside the bedroom window of his latest prospect . . .

Perfect.

Now all Edge needed was the right Maja for a psychic tip, one not quite powerful enough to trace the vision back to him. Luckily, he knew the perfect candidate—Gawain's little friend. He'd already made contact with her, touched her magic, so he could sense her even against the background buzz of the Mageverse.

Tightening his grip on the grail, he sent his mind questing for hers.

And slammed right up against a rock-hard barrier: the wards around Avalon. They seemed stronger than before. Evidently the witches had reinforced them recently. Fortunately, just holding the grail provided a certain boost, and anyway, he didn't need much of an opening for what he intended.

Even so, sweat broke out on his forehead and his temples began to pound as he pushed at the shield. Too much force, and they'd detect him, too little and he'd never get through.

Something gave. Yes! He had her now . . .

TEN

Lark had just picked up her first forkful of eggs when the table in front of her faded away. Suddenly she was sitting beside a bed in a darkened room. A sweet-faced little boy, about eight or so, lay on his side in front of her, deeply asleep. Moonlight streaming in through a window made his pale, tousled hair seem to glow like a halo. A bedraggled stuffed bunny lay in his arms, one ear flopped against his smooth cheek.

Smiling, she looked up.

A face filled the window, twisted with horrific lust. Lark opened her mouth to shout a warning . . .

And found herself staring at a forkful of eggs. What the hell . . . oh, God.

A vision. She'd just had a vision. That meant . . .

"Gawain!" Throwing the fork across the room, she leaped to her feet, called her armor, and ran for the stairs. "Gawain!" she yelled as she took the steps two at a time. "Kel! Armor up, we've got trouble!"

The bedroom door flew open as she raced down the hall. Gawain stepped out, already in his armor with Kel in his hand. His handsome face looked grim, yet like the combat veteran he was, he held his big body loose-limbed and ready. "What's going on?"

"I had a vision," Lark told him, stopping short to cast a spell. Her will brought a dimensional gate swirling into being in the hallway. Within its depths lay a deceptively serene view of a perfectly ordinary middle-class home in the center of a neatly-kept lawn.

Gawain threw the scene a narrow-eyed glance. "Edge?"

"No, somebody else. He's about to snatch a child. We've got to move now if we're going to save that boy." The dimensional gate started to form.

"I don't want to get caught off-guard again," Gawain snapped. "Kel . . ."

"I'll call Arthur."

"I don't think so," Tegid murmured under his breath, staring intently into the scrying pool, his tail lashing with excitement. This entire situation had real possibilities as something he could manipulate to his advantage. Merely getting Gawain killed would serve his purposes, since Kel would be left to die in the sword.

Sensing his nephew drawing power to call out to Arthur, he cast a spell of his own to block it. Kel's magic hit his barrier and bounced. Satisfied, Tegid smiled.

Oh, yes. This could work nicely.

Gawain shot a look at Lark. Her face was pale, but her eyes glittered with fierce determination as she started to step through her gate. He grabbed her shoulder.

"We go first." Lifting Kel and roaring his battle cry, he leaped through the gate. Lark ran after him.

On the other side of the gate, he scanned his surroundings. A small, neat yard populated by oaks and azaleas, a two-story house with white vinyl siding . . .

And a vampire in scarlet armor standing by one window. The sorcerer spun with a growl, flinging out his hands. His magical blast splashed off Kel's shields. A fireball flashed past as Lark returned fire. Gawain charged, swinging Kel up for a vicious overhead strike.

The sorcerer ran to meet him, howling a battle cry. "Geirrrooooolf!"

"Why do you idiots call that alien's name?" Gawain parried the blow and swung at his foe's head. The vampire ducked, agile and blindingly quick. Dammit, this one was more competent than they usually were. "He's as dead as you're going to be."

Fangs flashed white through the slits in the vamp's visor. "I don't think so." He blasted a spell into Gawain's face, knocking him back a pace. Shaking off the pain, Gawain lifted the Dragon Sword.

Kel's return shot took the vampire full in the chest, slamming him into the side of the house.

Wood cracked like a rifle shot with the impact, but the sorcerer landed on his feet, undaunted. *Okay, so we'll just have to hit him harder next time,* Gawain thought grimly, starting toward his foe.

The vamp was a wiry little bastard inside that scarlet armor, but probably stronger than he looked. A lowered visor hid his face, eyes glittering from behind its snarling demon mask. At Gawain's approach, he retreated, a glowing ball of mystical force gathering around his hand. It stunk of death magic. "Who the fuck are you?"

"Gawain, knight of the Round Table." The name alone had been known to shake opponents.

The sorcerer made a mocking half-bow. "Clayton Roth, your killer."

Gawain bared his teeth. "You've got an active fantasy life, Clayton."

Roth laughed and lifted his sword. "Oh, my fantasies would terrify you." His gaze flicked to Lark, who was circling around behind him like a cat creeping up on a canary. "And what's your name, Magic Barbie? Morgana Le Fay, perhaps?"

"How'd you guess?" Her eyes were cool and fearless behind her visor, and her sword was steady in her hand.

"You wish. You don't have that much power." He shot a spell at her head. It splashed off her shields in a showy burst of sparks.

Lark didn't even hesitate as she retaliated, lobbing blast after blast at him until he was forced to take cover behind a tree.

Good for you, Gawain thought. The girl might be green and lacking in self-confidence, but she was no coward.

Where's Arthur? he asked Kel in their link while Lark and Roth fired at each other. *I thought you called for backup.*

I did. Something blocked me.

Roth?

More juice than that. Almost felt like a dragon, but that makes no sense. I have no idea what's going on.

Oh, great. Just great. With a growl of frustration, Gawain charged in. Roth retreated, shooting a trio of fireballs at him. Gawain ignored them as they pelted Kel's shields, looking for an opening in the vampire's guard. *What's he done to the child's family?* Somebody should have run outside to investigate by now, considering the noise they were making.

He's got them under a sleep spell. Want me to break it, tell the parents to grab the kid and run? It's going to take some effort. Roth has a lot of juice.

Which means he's been killing a lot of kids. Go ahead and—

Suddenly a voice purred in his ear. "Remember me?"

Pain exploded in Gawain's throat as his feet flew out from under him. His back slammed into the ground so hard he saw stars.

"Gawain!" Lark cried out.

Unable to answer, unable even to breathe, he gagged

helplessly. *You took a neck blow*, Kel snapped. *Your gorget is dented.*

Magic rolled over his skin as he struggled for breath. Air rushed into his lungs as the obstruction abruptly vanished. The dragon had magically repaired his dented throat guard.

Coughing, Gawain rolled to his feet to find Lark and Roth exchanging a furious barrage, circling each other as they hurled blast after blast. Each glowing fireball lit up the night, throwing dancing shadows across the lawn. The night breeze carried the carnal stench of Roth's spells warring with the sweeter scent of Lark's.

Magic boiled from the tip of his own sword, only to splash off something approaching fast from Gawain's left. It looked like a spell shield, yet it seemed to surround empty air. *What the hell?*

Invisibility spell, Kel said. *It's Edge.*

So that was the voice he'd heard. *Where the hell did he come from?* Gawain retreated, bringing up his sword.

From the corner of his eye, he saw Lark swing toward him, obviously realizing they had a new player. She staggered as a blast from their unseen attacker slammed into her shields.

Another blast lit up Kel's shields. *Break that damned invisiblity spell!*

Working on it, Kel retorted grimly.

Gawain sensed more than saw an attack coming, tried to parry. Missed. The invisible blade rang on his armored ribs. He jumped back, staggered, managed to catch himself.

Kel, I need to see this asshole!

I know, dammit!

"*Who the hell* is that?" Lark tried to get closer as Gawain circled his new foe.

"Edge!" He staggered and shook his head hard, as if his invisible foe had landed a blow.

"Oh, hell." She started composing a spell to make their latest enemy visible, then froze with a jolt of unease.

What had happened to Roth?

She glanced around. No suit of scarlet armor. She instantly realized where he'd gone. "Shit!"

Gawain was going to have to fend for himself. Changing direction, Lark charged toward the boy's house and vaulted through the open window where the vampire had been standing.

A figure in scarlet armor bent over the child, about to snatch him from his bed.

With a snarl, Lark lobbed a fireball into the molester's helm, slapping him head first into the wall beyond the bed. Even as she went after him, sword lifted, he rolled to his feet.

"Stay out of this, Magic Barbie," Roth snarled. "That kid is mine. I chose him, and I'm taking him. And you don't have the power to do anything but get gutted."

Lark was way too pissed to be intimidated. Drawing on the Mageverse's distant psychic blaze, she hurled a blast at him. An explosion of light detonated in her face with his return shot, barreling into her shield like a truck. To her horror, the barrier began to bow inward, almost as if the spell were eating its way through. Desperately, she fought to reinforce it, drawing more power and feeding it into the shield. Roth's attack kept coming, and the shield's glow intensified, first a violent red, then blinding blue, then at last an aching white that made her skull pound with the effort she was expending. Finally, just when she thought it was going to punch right through, the attack faded away sullenly. Lark slumped in relief as her headache faded to a warning throb.

The sorcerer's grin flashed behind the slotted holes of his visor. "Like I said, I've stored up a lot of death magic, bitch. I don't mind adding yours to my stores. Be more available for fun and games with little Timmy over there."

"Bastard!" Furious, Lark swung her sword at his head with every bit of strength she had.

He parried the blow easily and shrugged. "Have it your way, Magic Barbie."

His return strike was so fast she barely had time to parry. Roth powered through her block as if it weren't there. The point of his weapon bit into the enchanted plate covering her shoulder, lodging deep in flesh and muscle. Pain knifed into her arm. Crying out, Lark almost dropped her sword.

Before she could scramble away, Roth punched her in the face, sending her reeling into the wall.

Through the stars flashing across her vision, she caught sight of his descending sword. Somehow she managed to block it and fire another blast. The sorcerer didn't even seem to notice as he struck for her ribs. Her parry was too slow. His blade cut into her cuirass and bit between her ribs. Lark wrenched free, sucking in a breath of agony as she scuttled to her left, trying to find room to defend herself.

Oh God, she realized in sick fear as blood rolled down her side, *he's going to kill me.*

And once she was dead, the boy wouldn't have a prayer. She thought of John and Tristan. They'd be so disappointed in her.

Roth smirked behind his visor. Just past his shoulder, Lark could see the boy lying on his bed, deep in the grip of the vampire's sleep spell. His white-blond hair gleamed in the moonlight over the round, sweet face she'd seen in her vision. He still held that stuffed rabbit.

Roth intended to rape and murder him.

No. Goddamn it, no. Rage splintered her fear, hot and empowering. *I may die, but Roth is not touching that child.*

Lark drove her blade at his chest, every ounce of her strength behind it. The sorcerer only laughed and parried without any visible effort at all. "Little slow there, Magic Barbie. Blood loss getting to you?"

It seemed she could hear Tristan's voice in her head. *You're not going to beat him with steel. It has to be magic.* Burning sweat rolled into her eyes as Lark summoned another blast and fired it at him. Again, it splashed off his shields.

Dammit, what was he, Superman? Every muscle in her body ached with exhaustion, but he kept right on coming.

His sword arced at her head. She brought up her blade but the weapon bit into her forearm through her gauntlet. Agony ripped a strangled cry from her lips as she retreated. Her back hit solid wood. A bureau. Plastic clattered and fell. She sidestepped and kept retreating, sending a toy skittering away from her booted foot.

"Give it up, Magic Barbie." Roth rotated his blade and grinned as he stalked her. "You just don't have it, and your friend's out getting his ass kicked. You're going to die, and I'm still going to take the kid."

Diera's voice flashed through her mind. *The next time you're in combat, remember the power is there. You just have to let yourself use it.*

But just how the hell did she do that? She was giving it everything she had as it was!

Roth swung his sword at her again, and she jumped back, simultaneously reaching for the Mageverse, dragging the power in like a swimmer taking a deep breath. It responded as it always had—but she knew even as the magic poured into her mind that it wasn't enough. Reaching for more, Lark parried his attack.

Or tried to.

Between her wounded arm and his sheer strength, his sword powered through her guard and bit into her thigh.

How many wounds was that? She could feel the blood rolling from them, cool and sticky inside her armor. Her hand was growing so slick on the hilt of her sword, it was all she could do to hang onto it.

Roth smirked at her. "That hurt, didn't it, bitch?" He inhaled. "Smell that blood. Yum. You're not my type, but maybe I'll feed on you after I get you down anyway. Be a shame to let it go to waste."

Fangs gaping, tearing into her throat, draining her life away. . . . Shut up! Lark told the fear savagely. *I do* not *have time for this!*

She had to keep drawing the power.

A stab of pain in her wounded thigh made her stumble, but she gritted her teeth and ignored it, retreating as the vampire stalked her, trying not to get backed into a wall.

Desperately, she fought to draw energy from the Mageverse, sucking it deep. The magic was beginning to burn inside her skull, a warning sizzle of pain that made her want to back off.

Almost, she told herself, extending her shaking left hand. The right still held her sword in blood-slicked fingers. *Almost there. Just a little more, and . . .*

BOOM!

The full force of the Mageverse blasted from her hand, searing her fingertips as it roared out, not in a ball, but in a blazing jet. Roth reeled back as the energy poured around him, fell to one knee . . .

Panting, her very eyes burning, Lark lowered her shaking hand and waited for him to die.

The sorcerer looked up at her. "Wow, Barbie," he said, his tone almost conversational. "I didn't know you had it in you."

Shit.

He rose to his feet. His smile flashed behind his visor. "There's a lot of magic in sacrificing a kid. That's why the ancients did so much of it. All that potential and innocence." For just an instant, his eyes glowed red in the shadows of his visor's eye slit. "I've sacrificed a *lot* of little brats."

He charged, lunging past her sluggish guard to grab her by the throat. Her injured thigh gave under her. His weight smashed her to the floor.

Roth jerked off her helm and threw it aside, then raised

his visor. His narrow face was contorted with predatory triumph. "Like I said, it's a shame to waste all that blood. I'll just have the kid for dessert."

Jerking his head back, he buried his fangs in her throat. Pain ripped through her flesh with his teeth.

There wasn't time for panic. Instead of drawing on the Mageverse, Lark threw her consciousness into it. Raw power boiled over her, inundating her in agonizing fire. She ignored it and grabbed Roth's sweaty head in both hands, sending all that blazing energy roaring into his skull.

He didn't even have time to shield.

The vampire screamed against her throat and tried to jerk free, but she held on and kept pumping the magical fire through her fingertips. It felt like her very bones were burning, but she didn't stop, pulling the power in and blowing it out with every bit of will she had. His scream built to a shriek.

And cut off as her hands suddenly met.

Roth's body hit her chest, the armor melting away as his magic failed. With a cry of revulsion, she pushed him away. Panting, Lark stared at him. And blinked.

His head was gone. His neck was a blackened stump.

"Damn," she husked. "I won."

Lark lifted her shaking hands. She was a little surprised to find them still attached, though she wasn't sure she wanted to take off her gauntlets. She let her arms fall as black spots rolled over her vision.

She hurt. Everywhere. Especially her throat. Breathing through her mouth, she lay still, grateful she could feel anything at all, even pain.

Unfortunately, she didn't have time to lie moaning on her laurels. She had to heal herself and go help Gawain with Edge.

Tears of agony in her eyes, she opened herself to the Mageverse again.

* * *

Tail lashing with excitement, Tegid stared into his scrying pool. In its wavering depths, Gawain and Kel did battle with some strange sorcerer.

Tegid had thought for a moment the ape thing must be Sidhe—he knew Magi couldn't work spells—but probing delicately with his magic, he quickly determined that wasn't the case. The creature's power carried the greasy reek of death magic, like that of the Dark Ones who had once victimized Dragonkind.

Normally, Tegid would be glad to see the destruction of anything connected to the Dark Ones. But as he watched the sorcerer fight Gawain, he changed his mind.

It was a good thing he'd blocked Kel's call for help. The enemy ape had potential.

The creature—it called itself Richard Edge—fought with a single-minded viciousness and impressive power. It had initially surrounded itself with an invisibility spell it used to good effect, but Kel had broken that.

Now the two apes fought hand to hand, swinging their long blades in soft, repulsive monkey paws.

Cachamwri's Breath, but Tegid hated humans. How Kel could have stooped to befriend one of them—it was revolting.

Narrow-eyed, he watched the creatures exchange furious sword blows and blasts of magic, grimly pounding away at each other. Dirt and blood smeared their metal carapaces, but they seemed oblivious to everything except their mutual hate.

Why, the Dark One's ape despises Gawain almost as much as I do, Tegid realized, intrigued.

Wouldn't it be convenient if he killed Gawain? Kel would be trapped in that blade, slowly dying a well-deserved death . . .

Tegid ran his forked tongue across his fangs and leaned closer to watch as the two circled. Slitting his eyes, he stretched his consciousness to sample the probabilities hidden in Cachamwri's River of Fate.

Feh! Tegid sat back in disgust. Despite his promising viciousness, Edge was going to lose. His magic was running out, and once it did, Kel and his ape would simply cut him apart.

Tegid was almost tempted to reinforce the creature's magic himself, but the idea of having even that much to do with a human was disgusting.

Still . . . his tail flicked thoughtfully. What if he did give the ape a little mystical boost? Not much. Just enough to let him kill Kel's pet.

It would be risky. Tegid huffed out a puff of smoke. Involving oneself in human affairs was strictly taboo.

On the other hand, no one would suspect Tegid if a human destroyed Kel.

He sampled the possibilities again, seeking to determine what would happen if he gave the ape a tiny little flash of extra power . . . ? He grunted in disgust at the results his Sight showed him. It still wouldn't be enough. He'd need to give the ape a more intense charge than was possible at this distance.

He could bring Edge here, of course. . . . An ape in his caverns. What a revolting thought.

Still, to rid himself of Kel and eliminate the danger . . .

It might be worth it.

Gawain circled Edge, watching the sorcerer's eyes through the narrow slits in his visor. In a distant way, he was aware of the sweat rolling into his own eyes, the ache of his sword arm, the low sizzle of pain from his wounds. But only distantly. His consciousness was focused on his opponent's every move, watching for that flick of an eye that meant an attack to the head, or the rising magical glitter around the hands that preceded a death spell.

The glitter, to his grim pleasure, was much dimmer. Edge was finally running out of power, just as Gawain had planned.

For the past twenty minutes, he'd been working to wear the sorcerer down, alternately battering at him while Kel shielded against his blasts but threw little magic beyond that. The idea was to conserve Kel's power while forcing the sorcerer to expend his.

Unfortunately, Edge had quickly caught on. He hadn't thrown any fireballs in the last five minutes, contenting himself with trying to get his blade through Gawain's guard.

Judging from the increasing desperation in those cold eyes, he knew he was in trouble. Gawain expected him to either try to gate out or launch some last-ditch magical attack in the next couple of minutes. Edge was out of other options.

What's Lark doing? Gawain asked Kel. He'd been relieved to hear she'd bested her opponent, especially since at the time, there'd been absolutely nothing he could do to help.

Gawain had tried to go to her when she'd gone down, but Edge had seen his distraction and blasted the hell out of him. By the time he'd fought the little fucker off, Lark had killed her attacker.

Just what she was doing the last six times you asked— healing. No, wait. Here she . . . Cachamwri's Breath!

Gawain, glancing past Edge's shoulder, saw light spill from the child's darkened bedroom window. For a moment, part of the wall seemed to melt away, and Lark appeared.

He was so startled, he almost let Edge hit him. Then the sorcerer spotted her, and he, too, broke off and scrambled backward in alarm.

Lark floated toward them like a ghost, bare toes a yard from the ground. Her armor was gone, replaced by a filmy gown that whipped around her long legs. Her hair streamed back from her head as if in a strong wind, and her eyes glowed like burning torches.

"Shit," Gawain whispered. The last time he'd seen a display like that, it had been a new Maja gone mad from the power of the Mageverse.

"Edge," Lark whispered. Her voice seemed to reverberate in his bones as she lifted slim hands that blazed with magic. "It's time for you to die."

"Uh, no." Edge whirled and ran.

With a shout, Gawain shot after him as a dimensional gate formed a few yards away. The sorcerer dove for the opening before it was completely dilated . . .

Only to sail through empty air as the gate abruptly winked out.

"You're not going anywhere," Lark said in that thundering whisper. "Except hell."

Edge hit the ground and rolled, coming up with his sword in his hand. "Fuck you, witch. I'll suck the magic from your . . ."

Before he could get the threat out of his mouth, a hole opened in the air over his head. He looked up, startled—and yowled as he was sucked off his feet and through the opening. The gate disappeared with an audible pop.

"What the fuck was that?" Gawain, about to charge after him, stopped dead in surprise. He looked over his shoulder at Lark. "Did you do that?"

"No." The magic glow around her vanished, and she sank to the ground. Her knees gave.

Gawain sheathed Kel and ran to her as she crumpled like a puppet with cut strings. Fear cold in his heart, he knelt beside her and scooped her off the grass. Her eyes were closed, her face pale as milk.

Is she okay? he demanded.

Uninjured, but badly drained. I'd say that little show she just put on was an elaborate bluff.

Her eyes fluttered open to look up at him. "Sorry. Lost him." Her voice sounded very faint.

"We'll worry about that later. What the hell was that all about? I thought you'd gotten Mageverse Fever for a minute there."

"Hardly," Kel told him. "Majae either get the Fever when they first change or not at all."

She let her eyes drift close. "Just trying to distract Edge . . . for you."

Gawain gave her a dry smile. "Good plan—or it would have been, if you hadn't shocked me as badly as Edge."

Lark opened her eyes a crack. "Where'd he . . . go?"

Gawain frowned and stood, cradling her in his arms. "Good question. He looked as startled as I was."

"It wasn't any of the Magekind," Kel said from his scabbard. "Actually, the remnants of the spell taste like dragon."

Gawain looked over his shoulder at his partner. "Didn't you say you thought a dragon blocked your call to Arthur?"

"The spell did have that smell."

"But why?" Lark asked. Her voice, thankfully, sounded stronger now.

"Most dragons want nothing to do with humans," Gawain agreed. "Why would one of them try to help Edge, of all people?"

"That," Kel said, "is a very good question."

Richard Edge hit the ground so hard he felt the impact even through his armor. Rolling to his feet, he fell into a crouch, his heart pounding as he warily scanned his surroundings.

He was in some kind of cavernous stone room with a ceiling that towered three stories overhead. At first he thought he must be in another sorcerer's temple, but the architecture was too alien for that. The walls curved into ceiling and floor, which in turn curved up to form irregularly spaced columns. The results were profoundly inhuman, an effect enhanced by shimmering green lighting.

Something moved—a whispering, sliding sound, like a massive object being dragged over stone. Richard whirled toward it. His heart seemed to simply stop.

The dragon stood looking down at him, its eyes shining like coals. Its head, topped by curving horns, was the length of his body on the end of a long, snaking neck.

Great wings lay furled as it sat back on powerfully muscled haunches.

As if in slow motion, he watched the beast's fanged jaws gape open. The massive head lowered—and breathed. Cursing, he threw up a magical shield and tried to duck.

Too late.

The spell hit the barrier and punched through as if it weren't even there, rolling over his head like a wave of acid. Cursing, he clawed at his face. The dragon hissed.

And the hissing became words. ". . . understand me now, ape?"

"What?" Disoriented, Richard looked around at his massive captor. "What was that?"

The dragon lifted its head, its expression somehow satisfied. "The spell worked."

Richard's eyes narrowed uneasily. "What the hell is going on?" Except for Kel and Soren, dragons hated humans.

The beast ignored his undiplomatic question, which was probably just as well. "So. You are the enemy of Kel and his ape ally, Gawain."

Studying the dragon's cold, alien gaze, Edge thought frantically. "What do you care?"

The dragon's voice dropped to a cold, menacing rumble. "Answer my question, ape!"

If this dragon was Gawain's ally, he wouldn't have removed Edge from danger. Which suggested he could be useful. "Yes, I'm his enemy."

"But not, however, a particularly effective one. It would have killed you had I not intervened."

"It?"

The dragon made an impatient gesture with one clawed hand. "Gawain. The ape."

Edge glowered and lied. "I'd have beaten them."

Laughter rumbled, sounding like icy stones grinding together. "Your magic was all but gone. Gawain and its female would have slain you."

Edge didn't answer. He needed to get the hell out of here. Did he have the magic to gate himself to safety?

Something huge swept out of the green shadows and slammed into his thighs, batting him against the wall like a tennis ball. Light burst in his skull, followed instantly by pain. He bounced and fell on his ass.

Dazed, out of breath, Richard watched the dragon's tail lash. The creature had hit him with it like Barry Bonds bashing a homer.

"When I lower myself to speak to you, you will pay attention," the dragon growled. "Now, ape, do you want the power to kill Gawain?"

He rubbed his aching thighs and considered attacking his captor. Better not. It would probably eat him.

Besides, this conversation was beginning to get intriguing. "I want the power to kill them all."

"Do you, now?" Something that might have been interest flashed across that inhuman face. "And who is *them*?"

"The Magekind." He curled a lip. "I want to wipe every one of the sanctimonious bastards off the face of the Earth. Either Earth."

"Now that," the dragon said, "sounds like a worthy goal."

ELEVEN

An hour after the battle, Lark listened as Gawain finished briefing the High Council with the emotionless dispatch of a professional soldier.

She wished they could get this over with and go home.

Tired to the bone, she glanced around the huge circular chamber where the combined councils of the Majae and Magi met in an emergency joint session. Arthur had called both bodies together after Gawain reported the fight with Edge and Roth, as well as the mystery dragon's bizarre involvement.

The two councils sat on a dais behind an imposing walnut semicircular table that was more an enormous desk than anything else. The table's wooden facade was beautifully carved with scenes from the Magekind's long history—Merlin and Nimue addressing the High King's court, both looking deceptively young; Arthur drinking from the Grail; the knights gathered around the Round Table; Morgana using her power for the first time as the ladies of the court looked on.

In contrast to the massive table, the council members

were informally dressed, the men in jeans or chinos and short-sleeved shirts, the Majae in slacks and knit tops or sundresses. They all looked serious and alert, leaning forward and frowning in concentration as they listened.

Except for Tristan and Diera. Unless she was very much mistaken, they both looked almost smug.

"What did you do about the boy and his family?" Morgana asked Lark. As usual, she wore one of those white power suits of hers, set off by a vibrant red blouse.

Lark surreptitiously dried her damp palms on the thighs of her jeans. She hadn't been able to stand wearing her armor any longer. "Timmy started to wake up after Roth was killed, but I cast a spell to keep him asleep while I helped Gawain with Edge. After Edge disappeared, Kel and I put the house back to rights and sent the family into a natural sleep."

"You're lucky the neighbors didn't call the cops," Diera observed dryly. As one of the senior Majae, she'd served on the Majae's Council for years.

Lark shrugged. "The house was pretty isolated. I don't think anybody heard us."

"This thing with Edge and the dragon concerns me," Arthur said, frowning heavily. "Kel, are you sure it was one of the Dragonkind who took him?"

Kel snorted from Gawain's shoulder. "Believe me, it's not the kind of situation I'm likely to mistake."

"Could the Dragonkind have formed an alliance with Geirolf's sorcerers?" Tristan asked.

"Not likely. It's probably one rogue individual."

"What leads you to that conclusion?" Arthur asked.

Kel flicked his wings and frowned, as if searching for a way to explain. "Ten thousand years ago—not long by dragon standards—Dragonkind and the Sidhe were enemies. They hunted us for our hides, and we sometimes ate them. Then the Dark Ones came to Mageverse Earth and started killing and enslaving everyone. They captured our king, Cachamwri . . ."

Lark looked over at him. "The dragon god you're always swearing by?"

Kel shrugged. "He wasn't a god then. Even the Sidhe were mortal. Anyway, the Dark Ones were torturing Cachamwri when a Sidhe warrior named Galatyn sneaked into their fortress on a raid. He found the dragon, took pity on him, and decided to help Cachamwri escape. Cachamwri started killing Dark Ones, and as he did, he absorbed their power, along with the life force they'd been hoarding."

"Which was a great deal of power," Morgana concluded.

"Enough to make Cachamwri a literal god. The remaining Dark Ones fled for their lives to Mortal Earth. In gratitude for Galatyn's help, Cachamwri made the Sidhe immortal and forbade the Dragonkind from treating them as enemies."

"So where did the taboo on relationships with humans come from?" Diera asked.

Kel furled his small metal wings. "My people have very long memories. Many don't trust the Sidhe or humans, regardless of Cachamwri's orders." He shook his head. "Even so, Dragonkind would never form an alliance with Geirolf's sorcerers. Geirolf was a Dark One, and his spawn practice the same kind of death magic he did."

"Yet someone has obviously decided to overlook all that," Arthur pointed out. "Any ideas who?"

Kel shrugged. "The only other dragon I know willing to have anything to do with humans is Soren . . ."

"Soren would never help those wretched sorcerers," Morgana said impatiently. "He gave us the spell to destroy the black grails in the first place."

"I never said he was involved," Kel pointed out. "I merely said he's the only other dragon I know of willing to befriend humans."

"Well, obviously another of them is doing it," Gawain said. "The question is, who?"

"Whoever it is has some pretty strong shields," Kel told

them. "I tried to trace the gate spell, but its creator blocked me."

"Curse him," Bors growled. "If he hadn't helped Richard escape, you'd have ended this. Now my son is going to start rebuilding his power. Merlin knows how many people he'll kill in the process." The knight looked haggard and drawn, as if, immortal or not, the news of Edge's treachery had aged him.

"We'll just have to get Edge before he starts killing in earnest," Arthur announced. "Or, better yet, we could find that last black grail and kill the whole lot of them." He turned toward the Majae's side of the table. "Any progress on locating it?"

"No." Guinevere dragged a weary hand through her blond hair. "We've been working with Llyr Galatyn, but we haven't been able to pin it down yet."

"We will." Cold rage made Morgana's eyes burn in her pale, elegant face. "I'm damned if I'm going to let some collection of jumped-up thugs prey on our people."

Everyone murmured agreement. Lark and Gawain exchanged a silent glance.

Edge was a lot more than a thug. And a lot less.

After the meeting, Gawain walked over for an intense, low-voiced chat with Arthur, Lancelot, and Galahad.

Lark just wanted to go home and take a nap. Despite that, she summoned a smile as she saw Tristan and Diera leave the dais and head toward her.

"I've always known you have so much potential," Diera said softly, drawing her into a quick hug. "I'm glad to hear you're beginning to realize it, too."

Lark hugged her back. "I was just trying to stay alive and keep that little boy from getting killed."

"And you damned near fried yourself doing it," Tristan said. For once, there was no reserve in his eyes. "I'm proud of you. And John's going to bust his buttons."

Lark smiled at the image. "I figured I was dead, so why not go for broke?"

"A great deal has been accomplished by people who had nothing to lose, Lark," he said. "It can be a valuable attitude."

"It was this time." She hesitated before admitting, "The power was incredible. I never realized I was capable of anything like that."

Diera smiled. "Which is the reason you weren't able to do it until now."

Arthur looked over at them. "Tristan? If you'll quit gloating over your great-granddaughter and get over here . . ."

The knight laughed. To Lark's astonishment, he gave her an awkward peck on the cheek and walked away.

She stared after him. "Whoa."

"I haven't seen him look that happy in centuries," Diera confided.

"Yeah?" Lark turned back to her friend. Who, come to think of it, was looking more relaxed and happy than she'd ever seen her. Particularly considering that Gawain was in the room. "How's it going with Antonio?"

Diera's expression softened even more. "He's . . ." She broke off and cleared her throat. "A very promising young Magus."

"Uh, huh." Lark grinned in delight. "You're falling for him!"

"Don't be ridiculous. I barely know the man." But her attempt at an aloof denial was spoiled by the flush on her cheeks.

"I've noticed that doesn't seem to matter a heck of a lot with the Magekind."

"Well, it matters a great deal to me." Diera's lips twitched. "Though he is very good. And very determined."

"And I can guess at what." Lark's teasing grin broadened.

"And how are things with you and Gawain?" Her friend searched her gaze, looking a bit concerned.

Erotic. Terrifying. I'm in deep trouble. Instead of saying what she was thinking, Lark shrugged. "Well, you know Gawain."

Sympathy gleamed in Diera's eyes. "I certainly do."

Richard Edge watched warily as his dragon captor considered him with cold, alien calculation.

"So," the beast said, "you draw your magic from death."

"Yes, but the most power comes from the death of someone with magic of their own." Richard curled his lip. "Particularly someone ancient. Like a knight of the Round Table. Though . . ." He frowned thoughtfully. "I suppose one of the really powerful Majae would be even better."

The dragon's tail tip flicked back and forth, drawing Edge's wary attention. After the last time the creature hit him, he was keeping an eye on that tail. "Yeessss. One of the females *would* have more magic to drain."

"The problem is getting to someone like that when she's not expecting it." Richard frowned. "Using sorcerers as bait isn't working well enough. The Magekind go in expecting a fight to begin with."

"Obviously, you must strike when they believe themselves safe," the dragon said. "When they're in their own nests in that city of theirs."

"In Avalon?" Incredulous, Richard stared at the beast. "Won't work. They've strengthened the city's shields. I can get a wisp of magic through, but that's about it."

The massive head lifted with a jerk, nostrils flaring. "I assure you, no barrier created by those creatures can keep *my* magic out. I will examine their shields and create a spell for you." The dragon paused, considering. "Then I will give you enough power to secure your first kill—I doubt you could slay one of the elder Maja without my assistance. After that . . ."

Edge grinned. "I'll take it from there."

* * *

Gawain tried to concentrate on the discussion of how to capture Edge, but it was tough going. As usual, in the aftermath of a battle, the Desire was awake and demanding to be fed.

But it wasn't hitting him the way it usually did.

Normally he'd be checking out every unattached Maja in the room—and there were several he knew who wouldn't turn him down.

This time, though, the only woman who interested him was Lark. Every move she made drew his eyes: the way she absently flipped a lock of hair away from her face, the roll of her hips when she shifted her weight, the elegant grace of her gesturing hands. She laughed at something Diera said, her voice musical and unconsciously sensual. He hardened at the sound. Damn, he wanted her, Edge and rogue dragons be damned.

Now.

"I'm afraid it's time to brace ourselves for the coming apocalypse," Lancelot said.

Jerked back to earth, Gawain turned to find his friends studying him with blatant speculation.

Arthur lifted a dark brow. "I don't think the situation with Edge is quite that grave, Lance."

"I wasn't talking about Edge—I meant Gawain." Lance grinned slyly. "Roomful of women, and he's only aware of one of them."

"I see your point." Arthur gave Gawain a sidelong glance and smirked.

"Kiss my ass," Gawain gritted. To his appalled surprise, he felt his cheeks heat.

Tristan's eyes widened in astonished delight. "Look at him—blushing like a virgin!"

"Awwww," Galahad drawled. "That's so sweet!"

Gawain flicked a finger in a very old, very obscene hand gesture.

"I think the mortals have a phrase for this," Lancelot said. "What is it again?"

Arthur grinned and supplied, " 'What goes around, comes around.' "

"That's the one."

Gawain had given Lance and Galahad hell a few months ago when they'd found their Truebond mates. "This is not the same thing!"

"Yeah, you keep telling yourself that, Pharaoh," Galahad said.

Deciphering the jibe, Gawain glared at him. "I am *not* the king of denial!"

"Son, you're so far up that particular creek, you need to hire oarsmen," Arthur told him.

"What I need is to get laid." Deliberately turning his back on his friends, he stalked toward Lark.

"Oh, yeah, that'll work," Galahad called.

"About like trying to put out a forest fire with rocket fuel," Lance agreed.

"Bet you a bottle of blood he's Truebonded this time next month," Arthur said.

"You're on," Galahad replied. "I give it a week before she's got him hog-tied with an apple in his mouth."

Lance snorted. "More like two days."

"And you wondered why I was so proud of my great-granddaughter." Tristan sounded downright smug.

Gawain pretended not to hear.

Hearing the hearty male ring of laughter, Lark turned to see Gawain stalking toward her, his expression thunderous, his eyes glittering.

Diera followed her gaze. "What's he so angry abou . . ." She broke off, her eyes dropping below his waist. "Oh." She skittered away as Gawain strode up, caught Lark's forearm, and started hustling her out of the council chamber.

"Gawain, what . . . ?" Lark tried to tug her arm free, but though his grip wasn't tight, she couldn't break it. "Hey, wait a minute!"

He flashed her a dark, hungry look that made something flutter and heat low in her belly. "I need you." Lust seemed to radiate from him like body heat.

Lark swallowed. Suddenly she wasn't even remotely tired.

Her nipples hardened. Gawain's gaze dropped to those tell-tale peaks and blazed even hotter. With a soft growl, he hustled her down the hall and into the nearest room.

Banging the door closed behind them, Gawain backed her against it. His head swooped down for a kiss that devoured with lips and tongue and teeth, making her head swim with its ferocity. His body pressed into hers, tall and hot and overwhelming, all hard-muscled strength.

Lark could feel his erection against her belly, a thick, demanding bulk. She gasped into his mouth and planted her hands against his chest to push him back. "What's gotten into you?"

His green eyes shuttered. "What do you think?"

The low, sexy growl in his voice made something clench between her thighs. Fighting to ignore it, she glowered at him. "You can't just haul me off for sex in front of half the Round Table!"

"It's nothing they don't do with their own women." Gawain's hands came up to stroke her cheek in a gesture as tender as his eyes were hungry. "On a regular basis, I might add." Tilting her head, he bent to string kisses along her jaw to one ear. He paused to tenderly bite the lobe, then swirled his tongue over it until she squirmed.

Her aroused embarrassment began to melt into simple arousal.

And he knew it. Boldly, he reached beneath the hem of her shirt, caught one cup of her bra, and tugged it down until he could reach her nipple. Pleasure slid through her as he strummed the little point, then twisted it gently. He palmed her, caressing her slowly until Lark purred and leaned into him. A small voice warned her someone could walk in on them, but with those skillful hands teasing and stroking, it was hard to give a damn.

She was panting by the time he stepped back and started towing her toward the table that dominated the room.

A circle of gleaming, polished wood. . . .

Lark stopped in her tracks. "Oh, no. Forget it—we are *so* not doing it on the Round Table!"

Gawain laughed, the sound deep and masculine. "It wouldn't be the first time. Arthur and Gwen . . ."

"Shut up! TMI! Too Much Information!"

But those strong fingers kept pulling her toward the table, so she hastily cast a dimensional gateway and babbled, "Look, your living room! With a couch and everything, just waiting for a bout of hot jungle sex . . ."

"TMI," Kel said dryly from his scabbard. Both of them ignored him.

"You talked me into it." Gawain swept her into his arms and stepped through the gate. Relieved, she banished it. "And in case there's any doubt, I'm not feeling patient enough to deal with all these clothes. So unless you want me to start ripping them all off . . ."

"All right, all right!" She banished their clothing with a flick of magic.

Naked, wearing only Kel's scabbard slung across his back, Gawain strode toward the couch. Lark met the dragon's jeweled gaze over a broad, brawny shoulder. "Is he always like this?"

"No, actually." Instead of the amusement she'd expected, the dragon's expression was thoughtful. "You seem to have gotten under his skin."

"Go to sleep, Kel." Gawain slid one hand out from under Lark's legs as he reached back to angle the scabbard out of the way. As she grabbed for his shoulders, he sat down on the couch. "We're about to get a little busy."

"I rest my case. He's not usually this rude." The dragon rolled his eyes, then obediently closed them and stiffened into solid steel.

Lark shook her head at Gawain, caught halfway between irritation and lingering desire. "I know you're hungry, but for God's sake . . . ahhhh!" She yelped as he caught her under the backside, lifted her like a rag doll and draped her thighs over his shoulders, then buried his face against her sex.

"Gawain!" Startled, Lark grabbed for his wrists as he lowered her torso until her head and shoulders rested on the floor, her back against his shins. She squirmed and yelped, feeling completely helpless. "What the hell are you doing?"

Wicked amusement rumbled in his voice. "Eating dinner." His tongue flicked over her clit, swirling around the hard little button before he closed his lips and suckled it into a red-hot knot of pleasure.

"Oh my God!" Lark gasped, bucking in his hold.

He chuckled and slid one hand down the length of her body to cup her breast. Licking and teasing, he simultaneously thumbed her nipple until her nervous system buzzed like a cricket.

"Gawain!" she moaned, squirming helplessly. She couldn't believe he was doing this. He'd been dominant before, but this stark sexual conquest was outrageous.

Not to mention wickedly arousing.

Ignoring her writhing struggles, Gawain slid his tongue deep in her sex in a wet, luscious caress while scissoring the tip of her breast between two strong fingers.

It felt amazing.

Groaning, she tightened her legs until she could roll her hips against his mouth.

Gawain lifted his head slightly and grinned at her, his mouth wet, his gaze wicked. "Like that?" Releasing her breast, he reached between her thighs before lowering his head to suckle her again. A long, skillful finger pumped deep in and out of her core, each plunge spiking her pleasure hotter.

"God, yes!" She felt utterly helpless in his powerful grip, her senses overcome by his mouth and plunging fingers. Any lingering outrage drowned without a whimper.

An orgasm began to gather low in her belly, coiling tighter as he closed his lips over her clit and sucked ruthlessly.

"Oh, God," she whimpered helplessly, rolling her head on the carpeted floor as the pleasure surged through her in a burning wave. "Morrrre . . ."

Gawain picked her up again, lifting her high and spreading her wide. Startled, she grabbed for his shoulders, meeting his fierce, satisfied gaze as he positioned her over his erection. As if she weighed no more than a rag doll, he lowered her onto his rigid cock.

Lark stiffened and gasped as its meaty length slid into her. "Gawain!" She dug her nails desperately into his shoulders. In this position, he felt a foot long.

"Yes?" His feral grin bared his fangs as he rolled his hips upward, driving that incredible cock deep.

Unable to answer, Lark could only writhe.

At first it was almost too much as she felt him pushing his way into her tight, slick flesh. She whimpered, the sound blending pain and pleasure.

He froze and searched her eyes. "You okay?"

She panted, her body adjusting slowly to his stark invasion. He was just so damned big. "'M fine."

"You sure?"

Her body was beginning to report its delight with his massive cock. "Yeah. Oh, yeah!" She gasped as her hunger began to rise again. "More . . ."

Gawain's smile was tight and feral. "Good." Slowly, carefully, he started thrusting.

Lark groaned. Each stroke felt luscious, overwhelming. She shuddered in pleasure, staring into his hot, green eyes. His handsome face was tight with fierce desire, his teeth gritted as he fought for control.

"That better?" he demanded, grinding up at her.

"Oh, God!" she whimpered. "Oh, man!"

"I'll take that as a yes." He bit his lip and increased the pace, delving his cock deep between her tight, slick walls.

Faster, then faster, each stroke tightening the spring of her orgasm until it pulsed on the edge of explosion.

Increasingly desperate for more of the sizzling pleasure, she began to meet his thrusts, grinding down on his thick shaft.

"Gawain!" She threw her head back and screamed as the climax boiled out of nowhere with a furious storm of delight.

A big hand locked in her hair, pulling her head to the side. He leaned in and sank his fangs into her throat.

Lark jolted, feeling Gawain's massive cock thrusting deep into her even as he began to drink. Overcome, she clung to him as the pulses of pleasure went on, as sweetly merciless as Gawain himself.

Gawain drank, rolling his hips upward into Lark's slim, lovely body. With every thrust, need curled tighter and tighter in his balls. He wrapped his arms around her, loving the silken feel of her skin under his hands. She shivered, a delicious little tremble that hit him like a punch in the gut.

His orgasm roared up in a hot blast. He stiffened and cried out against her throat.

The storm went on, pulsing fiercely, driving him to arch his back and drive himself to his full length. Gasping, he held himself there for a long, luscious moment before collapsing back against the couch.

"Man," Lark whispered.

"Yeah," he panted, his heart thundering.

"That was . . ."

"Yeah."

They fell silent as they fought for air, content to cling together for mutual support.

Suddenly a new impression made its way into Gawain's pleasure-saturated mind. Lark felt so delicate, so fragile in his arms.

And so . . . precious.

He'd made love to countless women, Majae and otherwise, since becoming a vampire all those centuries ago, but somehow the experience had never had such pure resonance to it. As if it meant far more than simply feeding a driving physical need.

Merlin's beard, he thought, stunned.

Were Arthur and the knights right after all? Was he falling for Lark?

TWELVE

Diera cried out as her climax broke over her like a wave of honeyed fire, sweet and burning at once. Automatically, she tightened the grip of her legs around Antonio's narrow hips, pulling him closer. That was all it took. He slammed to his full delicious length and roared out his pleasure.

At last Antonio collapsed over her, mantling her in his warm, sweating weight. "Christ, woman," he moaned into her neck, "you're killing me!"

"You're an immortal. You'll get better." She smiled, smug as a cat, and curled her arms around his powerful back. They'd already made love once tonight after returning from the High Council's Joint Session, and her throat still stung from his fangs. She didn't care. It had been exquisite.

"Insatiable wench." Antonio rolled over onto his back, tugging her on top of him. As he looked up at her, the smile faded from his face. "I can't believe how beautiful you are."

There was so much awe in his eyes, she found herself believing him.

What's more, he made her feel beautiful. Made her feel

young for the first time in a long time. Every time he touched her, she felt more and more of the old bitterness flaking away. Years of loneliness meant nothing in Antonio's arms.

"The beautiful one in this bed is you," she told him, stroking a hand through his long, tangled dark hair.

His lips twitched. "You do realize we're on the verge of getting gooey."

"I'll risk it if you will."

In answer, he threaded his fingers through her hair and pulled her head down for another of those long, dizzying kisses.

When they came up for air again, Diera let herself collapse across his chest, feeling as boneless as a silk scarf. She thought back over the months she'd known him, remembering how long she'd tried to pretend he was only a green boy instead of the warrior he was.

Bless Morgana's spell for uniting them. Antonio had instantly recognized the assignment as the opening he'd been looking for and had devoted himself to seducing her.

She'd managed to resist him for barely three hours. No surprise, really, considering the groundwork he'd laid over the past months.

"How did I stay away from you so long?" Diera murmured softly.

"I have no idea. I've been working on you for months. I thought I'd never get you into bed."

"I've been an idiot." Thoughtfully, she combed her fingers through his tangled hair. "Lark and Gawain looked good together tonight."

Antonio stiffened. "Do not mention that man's name in my bed."

She lifted her head and grinned, perversely pleased with his show of jealousy. "Cool that hot Italian blood. I only meant she's good for him. Better than I ever was." Diera sobered. "Probably because I was never really in love with him."

Her lover went still, searching her eyes. "What leads you to that conclusion?"

"You," she said simply. "I never felt the way about him that I do about you."

His muscular chest rose beneath her as he caught his breath.

"I thought I should love him," Diera said softly. "He was everything I thought I wanted, after all. But we never really fit, and he knew it. That's why he refused to True-bond with me. He was wiser than I was."

"He was an idiot."

"No. He just wasn't you."

"Truebond with me." Antonio's eyes widened, as if he'd spoken the words without intending to. "I mean . . ."

For a moment she thought the panic in his eyes was a fear she'd take him seriously when he hadn't really meant the words. Disappointment clutched at her soul.

Then strong hands clutched her shoulders. "Don't send me away. I know this is sudden—I can wait. But let me stay."

Diera stared down into his handsome, pleading face, re-alizing his panic was born of the fear she'd reject him. Warmth expanded in her chest, melting that last chip of bit-ter ice buried in her heart. She cupped his cheek in her hand. "Do you really think me foolish enough to throw away such a precious gift?"

Thick, dark brows furled, and he searched her gaze. "Don't be kind to me. Don't let me hope if you only mean to let me down gently."

She snorted. "Gawain could tell you I'm anything but kind."

"I repeat, Gawain is an idiot." Anger snapped in his eyes, mixed with a gratifying flash of jealousy.

"And I repeat, I never felt about him the way I feel about you."

Hope leaped in his gaze. "Does that mean . . . ?"

Her heart demanded she seize this chance with both

hands, but she was too honest for that. "I would love nothing more than to Truebond with you, Antonio. Sharing a link with that lovely soul of yours would be the greatest pleasure in my long life. But we've only known each other a few months."

"I can wait." His hands tightened around her waist. "Just give me a chance to win you."

She took his face between both hands. "Antonio, you already have. I've known countless Magi, seduced them and been seduced by them. I've never known a man like you. And I want to bind you fast to my soul. But you're so young . . ."

"Not so young that I don't know what I want." Anger tightened his deliciously masculine mouth. "I may not be centuries old, but I'm not a boy either. I've romanced more than my share of Majae, and I know when the Desire is trying to do my thinking for me. God knows you've got its enthusiastic support, but my heart, my soul, and my mind want you even more." He tilted up his chin in challenge. "Touch my thoughts and see."

Diera closed her eyes and let her consciousness flow through her fingertips. He made not the slightest attempt to block her, opening himself without flinching.

Contact.

She caught her breath as she saw him completely for the first time.

Antonio was right. There was nothing boyish about him. Instead, she found power, strong and sure and very male. Flaws, too—he battled a certain bitter jealousy of Gawain for holding her love for so long—but he didn't try to hide them from her.

But even more than that, she sensed Antonio's basic decency, the fierce desire to protect and nurture those weaker than he. Which, she realized as she touched him, was almost everyone.

Most of all, she sensed his love for her. It had grown in him slowly as he'd worked with her and Lark, but he'd thought it fruitless. He'd believed he'd had no chance against Gawain's memory. But when Morgana's spell had partnered them, he'd seen his chance, and he'd taken it.

He'd been thinking about Truebonding with her for days now, but he'd been afraid to say anything, fearing her rejection.

Rejecting him was the last thing on her mind. They belonged together. It didn't matter how briefly they'd known each other, or how long she'd known other men.

This was right.

Still, she had to remind him. *If we do this and one of us dies, it could kill the other.*

Or the healthy one could keep the injured from dying, he said. *Either way, I'll accept the risk. One thousand years or one hour, being with you will be worth it.*

Diera smiled into his handsome face. *That's all I needed to hear.* Closing her eyes, she called her magic and let it spill over them in a warm flood. In seconds, its intensity built to a white-hot burn that melted their mental barriers like mist in the sun.

She felt him. Felt him far more profoundly than she had a moment before, felt him sinking into her very bones and blood, felt his strength and sure power and keen intelligence wash over her like warm, sweet sunlight. And he felt her. In the mirror of his mind, she saw herself as he did, all fierce will and pride and wit. Saw the beauty that took his breath.

As the Truebond snapped into full force, Antonio's eyes widened with a child's wonder, then narrowed with a man's satisfaction. *There you are.*

She could feel him like a sweet and glorious dimension just waiting to be explored. *Yes, here I am.*

Silent as a wolf, wrapped in an invisibility spell, Richard moved around the outskirts of Avalon. His heart pounded in long, strong beats, and his palms were damp. Yet beneath that anxiety, his entire body thrummed with borrowed magic.

The spell his dragon ally had given him had worked, allowing him to punch through the city's shields without being detected. Still, Richard knew all it would take to doom him was some clever Maja sensing the death magic at his heart. Even the dragon's power couldn't save him from the collective rage of the Magekind.

Perversely, Richard found that thought only added to the knife-edged excitement pouring through him. Despite the odds, he was going to pull this off. He could feel it in every cell. He was going to find the Maja he was looking for, kill her, and steal her magic.

And Bors was next.

Luckily, he had a good idea of his target's location. Richard knew this section of the city well; he'd spent his boyhood playing knight in the manicured gardens of the surrounding homes. He'd dreamed of being a hero then. Becoming a Magus like his father, fighting evil, and feeding from beautiful Majae.

Living forever.

Instead Bors had told him he didn't deserve to be a Magus, and the Magekind had turned their backs on him. Even his own mother had washed her hands of him.

She was dead now, killed by one of Geirolf's sorcerers. Somewhere deep within him, the boy Richard had once been grieved for her.

But the man he'd become thought it was no more than she deserved. After all, she'd rejected her own flesh and blood.

Still, every time he killed one of the cultists, he thought of her.

And now, there was nothing to stop him from killing Bors, or anybody else for that matter. They were all bought and paid for as far as he was concerned.

Like the one whose house he slipped toward now.

He knew her well. She'd served him cookies as a child and made him laugh with her magic. He'd dreamed about her as a teenager—hot, sweaty dreams of becoming a Magus while thrusting between her long legs.

When Bors had rejected him, he'd used the charm she'd once given him to call her. She'd come, and his heart had leaped with hope.

But when he begged her to give him Merlin's Gift, she'd refused, her gaze level and cold. She'd come, she said, to tell him she'd heard about his teenaged indiscretions. "Turn away from the path you follow, Richard. You can still live a productive life as a mortal." Her eyes had hardened even more. "But a mortal is all you can ever be."

Humiliated tears in his eyes, he'd cursed her. She'd had the gall to look pitying before she gated away.

Well, she was the one who'd deserve pity by the time he was done with her.

Richard went through the wards against her elegant French chateau as if they weren't even there. Even the massive double doors melted away at his approach. He stepped into the marble foyer with a sensation of triumph. A cool smile on his face, he scanned the crystal chandelier high overhead, then flicked a glance down to the bronze statue of Diana that held a place of honor directly beneath it.

Such elegance. Such riches. Too bad none of it would save her.

Still wrapped in the invisibility spell, he stepped down the corridor, moving silently, nostrils flared. His sensitive vampire hearing picked up a familiar sound, and his head came up.

Oh, yeah. He didn't have to worry—they wouldn't hear him.

Grinning now, confident, he headed for the bedroom that stood at the other end of the house. And walked right in.

A naked Magus stood with his back to the open door, the Maja on her knees in front of him. Edge paused a moment to appreciate her technique before he drew his sword.

Though the spell blocked any sound he made, the Magus seemed to sense him. He started to turn . . .

Richard decapitated him with one blow of his sword. The Maja leaped to her feet with a scream as her lover fell, his head rolling away.

Dropping the invisibility spell, Richard smiled. "Hello, Diera."

It felt as if Antonio was being torn out of her by the roots. Diera screamed, a howl of denial that rang all the way to the depths of her soul. *No! We just found each other!*

She sensed his helplessness. *I've failed you.* She could feel him being drawn away into light, into the distant sound of music.

In anguish, she realized he could not stay, and she could not let him go.

That left only one thing to do: *let everything else go.*

She called the Mageverse one final time and remorselessly used its power to stop her own heart. As her knees buckled, Diera saw Edge start toward her, a savage grin on her face and his sword in his hand. His grin turned to rage as she swirled into the light.

Diera felt Antonio's warmth envelope her again and wrapped him in her own.

I failed you, he mourned again.

Don't be ridiculous, she said, and drew him with her deeper into the pure and pulsing light.

"You bitch!" Edge screamed in rage as he stared down at Diera's lifeless body. She'd toppled the moment he'd taken the man's head. "You were Truebonded with him!"

Furious, he brought his sword down on the corpse, but it was useless. Her life force was gone; he couldn't drain it. He had the man's, but the Magus had been so young, it scarcely made a difference.

All this for nothing.

The dragon was going to be pissed.

Lark lay on the couch in a boneless sprawl, half-dozing. Gawain and Kel were having one of their soundless conversations, but she didn't care. Between fighting Roth and making love to Gawain, she was done. She doubted she could . . .

The flash of a blade. Diera's scream. Lark jolted upright with a cry of horror.

"Hey, it's okay," Gawain said. "You were dreaming."

"That wasn't a dream." Wide awake, she shot off the couch and called her armor. "Something's wrong with Diera."

"What?" Alarm widened his eyes.

"I don't know, but we need to get to her villa. Now!" Even as she cast the gate, Kel was conjuring Gawain's armor.

"It's probably that fuck Edge and another one of his traps." The knight looked over his shoulder at Kel. "Call Arthur and the other knights. We're going to need them."

"Let's hope I don't get blocked this time," the dragon growled.

As he sent the call, Gawain plunged through the gate. Lark dove after him, and they burst into Diera's bedroom.

Edge stood over a still female body. At first glance Lark thought Diera was naked from the waist down, wearing only a red shirt.

Then she realized the "shirt" gleamed wetly.

Blood.

Edge looked around at them. "When I was a boy, I wanted her heart." He opened his hand to display something bright red. "Now I've got it."

"You *fuck*!" Gawain leaped for the vampire, who threw his dripping burden aside and drew his sword.

As the two men engaged in a fury of blows, Lark stood frozen, staring down at her friend's butchered body.

This couldn't be happening. *Not Diera.*

Then Edge blasted Gawain so hard, the knight staggered even behind Kel's shields. Jolted out of her momentary paralysis, Lark shot a spell of her own at the sorcerer.

He ducked and whizzed a fireball at her. Lark blocked it, taking a step back. One foot slipped in something wet. Automatically she glanced down. Blood.

Beside her foot was a naked body, broad-shouldered and headless. Cold spilling across her skin, she realized who it must be.

Antonio.

Her gorge rose as she put two and two together. He and Diera weren't naked because their clothes had vanished when they died. They hadn't been wearing any. *Edge had killed them while they were making love.*

Rage came at last, hot and welcome, bracing her with its feral strength. Teeth bared, she looked around for the sorcerer. Spotting him locked in combat with Gawain, she lurched toward him, wanting only to kill the man who'd murdered her dearest friend.

"I'm going to gut you, you sick son of a bitch!" Gawain snarled, circling the killer. "And I'm going to take my time!"

Edge laughed, the sound chilling. "You're the one who's going to do the dying. I've got more than enough power now to do the job." He leaped back, avoiding Gawain's sword-thrust, then darted forward like a snake, striking for the knight's heart. Gawain twisted away, all agile power.

Eyes burning, hands shaking with her rage, Lark hesitated, looking for an opening. She was no match for Edge with a sword, but she could force him to split his attention between her and Gawain.

Spotting her moment, she swung up her sword and charged, hacking at the sorcerer's chest. He saw her coming and leaped back before she could cut him in two. The blade jolted in her hands as he parried, steel ringing on steel. Lark spun away and fired a blast at his face. He ducked, then lobbed his own fireball in return. Watching the seething mass of energy fly toward her chest, Lark automatically shielded.

The death spell hit her barrier, which blazed blue white, then dimmed alarmingly as the energy started eating right through it. Hastily, Lark poured power into the shield and ducked aside, her heart pounding with fear. Edge's fireball finally dissipated with a sullen pop and one final rolling reek of brimstone. Shaken, she realized that if it weren't for her own increase in power, the attack would have killed her.

Edge met her eyes and smirked, conjuring another fireball with his free hand as he spun his sword with a lazy rotation of the opposite wrist.

He didn't get a chance to use either. Gawain roared in fury and attacked, swinging Kel like a scythe. Edge cursed and parried, but Gawain kept coming. The blades rang together in a demonic chorus as he drove the sorcerer from the bedroom and out into the hallway beyond.

Lark didn't hesitate as she followed. One way or another, they couldn't let Edge get away. Moving up beside her lover, she joined the attack, tossing fireballs while he pounded at Edge's guard. She gave each one of them everything she had. Within seconds, her face streamed with sweat from the magical effort, and her head ached. She ignored the pain, intent only on revenge.

Together, Lark and Gawain hounded the sorcerer down the corridor, alternating blasts and blade attacks. Edge retreated, hurling spell after spell at them. The fireballs hit their shields in a relentless pounding until Lark's skull seemed to ring with each impact.

Magic abruptly rose at her back, the sensation strengthening her in her exhaustion. Thank God—somebody had just gated in. A familiar male voice bellowed in rage. "Edge, you bastard, what have you done?"

Lark dared a glance over her shoulder and saw Guinevere and Arthur striding toward them, both in full armor.

Excalibur flashed as the Magus broke into a run, lifting the great blade high. Lark grinned savagely as she and Gawain ducked aside, giving him room for his attack.

No matter how much power Edge had stolen, he was finished now. The killer didn't have a prayer against all four of them.

He knew it, too. His eyes widened as he leaped back, narrowly avoiding Excalibur's savage descent.

Arthur snarled something in Latin—he really was pissed—and spun the great blade around in a glittering figure eight. "You're dead, boy!"

Edge grinned at them, baring gritted teeth. "Not yet, old man!" A flick of his wrist summoned a dimensional gate as he parried Arthur's ringing attacks.

Lark shouted a warning, but the vampire turned and leaped through before Arthur could stop him.

Guinevere promptly cast what Lark recognized was a mirroring gate that would track him to his destination. Only a fool would have used the gate Edge had cast, since he could have collapsed it when his pursuers were halfway through.

"Leave a trail for the others," Arthur said. "We've got him this time." He turned and jumped through, Gawain, Kel, Lark, and his wife at his heels.

Lark threw a shield over all of them the instant they landed on the other side of the gate. Just in time—a blast lit up the barrier with fire.

The magical buzz of another opening gateway rolled over Lark's skin. She threw up a mirrored gate of her own to track it and was the first one through.

Mistake.

Steel flashed as her vision filled with Edge's snarling face. Lark barely got up her sword in time to parry. Her arm went numb to the shoulder as Edge hit her with his full vampire strength. She fell back, going down on one knee as Edge loomed over her.

A blade appeared before her face, deflecting the

sorcerer's attack. Gawain thrust him away, and Kel kept him going with a spell blast. Lark struggled to her feet as the two men fought. Arthur charged in to join the battle, Guinevere striding after him.

Around them, tall city buildings suggested an urban neighborhood, possibly in New York. As the men hacked at each other, Lark searched for her shot. Guinevere turned toward her. "Let's combine our power. We need to . . ."

Before she could get the rest of the sentence out of her mouth, Edge whirled, conjured yet another doorway, and jumped.

"Dammit!" Lark growled.

Kel cast the gate this time. The two women leaped after Gawain and Arthur, shielding all four of them when they hit the other side. Another blast lit their joint barrier and splashed helplessly.

"Might as well quit running," Gawain told Edge, who backed away as the two knights stalked him. "There's nowhere you can go that we won't track you. You'll just use up all your power, and we'll butcher you like a suckling pig."

Edge's eyes narrowed. "There's one more place."

He spun aside, leaping through yet another gate that popped into being. Lark cast her own to follow . . .

It felt like she'd slammed into a brick wall. She yelped and staggered. Guinevere tried next, only to drop her arms and curse.

"What the hell's going on?" Arthur demanded in frustration.

"He's jumped behind a really powerful set of wards," Guinevere told him absently, her gaze fierce with concentration as she again fought to punch through. "It's somewhere on Mageverse Earth, but I can't tell . . ."

"The Sidhe kingdom?"

"No, I'd have recognized that magic. This is something else. It feels almost like . . ."

"Dragon," Kel said flatly.

"But why in the hell would one of the Dragonkind work

with Edge, of all people?" Galahad demanded. Caroline stood by his side, white-faced. The two must have just gated in. Lark had been so focused on Edge, she hadn't even noticed.

What's more, Morgana was there, too, along with Bors, Lancelot, and his new wife Grace. Even as she watched, Tristan and Kay appeared with Helen and another Magus she didn't recognize.

"Must be the same bastard that rescued him the last time," Gawain growled. "But who?"

"I have no idea," Morgana said grimly. "But I do know someone we can ask."

As the senior Magekind discussed who best to bring in on the problem of the mystery dragon, Lark stood numbly listening. With the battle over, her rage had been overcome by a nagging sense of unreality.

A slender arm slipped around her shoulders, jolting her out of her fog. She looked around to see Caroline watching her with dark, sympathetic eyes.

"He killed them while they were making love." Lark blinked hard, feeling helpless. "It didn't look as if Diera even got off a shot."

Caroline's arm tightened. "It must have been really quick then. She wouldn't have suffered."

"He cut out her heart, Caroline!"

"I know, sweetie." Her face, normally alight with mischief, now looked grim and blasted with grief. "I saw the bodies. Diera and Antonio. . . Oh, God. I can't believe it."

Lark rested her temple against Caroline's as she stood in the circle of her friend's arms. "She was so damned wise. She understood everything I didn't." Blinking hard, Lark bit her lip, looking away from the group who still stood in low-voiced conversation. "I'm not going to cry, dammit."

"Lark," Caroline said, lowering her head and her voice, "I think they'd understand. She was their friend, too."

"We all lost too much today."

Lark turned to see Arthur walking toward her. He dropped a hand on her shoulder. "There's no shame in grieving for her, Lark. We all loved her." His smile was faint and sad. "She made it easy."

"Yeah," Lark said softly. "She did." Rage flared in her heart, cold and bitter. "And that bastard took it all away."

"He'll pay for it," Tristan told her. His face was white inside his lifted visor. "He's going to pay dearly."

THIRTEEN

The tail caught Richard in the side and knocked him fly-ing. He smashed into the rock wall so hard he saw stars, then saw them again when he hit the floor.

Despite the pain of what he suspected were broken ribs, he rolled to his feet and backed away from the dragon that stalked him in the green darkness.

"You nasty little ape," it snarled. "You *dare* come here when I have not summoned you! And you *dare* use the spell I taught you to do it? I'll rip you in two and eat the pieces!"

"They were gating after me! It was the only way I could lose them!" He'd known he was taking a risk when he'd gone through the Dragonkind's wards with the same spell the dragon had taught him to use on Avalon. But he hadn't realized the creature would be so enraged.

"And you think that matters to me? When I honored you with knowledge and a piece of my own magic, it was not an invitation to take advantage of my good nature!"

What good nature? Somehow Richard bit the words back. He had to talk fast. "Don't you want to be free of the Magekind?"

"Do you think me such a fool that I'd believe protecting a worm like you would have any effect on them at all? You can't even fight off a handful of apes!" The dragon reared, fanged mouth gaping, obviously about to swallow Edge whole. "You didn't even manage to steal that one female's magic! *You're weak!*"

"She died before I could take it!"

"Excuses!" The dragon gathered itself to lunge.

"No, listen to me!" Richard scuttled back as the words tumbled out in a desperate rush. "Geirolf created a spell to destroy the Magekind. I know what it was. I can replicate it! Think of it—the stench of the apes gone from this Earth. . . ." He braced, ready to leap aside if the beast didn't listen.

"If you had such a spell, you'd have used it by now." But the dragon didn't lunge for him.

"I didn't have the power. But you . . ."

The dragon rocked back. "Me? Use some perverted magic from the Dark Ones against the Magekind? My people would have me executed!" But despite the denial, Richard thought he saw a flicker of interest in those alien eyes.

He licked his dry lips. "They don't have to know."

The dragon made a sharp, grating sound, its version of a laugh. "Oh, they'll know, ape." Calculation flickered in the creature's eyes, and that massive tail snapped, spines grating on the stone floor. "But you, now . . . you could work it."

Richard swallowed and took a gamble. "If you lent me more power . . ."

"I told you, no! Pah, I waste my time with you, you stupid, smelly ape." The dragon peeled its lips back from its teeth and coiled to lunge.

"There is a way I could get enough power," Richard continued hurriedly, backing away. "If you can help me with the spell." Maybe. He thought. He prayed . . .

The dragon hesitated, then growled in disgust. "You lie. Again. You do nothing but lie."

"No, look." Richard opened a quick dimensional gate back to his sanctuary. A spell drew the black grail from its hiding place and brought it floating toward him.

"Feh." The dragon's head came up, lip curling in revulsion. "That thing stinks worse than you do, ape."

Richard cradled it protectively. "It's the last of Geirolf's black grails. He used this to create us." *Time to take a gamble.* "Arthur and his knights are searching for this, because they've got a spell that would destroy the grail—and with it, all of us."

The dragon cocked its head, cruel interest in its eyes. "Including you?"

"Including me. When Geirolf died, one of his lieutenants sent his life force, his magic, into each of us." He looked down at the cup. "If I could figure out a way to survive the grail's destruction and gather that energy, I'd be able to call on vast forces." Richard met the dragon's gaze, silently demanding belief. "Vast enough to perform Geirolf's sacrificial spell and wipe out the Magekind, just as he intended."

"And with the Magekind gone, Kel will die." The dragon's eyes narrowed. "Did you say *sacrificial*? What sacrifice do you intend?"

Yes! I've got you now, you scaly bastard. With difficulty, he hid his triumph. "Originally, Geirolf intended to sacrifice a Magekind couple, but those he intended to kill trapped and slew him instead. If he'd only listened to me, he'd have made another sacrifice and survived."

"You? Why would he listen to *you*, worm?"

"How do you think he knew about the Magekind to begin with? Merlin had him locked in a magic cage for sixteen hundred years. When he finally freed himself, he didn't know a damn thing."

"But you did." The dragon curled a lip. "You're lying again, egg-sucker."

"No. I'm not. I suggested the ultimate sacrifice, the one that would liberate all the power he wanted. But Geirolf thought that target would be too risky."

The great tail lashed like a hungry cat's. "And who was that?"

"Who is the heart and soul of the Magekind, even in the minds of mortals who don't even believe in him?" Richard grinned, watching that flash of interest intensify. "Whose abduction would leave the Magekind in a panic?" He paused a moment, letting the thought penetrate, letting the dragon draw its own conclusions. "Arthur, the Once and Future King." He grinned savagely. "Or should I say—the Once and Never King."

Lark and Gawain returned home barely half an hour before the sun would force him into the Daysleep. He felt weary to the soul in that particular way he associated with a serious defeat.

And Lark . . .

She looked grief-dazed, more like a woman who'd lost a mother than a good friend. Yet despite her pain, she'd returned to Diera's home and used her magic to ready the lovers' bodies for their funeral the next night. Gawain had gone with her to lend emotional support and Kel's help.

It was as she wrapped the bodies in her magic that Lark sensed Diera's gruesome injuries were all postmortem. She'd been dead before Edge even touched her.

Gawain had instantly realized what happened; he'd seen it before. "Diera and Antonio must have Truebonded."

"And Antonio's death killed her." Lark had stared at him, puzzled. "But she didn't mention they'd Truebonded when I saw her at the meeting. In fact, she was still denying she loved him."

Gawain shrugged. "They probably hadn't done the ritual yet. It was likely impulse." Brooding, he shrugged. "If not for the Truebond, Diera might have been able to fight Edge off."

"Or not. She loved Antonio. The shock of seeing him

dead like that . . ." Lark shook her head. "I'm glad they did it. At least they were together."

Thinking about it now as he and Lark trudged up the stairs to the bedroom, Gawain found himself sharing her gratitude. Though Diera had never believed it, he'd loved her. Not enough to give her the Truebond link she wanted, but he had loved her.

When she'd found Antonio, he'd been happy for her, had hoped they could finally be friends again.

Edge had destroyed it all like a heedless toddler in a temper fit.

And the little bastard could not have hurt his father more if he'd cut out Bors's heart instead. Gawain had seen men look less devastated on the way to the executioner's block.

"Think Morgana and Gwen will have any luck?" Lark asked him as they walked into his bedroom.

Since the men had no choice except to sleep, Morgana had announced her intention to talk to Soren that morning. Guinevere intended to request an audience with the Sidhe king, Llyr Galatyn. Galatyn was the Heir to Heroes, with a special magical connection to Cachamwri, the dragon god. Perhaps he'd be able to find out something if Soren couldn't help.

"It's hard to tell. Neither the Dragonkind nor their god is known for being cooperative."

"Good point." Lark grimaced and banished her armor with a flick of the fingers.

Gawain blinked. She'd replaced it with a white cotton sleep shirt that seemed to swallow her slim body. All she needed was a slogan across the front: "Keep off the Maja."

Then again, he was too exhausted to even think of making love himself. There'd been one too many battles tonight.

With a sigh, Gawain shrugged off his scabbard, barely noticing as Kel replaced his armor with loose cotton pants.

Instead of hanging the scabbard on the bedpost, he put it down on the floor. Considering Edge's new talent for gating past Avalon's wards, he wanted the sword in easy reach.

As Lark gestured the lights off, he got in next to her and tugged her gently against him, wrapping her in his arms.

With a muffled cry of grief, she turned and burrowed against him, her body shuddering as she wept.

"I loved her, too." He stroked Lark's hair and kissed her forehead. "It wasn't enough for her, but I did. She was warm and funny, and she never backed down."

"They were in love," Lark said against his neck. "She was actually happy. And then that bastard took it all away."

"I'm going to kill him."

Her arms tightened around his waist. "I know."

Gawain woke before Lark did, something which told him just how exhausted she must be. The Desire was awake and prowling, of course—it always was after a battle—but he had no intention of indulging it. Not after what she'd gone through last night.

He'd just have to go hungry.

Instead, he rolled over and propped his head on his forearm, the better to watch her as she slept. Now that the sun had set, the bedroom's magical shutters had opened, admitting a spill of moonlight to caress her cheek.

Brooding, he studied her elegant fragility. She looked pale, her closed lashes long and dark against her cheeks.

Was he going to fail her the way he had Diera?

OK, enough of that, Kel said in their mental link. *Pick me up. I want to talk to you.*

He supposed he needed to touch base with Arthur, Morgana, and Guinevere, find out if they'd made any progress during the day on tracking down Edge . . .

Hey, you!

. . . though if he hadn't let the little fucker get the better of him, none of this would be necessary, and Diera would still be alive.

All right, dammit, I'm coming to you.

Gawain felt the covers tug across his hip as if something were pulling on them. With a sigh, he reached down to pick the sword up. Teeth snapped at his hand. He snatched back. "Hey! You said you wanted me to pick you up!"

"By Cachamwri, I'm going to do it myself now." The dragon sniffed. "I've decided I need the exercise." With his ferocious pride, Kel often insisted on forcing his tiny, awkward metal body to do his bidding.

Gawain lay back and waited, alert for any sign the dragon might lose his grip on the sheets and fall. It wouldn't hurt him, but it would piss him off even more. Neither of them needed the frustration.

A moment later, the dragon's tiny head appeared over the side of the bed. His neck snaked out, and he bit down fiercely on a fold of sheet as he used claws and wings to drag himself the rest of the way onto the bed. Behind him, the sword blade dangled like some awkward tail. Gawain scooped the length of steel up and arranged it into its proper position. As soon as it was straight, the blade solidified. Kel sighed in relief.

One of these days, I'm going to eat the egg-sucker who did this to me. Cannibalism was the most vile, insulting threat one dragon could make against another, implying as it did that the other was prey.

Kel meant it.

I'll slice him up for you, Gawain thought with a black grin. *We'll have dragon steaks.*

Jeweled eyes gleamed. *Even better, dice him into dragon stir-fry and cook him in my mother's memory.*

Dragon burgers.

There you go. We'll invite the Majae and have a little cookout. Kel's jaws gaped in a vicious grin. *Edge can provide the appetizer.*

Gawain curled his lip. *There's not going to be enough left of the bastard when I get done with him.*

They lay silent for a long moment, each pondering his own bloodthirsty revenge. But after a moment, Gawain's attention returned to Lark's delicate little face.

The dragon watched him. *She may be young, but she fits your soul as none of the others ever did.*

Gawain blinked. *Even Diera?*

Especially Diera. She was a lovely woman, but the two of you weren't really in love. And deep down, you knew it, which was why you never wanted a Truebond with her.

I only wish we'd been in time to save her. Five minutes sooner . . .

The dragon gave him a sharp look. *You know better than that. You've lived long enough to know that some things can't be done, no matter how powerful you are. And in this case, you literally could not have gotten there any faster than you did.*

I know that, and yet . . .

. . . Blaming yourself gives you the comfortable illusion of being in control.

Gawain blinked at his friend. *You know me entirely too well, don't you?*

I should, after all these centuries. Now, what are you going to do about Lark?

He had no idea.

Lark strode down the marble corridor of Diera's villa, her sword in her hand. She was alone this time. Alone in the chilly, ringing silence.

She stopped, horror and dread creeping over her. The hair on the back of her neck rose as she heard a faint liquid sound. A suckling.

Her hand began to sweat around the hilt of her sword. Her instincts shrieked at her to run, but she couldn't. Diera and Antonio needed her.

This time, she would be in time.

Licking her dry lips, she forced her leaded feet to keep moving. The bedroom doors stood ajar. The liquid sound was louder now.

She swallowed, then extended the blade of her sword and used it to nudge the door open. Stepping inside, Lark felt her eyes widen in surprise.

Diera knelt before Antonio, suckling him.

"Oh, I'm sorry!" Lark stepped backward as her cheeks flamed hot. "I thought . . ."

Antonio's head slowly turned to look at her. His blue eyes were fixed and staring. Dead. Dead as his gray face. "Why didn't you come in time?" His voice echoed, hollow and moaning. A red crack spread across his throat, widening. Blood spilled down his muscular torso as his head tumbled off his shoulders. It hit the carpeted floor with a wet thud.

Slowly, so slowly, his body toppled, revealing the bloody, gaping hole in Diera's chest.

"Too late." A tear rolled down the Maja's dead, decaying cheek. "Always too late. I thought you were my friend."

Lark jolted up with a scream. Masculine arms snapped around her, and she fought them in instinctive panic.

"Hey!" Gawain's deep voice penetrated the mental fog. "It's me! You're having a nightmare."

Blinking, dazed, she quit flailing at him and let him gather her against his warm, strong chest. Images from the dream flickered through her mind. She had to swallow hard against her rising gorge.

A big hand came to rest against her hair, gently stroking. "Want to talk about it?"

Lark closed her eyes and shuddered. "Not really. It was just the same damned dream I had half a dozen times last night. Or today. Whatever." She let her head rest against his brawny shoulder. He felt good, so warm and strong, just touching him freed something wound tight in her.

Gawain lay back, pulling her over on top of him and

curling his arms around her. Lark sighed, letting the comfort of his warmth roll over her. "How long have you been up?"

He shrugged, his chest rising and falling under her cheek. "An hour or so."

Guilt stirred, and she lifted her head. "You shouldn't have let me sleep so long. The funeral . . ."

". . . Isn't for another couple of hours. Everybody's been busy trying to get the Dragonkind to believe one of their own was involved in the murders."

Lark stared at him. "But Edge was using Dragon magic. I could sense it."

A muscle flexed in Gawain's jaw. "The Dragon Lords have flatly denied any of their people would have anything to do with a Dark One's spawn."

Kel's grumble emerged from the sheets. "Basically, it's a variation on the same song and dance they've given us about the dragon who trapped me." He raised his voice in a mocking singsong. " 'It was probably a human magician, Kel. That's what happens when you associate with humans.' Like I don't know dragon magic when I feel it."

Lark thumbed the sleep out of her eyes. "Why are they so blind about this?"

"Because it suits them." The sword made a low growling sound. "You know, I think I'll go work on a locator spell. I'd really love to confront those idiots with proof they can't deny their way around."

The sword went still, the way he did when he slept. This time though, Lark could sense magic building around him like an electrical field, almost crackling with his fierce concentration.

Gawain rolled over to pick him up and return him to the scabbard lying beside the bed. "Well, that'll keep him occupied until it's time for the service. When Kel latches onto a problem, he never lets go." He sighed. "Sometimes it's the only thing that keeps him sane."

"I've wondered about that." Lark sat up against the headboard. "I can't even imagine what it would be like being trapped like that. I don't think I'd be able to hold on."

"If it wasn't for our mental link, I'm not sure Kel would have made it either." Gawain extended his powerful arms in a broad stretch before settling back down again. "As it is, he experiences life through my senses. It was really rough for him before we established the link."

Lark watched him, admiring the ripple and play of tanned muscle as he moved. "How do you go about Truebonding with a dragon?"

A corner of his lip twitched up. "It's not exactly a Truebond. For one thing, Truebonds are sexual. I may have an interesting reputation, but I assure you, I ain't banging my sword."

She winced. "God, the mental image that leaped to mind . . ."

Gawain laughed. "Imagine how I feel."

"Actually, I've got a pretty good idea how you feel." She said it without thinking, the sort of automatic flirtation that felt natural with Gawain.

The smile froze on her lips as she remembered Diera. How could she joke at a time like this?

Reading her stricken gaze, Gawain cupped her cheekbone. "You know what Diera would tell you right now?"

Lark could almost hear her friend's voice. *Being alive isn't a betrayal. Being afraid to live is.* "I've got a pretty good idea." She sighed. "I'm glad she found Antonio. I hope they'd made love all night long."

"There's something to be said for seizing every chance you get. Fewer regrets that way."

For a long moment they went silent, each lost in memory.

Despite her emotional scars, Diera had found the courage to reach for happiness with Antonio. And maybe, Lark thought suddenly, it was time she did the same.

She knew better than to believe Gawain would ever Truebond with her—she wasn't even sure she wanted to—but they could make the most of the time they had.

Lark looked up into his handsome face and let the need show in her eyes. "I know if it was me, I'd rather remember making love to you."

He went very still. Then he visibly reined in his leaping hunger and eased back. "Might be better if you didn't say that kind of thing to me right now. After last night's fight . . ."

"Maybe I need you as much as you need me. Maybe I need to forget."

She watched his Adam's apple bob as he swallowed. He took a deep breath and searched her face. "Are you sure about that?" Despite his obvious attempt at control, something feral showed on his face.

Need, wild and reckless, rose in her. A need to forget her guilt and grief, to celebrate being alive. To be in control, when it seemed she'd been in control of so little for so long. "I'm sure."

He started to reach for her. She slapped a hand in the middle of his chest. "Not so fast."

For a moment, the Desire glared, frustrated, out of his eyes before he yanked it into submission. He eased back. "It's your call, sweetheart. You're in control."

Control. Yeah, that's exactly what she wanted. Hungrily, she eyed his handsome face. "You know, I think it's time you were on the receiving end."

He lifted a blond brow, warily interested. "What do you have in mind?"

"You. All tied up." She gave him a hot smile of raw anticipation. "At my mercy."

"When you say tied up, are we talking silk scarves or . . . ?"

"Magic." Lark grinned. "Like I said, I want you at my mercy." He could probably snap solid steel shackles like wet pasta. Anything less than a spell wouldn't hold him.

Gawain swallowed, his expression a blend of unease and intrigue. "That's what I thought."

She realized she was enjoying this. "The question is, do you have the guts to do it?"

Green eyes narrowed. "I assure you, my *guts* are not in question."

"That's just what I wanted to hear." Lark flicked her fingers and cast the spell.

It felt as if something clamped around Gawain's wrists and ankles and jerked them spread-eagle. "Whoa!"

Sitting up on the bed, her breasts thrust out beneath that white cotton shirt, Lark gave him the kind of smile a cat gave a caged canary. "A little disconcerting?"

Gawain pulled at his right wrist. Though it didn't seem bound to anything, it wouldn't budge. "A bit."

She shuttered those hot chocolate eyes and crawled up his body to lay down at his side, one elbow braced on the mattress. "It can be intimidating, being held like that, knowing you can't escape."

He met her gaze steadily. "Depends on whether the one doing the holding is trustworthy."

"That's the whole question, isn't it?" A long forefinger traced over his nipple. Hot, flickering sensations trailed it, so fast he could barely process them all—the stroke of a tongue, a quick pinch, teeth scraping gently. And over it all, he could sense the tingling rise of her power.

Gawain caught his breath. "You're . . . using magic."

"Ummm hmmm." The finger slid across his chest, circled the other nipple in a kaleidoscope of sensation. Even that small magical contact brought him arching off the bed.

"Dirty pool." He gasped it, barely able to catch his breath.

She grinned wickedly. "Want me to stop?"

"Hell, no!"

"That's what I thought." She started touching him.

Everywhere. Light little brushes of her fingertips—his collarbone, the top of one thigh, his knee, his biceps. And wherever those long nails moved, starbursts of delight trailed until it was all he could do not to writhe.

Gawain had heard of other Majae using magic like this, but none of them had ever tried it on him. Probably, he realized, because he hadn't given them the chance. He'd kept them far too busy wondering what he'd do to them.

But there was definitely something to be said for being on the receiving end.

Lark watched his face, those dark eyes wicked with knowledge and arousal. She knew exactly what she was doing to him, and she loved it.

"God," he moaned. He was usually the one who made other people moan. "You're good at this. Do you do it often?"

Her lips quirked wickedly, and she bent her head down over his. "First time."

And then she took his mouth.

The kiss was soft at first, gentle and questioning. Longing to taste her, he thrust his tongue into her mouth in a careful, licking stroke. She suckled it in . . .

And it felt as if a wet female mouth had engulfed his cock in one hot swoop. Startled, he cried out against her mouth.

"Like that?" Lark purred, and licked his tongue again, a stroke along its underside. A hot echo caressed his cock.

She suckled his tongue slowly, swirling her own around it, tugging gently. And every move she made, he felt in his dick.

Gawain had enjoyed blow jobs by very skilled partners, but none of them had ever felt like this. He was well-endowed enough that it wasn't physically possible for a woman to suck him so fast and deep, but Lark and her magic could do just that.

Even as she worked his tongue and cock, her slender hands stroked him, spilling exquisite sensations over every inch of his skin. It was like being taken by a harem of women, all licking and caressing and sucking at the same time.

Gawain felt the orgasm coil tight in his balls, ready to pump him dry. "I'm coming!" he groaned. There was no way he could hold out against the pleasure.

Lark lifted her head and breathed, "No."

And the rising pulse of his climax just . . . stopped.

For a moment, he couldn't believe she'd dared.

Blazing green eyes met hers. "You little . . . witch."

Lark reached down a hand and closed it gently around the long, smooth length of his erection. "Yes, as a matter of fact, I am." She sent a burst of magic into her fingers and watched with satisfaction as his eyes rolled back in his head.

She liked this.

She'd never experienced anything so erotic in her life as having this big, delicious male animal so thoroughly at her mercy.

And the turnabout was wickedly satisfying. Though he hadn't treated her with condescension, he'd never let her forget which of them was the vampire knight of the Round Table.

Now he writhed in his magical bonds, all that powerful muscle jerking under her fingertips as she stroked him, green eyes burning as he stared hungrily into her face.

If she made the mistake of turning him loose, he'd be all over her, driving that rock-hard cock into her sex and his fangs into her throat.

She was almost tempted. . . .

No. He could damn well just lie there and writhe. A little payback for Diera's broken heart—and the one she suspected was on the way for her.

FOURTEEN

Lark left off kissing Gawain and began to nibble her way along that stubborn chin to the muscled column of his neck. His skin tasted salty with sweat, flavored with the rich musk of vampire.

God, I love that taste.

She continued down his body, licking here, biting there, hands stroking everywhere else. Several times on the way, she felt the boil of his climax on the verge of breaking free and had to stop to calm it. She really didn't want him coming yet.

Besides, it drove him insane when she blocked his orgasm, and she loved that, too.

By the time she stopped off to nibble his belly button, he was grinding his hips against her in furious demand. "You'd better watch it," he growled. "The next time I get you at my mercy, you'll think you were thrown to the big bad wolf."

"What're you going to do, wolfie?" Catching the hard length of his cock in one hand, she watched him out of the corner of one eye and opened her mouth just over the flushed head. "Huff and puff and . . ." A teasing tongue flick tore a gasp from his throat. ". . . blow my house down?"

His green eyes glittered. "Actually, I think I'll just fuck you." He rolled his lips up to expose gleaming fangs. "Hard."

"Wicked man." She swooped her head down over the head of his cock and sucked, simultaneously sending a wave of magic into the hot, smooth shaft.

"Jesu!" His back arched helplessly at the blend of magic and stark carnality.

Oh, yeah, she definitely liked this. Feeling inspired, she cast another spell, this one on herself. Scrambling onto her knees, she angled his cock up with one hand, poised her open mouth over its flushed head, and met his eyes. And watched with satisfaction as his widened in shock.

Lark had fangs.

The white length of them was pressed against the flesh of his cock head, not quite biting. But the threat was definitely there. After that first startled kick of adrenaline, Gawain realized she'd conjured them. "What are you going to do?" he demanded. "Bite me?" His voice sounded hoarse to his own ears.

"Well . . ." She gave him a slow, contemplative lick, as if tasting him. "You certainly seem to enjoy biting *me.*"

His heart was pounding. "Not using my fangs. Or at least, not on your equivalent anatomy."

Lark closed her lips over his cock and suckled, sending yet another wave of delight down the shaft and straight into his balls. His back arched in involuntary reaction. She lifted her head and purred, "How do you know you wouldn't like it?" A mind-blowing lick. "I'll bet I could make you."

"I'd advise against it. You have to let me go sometime. And then . . ." He'd intended the statement as a silken threat, but panting ruined the delivery.

Appearing to consider the point, she gave him a long, slow lick. "On the other hand, I *am* the witch. How are you going to hold me? Any bonds you create . . ." Another lick. ". . . I can magically dissolve."

He bared his teeth. He'd never been more violently aroused in his life. "Maybe I'll just hold you down."

"And maybe I'll tie you up with another spell and . . ." Gently, she raked her false fangs over his cock head. This time he managed not to twist in pleasure. ". . . do this all over again."

He ached to drive his cock into that tight, creamy little body. He ached to bite her. Claim her. Make her beg the way he was so tempted to beg himself. "Remember, darling—fangs or no fangs, you're not the vampire here." He bared his own at her. "I am."

"And I'm the witch." Suddenly she sat up, flung one long leg across his hips and planted a foot against the mattress. Angling his cock upward, she sank down as she met his gaze. "I'm the one with the power."

Feeling tight, wet flesh engulf his length centimeter by silken centimeter, Gawain threw back his head and surrendered. "You certainly are. Merlin's beard!"

"Oh, God." She shuttered her lids, shuddering as she impaled herself. "You feel so . . ."

Her satin ass came to rest on his thighs. He was buried all the way inside her, right to the balls. Unable to resist, he ground upward. "Jesu, Lark, fuck me!" It was a naked plea, but he didn't care.

Gasping, she rose. Slowly, so slowly, wet, snug flesh caressing him, milking the thick shaft. At the apex, she braced her hands on his belly and paused, then ground downward again.

"Let me go," he groaned. "I want to . . ."

Dark eyes met his and narrowed. "No."

"Dammit, Lark . . ."

She growled something defiant under her breath and went right on taking him in slow, torturous strokes that threatened to drive him out of his mind. Losing patience, he surged upward, fighting her for control.

Suddenly he couldn't move. "Lark, dammit!"

Her gaze met his fiercely. "I'm doing you, remember?"

He snarled. "I'm going to get you for this."

She closed her eyes and sank down over him. "I don't care."

Another slow stroke and then another. He wondered if she was ever going to let him come. He wondered if he was going to go insane.

Probably.

But he was damn well going to get her at his mercy, if he had to have Kel put a spell on *her*.

She'd picked up the pace, slick stroke following slick stroke with the weight of her body behind them, maddening and delicious. Gawain felt the pressure building in his balls again and prayed she wouldn't stop him this time.

Lark threw her head back so hard her long hair whipped across his thighs. Gasping, she plunged up and down, until he could feel the tiny pulses of her orgasm start to milk his cock. "Oh, I'm . . . aaaaaaahhhhhhhh!" She twisted.

At last, his climax exploded out of his balls like a cork blasting from a champagne bottle. Gawain roared as he shot and shot, caught in the grip of the most savage orgasm he'd ever had in his long life. Lark's suppression of it had intensified its fury.

At last she collapsed on top of him, sweating and limp. Even if he hadn't been bound, he realized he couldn't have moved if his life depended on it. She'd drained him dry.

"That was . . ." He had to stop, unable to find a word to do it justice.

"Oh, yeah."

"But I'm still going to get you."

Lark lifted her head and gave him a cheeky grin. "I'm looking forward to it."

* * *

An hour later, they attended Avalon's second funeral in a week. Diera and Antonio lay on the flower-decked biers Lark had created for them, the Maja in an elaborate white velvet gown, a bouquet of white roses in her folded hands. Antonio, his body whole again thanks to Lark's magic, wore white hose and boots, and a white velvet doublet that emphasized the width of his shoulders. His hands were folded around the hilt of the sword that lay over his body. Mounds of flowers surrounded them, along with tall candelabra in gleaming gold. Just as Lark intended, the effect suggested a wedding as much as a funeral.

When her time came to speak, she stepped forward and told the Magekind what her magic had discovered about the couple's deaths. Her voice broke only once, and it was only as she returned to Gawain's side that the tears began to roll down her cheeks.

He rested a comforting hand on her shoulder before walking out to the center of the square to speak.

They weren't the only ones. It seemed everyone had something to say about the lovers.

Finally, Lark joined the other Majae in shooting her magic into the biers. She watched the fountain of light explode upward in their final tribute to burst against the stars.

We'll get him, she told her friend's memory. *Richard Edge is a dead man.*

After the ceremony, the knights and selected Majae adjourned to the Round Table chamber to plan their next move. Lark and Gawain entered just behind Soren and Morgana, who were locked in a fierce, low-voiced argument. The dragon had attended the funeral in his human form—a regally handsome man dressed like a medieval courtier in a black tunic and hose. The faint blue tint to his skin was most noticeable on his smoothly shaved head.

"I spent the day arguing with members of the council," Soren said. "They adamantly refuse to drop the wards around the Dragon Lands long enough to let you scan for Edge."

"Then you tell those scaly bastards that we're holding them personally responsible for the next one of our people Edge kills!" Morgana snarled.

"Does she seriously think they'd care?" Kel murmured to Gawain.

"She's always been an optimist," Gawain told him dryly.

Arthur and Guinevere had already seated themselves at the Round Table next to King Llyr Galatyn and his were-wolf wife, Diana, who was visibly pregnant. Llyr was a tall, leanly muscled man whose blond hair fell in a silken stream to his hips. Like the others, he was dressed in full court mourning, the black providing a dramatic contrast to his glorious hair. The tips of his pointed ears protruded through the pale strands, making him look even more elegantly alien. "I've been attempting to call Cachamwri, but he refuses to respond," the king said. "He hasn't cut me off like this since before he helped me defeat Ansgar."

"Well, he is the Dragon God," Diana pointed out. "Maybe he doesn't want to take our side against his people." She was lovely, with her short dark hair and gray eyes so pale they looked silver. Athletic and tall in a black and silver gown that draped over her pregnant curves, she was surrounded by a fierce, restless energy.

"Or maybe he's playing some game we can't even comprehend," Kel pointed out. "You can never tell with Cachamwri."

"Very true." Llyr nodded a greeting. "It's good to see you again, Kel. Gawain."

"Your Majesties." Like the courtier he'd once been, Gawain made a graceful bow, then extended a hand to Lark. "May I present Lark McGuin, my apprentice?"

The Sidhe king turned an iridescent gaze her way and gave her a regal nod. "It's always a pleasure to meet one of Arthur's Majae."

His wife's smile was wide and genuine. "Hi."

Lark blinked at the queen's American manners and managed a curtsey without falling on her face. "Your Majesties."

She listened to Gawain exchange small talk with the royal couple for a few more moments. It was difficult to concentrate on the pleasantries, given how grief-blasted and exhausted she felt.

Though Lark had briefly escaped the reality of Diera's death in Gawain's arms earlier that night, the funeral had brought it all home. Now all she wanted was to escape somewhere and have a good cry.

After that, she'd like to hunt Edge down and gut him with a dull melon baller.

Social amenities finally concluded, Lark and Gawain dipped bows to the couple and headed for the other side of the Round Table. They found empty seats next to Tristan, who was holding a low-voiced conversation with Bors while the knights' respective apprentices flirted.

Not surprisingly, Bors looked even more haggard.

"How long has it been since you had anything to eat?" Gawain asked his friend in a low voice.

Bors shrugged his broad shoulders. "Discovering my son murdered one of my dearest friends seems to have stolen my appetite."

"Merlin's balls, Bors," Tristan said, "you're not responsible for what that vile little creature does."

The knight's eyes glittered. "I raised him. I taught him the blade skills he used to butcher Diera and Antonio. If it's not my fault, who the hell's is it?"

"His, maybe?" Regretting the irritated growl in her voice, Lark rubbed a hand over her forehead and reached for patience.

"We all have regrets." Tristan rested a soothing hand on Lark's shoulder. "I regret not spending more time with my son. If I had, I would have met Lark much sooner, and I could have saved both her and John a great deal of suffering."

"Perhaps it's just as well you didn't," Bors said. "She seems to have turned out well enough."

Lark suddenly discovered she just didn't have the patience for this. "You know, for a guy not much younger than Jesus, you're kind of dumb."

Gawain's eyes widened. "Lark . . ."

She turned on Tristan. "And for the record, you might not have been there the past few years, but you were there long enough to teach Granddad to be a hero." She jerked a thumb at Morgana, who was staring at her in amazement. "That lot might not have thought he was good enough to be a Magus, but by God, he charged those Nazi machine guns on D-Day. And he's still got the barbed wire scars to prove it. Once he pulled an eight-year-old girl out of a burning house and chopped open a blazing roof to save his trapped men. He did that because of you, Tristan. And you." Her eyes went to Bors, then to Gawain. "And you."

She rose to her feet in the ringing silence, breathing hard, suspecting she was making an idiot of herself. And not caring. "You know what? He raised me to be a hero, too. He raised my mom the exact same way, only she decided to become a drunk instead. *She* decided. Not him." Lark gave Bors a burning look. "Just the way Richard Edge decided he wanted to become a monster when he grew up."

Bors stared back. "Lark, I . . ."

Her eyes stung. "Now, if you'll excuse me, I'm going to see my grandfather." With a gesture, she opened a dimensional gate and stepped through.

For a moment Gawain stared at Lark's retreating back, caught somewhere between shock and a desire to cheer. "I'd better not let her go alone." He jumped up and hurried through the gate after her.

He found her standing in a small living room where a tall, elderly man sat in front of a television set. The man, who bore an uncanny resemblance to Tristan, stared up at them in surprise.

"Lark, honey!" He rose to his feet and stepped toward her.

"Granddad . . ." Her breath hitched.

"What's the matter, honey?"

"Diera's dead!" She threw herself into his arms and began to sob.

"Ahhh, honey," the old man said, and stroked her hair, crooning to her as she cried.

Aching to comfort her himself, Gawain instead stepped back to give them privacy. His own eyes stinging, he watched as her grandfather rocked her in his arms.

The following night

Sweat rolled down Richard's naked chest, burning the cuts that marked his flesh. He barely noticed, intent on watching the dragon use a single claw to trace glowing runes into the magical shield that covered him. The pain of sweat salt in his wounds was nothing compared to the sensation of that claw biting deep, carving the intricate pattern of protection directly into the flesh.

Intricate, bloody shapes now covered every inch of his body. Whenever he looked at them, they seemed to writhe. Carving them had taken endless hours of torment.

Richard had the distinct impression the dragon had enjoyed each second of his pain.

Sadistic fuck.

The two of them had worked for two days to create the spell. It was the most complex piece of sorcery Richard had ever participated in, since it was designed to protect him from the grail's destruction, collect the energies liberated in the process, and funnel them into him.

If it failed, he'd be incinerated.

Through the glowing shield, Richard met the dragon's crimson eyes. Yet again, a thought gnawed at his confidence, the same one that had circled his mind through the agonizing process of cutting the runes: *What if he's playing me for a fool? What if he intends to simply destroy us all?*

It was certainly possible. Yet despite Richard's paranoia, he sensed that the dragon hungered for the Magekind's destruction as much as he did. He had no idea why, and in truth, he didn't much care. All that mattered was that the spell work.

"It's done." At last the dragon moved back from the shield and tilted its head, studying the glowing hemisphere. A third set of runes had been carved into the floor of the cavern, forming the circle Richard sat within.

All that work had made him feel better about the process. Surely the dragon wouldn't have spent so many hours creating the patterns if it had only been playing some kind of sadistic game.

"Are you ready, ape?"

Richard was getting royally sick of being called an ape, but he wasn't about to protest now. "I'm ready."

The massive head nodded. "Good." Huge jaws opened, and the creature breathed. Magic rolled from its mouth, forming a dimensional gateway directly over him and the protection spell.

But this was a gateway unlike any Richard had ever seen. It formed a spiraling shape that reminded him of a huge funnel, the spout of which was pointed down at his head. Looking up into the unearthly green swirl, he swallowed.

Then the dragon turned to lift the black grail from where it sat by its side. Balancing the cup on its reptilian palm, it closed its crimson eyes and began to chant.

And the grail began to glow.

Richard's heart started pounding. With each rolling syllable, the cup glowed a little brighter, the light intensifying. First like a stoked bonfire, then a white-hot molten blaze that built steadily into a searing blue-white that made his eyes ache and tear.

Just as he thought he couldn't bear to look at it any longer, the grail exploded. Richard gasped and flinched, but instead of engulfing him as he half expected, the fireball of sparks was sucked upward, flying into the energy funnel like flames up a chimney.

An instant later, the screams began.

He heard them not with his ears but deep in the center of his being, as if his very psyche vibrated to the sound of those mental shrieks.

His cup-mates were dying.

Two minutes earler

Desperation sat like lead in Lark's belly as she scanned the ring of hostile fanged faces that jostled around her, murder in their eyes. Her fear was only slightly relieved by the solid male presence of Gawain at her back, swinging Kel in great glittering arcs as he fought the sorcerers that had them surrounded. To her left, Caroline and Galahad fought back to back, just as Lark and Gawain did. It was the only way to avoid being overrun.

They'd gated in to the cultists' underground temple fifteen minutes ago after Caroline had a vision of its location. Buried deep under the city of Miami, the temple had been magically constructed of bloodred marble and entirely too much gold leaf. Gawain had taken one look and pronounced it a cross between a whorehouse and a mausoleum.

God knew it smelled like there was something dead around there somewhere. The stench of death magic rode the air in a nauseating fog.

A spell sizzled against Lark's shield. Grimly, she shot back with a blast of her own, simultaneously parrying a sword stroke one of the sorcerers aimed at her head.

"You know, Caroline, you might have mentioned there were thirty of these bastards in the nest—before we gated right in the middle of them!" Gawain yelled over the din of screaming voices and hissing fireballs.

"Sorry!" Caroline called back as she battled at her husband's side. "My vision said they had a nest here, not how many of them were in it."

"Maybe we should have checked on little details like that before making the jump." Galahad beheaded a shrieking vampire in mid-lunge. "I'm beginning to feel like Custer at the Little Big Horn."

Lark wasn't feeling all that optimistic herself. She and Kel had formed a joint spell shield, yet it was still all they could do to repel the constant rain of attacks.

Something flashed overhead, so bright and blinding she instinctively ducked, throwing a quick glance at the marble ceiling. Sparks flurried downward, swirling like a blizzard. "Oh, hell!" Lark gasped as they began to drift over the barrier spell she'd created with Kel. "What *is* that?"

To her horror, the flecks of light cut right through the joint shield like tiny razors. Gawain cursed. "Damned if I know. Kel?"

"Death magic," the dragon said grimly.

"I figured. Ow!" Lark flinched as the sparks sank through her armor, only to straighten in surprise. They felt oddly cool as they struck her skin, like snowflakes. "Now, *that* was unexpected."

A sorcerer screamed, a howl of abject terror.

Lark jerked around, her heart in her throat, as a cultist fell back, a swarm of sparks whirling around him like attacking bees. He screamed as they blazed brighter, eating right through the enchanted plate of his armor. A moment later, his bellow spiraled into a shriek of true agony.

"No!" another sorcerer cried. "It's the grail!"

Lark blinked. "What, again?"

As the Magekind stared around in confusion, the cultists fell, writhing, their bodies catching fire under the pelting rain of light. The stench intensified until Lark gagged. Even Gawain coughed.

Until, with a final chorus of screams, the sorcerers dissolved in a collective shower of sparks that rushed upward as though caught in a whirlwind. As Lark watched in wide-eyed awe, the whirlwind vanished into the temple's marble ceiling with a final singing hiss.

The marble ceiling instantly began to glow a sinister red.

"Shit!" Galahad gasped. "The temple's going!"

And since the temple was a hundred feet underground . . .

"Run!" Kel roared, pouring energy from his metallic length to swirl into a dimensional gate big enough for all four of them to leap through at once. Blessing the dragon's quick thinking, Lark dove.

She hit the ground rolling. Gawain landed on top of her, shielding her with his body as dust and bits of rock blew through the gateway, pattering against their armor to the grate and rumble of imploding stone.

A fraction of a second later and they'd have been trapped in the collapse.

Heart in her throat, Lark looked around for her friends. Caroline's gaze met hers through the slit in her visor, eyes wide as she clung to her husband's armored shoulders.

Thank God. Lark blew out a breath in relief.

"You know," Gawain said in her ear, "if somebody was going to destroy that last grail, the least they could have done is warn us."

"Does this mean it's over?" Caroline asked as Galahad rolled to his feet and reached down a hand to help her up.

The two knights looked at each other. "Merlin's beard, I hope so," Galahad said fervently.

Lark frowned as she and Gawain stood and brushed themselves off. "Why do I have the nagging feeling that something's wrong with this picture?"

Gawain snorted. "Because you're justifiably paranoid."

"Or maybe you're just a worrywart." Caroline grinned

at them like a fool. "Some Maja got lucky and found the grail, and she just didn't wait for permission to blow it all to hell."

Lark met Gawain's uneasy gaze. "Let's hope so."

Kel grunted. "Sure didn't smell like Mageverse magic to me."

The ape was howling.

Despite himself, Tegid took a step back. Just as they'd intended, the raw energy of the sorcerers' destruction had roared into the collection spell, then poured down through the shield that covered the creature.

Now the hemisphere was one solid, roiling mass of fire. Somewhere in the middle of it all the ape screamed in howl after high-pitched howl of agony, as fast as it could draw breath.

Tegid frowned. Had he miscalculated? He thought he'd taken all the elements into account . . .

Abruptly the fire died and the screaming stopped. Even the glowing runes winked out. The shield collapsed, leaving the cavern in comparative darkness.

Slowly, Tegid's eyes adjusted until he could make out the ape lying motionless in the center of the circle of runes on the floor.

The creature looked . . . odd. There was something wrong with its head. And its flesh was a deep, dark red, as if it had been burned.

It moved.

Power.

Tegid took a hasty step back as the sensation of raw magic suddenly rolled off the ape's body. The stench of death flooded the room in a cloud rank enough to make even the dragon gag.

As his gorge heaved, the thing groaned and got to its hands and knees. Slowly, it pushed itself upright and rose to its feet.

Tegid blinked in astonishment. It looked . . . bigger. Much bigger. And it had horns. Curling horns that extended from either side of its head. What's more, the ape's red color wasn't a product of burns after all, not as deep and even as it was. The ape's skin had turned crimson, though the runes Tegid cut into it still marked its skin in black, seared lines.

Cachamwri's Breath, Tegid realized, suddenly recognizing the ape's horns and alien coloring. *It looks like a Dark One.*

The thing opened eyes that glowed a bright and reptilian red. "Oh," it said in a sinister rumble, "that's *much* better."

FIFTEEN

Lark listened from the audience as Reece Champion and his wife, Erin, made their report to the High Council.

"I'd just thrown an energy blast when the sorcerer screamed and disintergrated," Erin said. "For a moment, I thought I'd done it, but then I realized my spell wouldn't have had that effect."

"My FBI contacts have reported the same thing," Reece agreed. "They're getting calls from across the country of people exploding." He grimaced. "The press is all over the story, entertaining whatever wild speculation anybody cares to spin. The current theory is that it's some kind of new terrorist superweapon."

Arthur snorted. "They'll get over it. In a year, these *disappearances* will be featured on some program about UFOs." He grinned at Guinivere. "How many of those have we been on now?"

"At least four," she said dryly.

Morgana frowned, obviously in no mood to join the rising tide of relieved joy. "The question is, who did it? Everybody's reported in now, and it wasn't any of us. Soren said it wasn't him either."

"And Llyr swears none of his people was involved," Guinevere agreed, looking no happier. "It couldn't have been one of the werewolves, because they don't work magic." The Magekind had been stunned to discover several weeks ago that Merlin had created a race of werewolves to keep an eye on the Magekind. They'd been living undetected among the mortals for hundreds of years, guarding the secret of their existence ferociously.

"Maybe one of the sorcerers did it accidently," Gawain suggested. "Tried some kind of spell and blew himself right to hell, along with all his little vampire friends."

Next to Lark, Caroline murmured, "Let's hear it for stupidity."

Morgana frowned uneasily. "That seems a little too easy, don't you think?"

Caroline leaned closer to Lark's ear. "Yeah, here we were all set for another battle to the death, and the bad guys went and spontaneously died on us. Doesn't that just suck?"

Lark snorted. "Yeah, tacky of them."

Noticing she'd drawn Morgana's icy gaze, she sank down in her seat. Pissing off the witch was never a good idea.

Bors spoke suddenly from the audience. "What about Richard? Did anyone see my son die?"

Arthur's gaze softened. "No, but if the others are gone, he would be, too."

The knight frowned, his expression caught between pain and hope. "What if he shielded himself somehow?"

Morgana and Guinevere exchanged a glance. "I suppose it's possible, but I doubt seriously he'd have that kind of power," Gwen said. "I detonated a grail myself a few days ago. Those things generate an astonishing amount of magical force. I just don't think he'd be able to shield himself against something like that. And he'd have had to know it was coming."

"What if *he* worked the spell with the help of this dragon of his? If his ally shielded him . . ."

Guinevere and Morgana exchanged another long look. "The thought has crossed my mind," Morgana admitted. "It's certainly worth looking into, but I'm just not sure why he'd do something like that. What would it gain him?"

A muscle worked in Bors's jaw. "Why did he murder Diera and Antonio? Power."

Arthur shook his head. "It would make more sense to simply unite all those sorcerers under his leadership. They'd be able to do more damage collectively than he could with whatever magic he collected from their murders. Even Geirolf, for all his alien power, wanted an army."

Bors considered the idea, his face working with emotions so complex Lark couldn't even read them. "So you think he's dead."

Guinevere studied him, quiet compassion in her eyes. "Yes, Bors, I do."

"I agree," Morgana said crisply. "We'll investigate further, but the odds would seem to favor it."

Bors did not look comforted.

Arthur sat back in his seat with a huff of relief. "If that's the case, this mess is over." A grin slowly spread across his bearded face, white and blinding. "I think it's time for a party."

Tegid watched nervously as the horned ape strode around his chambers. The creature had definitely grown, and not just in size. Magic radiated off it like heat from flowing lava.

Tegid had the uncomfortable suspicion it was now more powerful than he was. *What have I done?*

"Perhaps you should leave before my people detect you," he suggested.

That was all Tegid needed—for Soren or one of his other rivals to sense the power this creature radiated and come to investigate.

The ape made a dismissive gesture. "I've shielded this

chamber. No one can sense anything beyond it. As to leaving, I see no reason to spend power on wards when yours are so strong. And there are all those lovely dragon diplomatic and political forces to keep the Magekind at bay." He grinned suddenly, baring teeth that looked very white against his crimson face. "Besides, by now they'll have realized the other cultists are dead, and they'll assume I am, too. They'll drop their guard, and it will be that much easier to take Arthur."

Tegid drew himself up to his full height and glowered down at the ape. "I do not want that spell worked in my chambers. My people will smell death magic, and they'll know I was involved."

The ape regarded him, horned head tilted. "Why would they care? Oh, I'm sure they'll make all the appropriate sounds of outrage, but secretly, they'll be as delighted to be rid of Avalon as you are. In the long run, it will probably prove to be a political benefit."

Tegid lashed his tail nervously. "Not if I'm a party to working death magic."

"Spray a little air freshener. No one'll know the difference."

Dismayed, Tegid watched the creature pace. It was mad. Yet if he tried to kill it. . . . Well, there was no guarantee he'd win, was there? Not considering the thing's raw power. It not only looked like a Dark One, it felt like one, too.

Better to wait, he decided. An opportunity might present itself to eliminate the ape with minimal danger to himself.

"*Am I the* only one with the nagging feeling that this was all a little too easy?" Lark called over the skirl and thump of an enthusiastic Magekind band.

Gawain snorted. "You call *that* easy?"

She thought of Diera. "God, no. Still, it's hard to believe

Edge just lay down and died without one of us chasing him down and sticking a sword in him. Repeatedly."

"I was kind of looking forward to it myself," Gawain admitted. "But at least we didn't lose any more people."

"Good point." Lark looked around the central square, which was packed with partying, tipsy Magekind. The main fountain bubbled with something amber and alcoholic—a medieval punch that kicked like a mule. Even the vampires were drinking it, though most of them looked as if they were more interested in diluting it with a little Maja first. Almost everybody was either paired off or visibly on the prowl for someone to pair off with.

And they were all dressed for it, too, in jeans, short skirts, and T-shirts, or for the more self-consciously sexy, snug black leather. That included a large number of Sidhe guests and several intimidated-looking mortals—actually werewolves who'd been invited to the party.

"I hope we've seen the last of the full court garb for a while," Lark said. "Velvet makes me itch. And I'm really sick of funerals."

"A wedding or two would be nice, though." Caroline slipped up behind Lark and slung an arm around her neck. She gave them both a tipsy smile as Galahad joined them. "How about it, guys?"

Lark shot Gawain a wary glance, but his face showed none of the panic she'd half expected at the suggestion. Instead, he looked . . . oddly thoughtful.

Her heart began to pound.

But before she could try to decide what he was thinking, the Magekind musicians segued off into a familiar tune. Bors stepped into the center of the square and lifted both hands, one holding his sword. "Blade dance! Come on, fellow knights—let's give the ladies a show!" His eyes were a bit too bright, his grin slightly too wide. When the others hesitated, he brandished the weapon. "Come on, come on! We have a lot to celebrate! A great evil is dead!"

"Excuse me," Gawain said, a hint of a frown between

his brows as he stared at his fellow knight. "I'd better join him before he falls on that sword." His voice dropped to a mutter. "Possibly on purpose."

"I'll go with you," Galahad told him. The two men started threading their way through the crowd.

Bors had spotted Arthur and was dragging him out of the crowd. Laughing, the group drew back to give them room.

"That man is potted," Caroline announced, watching them.

Lark shot her a look. "So are you."

"I'm entitled."

Lark looked at Bors, taking in the strain on his face that neither joking nor alcohol could fully relax. "So is he."

The knights of the Round Table formed a laughing, clapping semicircle, catcalling and taunting each other. They were the elite warriors of the Magekind, the oldest and most skilled of the vampires.

Looking at all twelve together, Lark felt almost over-whelmed by the solid weight of legend: Arthur, Lancelot, Galahad, Bors, Gawain, Tristan, Percival, Marrok, Kay, Cador, Lamorak, and Badulf. They weren't all convention-ally handsome—Kay in particular had just a touch of thug to him—but they were all muscular and athletic, radiating a kind of raw masculinity that would make any woman's li-bido hum.

Then, one by one, they stepped to the center of the half-circle and began to dance as the crowd stood back to watch.

Being men, they turned it into a contest—vying against each other in blurring swordplay and stomping, dazzling footwork, leaping and spinning to the sprightly music of drums, fiddles, and flutes. Some of the single men pulled their shirts off, apparently to ensure the Majae got a good look.

"I'm hot!" Badulf explained over the catcalls of his brother knights.

"You certainly are!" a Maja called back.

He tossed her his shirt. She caught it, grinning like a

woman who'd just captured something a lot more interesting than a little sweaty cotton.

Lark hooted and clapped as Badulf began to dance in a blatant bump and grind.

"Hell of a show, huh?" Caroline yelled over the crowd noise, appearing at her side with two cups of that deadly Mageverse punch. She handed Lark one and took a drink of her own.

Lark was just tilting her cup up when Tristan swaggered into the center of the circle, pulling off his shirt. She choked. "Ack! Noooo!" Slapping her free hand over her eyes, she spun around as Caroline hooted at her. "Tell me when it's over!"

"Oh, come on, Lark! Tristan's a stud."

"Shut. Up!"

"Man, look at those abs."

"You're married!"

"But I'm not blind. Oooo! *Nice* move."

"That's my great-grandfather you're lusting after, you perv!"

"Yeah, but you've gotta admit, he's extreeeemely well-preserved."

Lark shuddered. "Just tell me when it's over."

Five interminable minutes later, Caroline, giggling like a hyena, told her it was safe to turn around.

Arthur had stepped into the center of the group. Lark settled back to watch, sipping her concoction.

He wasn't the handsomest of the knights—that was Tristan, much as she hated to admit it—nor was he particularly tall, though he was solidly muscled. But there was something about him that riveted the eye, something he seemed to radiate like his own kind of magic. Looking at him, Lark suddenly saw why his knights were willing to follow him without question, despite his sometimes spectacular temper. He might hold an elected position on the High Council now, but he was still king. And he always would be.

Then he began to move, slowly at first, a slight smile quirking his dark beard as he rolled his narrow hips. Almost lazily, he whirled Excalibur, first simply by rotating his wrist so the great sword described a glittering circle. Then he tucked his left arm in close and broadened the movement so the blade spun around him in a blur of light. His feet moved faster and faster, heels clicking on the cobblestones. Lark grinned, realizing he was wearing cowboy boots. As the drums beat faster, he segued into more complex sword work, as though fighting imaginary enemies, powerful shoulders flexing under the thin black fabric of his T-shirt.

"You know, Arthur is really sexy." Caroline said in her ear, sounding increasingly tipsy after all that lethal punch.

Lark shook her head. "You really are a perv."

"Oh, God, you're right." Caroline's eyes widened in horror. "I'm lusting for King Arthur. Is that, like, blasphemy or something? I'm going to hell, aren't I?"

"Hey, Arthur!" Galahad promptly called. "My wife thinks you're hot!"

Arthur stopped dancing to throw his head back in a roar of laughter.

From somewhere in the crowd, Guinevere yelled, "Keep your distance, wench!"

"Oh, God," Caroline moaned, covering her face with both hands. "Just kill me now. Please."

Lark grinned, watching Arthur walk over to Galahad and slap him on the back as the two laughed. "Don't sweat it, Caro. I think he's flattered."

She parted her fingers, revealing glittering dark eyes. "I'm going to kill my husband. I'm going to turn him into a frog. Better yet, something without a dick. Do frogs have dicks?"

Biting her lip to suppress her hoot of laughter, Lark managed, "I have no idea."

"Don't you 'Now, Caroline' me!" her friend called across the crowd, apparently reacting to something Galahad

had said in their Truebond link. "Keep it up, Kermit, and you'll be guest of honor on a plate of frog legs."

Lark wrinkled her nose. "Ewww."

"Dream on!" Caroline shouted, apparently still arguing with her husband.

Galahad left the line of knights and stalked toward them, a gleam of heated determination in his eyes, a half-smile on his lips. The crowd around them broke into cheers.

"Yeep!" Caroline retreated, holding out a hand to ward him off. "Keep your distance, Kermie!" She squealed when he pounced, snatching her into his arms. "You put me down right this minute, or I swear you'll be looking for a froggy wheelchair!"

"We'll just see who eats whom, Miss Piggy," he rumbled, striding away. "I find I have a sudden craving for witch."

Lark wasn't at all surprised when Caroline twined her arms around her husband's muscular neck and kissed his ear, giggling boozily.

Grinning, Lark turned to see Gawain step to the center of the circle. His eyes were fixed on hers, so hot and male with sexual demand, she forgot her amusement in a surge of instant heat.

He swung his sword up in an arc over his head, and as he did, Kel spilled a river of sparks in his wake.

"Show off!" Arthur shouted.

Gawain laughed, but he didn't stop, spinning the sword over his head and around his body. With every move he made, sparks fell over his rocking hips, or the bunch and play of his thighs under his jeans.

In contrast to the frenetic athleticism the other knights had displayed, Gawain moved almost lazily, forcing the music to slow into a suggestive, rocking beat.

And his eyes never left hers.

Lark stared back at him, enthralled by the play of muscle in his arms and shoulders as he spun the sword. The drifting flecks of light illuminated his face, throwing the strong facial bones into stark relief. His mouth parted, and she felt the sheer sexual kick of it all the way to her heart.

Still rotating the sword, he turned his back, leaving her to stare at the sweeping line formed by broad shoulders and narrow waist. The muscled cheeks of his backside worked as he danced, each rock of his hips reminding her of the sensation of his cock sliding deep into her sex in a long, thick glide. Her nipples peaked and her mouth went dry.

Slowly, he pivoted to face Lark again. His gaze locked on hers. She gasped at the blatant sexual promise in his eyes.

"Dammit," some Maja in the crowd said, "he never looked at me that way!"

Everyone laughed—except Lark and Gawain. She was too hypnotized by him, by each move and flex of his big body. She barely noticed as the lights of the square began to go out one by one, extinguished by Kel's magic, until the only illumination came from the slowly rotating sword.

The laughter died to silence as a mood of thick, heavy sensuality descended over the Magekind crowd. Behind Gawain, even the knights had gone still, their attention focused on their chosen partners in the crowd.

The music swelled to a crescendo as Gawain suddenly thrust the sword over his head. Kel stopped spilling sparks and began to glow like a torch, so bright Lark's eyes stung.

Abruptly the light went out, plunging the square into darkness.

A sound rose, a kind of collective male growl, starkly sexual with hunger. A woman gasped a man's name. Another woman squealed as her partner grabbed her.

Lark's heart was pounding. She blinked hard, trying to clear her dazzled vision.

By the time her eyes adjusted, Gawain was standing right in front of her, stark hunger in his eyes.

"Run," he breathed.

Without thinking, she obeyed, whirling to push her way

through the crowd with him right behind her. Somebody laughed. "In a hurry, Gawain?"

She ignored the woman and kept going until she shoved her way clear.

"Run," he rumbled again.

Lark flung herself into a sprint, not questioning why, knowing only that her entire body throbbed with erotic heat. Behind her, she heard the swift pad of his running feet. Her nipples drew into tight points as she imagined what he'd do when he caught her.

And he would catch her.

The racing thud of his feet grew closer as he gained on her with every step. Her heart began to pound in the hard rhythm of arousal. He'd pounce on her in a moment, just take her down and . . .

Lark sensed him grab. Instinctively she veered, grinning at his growled curse as he missed. Shooting through a stone gateway, she fled into the park that lay beyond it. The air smelled sweetly potent with the scent of Mageverse flowers. Banks of pale blossoms nodded in the cool breeze as she ran, and a fountain tinkled somewhere nearby. Hearing the crunch of a footstep right behind her, she darted behind an oak. A big hand flashed past, barely missing her as she ducked. Laughing, she whirled around the tree—

And ran right into Gawain's brawny arms. They snapped around her like a trap springing shut, strong and warm.

His grin at her startled yelp was more than a little predatory. "Dinnertime."

"Not quite." Lark grabbed him around one shoulder, hooked an ankle behind his, and tried to throw him as she'd been taught. It was like trying to toss a marble statue.

Gawain's grin only broadened. "You must be joking."

The next thing she knew, she was the one on the ground, pinned under his hard strength. Lark gasped, helplessly, impossibly turned on.

He reared over her and flipped her onto her belly. Something rattled, and Lark felt metal encircle her wrists and click shut.

"Hey!" She squirmed, but Gawain had already hauled one of her feet up and back. *Click.* Lark glowered over her shoulder and saw he'd locked one cuff of a set of shackles around her ankle. "Are you chaining me up?"

Gawain grabbed her left foot and clicked another cuff around it. Chains rattled musically. "Yep." His eyes glittered at her. "If you'll recall, I told you I would when you tied *me* up."

Kel must have conjured the bonds for him; he hadn't had them earlier. Her gaze flicked to the sword, but the dragon had gone stiff and metallic again.

Gawain grabbed the back of Lark's T-shirt and pulled. *Riiiiiip.*

"Cut that out!" She tried to kick at him, but with her ankles and wrists bound, she couldn't move. "You're not stripping me in public!"

"Yes. . . ." *Snap.* Her right bra strap collapsed. "I am." He pulled again, and her left strap dropped to the grass in front of her eyes.

We'll just see about that, buddy. Lark concentrated, trying to dissolve Kel's cuffs with her magic, but the steel remained stubbornly solid.

Another series of tugs and ripping fabric, and Gawain calmly pulled off her bra. She thought about conjuring a new one, but a blade of grass stroked over one hard nipple.

Oh, what the hell. Everybody in Avalon was off getting laid anyhow.

Riiiiiiip. Gawain had started work on her jeans.

"You know, I could make those disappear for you."

"But I want to tear them off." Desire and wicked humor deepened his voice to a rumble of lust. A minute later, he tossed the last scraps of fabric aside.

And Lark was definitely creaming.

He turned her over on her back, and she tensed, waiting

for his touch. Instead he rose to his feet and reached for the hem of his shirt. As she watched, he pulled it off over his head, revealing the ripple and play of tanned muscle across his broad, powerful chest. Toeing off his running shoes, he reached for the fly of his jeans.

A long, magnificent erection angled upward under the tough fabric. Lark licked her lips as his zipper hissed. His eyes never left her face as he grabbed his waistband and pulled jeans and boxers down. His cock thrust free, bobbing hungrily as he pushed his pants down his brawny thighs.

Lark's heart was pounding like a kettledrum by the time he threw his jeans aside. She swallowed. "What exactly do you have in mind?"

Gawain sat down on the grass beside her and calmly took off his socks. His green eyes were hot with hunger and pure possessive male satisfaction as he looked over her bound nudity. "Payback."

That was what she'd been afraid of. She licked her lips. "What kind of payback?"

Gawain flipped her across his thighs and lifted one big hand over her ass. He grinned toothily. "What do you think?"

Lark stared at him, outraged. "You are *not* going to spank me!"

"Actually, I am." His palm smacked down. She jolted against his legs with a yelp born more of astonishment than pain. The swat had been too light to really hurt.

Another swat, this one stinging. She yowled in earnest. "I'm going to turn you into a rabbit!"

"Not a frog?" Another meaty slap.

She tried to kick with her bound feet. "Poetic justice. All you want to do is fuck!"

"Not so." A rain of quick smacks hot enough to make her squirm. "I also like to bite."

"Ooow! I'm warning you, Bunnicula . . ."

"I should have asked Kel for a gag." *Smack!*

"Jerk!"

"Jerk? Is that the best you can do?" *Smack!* "No threatening to turn me into rabbit stew?" *Smack!* "A rabbit fur coat?" *Smack!* "A rabbit's foot?" *Smack!*

Panting, she managed, "How about a rabbit-shaped vibrator? That way I can shove a D-battery up your . . ." *WHACK!* "Oooww!"

"If anybody's going to shove anything anywhere, it's going to be me." He ran caressing fingertips over her backside, soothing the sting. Lark drew in a quick breath at the sensation. "You know, your ass has turned a really pretty pink. It's giving me an erection."

"What *doesn't* give you an erection?"

"Where you're concerned, not much." He ran a hand down her bottom and between her thighs. A finger stroked, probed. She moaned as it slid deep. "Why, you kinky little witch! You're creaming."

"Duh." Another deep stroke. She laid her cheek against the grass and groaned.

"I think I've made an error in judgment."

Oh, God, please don't stop! "Yeah, you've pissed off a witch."

"No." Another delicious stroke. "I chained your legs *together.*"

She grinned into the grass. "Dummy."

He caught her by one calf and pulled her legs up until he could reach the chain around her ankles. But instead of freeing them both, he only unfastened the right cuff.

A moment later, he had her left wrist chained to her left ankle. Her jaw dropped in outrage. "You are *so* not hogtying me!"

"Don't bet on it, Miss Piggy." He was already repeating the process with her right arm and leg.

"I'm going to get you for this. I'm plotting my revenge right now!"

"I really should have asked Kel for that gag." He turned

her over on her back. "Well, at least I know one way to shut you up."

She glowered at him, halfway between laughter and arousal. "Only if you want me to bite it off."

He pushed her knees apart and settled between her thighs. As he lowered his head toward her deliciously spread sex, he lifted a blond brow. "Want to reconsider that suggestion?"

Her eyes widened as he swirled his tongue over her clit. "Sir Gawain, I promise I would never, ever bite any—Oh, God!—sensitive parts of your anatomy." His next long lick had her throwing her head back. Panting, she added, "And I really hope you won't use those big, sharp teeth on mine!"

Gawain grinned wickedly as he caught her nipples in both hands. "Would I do that to you?" Tracing the tip of his tongue around her clit in a delicious figure eight, he tugged the captured peaks. The stark pleasure made her squirm, despite the friction of the grass against her well-paddled butt. He drew back, twisting her nipples delicately. Green eyes glittered up at her. "Especially after the way you teased me and tormented me and wouldn't let me come?"

"What was I thinking?"

"You were thinking I wouldn't do this." His stiffened tongue thrust up her core in a long, taunting stroke.

Her spine arched. "Actually, I kind of hoped you would."

"Bad girl." Another delicious, liquid tongue swirl as he teased and stroked her breasts.

Lark lifted her head and smiled hopefully. "Maybe you should punish me with your cock until I beg for mercy?"

His head lifted, revealing a truly evil grin. "Now, there's a thought."

One minute his face was between her thighs. The next, he loomed over her, his body covering hers. She blinked up at him as he reached down to aim himself. "You're fast."

He lifted a brow. "Not that fast."

He proved it as he slid into her one slow, delicious inch at a time, in a seductive satin glide. "Oh, Merlin's Beard!"

"You know . . ." Another inch. ". . . he didn't really have a beard."

"Who cares?" She threw her head back. "God!"

Gawain's balls rested against her backside now, and she could feel his entire length stuffing her. Slowly, he began to pull out. She writhed against him, pulling helplessly at her bonds.

With a dark smile, he settled down over her until every inch of his hard, powerful body pressed against every inch of her soft one. Taking his time, he pumped, slow and deep at first, each stroke teasing her tight, creaming channel. The fingers of one hand threaded through her hair, pulling her head back and to the side. He breathed against her neck and drove his cock a little deeper, a little harder, a little faster.

Lark shivered, knowing what he was going to do, feeling the first hot pulses of her orgasm. She tried to wrap her arms around him, but she was still trussed and helpless.

And he was anything but, pumping that massive cock in and out as he slowly licked the pulse in her throat.

She was so close, she couldn't stand it. "Gawain, oh! Please . . ."

Pump. Pump. Pump. Relentless as a machine. The tips of his fangs brushed her skin as he opened his mouth.

"Gawain!" Teetering on the edge.

He bit deep. A sting of pain, barely felt in the hot pleasure of his surging cock. He began to drink, thrusting in short, hard digs.

With a helpless shriek, Lark came, pleasure surging in a foaming burn over her body, making her writhe.

He shoved his cock to the balls and stiffened, growling against her throat as he came, pumping her full of his come as he took her blood.

SIXTEEN

"Help," *Lark moaned* sometime later, as Gawain turned her over and unlocked her cuffs. "I've been eaten by the Big Bad Wolf." Her freed limbs flopped, limp as noodles. She felt way too sated to move.

He laughed. "And a delicious meal you were, too, little pig."

She opened one bleary eye. "Little Red Riding Hood. I refuse to be a pig."

Gawain threw himself down next to her and pulled her into his arms. "Well, you do have a very nice basket of goodies."

"On the other hand, you don't look like anybody's grandma." She worked up just enough energy to manage a slow kiss. "Though you do have really big . . . teeth." Smiling lazily, she ran her tongue over one of them.

With a mock growl, he dragged her close and kissed her thoroughly.

Just as she put a hand down to discover whether any other parts of him had gotten big, again, Morgana's voice breathed into their minds in a general psychic call—the last part of the assignment spell. *In case you haven't*

*realized this yet, Arthur would like me to announce that
with the war over, the apprenticeships are now officially
dissolved. Good work, everyone.*

Lark froze.

"And that couldn't have waited for a phone call sometime *tomorrow?*" Gawain rolled his eyes. "That woman
loves to stick her mind in other people's heads."

She looked into his face, feeling stricken. He no longer
had a reason to stay with her. And without the pretext of the
mission, how long would it be before his attention began to
wander? "I guess that's it, then." Lark started to pull away.

His arms tightened, holding her in place. "Hey, wait a
minute. You're not going anywhere." He flashed her a ro-
guish grin. "The Big Bad Wolf's not finished with your
goodies yet."

But what happens when you are?

Gawain frowned suddenly, arching his back. "On second thought, I think I want to eat my goodies in a real bed.
Preferably one that doesn't have rocks digging into my
ass." He smiled into her eyes. "Let's go home."

She stared into his face, hesitating. What should she do?

Gawain went still. "What?" Alarm stirred in his eyes.
"Did I hurt you?"

"No." *Not yet.*

He looked relieved a moment before his frown returned.
"Then what's the problem? Because you're definitely not
happy."

Lark sat up and started looking for her clothes, then remembered he'd shredded them. After conjuring a set of re-
placements, she got to her feet.

"Would you talk to me?" He was looking irritated now.
"What did I do to piss you off?"

"Nothing."

He grabbed his jeans from the rosebush they lay across
and began putting them on. "That sounds like one of those
nothings that's definitely a something. *What is the problem?*"

Gathering her courage, she met his eyes. "Why do you want me to go home with you?"

"What do you mean?" He looked around for his shirt, found it balled up on the grass, and put it on.

She watched him look for his shoes and scuff his feet into them. Was there any way to ask this without sounding like an idiot? Probably not. But she had to know anyway. "Is it just for sex?"

For an instant, she thought she saw a flicker of fear in his eyes before he grinned. "Isn't that enough?"

She turned away and started toward her brownstone.

Gawain cursed, looked around for Kel, snatched the sword up off the grass, and hurried after her as he looped the scabbard over his shoulder. "I was kidding. Look, you took me off-guard. If this is one of those do-you-love-me things . . ."

"I'm not looking for a declaration of love." She'd have to be an idiot.

"Then what are you looking for?"

Lark stopped and turned to face him. "I don't know." She sighed and raked her hands through her hair. "Everybody says you're going to break my heart. As long as we were together because of the assignment, I didn't have to worry about it. But if we're going to be *together* together . . . that's another thing."

"Lark, we've only known each other a week."

"Which means I can still cut my losses." She turned away again.

"So you're just going to walk off because of something I *might* do?" He glared, temper steaming off him in waves that were almost visible. "I didn't think you were a fucking coward, Lark!"

That stopped her in her tracks. For a moment, she looked down at her feet, searching for the words to make him understand. "It's like Tristan said. You've had some of the most beautiful, powerful women in Avalon. What am I?"

"A hell of a lot more than you realize, apparently.

I think I'm falling in love with you." He said the last quietly, so quietly she almost believed him.

She met his demanding gaze. "See, that's the thing. If you were in love with me, you'd *know* it."

Gawain watched as she turned and walked away again. "Dammit, Lark!" He started to charge after her.

Give her a minute, Kel said.

She's doing the exact same shit she always does—convincing herself she's not good enough!

And just like all the other battles she's fought, this is one she's going to have to win on her own. You need to give her time.

Fuck that. He wanted her. He wanted to hold her and take that pretty mouth and shake some sense into that stubborn head.

The dragon craned his head around until he could look up at him. *Are you in love with her?*

He sighed. *Just how much of the conversation did you hear?*

Morgana woke me.

In other words, all of it. *Yeah. Yeah, I am.* Though he hadn't realized it until the words came out of his mouth. *And yes, I know it's only been a week. Doesn't seem to matter.*

You've never had a problem recognizing what you want.

No. He sighed. *Wish I'd handled it better, though. Maybe if I'd done the hearts and flowers thing when I saw where the conversation was going, I could have headed her off. Instead I panicked. Dammit.*

So give her a day to think about it and try again. Flowers. Boxes of candy. All the human mating rituals.

Gawain snorted. *In my day, the human mating ritual was to give her father a cow.*

Perhaps . . . something a little less old-fashioned.

"Damn it, Bors, would you at least try being reasonable?"

It was Arthur's deep voice, rumbling somewhere behind him. "The man is dead."

Merlin's Beard, what now? For a moment Gawain considered going after Lark anyway before reluctantly turning and heading for the sound of his liege's voice.

"I'm telling you. He's. Not. Dead!" Bors gritted. He, Arthur, and Guinevere stood in the light of a street lamp a block or so back. The royal couple looked frustrated. Bors stood with his arms folded, a stubborn expression on his face. "This is not over," he told them.

With a sigh, Gawain broke into a trot.

"Bors, when that last black grail blew, it killed everyone," Gwen said patiently. "Arthur and I were there when it took out the nest in Dallas, and I sensed the amount of power it generated. Every vampire there died instantly. You heard the reports—the same thing happened everywhere. Nobody survived, including Richard."

"*He did it,* Gwen. I can feel it in my bones. He's responsible for this, and he's still alive."

"Bors . . ." She broke off, stiffening, her eyes going wide.

"Gotta admit, Dad," a deep voice rumbled from behind her, "when you're right, you're right."

A monster materialized right behind Guinevere, one huge crimson hand wrapped around her head. Fingers the size of cucumbers opened, and she dropped in a heap. The thing grinned. "I'd have killed her, but you know, that True-bond thing . . . can't have you dying, Arthur. Yet."

"Fuck!" Gawain broke into a run. "Kel!"

"On it."

The Dragon armor materialized around him between one racing step and the next.

"Guinevere!" It was a roar of agony. Arthur grabbed for the sword he always wore sheathed at a blue-jeaned hip.

WHOOOOM!

As if in slow motion, Gawain saw the blast hit Arthur and Bors, picking them up and throwing them like poker chips in a hurricane. Arthur crashed backward into a tree. Gawain didn't see where Bors went.

He didn't break stride as he reached his foe, swinging Kel with all his strength right at the monster's gut.

A sword materialized in one big red hand, and the thing parried his blow as it backhanded him with the other.

It was like being hit by a train. The world went white in an explosion of pain.

Get up! Kel howled in Gawain's head.

He lay on the ground. He didn't even remember falling. Despite his helm, the side of his head throbbed viciously. Somewhere close by, he could hear the clash of swords and shouted curses. "Arthur?" Gawain scrambled to his feet, swaying, and looked around.

The liege of the Magi sagged in the cradling limbs of a nearby downed tree, limp as a broken doll. The jagged butt of a tree branch protruded from one thigh, and his body was covered in blood. Apparently the branch had punctured the something critical.

Looking beyond him, Gawain could see Bors and the monster battling each other, their swords ringing with every blow. He needed to help his fellow knight, but first he had to tend Arthur, who was in no shape to transform and heal. He staggered toward his liege.

We've got to make this quick, Kel told him. *I armored Bors and gave him a sword, but Edge is kicking his ass. Let's heal Arthur and help.*

Edge? That monster is Edge?

'Fraid so. Kel beamed a spell at the branch, which flared white and vanished. Another spell stopped the scarlet flow. Gawain sheathed Kel and gingerly lifted his liege in his arms, ignoring the copper reek of blood.

As he lay Arthur on the grass, the Magus stirred and moaned. Dazed eyes opened and promptly filled with fear. "Guinevere! Where's Gwen? I can't feel her!"

"Comatose but alive. She's still lying in the street where we left her, but I can't seem to snap her out of it," Kel told him. "Edge took her out with some kind of spell. She'll be fine if we can kill him and break it, but I doubt we'll be able to wake her in the meantime."

Arthur's eyes snapped wide. *"That* was *Edge?"* With a grunt of effort, he sat up and looked at Kel. "Have you called for reinforcements?"

"Can't get through. He's got some kind of barrier spell up. The bastard must have power to burn."

A voice spoked from behind them. "As a matter of fact, I do."

Still supporting Arthur, Gawain turned.

The towering monster that had been Richard Edge gave them a mocking little bow. Behind him, Bors sprawled on the grass, dead or unconscious.

"What the hell did you do to yourself, boy?" Arthur growled.

Edge grinned, revealing a mouthful of razored teeth. "Just a little spell. Or two."

He was more than seven feet tall, his body heavily muscled. Black horns curved to either side of his head, massive as those of a water buffalo. His feet had become cloven hooves, and his hands ended in long, knife-like claws. He wore only a black loincloth that revealed a great deal of crimson skin, every inch of which seemed to be covered with Draconian runes that looked as if they'd been burned into his flesh.

"Tegid," Kel snarled. "I recognize his marks. My uncle is your partner, isn't he, you bastard? I can smell him on you, underneath the stench of rot."

Edge tilted his horned head, looking interested. Then he shrugged. "Actually, he never mentioned his name." He grinned, flashing those horrific teeth again. "I do know he doesn't much care for you, though. You don't suppose he's the one who put you in that sword?"

Quick as a fastball pitcher, he hurled a spell blast that blazed at it struck Kel's shield. To Gawain's horror, it started sinking inside, slowly penetrating.

"Richard!" Bors's voice was a raw howl of rage.

Edge spun as the knight raced toward him, his sword drawn back. "Ooops. Daddy's up, and he's pissed." He ducked as Bors swung at him.

As the two began to fight again, Gawain threw another glance at the death spell that was still trying to eat through Kel's shield.

"Damn, this bastard's powerful," Kel growled. Gawain felt him pour more magic into the shield until the spell finally winked out. "He's almost as strong as Geirolf."

And Geirolf had nearly destroyed them all.

Arthur's face went cold and blank behind its mask of drying blood. "Well, we killed Geirolf, and we'll get this bastard, too. Can you armor me?"

"Yes, but can you fight?"

"I can always fight."

Armor materialized around Arthur as Gawain spotted Excalibur and dragged it out of the wreckage of the tree. He handed it to his liege, one eye on Edge and Bors, whose battle had carried them farther into the garden. They circled one another, snarling insults as they searched for an opening to attack.

Arthur roared his battle cry and charged toward the combatants. Gawain leaped in his wake.

They'd fought together for sixteen hundred years in battles with everyone from Modred to Al Qaeda. As if the move were choreographed, the three knights split to encircle Edge like a trio of wolves, settling into the cold clarity of combat.

Edge pivoted, more bullfighter than bull, the biggest damn sword Gawain had ever seen in one hand. Gawain and Bors shot a glance at one another and went for him. With one hard sweep of his blade, he parried their simultaneous attacks, then whirled aside as Arthur tried to take his head from behind. His sword licked out and sliced into the knight's right shoulder, cutting deep. Arthur reeled backward, struggling to hold on to Excalibur.

"Traitor!" Bors swung at Edge's gut, but missed when the creature leaped aside. "I'm glad your mother didn't live to see what you've become!"

"I'm exactly what you made me, Dad." Edge dropped to one knee, grabbed Bors's sword hand, and jerked him forward, right onto those waiting horns. Twisting his head like a bull, he threw the knight across the clearing with a splatter of blood. He hit the ground and didn't move.

"Bors!" Gawain stepped in with a hard, flat sword stroke, only to be deflected by another teeth-rattling parry. Before he could sweep in again, Edge reversed his stroke and caught him hard across the ribs.

With a strangled cry of agony, he staggered, fighting to keep his feet.

The killer bared his teeth in a grin. "Bet that stings."

And it did. Cold fire burned along his side, so vicious he barely managed to duck Edge's next swing.

Excalibur flashed as Arthur moved in, hacking at Edge with the sword in his left hand. His right arm hung, blood rolling down it to drip on the grass. The killer parried with no apparent effort.

Spotting an opening, Gawain struck out at Edge's thigh, forcing him to leap back. Daring a quick look, he saw that Bors still wasn't moving.

Is he dead?

No, but Edge gored him badly. And he's bloodied you, too, the dragon told him. *He cut right through your cuirass.*

Kel was right. Something hot rolled down his side from the source of the cold pain.

Grimly, he parried three teeth-rattling sword blows, aware of Arthur circling, limping on his wounded leg as he looked for an opening. The blood was flowing faster now, pouring from his injured arm.

Realization hit Gawain, cold and sickening: they were losing. Retreat was their only chance. They'd have to gather reinforcements and come back for the bastard. *Can you cast a gate?*

I've tried. The same shield that's keeping me from calling out is blocking that, too.

The two knights engaged Edge grimly, trying to break through his guard. He parried every attack almost casually. The creature was fast—much faster than either of them. And worse, he was even stronger; it was all Gawain could do to block his attacks.

Then, abruptly, Edge lowered his weapon and straightened from his fighting crouch. "I think it's time to wrap this up. I've got a busy night planned."

Gawain opened his mouth to sneer a retort, but before he could speak, Edge lashed out, hitting Arthur in the helm with a blurring backhand that sent him flying.

With a roar of rage, Gawain charged in, bringing his blade up and around in a scything blow intended to decapitate.

Edge parried, stepped inside his guard, and buried his hand in Gawain's gut so hard, it lifted him off his feet.

Hot agony stabbed into him, and he lost his grip on Kel. The dragon's wings slipped from around his hand and the sword tumbled to the ground. Gagging, Gawain clawed at the hand that held him off the ground.

With a sense of horror, he saw blood dripping from around the creature's fingers. Edge had impaled him on those knife-like claws, punching right through his armor.

From the corner of his eye, he saw that huge sword lift over his head. The bastard was going to decapitate him as he hung there helpless.

Before Edge could strike, an energy blast boiled upward from his feet—Kel, launching a desperate attack. The monster staggered back, losing his grip. Gawain screamed as his own weight tore him free from those claws. He hit the ground in a rattle of armor, paralyzed by the tearing agony in his gut.

As if from a great distance, he heard Arthur roar. Sword clashed on sword, and light exploded over his head. Arthur bellowed in pain.

"Enough of that," Edge snapped. "You and I have business, Pendragon. We're going to finish what Geirolf started."

"Fuck you!" Arthur rasped, his voice weak.

Blood filled Gawain's mouth, but he struggled to lift his head and push himself to his hands and knees. Magic foamed to his left with the telltale tingle of an opening dimensional gate.

Edge had picked Arthur up and thrown him over one shoulder like a sack of meal. He held Excalibur in the other hand.

Gawain tried to lunge at them, but his treacherous legs gave, dumping him on the grass. Clutching his bleeding gut, he watched the gate wink out behind Edge and Arthur. "No."

A swarm of black fireflies descended on him and carried him away.

Irritated with herself, Lark stalked down the cobblestone street, looking for Gawain.

She'd been about to climb the steps of her brownstone when she realized he was right. She was being a coward.

They needed to talk.

Assuming, that is, she could find him. He wasn't at his house; she'd checked there first. And Kel wasn't answering her calls.

If Gawain was already off getting laid, she swore to Merlin she'd . . .

Something was lying in the illumination of a street lamp. It looked like a body.

Frowning, Lark broke into a run, then skidded to a halt as she stared down at the still, familiar form. Cold horror rolled over her. "Guinevere?"

And if Guinevere was here, where was Arthur?

Heart pounding in sickly beats, Lark dropped to one knee and laid two fingers against the unconscious woman's throat. There wasn't a mark on her, and her pulse was steady and strong.

But she stank.

Oh, shit. Lark recoiled, her sense of sick dread increasing. She knew that smell. Death magic.

But all the sorcerers were dead. . . .

Apparently not all of them, idiot. Grimly, Lark sent a spell rolling across the unconscious woman's still form, trying to break the enchantment that held her. Nothing happened.

Don't panic, just call Morgana. She'll know what to do. Summoning her magic, Lark reached for the Maja's mind.

And slammed right into yet another magical barrier that was obviously designed to prevent communication from anyone in the area.

What the hell was going on?

Frowning, she sat back on her heels, and conjured a pillow and blanket to cover the unconscious witch.

It was apparently all she could do. Damn it to hell.

In the distance, someone groaned.

Lark looked around spotted something shining in the moonlight between the trees of the park next door. Armor?

"Good God!" She leaped to her feet, conjured her own armor and sword, and ran.

There, in the middle of a circle of trampled, bloody grass, lay two men, both bleeding and still. One was wearing armor that was all too familiar. There was no sign of their attacker, though the soft earth was churned with tracks.

Hoofprints?

"Gawain!" Her heart in her throat, Lark dropped to her knees beside him. He lay facedown. She started to turn him over, then hesitated, not sure how badly he was hurt.

"Help him." Kel's voice sounded from the grass a few feet away. "I can't heal him. Hell, I can't even get him to come around. He's too badly wounded. There was something nasty on that bastard's claws."

Claws? "What about Bors?"

"Here." The knight groaned again, and she realized his was the voice she'd heard. "I think . . . I think I can change."

Magic flared around him. When it faded, a black wolf lay sprawled on the bloody ground. He rose to his feet and shook himself, whole again, before trotting toward her.

Gawain, however, wasn't even conscious, so changing was out of the question for him. And since he was the source of Kel's major magic, if he was too badly hurt, Kel had nothing to draw on. She threw a look at the sword. "Drop his armor. Let me touch him."

Even as she reached for him, the enchanted scale and plate melted away. Lark rested a hand on the small of his bare back—and winced at what she sensed.

He'd been all but gutted. A human would already be dead of such wounds.

Closing her eyes, Lark let the Mageverse pour through her hands and into him, healing his horrific injuries, forcing his body to regenerate the blood he'd lost.

"Arthur . . ." The word was so faint, at first she wasn't sure he'd spoken at all. "He's got Arthur."

Lark went cold. "Who?"

"Richard," Bors said. He'd returned to human form while she'd been distracted. "He attacked us."

Gawain lifted his head. His hair was matted with blood, his eyes wide. "He took Arthur."

Lark stared at him in horror. "Edge is dead. He must be—the last grail was destroyed!"

"He survived," Kel said, sounding stronger now that Gawain had recovered. "My uncle helped him."

"What? How?"

Gawain pushed himself onto his hands and knees. Magic rolled over him as Kel clothed him in his usual jeans and shirt. "He said he and Arthur were going to finish what Geirolf started. Then he took Arthur with him."

"Why would he . . . ?" Lark's eyes widened. "The sacrifice! Oh, God, the spell that would have destroyed the

Magekind! But I thought he needed a Magekind couple for that?"

"Arthur would be even better," Kel said. "Magically speaking, he's the heart of the Magekind."

Lark bunched her fists, fighting panic. "Where did he go, Kel?"

"Where else?" Kel asked bitterly. "The Dragon Lands. He knows he'll be safe there."

Bors stood. "We've got to gather our forces and attack before . . ."

"There's no time," Gawain interrupted, sitting up. "We'd all be dead before we finished. There's only one thing we *can* do in time."

"No," Kel gasped in horror. "Oh, fuck no. Forget it, Gawain!"

His partner's expression was cold with determination. "In dragon form, you'd have the power to get through those shields and save Arthur."

Lark stared at him in sick horror. "Only if he killed you! Gawain . . ."

"If we don't get Arthur back, I'm dead anyway." He rose to his feet and handed the sword to Bors. "You'll have to take my head."

"Oh, for Cachamwri's sake, Gawain!" There was panic in Kel's voice. "Don't do this to me."

"No!" Lark leaped to her feet and grabbed his forearm. Her heart was hammering, and it was all she could do not to throw up. Gawain dead, his head cleaved from his shoulders. Like Antonio. "You can't seriously . . ."

"We don't have time to argue about this, Lark." Gawain's expression was emotionless, but his eyes burned in his pale face. "Kel could penetrate Dragon Lands' wards and rescue Arthur, but only in dragon form. He's the only one with a prayer of saving the Magekind. It's better to lose me than all of us."

"What if I can't, Gawain?" Kel demanded, sounding as frantic as she felt. "This all would be for nothing!"

Lark's panicked mind worked desperately. "Wait—
what about a strike through the heart? What if I could heal
you—"

"We tried that a thousand years ago," Gawain interrupted impatiently. "Morgana couldn't leave me dead long
enough. It didn't work." He looked at Bors. "Bors."

"Shit, Gawain." The knight shook his head and lifted
the dragon sword. "I wish to God you weren't right."

"Truebond with me!" Lark reached out and grabbed
him. Tears spilled down her cheeks, but she didn't care. "He
could run you through the heart instead. It would be enough
to kill you, but I can hold your soul here and heal you once
Kel is free."

He looked at her, sadness in his eyes. "It won't work,
Lark. You'd only die with me. Just like Diera and Antonio."

SEVENTEEN

Tegid growled under his breath, pouring more power into the wards around his cavern, but the pressure built as the ape fought him, forcing his way through.

Abruptly the spell imploded, and the ape's gate burst wide in the cavern's main chamber. Cloven hooves clicked as the creature stepped through, another mammal draped limply over one crimson shoulder. Its prisoner was tightly bound in shimmering bands of magical force.

The ape's eyes glowed yellow, and its black lips peeled back from its fangs. "You tried to block my gate, reptile. I don't like that." Malevolent power boiled around it like lava. Cachamwri's eggs, the thing was powerful.

Nothing to do now but try to bluff. Tegid drew himself up, fanning his spines as he stalked toward the ape, smoke drifting from his nostrils. "I've decided I don't want you here, ape. Work your death magic somewhere else."

The ape lifted its horned head, glowing eyes narrowed. "We've been through this, Tegid. That is your name, isn't it? Tegid?"

Tegid's spines flatten in alarm. "How did you know that?"

The ape bared its teeth. "Your nephew sends his regards. I think he recognized your handwriting."

His heart began to pound, a thick, slow beat. "I trust you told him he was wrong."

"Would he have believed me if I had?"

"Ungrateful ape!" Tegid lashed his tail in a rage that grew even hotter when the creature only looked amused. "If Kel tells Soren . . ."

"Kel isn't going to be telling anybody anything," the ape said dismissively. "When I'm finished with this spell, Gawain will be dead, and Kel will be well on his way to turning into a very large razor blade."

And Tegid's problems would be over. He blew out a puff of smoke and reluctantly yielded. "Very well, ape. Work your magic and get out."

The creature lifted one shoulder. "I'm afraid it's not that simple. This particular spell will require considerable preparation." He looked toward the entrance of Tegid's chambers. "And I'd better get to work. I don't care to be caught by the sunrise."

Tegid hissed a dragon curse and turned. Catching a stalagmite between his claws, he climbed up to his sleeping chamber and settled down to watch.

However quickly the ape worked his magic, it wouldn't be fast enough. The sooner the Magekind was dead, the safer Tegid would be.

"*I will save* you," Lark insisted, her eyes locked on his, willing Gawain to agree. "Just give me the chance."

He only shook his head. "Lark, you don't have the power to hold me here that long. It would kill you."

"I won't let it," she said through her teeth. "I will *not* allow you to die like this."

"No," he snapped. "Look, we don't have time to stand here arguing. Bors . . ."

She stepped against him, grabbed his face in both

hands, and dragged him down for a hard, desperate kiss that tasted of tears. "He might as well kill me, too, Gawain," she said against his mouth. "Let me do this. Please."

"Dammit!" Bors growled. "Kel, this is ridiculous!"

They looked around. The sword had gone limp, hanging in Bors's hands like a piece of wet spaghetti. "Let her try, Gawain! I didn't endure sixteen hundred years of hell only to kill you."

Bors gave a snort and waved the blade, which flopped in his hands in silent demonstration of Kel's refusal to cooperate. "Gawain, we don't have time for this argument. Truebond with the girl before my son kills Arthur and we *all* die."

Gawain spat a vile curse, helpless anger in his eyes as he realized they had him outmaneuvered. "Dammit, Lark, I love you! I don't want to kill you."

In her frenzy, his confession barely even registered. She rested her forehead against his and stared into his face. "Neither of us is going to die."

He took a deep breath. "Then do it."

"God, thank you." Ignoring the tiny, panicked voice that told her she didn't know what the hell she was doing, Lark opened herself to the Mageverse and drew its power deep, inhaling it, letting its warm, foaming energies fill her until her mind seemed to burn. She'd need every last erg of magic she could absorb to heal Gawain's injuries.

Once she had as much as she could hold, Lark sent a gentle spell rolling through her fingertips and into the warm, bearded skin between her palms. Without protest, Gawain opened himself to her. And for the first time, she made contact with his mind.

Power. Deep, ancient, profoundly masculine, yet incredibly compassionate. He had a craving for justice, a need to protect those weaker than he was, which had been born from his centuries of seeing the best and worst mankind was capable of.

And he loved her. She felt the warm purity of it shining through his consciousness like sunlight. Her willingness to risk herself for him had brought that love to the surface in all its sweet devotion. Though they'd known each other so little time, the depths of Gawain's love stunned and humbled her.

I haven't been around all these centuries without learning to recognize someone worthy of love.

God, Gawain, I love you! The thought burst from the core of her consciousness, almost vibrating with its intensity.

She sensed his male satisfaction. *Good.*

Despite the circumstances, Lark found herself laughing.

Another voice spoke in their joined consciousness. Kel. *I've got to end our bond, Gawain. We won't be able to break the spell if we're linked.*

Lark blinked in awe. Now that she'd become aware of him, she realized the dragon was an astonishingly massive presence in Gawain's mind. Touching Kel's consciousness, she glimpsed a kaleidoscope of alien memories: flying into the aching blue of the sky, the feeling of wings biting the air. Scaly, reptilian faces, dragon voices hissing and roaring.

You're right, Gawain said in their link. *Warm winds, my friend.* It was the traditional Draconian farewell.

Warm winds, Gawain.

Even through as he started to draw away, they could feel Kel's regret, his fear that he'd end up killing them both. Worse, that their sacrifice would be for nothing.

I won't fail you, Gawain, he told them silently, thrusting the fear away. *That I swear.*

I know, Kel. You've never failed me.

Then the dragon was gone.

They were alone together, floating in warm delight of their nascent link. *Closer,* Gawain said, reaching for her with his mind. *We need to be closer. We're not completely bonded yet. You're still holding back.*

And he was right, she realized. Some part of her was afraid. What if he saw her as she really was and turned away? What if he. . . .

I love you. His soul wrapped itself around hers like warm silk. *I love your strength. I love your intelligence and will and humor. And now that I've touched you, I know you can do this. You can save us.*

And he did. His certainty felt like sunlight cutting through the cold of her fear, like warm, fragrant water, like music, deep and low. Feeling that certainty, she couldn't help but believe it, too. Releasing the last of her fear, Lark opened herself completely.

And with a psychic click, their bond became complete. She could feel him in all his fierce courage, the love and loyalty, his devotion to the cause of saving humanity from itself.

What could she do but love him?

What could I do but love you? he whispered.

"Are you ready?" Bors's voice, breaking through the moment of peace, bringing them back to awareness.

Gawain's hands caught her shoulders and pushed Lark gently back. "We've got to do it now, Lark," he said softly. "There's no more time."

For just a moment, she felt fear stir again. Then she saw a memory in his mind: herself, stepping from the boy's home after the fight with Clayton Roth, blazing like a torch. Gawain believed her.

Her mouth firmed as she drew herself upright. She rose on her toes and kissed him just once, a brush of the lips that more promise of the future, then stepped away.

Looking over at Bors, Lark nodded tightly. "We're ready."

The knight moved and took her place in front of Gawain, Kel gleaming long and solid in his hand. The little dragon's ruby eyes were very wide. Bors himself looked pale, his jaw tight. He lifted the sword and hesitated. "Gawain . . ."

Gawain gave him a bracing smile. "I know."

"Dammit." He took a deep breath and closed his eyes a moment, gathering himself.

Lark watched as Kel dissolved Gawain's armor away, leaving him standing bare-chested, wearing only his jeans. He squared his broad shoulders and met her gaze.

I love you, he told her in the Truebond.

She licked her lips and fought the rise of terror. *And I love you.*

Bands of magic bound Arthur so tightly, he could barely breathe. He was intensely aware of the icy stone floor he lay on, and the click of Edge's cloven hooves as he paced around the huge, echoing chamber. The sorcerer's voice rose and fell in a rythmic, alien chant that made every hair stand up on his body.

Arthur closed his eyes and concentrated again, trying to reach out to Gwen's mind. He touched only utter blackness. The bastard had her in a coma so deep, even Arthur couldn't wake her.

God, he missed her. And unless he did something now, he'd never touch her bright, lovely soul again.

His mind worked furiously as his thoughts went back to Gawain and Bors. Both men had been seriously injured, but Arthur didn't think it was anything a healer couldn't fix. As long as they were found in time, anyway.

But even if they were, what about the wards around the Dragon Lands? They hadn't been able to break through them before . . . but maybe Soren could help. If they could get to him in time.

Fuck. Arthur eyed Edge's broad crimson back with its seared magical scars. Somehow, he had to buy some time. If he could only distract the bastard. . . .

"Just for curiosity's sake, what exactly are you doing, Richard?" With an effort, he made his voice sound level and politely interested rather than furious and pissed off.

The chanting fell silent. Hooves clicked slowly closer,

giving Arthur time to wonder if he'd just made a tactical error. "Preparing to work the spell Geirolf should have worked to begin with. I told him from the start he should have sacrificed you in that spell—I even suggested using Excalibur as the sacrificial knife. But Geirolf thought you'd be too closely guarded. He decided he could use a Magekind couple as a substitute. If he'd listened to me, he wouldn't be dead." Edge smiled in a chilling expanse of razored teeth. "But hey, looks like it's all going to work out in the end." He leaned over Arthur, his breath smelling of death. "I'm going to wrap this spell around that sword of yours, Artie. And then I'm going to drop it right through your heart."

Gawain watched Bors draw back the sword. This was going to hurt. He clenched his fists and braced himself.

With a grunt of effort, Bors thrust the sword with his full weight behind it. Gawain sucked in a gasp at the pain of ribs cracking under the impact. The point of the sword shot through his heart.

Fire exploded in Gawain's chest. Lark's scream echoed his. Bors jerked the blade free as Gawain fell to one knee, cold racing over his body as his dying heart struggled to beat. Lark grabbed for him as he toppled to the grass on his back. The pain bled rapidly away as his body began to go numb and distant. Staring up at the spinning stars, he struggled to draw breath.

Gawain! Lark flooded his consciousness, so warm with life she almost burned. *I've got you! Hang on . . .*

But above them, the stars were exploding, spilling down a river of light that poured over his cold, bleeding body. He felt himself start to float . . .

No! Fiercely, Lark wrapped herself around him, anchoring him in place, holding him inside his body. *No! You have to stay. We have to save Arthur! Gawain, please!*

He wanted to. God, he wanted to. Yet the pull of the

light was so gentle—and so incredibly powerful, dragging him from her desperate arms as it sung sweetly of peace. . . .

No! *Lark would die if he died.* He jolted, trying to fight the light, trying to fight the pull that threatened to kill the woman he loved.

Lark tightened her grip, holding on with everything she had against the seductive pull of the shining warmth.

The strong, bright warmth that breathed offers of an end to battle, an end to the fight that never ended . . . Despite herself, she looked up into the light.

Gawain's eyes flared open. *No.* His voice rang in her mind, and he was fully with her again, his consciousness locking onto hers. *You're not going to die.*

He was back! Quickly, she reached for the Mageverse, trying to call the magic, restart his stopped heart.

Nothing happened.

Oh, God. She'd waited too long. She'd gone too far. She couldn't reach her power. . . .

I said you're not dying! His iron will poured into hers, extending her reach, strengthening her until the power flooded in again, sweet and life-giving. Desperately, she dragged it deep and sent it spinning into his body, repairing his damaged heart, forcing it to beat.

Thud.

Silence.

Grimly, she dragged in more power, sent more magic into his healing heart.

Thud. Thud. Thud.

And the singing light winked out.

Gawain sucked in an agonized breath as Lark did the same, her body instinctively echoing his. His heart began beating hard now, uneven thuds that settled quickly into strong rhythmic thumps.

Green eyes opened and met her dazed stare. Slowly, painfully, he smiled.

A tall, handsome man loomed over him, his hair a long fall of silken blue around his face. He smiled, the light catching the faint blue shimmer across his cheekbones. "You back now?"

Belatedly, Gawain recognized the face he hadn't seen in sixteen hundred years. "Kel?" His chest ached, and his voice sounded faint.

Lark, sprawled next to them in the grass, asked the question for both of them. "Why aren't you a dragon?"

Kel looked up at her with a faint smile. "I feared I might need a man's hands to help him."

"Arthur." Gawain remembered. He sat up with a grunt of effort. "We've got to get to him now."

Kel lifted him easily to his feet as Bors moved to help Lark to hers. She braced her feet apart, feeling battered, and reached for the Mageverse. To her relief, she sensed it shimmering on the edge of her consciousness.

Just like Gawain. He almost glowed, strong and warm and so wonderfully alive. She wanted to kiss him, wrap herself in his body, but there wasn't time.

Instead she called the magic and clothed them all in armor.

But when she tried to call out to Morgana, she slammed into the same magical wall that had blocked them before. "Dammit!" She looked at Kel. "Should one of us go for reinforcements?"

"By the time Morgana gathers the army, Arthur would be dead."

"What about Gwen?" Lark glanced through the trees, worried. "She's still lying under that street lamp, out cold."

"We can't take her with us, Lark," Gawain pointed out. "And there's nothing in Avalon that can or would hurt her."

"Yeah, but I hate leaving her like that." Lark flung a quick protection spell at Gwen just to be sure.

Turning, she saw Kel striding away through the trees. She started to follow him, but Gawain grabbed her arm and pulled her to a stop. "Give him room. He'll need it."

Reaching a clearing, the dragon man stopped and threw back his head. Blue black hair flew around his face as he lifted his voice in a shout.

His voice deepened, simultaneously growing louder and louder as magic boiled out of the center of his chest, so bright Lark had to jerk her eyes away.

When she looked back again, a dragon filled the clearing, big as a passenger jet, its great wings spreading wide as its tail whipped, crashing into a small bush that ripped free of the ground and went flying.

Lark gaped at it in frozen astonishment. She'd never seen one up close before, never realized how huge they were.

The massive skull swung toward them, enormous ruby eyes narrowing. "What are you waiting for?" Kel's familiar voice demanded, though it rumbled far deeper and louder than it ever had before. "Climb on."

"Jesu," Bors muttered before the three of them sprinted toward the huge creature. Gawain was the first to climb on, planting a foot on the dragon's elbow and vaulting atop the broad, muscular neck. Bors caught Lark around the waist and lifted her up until Gawain could slide an arm around her and settle her into place astride Kel's neck. Bors scrambled up behind him.

"Hold on," the dragon rumbled, coiling his massive body.

Oh, God, Lark thought desperately, grabbing for one of the spines that protruded from his powerful neck, *I'm not ready for this!*

I've got you, Gawain told her through the Truebond. His strong arms tightened comfortingly around her waist.

And then the great beast leaped skyward with a roar.

Gritting her teeth shut against an instinctive scream, Lark clung to Gawain's arms and clamped her armored legs around the dragon's huge neck.

"Try calling Morgana now—we're beyond the range of Edge's spell," Kel called over the heavy beat of his wings. "I've got to generate a gate to take us to the Dragon Lands."

"Why not just gate directly there?" Bors asked.

"The wards are still blocking me. They're similar to a combination lock, and the Dragonkind changed the combination on me. But once we're close enough, I should be able to find a way to break through."

Lark certainly hoped so. Trying to ignore the sight of the ground dropping rapidly away—taking her stomach with it—she closed her eyes and reached for Morgana.

It was not a conversation she was looking forward to.

Kel soared through the dimensional gate. Ahead of him, for the first time in centuries, he could see the Dragon Lands lying spread under the moon.

Despite the grim situation, despite the rage burning in his heart, he couldn't help but glory in the sight. Finally, after all these years, he was free again.

Then he frowned, realizing that the thought of seeing his people again held far less pleasure for him. All his fellow dragons had done was give him pain, from his own imprisonment to the shattering loss of his mother centuries ago.

No, his true people now were those who rode his back— Gawain, Lark, and Bors, not to mention all those back in Avalon who were in such deadly danger. He was damned if he'd fail them, especially since Gawain had finally found a woman he could be happy with.

Extending his magical awareness, Kel could sense the complex energies of the Dragon Land's wards ahead of him. They'd defeated him repeatedly over the past days as he'd tried to search for Edge, but he was a hell of a lot more powerful now that he was back in dragon form again. More, he had the experience of centuries of magical combat at Gawain's side.

If Tegid expected him to have been weakened by his imprisonment, his uncle was in for a very nasty surprise.

Kel reached out his consciousness, exploring the pattern of forces, looking for the counter spell that would open them.

There. He spotted it and sent a wave of magic into the barrier. If he'd still been trapped in the sword, he wouldn't have had the power to do it. But as it was now . . .

The wards silently gaped wide.

With a rumble of victory, Kel flew through, arched toward his uncle's caverns and began to beat his wings harder.

Here I come, you egg-sucking son of a bitch.

Arthur bucked and fought, but it did him no good as Edge's spell lowered him onto the pentagram-shaped altar the monster had created in the center of the cavern.

His armor had vanished, melted away by Edge's spell. Beneath his back, the runes cut into the stone seemed to burn his flesh. In his mind, he howled his wife's name with every ounce of his strength, trying to break through the magic that held her. If he could only reach Gwen, she could mobilize the Magekind for a rescue. Otherwise his people were lost.

The prospect of his own death had long since lost its fear for Arthur, but the destruction of his people did terrify him. Worse, if the Magekind fell, humankind would lose its most powerful protector. Protection Earth desperately needed now that the forces of hate and bigotry were coupled with the potential of planetary destruction.

Gritting his teeth, he strained to reach his wife's mind. And touched only silence.

"You're wasting your energy, Arthur," Edge told him. "Nothing's getting through my shield spell, no matter how loudly you scream."

"You bastard!" Arthur snarled. "Bors should have strangled you in your cradle!"

A flash of razored fangs. "Yeah, but he didn't, so I got

him first. Felt good goring him, too. I just wish I could see his face when this spell kills you all." Cruel black eyes scanned his expression. "Though yours is almost as satisfying."

"Go to hell, coward." He bared his teeth.

Rage flared in those inhuman eyes. "If I'd been a coward, I would have contented myself with the miserable mortal life you and my loving father consigned me to. Instead I did this." He spread his massive arms, displaying the black runes seared into his flesh. "I could have easily burned like all the others, but I endured, and I won. Now you're the ones who'll burn."

As Arthur watched in helpless fury, Edge gestured. Excalibur floated into the air and positioned itself point down over Arthur's bare chest.

Edge began to chant again. Growling in helpless rage, Arthur fought his bonds.

Around them, malevolent energies began to rise, swirling and stinking of death like the wind from a tomb.

EIGHTEEN

Rage. A great wave of it, headed straight for Tegid's chambers.

He jerked his head off his forelegs in horror, realizing at once what had happened. Bolting to his feet, he dove off the second level and hit the cavern floor, racing for the entrance. "Kel's free of the sword! He's coming!"

The ape didn't stop his chanting, but his mental voice rang magically. *Stop him. I need another three minutes to finish this.*

For once, Tegid didn't quibble about taking orders from the ape. He galloped to the entrance and threw himself into the air, wings beating desperately toward his foe.

Lark gasped as the red dragon shot out of the cavern like a cannon shell, headed straight for them.

"Can you fly?" Kel shouted.

"I don't know!" she yelled back, her heart stuffing its way into her throat. She knew it was possible, she'd even seen Morgana do it. But she wasn't Morgana. "I've never done it before."

The red dragon opened its mouth. Lark knew whatever came out was not going to be good.

"You'd better learn!"

Flame roared toward them, only to splash off Kel's shields. Struggling to compose the spell, she watched the red dragon fly closer and closer, about to slam into them all like an eighteen wheeler hitting a school bus.

"Jump!" Gawain roared. He didn't wait for her to obey, instead tightening his grip around her waist as he threw both of them off Kel's back. Bors did the same. All three of them fell like bricks. The cliffs rushed toward them. . . .

Lark grabbed for the Mageverse and sent a wave of energy shooting out in all directions, forming a great golden bubble around them. Their collective weight hit the bottom of it . . .

And she felt it give.

"Shit!" Frantically, she poured more magic into the barrier until the bubble solidified.

"Let's go!" Bors shouted. "We've got to get into that cave."

Lark eyed its glowing green mouth and thought about casting a gate, then realized she wouldn't be able to do that and keep them airborne at the same time. Gritting her teeth with the effort, she sent the bubble soaring skyward.

Between the three of them and all their armor, they probably weighed more than eight hundred pounds.

Don't think about it, Gawain growled in the Truebond. *Just do it.*

What are you, a Nike commercial? Clenching her teeth harder, she drove the bubble faster. Behind them, they could hear the furious sounds of the two dragons fighting—massive, meaty sounds of impact, ear-splitting roars of fury, and the hiss and boom of magic.

Through the Truebond, Lark heard Gawain say a prayer for his friend. Grimly, she concentrated on keeping the bubble moving.

* * *

Kel sank his fanged jaws into his uncle's shoulder and bit down, tasting the sweet hot rush of dragon blood. Tegid's roar of pain sounded like music. The older dragon jerked away, wings beating as he retreated. Kel flew after him, lost in the hot madness of the duel.

Finally—finally, after all these centuries! Freedom and revenge, the two things he'd dreamed of endlessly, trapped in that tiny shell of metal.

Distantly, he was aware of other dragons swooping around them in a frenzy of agitation, but he didn't care.

After all, they'd never cared about him.

"What are you doing, Kel?" It was Soren, flying close as he chased Tegid over the cliffs.

Kel bared his teeth. It was all so devastatingly clear now. "Tegid trapped me in that sword, and he plotted with a spawn of one of the Dark Ones. And I'm going to kill him for it!"

A hissing murmur rose from the watching dragons.

Tegid looked around at them, his eyes going wide with fear and fury. "He's mad! Being trapped in that sword has driven him insane!"

Wheeling in the air, he flung himself at Kel. The impact tore them both from the sky, and they fell together, tearing at one anther with claws and teeth as they dropped.

Sweating, driven by an increasing mental drumbeat of urgency, Lark drove her improvised bubble faster, conscious of the dragons circling above her. With Kel battling his uncle, anything magical was her responsibility.

The thought made her stomach knot.

You can do it, Lark. It wasn't so much the words that touched her as the certainty she could feel in Gawain's mind. He believed in her.

Her eyes narrowed, and she flung the bubble forward even faster, shooting it right for the opening of the cavern.

It blasted through the hole like a cannonball. In the center of a huge central cavern, Arthur lay nude on a star-shaped altar. A huge horned creature stood over him, Excalibur hanging point down directly over his chest.

With a wordless snarl, she flung the bubble toward them. The horned thing whirled at their entry. It had to be Edge. He flung beefy arms up in the start of a gesture, and she realized he was going to drop the sword on Arthur. A spell hung swirling around the altar, just waiting for the Magus's death to power it.

Lark dissolved the bubble. She, Gawain, and Bors crashed to the floor.

Even as she hit, Lark flung every bit of the Mageverse she had in a concentrated blast of force, aimed right at Edge. He tried to fling up a shield, and she poured more power into her blast.

Excalibur plunged downward.

The instant before it hit, her spell shattered Edge's shield with the full power of her desperation. The wave of force blew the sword, Edge, and Arthur across the cavern like leaves in a hurricane. Still bound and paralyzed, Arthur hit the rear wall of the cave and collapsed in a heap. The sword rattled to the floor, unbloodied.

"That's my girl!" Gawain crowed. He and Bors raced toward the demon.

Edge roared in rage and lunged to his feet, armor appearing around him, twin blades filling his hands. He charged them like a bull.

Lark took one teetering step forward before her knees gave, dumping her in a sweating, panting heap.

Through their Truebond, she felt the jar as Gawain's sword crashed into Edge's, heard guttural, snarling curses.

Get up, she told herself grimly. *Dammit, get up!* But her body refused to obey. She'd spent everything she had in that blast.

But without her magic or Kel's, Bors and Gawain didn't have a prayer against Edge.

* * *

Gawain sensed Lark's fear and helplessness through their Truebond, but he was too busy parrying Edge's teeth-rattling attack to reassure her.

"Arthur!" he shouted, sparing a glance at the still, naked figure curled on the ground behind Edge.

"Here," Arthur grunted. "I just can't move."

"Patience, Artie," Edge snarled, wheeling to drive Bors back with a brutal sword swing. "I'll be with you in a minute."

"Don't bet on it." Gawain danced forward and swung his blade with both hands, trying to cut the sorcerer in two.

Edge parried the blow with his left hand sword. The big weapon began to blaze with magic. Before Gawain could leap away, Edge flicked the blade forward, slinging the blast into his face.

It burned!

He fell back with a shout of agony as the magic started eating through his enchanted armor like acid.

Gawain! Lark's voice rang in his mind. He sensed her fighting to cast a spell and shield him, but her magic still wouldn't respond.

Edge laughed, the sound coldly evil, and took a step toward him.

"Get away from him!" Bors roared, swinging his sword like an axe.

Edge parried with both blades, trapping the knight's weapon between them. Rearing back on one leg, he sent a hoof slamming into Bors's gut. The kick sent the knight flying to crash into the cavern's stone wall.

"Damn, that felt good!" Edge crowed.

The taste of blood flooded Kel's mouth, so hot and heady he barely felt the wounds marking his own flesh. His left rear leg screamed as his weight came down on it; he must have hurt it in that fall.

Tegid's jaws gaped wide, releasing a flaming plume of magic that forced him to release his clamping bite on his uncle's foreleg. Panting, half-blinded, he sensed the dragon scrambling away. He blinked the dazzle from his eyes and went after his foe.

He knew he was teetering on the edge of blood rage, his people's version of a berserker fury, but he didn't care.

"Why?" Kel growled, stalking Tegid. "Why trap me in that sword? Why that particular spell?"

"You weren't trapped!" Tegid scrambled over the great rocks at the base of the cliff. Snarling, Kel leaped atop one of the huge boulders and watched for an opening. "Had you not been so stubborn, you could have freed yourself at any time."

"By killing my friend!"

"He's an ape! How could you call one of those smelly, revolting creatures a friend? Unnatural!" Tegid roared a blast of magic at Kel, but he opened his wings and leaped, shooting through the air to slam into his uncle. They hit the ground tumbling, raking and biting one another.

Tegid clamped his teeth into the base of his neck. With a roar of pain, Kel twisted and blew a plume of raw fire right in his face, forcing him to let go and leap away. Too bad his kind were virtually fireproof; it took a prolonged blast to do real damage.

Smoke curling from his nose, Kel limped after his uncle. "You're one to talk about unnatural allies—you made Edge a Dark One! You plotted with an ape to destroy the Magekind!"

"What?" one of the dragons overhead called. "What is this, Tegid?"

"He lies!" Tegid lowered his head, growling viciously. "He's just like his mother—always questioning me, showing me up, exposing me to ridicule since the day we were hatched. She changed her tune once you were in that sword, though, didn't she?" A vicious smile curved his mouth. "She wanted me to help her prove Evar had trapped you, so I told her she had to keep to her place. That was all it took."

Kel stopped in his tracks as a great deal became clear. "It wasn't only about me, was it? It was her. You kept me in the sword to control and punish her."

"She had too much influence on the Bloodstone females!" Tegid drew his neck to its full, towering extension. "She was always making trouble. Maneuvering, trying to make you a Dragon Lord. Boasting that you'd unseat me. But I ruined her plan, didn't I?" He laughed. "And she thought it was Evar! Evar didn't have the brains!"

A curious calm rolled over Kel, cold and still, replacing his rage. "You're the one who told her Evar trapped me. That's why she challenged him, even knowing he was bigger and more powerful than she was. And he killed her."

Tegid lowered his head. "All you had to do was kill the ape, and none of this would have been necessary."

Kel showed every tooth he had. "You're dead, Uncle. I'm going to eat the heart out of your chest."

And he charged.

She had it! The Mageverse was back! Lark felt the warm wash of magic respond to her desperation. Just in time, because Gawain was on the ground now, writhing in the grip of Edge's spell. It had eaten its way through his armor and was beginning to sear his skin. His pain flayed her through their Truebond like a whip.

Gathering the magic, she sent it pouring into him, stopping the spell in its tracks and healing his injuries before repairing his damaged armor. They both gasped in relief.

Scrambling to her feet, she hurried over to join him as he rose, picking up his sword.

Edge was circling his father, taunting him. Lark and Gawain moved in, looking for an opening.

"There's something I've always wanted to tell you, Dad." He watched Bors through glittering eyes, a smile curling his mouth. "Looks like this is my last chance."

Bors swung his sword in a powerful, two-handed blow that by rights should have taken his foe's head off his shoulders. Instead, the sorcerer easily parried with one sword and struck at him with the other.

The knight leaped clear, panting. "You think I care what you have to say?"

Edge ignored that, stalking him. "Ever since I can remember, you kept trying to fill my head with honor and duty and the importance of protecting mortals. And it was all just bullshit." He grinned. "I've been dying to tell you that since I was five." The two circled, hooves and armored boots clicking on the stone floor. "You'd talk and talk and talk, and I'd think how stupid you were."

Edge pounced, swinging both swords like scythes. Bors leaped over them in a move only possible for a vampire. Landing in a crouch, he slashed at Edge's thighs. The monster dodged away with a low, ugly laugh. "But you probably know that now, right? I mean, where's your honor got you? You think any of the mortals will care when you're dead? Fuck no. They'll be too busy trying to blow themselves to hell. Because they're like me. None of them really cares about anything but eating and sleeping and pussy. The rest is just noise."

"Yeah, you're good at noise." Lark hurled a spell blast, catching him right in the head. Edge staggered. "And we're sick of listening to you."

Taking advantage of their foe's distraction, Gawain raced up and swung hard, catching the sorcerer across the chest. His blade sliced into Edge's cuirass.

The monster roared in pain and struck out at him, but he ducked as Bors darted in. Catching his son's left-hand sword with his blade, the knight twisted it with a skillful flick of the wrist and sent it flying. Edge snarled and swung at him with the right blade, but Bors parried and danced back.

Lark powered another spell into Edge's chest, knocking him back a pace. Gawain circled behind him and chopped viciously across his thighs. With a roar, Edge fell to one knee and turned to hack at Gawain. Nimbly, the knight retreated even as Lark shot yet another volley of spells at him. Edge threw up a shield and lunged to his feet again.

That spell he tried to cast on Arthur must have weakened him. *We've got him on the run,* Gawain said in the link. *Blast him again.*

Lark reached for more magic as Bors and Gawain closed on the sorcerer, swords lifted.

"Fuck this." Edge spun on his cloven hooves and shot across the chamber.

Straight at Arthur.

Around them, the death spell he'd begun seemed to vibrate, gathering itself. Waiting for the sacrifice.

"Cachamwri's Egg!" Perched on the face of the cliff with the other watchers, Soren looked away from the combat raging below as a sense of violent evil suddenly blasted out from somewhere overhead. He craned his head upward. "That's coming from Tegid's chambers!"

If Kel's accusations about the Dark Ones were correct . . .

With a growl, he flung himself upward. "Where are you going?" another dragon called.

"I'm checking that chamber!"

"Noo! Let me go!" Tegid lashed and fought, but Kel only clamped down harder on his throat, grimly intent on ripping his way through. His uncle clawed at his face with a foreleg, catching him across the eye. Blood spurted. Kel jerked and lost his grip. With a furious wrench, Tegid tore free and launched himself skyward. Kel roared, shook away the blood, and flung himself after his uncle.

Around them, the watching dragons launched themselves skyward, hungry to see the rest of the fight.

Tegid, however, seemed to have forgotten all about it as he shot for his cavern, beating hard as he tried to catch Soren's whipping tail.

Gawain leaped at Edge, only to take a spell blast in the chest that batted him across the cavern like an empty tin can. Bors charged, but Edge had already reached Arthur and snatched him off the ground.

Wrapping a massive forearm across the knight's neck, he pressed his remaining sword to Arthur's throat. "Back up, Dad." Bors growled and lunged. Edge shot a blast at his head, forcing him to duck.

Spotting a glint of silver, Lark dove on Excalibur, still lying forgotten on the floor. She snatched the blade up and retreated. "Aren't you forgetting something, Ricky? Spell won't work without Excalibur, will it?"

Stymied, the monster snarled at her. He dug the tip of his blade against Arthur's throat. "Maybe not, but I can still cut Artie's head off." His eyes narrowed and flicked to Gawain, who was up again and circling around to his left. "Uh, uh, Gawain."

"Well, now," A big blue dragon drawled from the mouth of the cavern. Tail lashing, he advanced on them. "Isn't this interesting?"

Instinctively, Lark moved back, her attention sliding from Edge to the dragon and back again. Edge watched her like a cat.

With a thud, a red dragon scrambled through the opening, crimson eyes wide with panic. "What are these apes doing here?" Lark barely understood its rapid-fire Draconian hiss even with her magic. "Get out of my cavern!"

"Oh, give it up, Tegid," the blue dragon mocked as Kel came in for a landing, trapping the red dragon. "Your runes are all over that creature."

Lark's eyes narrowed, her mind working frantically. So this was the dragon who cast the spell that had allowed Edge to survive the black grail's destruction. But why were the runes still burned into his skin? Why hadn't they healed?

Unless they were still part of an active spell. What if they were still at work containing all that dark magic? And what would happen to Edge if that spell broke?

"You outsmarted yourself, Uncle." Kel, covered in blood and limping, stalked his foe, who backed away, hissing. The red dragon's tail slashed toward Lark, and she jumped back . . .

Quick as a snake, Edge drove his sword through her shoulder and snatched Excalibur from her hand. With a screech of pain, she fell. As if in slow motion, she saw Edge lift the sword toward Arthur's neck . . .

And thought in the Truebond, *Kill the Red Dragon!*

Centuries of living with Kel's consciousness had taught him exactly how to do it. Gawain whirled as Lark conjured a spear into his hand and hurled it with every ounce of his strength.

It thudded home squarely in Tegid's right eye. With a howl of agony, the dragon tossed up his great head, convulsing, his tail whipping back and forth. Gawain barely leaped aside in time as the huge creature toppled to the stone floor with a meaty thud.

The blue dragon reached out a forepaw and snatched Bors back as one of Tegid's clawed rear feet gave a last lethal dying kick.

"Noooo!" Edge roared, his eyes widening in horror. All over his crimson body, the runes flared red and began to vanish one by one. The sorcerer's frantic gaze darted around the cavern, his sword dropping from his lax fingers as his mouth worked helplessly.

Seeing his chance, Arthur tore himself free from the monster's grip and scrambled to get as far away from him as he could. Lark and Gawain ran to join their liege and

dragged him behind a stalagmite, all three of them hunker-
ing into its shelter. Lark threw a spell shield around them
all as, from the corner of one eye, she saw the blue dragon
throw a similar barrier around himself and Bors.

Edge's mouth gaped, but instead of a scream, light
poured from his lips in a blinding torrent. The silent blaze
quickly spread to his entire head. He threw out a hand to
his father, the gesture oddly pleading as the blinding light
spread down his torso. The light was so fierce, Lark's eyes
began to tear.

Then, without any sound at all, Edge exploded. A blast
of liberated energies roared over them all, staggering even
the dragons, who crouched against its battering fury.

Gagging at the smell of death magic, Lark desperately
strengthened her shield as the energy roared around them
like a hurricane.

Finally, with a whining moan, the last of the liberated
energy swirled from the cavern and disappeared into the
night, leaving them all in complete darkness.

For a long moment, there was no sound except the rasp
of breathing and the slither of scales.

Light blazed up, and Lark ducked, covering her head instinctively. Daring a glance through her spread fingers, she
realized it was only Kel, summoning a light spell.

"I trust that proves my accusation, Soren," the dragon
said. "Without Tegid's spell to control it, the black grail's
magic destroyed Edge."

The blue dragon studied Tegid's bloody body with dis-
taste. "Yes, I'd say so." Shrugging, he raised one wing, revealing Bors huddled against his side wearing a dazed
expression. "Are you all right?"

"Yeah," the knight said hoarsely, climbing to his feet.

"How about the rest of you?"

"Lark?" Arthur asked in a deep voice. "Not that it's a
hardship wearing you like a mink stole, but Gwen might
not understand."

She lifted her head and belatedly realized the Magus

was no longer bound—but he was very thoroughly naked. "Sorry." Quickly, she straightened off him and conjured clothing, averting her eyes.

Gawain grinned and rose to help her up.

"What was that?" a deep outraged voice asked in Draconian. As they looked up, several very big heads poked into the cavern. The dragons gasped in horror at the sight of Tegid's body, Gawain's spear still lodged in one eye. "What happened?"

"He got what was coming to him." Kel turned toward Soren. "I'm going to take my friends home now."

The great dragon nodded. "When you return, we'll discuss your seat with the Dragon Lords."

"Actually, I don't plan to return." Kel lifted his great wings and shook them out. "I have no interest in the Dragon Lords. I'm sure there are those among you who'll be more than happy to duel over Tegid's seat."

"What?" A babble of voices rose. One of the dragons pushed its way into the cavern, which began to seem more than a little cramped. "What do you mean?" the newcomer demanded.

Kel turned a cold red gaze on them. "You left me in that sword while you accepted a bigot and a murderer as your leader. You let him engineer the murder of my mother, and again, you did nothing." Light swirled around him, leaving him in human form. Except for Soren, the dragons recoiled in horror. "I have no interest in living among such as you. I'd rather be human."

Ignoring his people's collective hiss of outrage, Kel summoned a gate with a flick of his wrist. He turned to the four Magekind. "Let's go, my friends. The sun will be up soon, and our people are waiting for us."

Without another word, they followed him through the gate.

NINETEEN

The gate took them to Avalon's central square, where it seemed the entire population of the Magekind waited under a sky going pink with uncomfortable speed. As they stepped from the portal, the gathered company burst into deafening cheers.

Squealing like a young girl, Guinevere ran to meet them and leaped into Arthur's arms. With a complete disregard for anybody's dignity, she wrapped slender arms and long legs around him and kissed him soundly. "You're all right!" he breathed when she let him come up for air.

Gwen stroked his hair back from his forehead. "Of course I'm all right. The minute Edge died, his spell snapped like wet pasta."

He wrapped a big hand around her head and pulled her in for another devouring kiss as the Magekind roared its collective approval.

Finally Arthur put his wife down and held out a hand to Lark, Kel, Bors, and Gawain. "Thanks to these gallant warriors, I live. And so do we all!"

The roar of approval was even louder this time, making

Lark's ears ring. She distinctly heard Caroline's voice shout, "You go, girl!"

When at last the thunder died, Arthur turned to Kel and dropped a big hand on his shoulder. "Normally I like to do these things with a bit more ceremony—but the sun is coming up, and our time runs short. Kel, you have fought beside me, Gawain, and our brother knights for sixteen hundred years. And you have always done it with unflinching courage and breathtaking power. Given all that, it's my hope you will consent to becoming one of my knights of the Round Table."

A stunned silence fell as Kel's red eyes widened. "But . . . but Arthur, you haven't added a new knight in three centuries!"

"Four." Arthur smiled. "But, as far as I'm concerned, you've always been one of us. Just not in this form."

Kel stared at him for a long moment as the watching crowd waited breathlessly. Lark thought she glimpsed a suspicious sheen in his crimson eyes. "It would be a great honor, my Liege," he managed at last. As the cheering rose again, he started to drop to one knee.

Arthur hooked an arm around his neck, dragging him back to his feet. "Oh, cut that out. You know we don't do that anymore."

The stunned amazement in Kel's eyes lightened into a grin, and he thumped the former High King on the back.

Arthur turned toward the waiting Magekind. "As much as I'd love to celebrate all day, the sun is getting dangerously close to the horizon. We'll meet to postmortem this mess tomorrow, and then we'll all get drunk again." He waved a big hand. "Scram."

Gates began hastily opening as Majae started transporting their male allies home.

As Lark turned to cast one of her own, she saw Bors standing off to the side, lost in thought. Gawain, following her glance, moved over to their friend. "How are you holding up?"

"Honestly, better than I expected." He took a deep breath and blew it out. "When we were fighting Richard, I finally realized something in him really was missing. And it always had been. Maybe it was a conscience, maybe it was a soul. Whatever it was, he just never had it. And there was absolutely nothing anyone could have done to give him one."

"No." Gawain slapped him on the back and threw another glance at the sky. "Now let's get out of here before we all get sunburn."

"Where do you want to go, Bors?" Lark asked.

He smiled. "My own bed'll do."

After he vanished through the portal she cast, she conjured a final gate. As Gawain reached out and took her hand, she looked at Kel. "You coming?"

"No." He was staring skyward, his face naked with longing. "Actually, I think I want to fly."

"Enjoy it, brother," Gawain told him as he towed Lark through the gate and into his own bedroom.

"I can't believe he walked away from Dragonkind," she said as she undressed them both with a gesture. "Think he's going to be okay?"

"He'll be happier with us than he ever was with them," Gawain told her, falling into bed with a sigh. He looked up at her, looking deliciously sexy as he sprawled there nude. "Think we've got time for a kiss before the sun comes up?"

She grinned and leaped into bed, landing on the mattress beside him. "Let's give it a shot."

Their lips met in a hot, silken slide, tongues swirling in a passionate dance of love and relief. Lark lifted her head. "I love you."

"And I love . . ." He broke off, his eyes sliding closed as the Daysleep hit.

With a happy sigh, she wrapped her arms around his powerful waist and rested her head against his shoulder.

She was asleep almost as fast as he was.

* * *

Lark was the first to wake. Which meant the sun had not yet gone down, though the windows that filtered out the light left the room in darkness. She lay still against him, listening to the slow, reassuring thud of his heart. She'd had a nightmare about feeling his heartbeat stop today as Kel's blade pierced it. She shuddered.

She'd come so close to losing him.

But I didn't, Lark thought, half-wondering. *I did it. I saved him.*

And he saved me. And we saved everybody.

Slowly, she ran a hand along the warm rise of his chest, savoring the ripples and hollows under her fingers. Silken hair curled under her nails, forming a trail downward. Mischievous, she followed it along his abdomen to the soft sleeping weight of his cock.

He didn't, of course, wake. It would be another hour before the Daysleep would release him.

With a sigh of resignation, she released him and rolled from the bed. After last night's fight, she felt grubby. Time for a shower.

Or, better yet . . .

She padded to the French doors at the end of the room and slipped through the curtains that covered them. Holding the fabric panels carefully closed with a spell so no light would flood beyond them, she opened the doors and stepped out on the balcony. Gawain wouldn't burst into flames if the sun touched him, but she didn't want him getting a sunburn either.

The sun hung over Avalon's fairy-tale skyline in a huge flaming ball, painting the sky in shades of crimson and gold. Closing her eyes for a moment, she savored the warmth on her naked skin before padding across the balcony to the railing.

Kel had constructed an immense pool on the ground just outside Gawain's window, designing it to look like a natural pond. Extending her magical senses, she realized it was so deep, she could easily dive off the balcony and plunge into its cool depths without risking a broken neck.

Regretfully, she decided against it. Instead, she summoned her magic and floated over the railing like a leaf, drifting slowly downward until she sank to her neck in the water. It was the perfect temperature—just warm enough without being too hot. With a sigh, she dove under and let it stroke over her body and through her hair as she swam. Finally surfacing, she rolled over on her back and allowed herself to float.

Something huge flashed by overhead with a glint of blue scales and the whip of a long tail. "Hi, Lark!" Kel called.

Startled, she jerked upright in the water and conjured a bikini. "Ummm, hi!"

"Watch this!" the dragon soared upward again and went into a barrel roll, simultaneously breathing flame. The plume of fire corkscrewed around him. "Cachamwri's Egg, I love doing that."

He circled around again in long, lazy beats of his wings, then transformed to human form and drifted downward, a big, handsome man in tailored slacks and a silk shirt.

She grinned at the child-like pleasure lighting his handsome face. "You seem to be enjoying your freedom."

"Oh, I am." He flung himself down on the grass beside the pool. "You have no idea what it's like to fly again after being trapped for so long." The smile faded from his face. "Thank you for saving him."

She snorted. "Believe me, it was my pleasure."

Kel grinned wickedly. "Or it will be once the sun sets, anyway."

A blush heated her face at the thought. "Bad dragon."

Kel laughed. "Baby, if you weren't taken, I'd show you how bad a dragon I really am." Wickedly he added, "Think they'll let me in the Ladies' Club?"

Lark grinned at him. "Since you're a brand new knight of the Round Table, hell yeah. Planning to pick up a girl?"

"Or two." His grin broadened. "Or possibly even three. I've got sixteen hundred years of celibacy to make up for."

She laughed. "Have fun, dragon."

He rolled to his feet. "Tell your Truebonded I'll be by later. I miss having the big lug in my head."

"He misses you, too."

Kel flashed her a look. "Not with you in there."

Lark watched him saunter away before banishing her suit again. She definitely wanted to be ready for Gawain's arrival.

Floating there, she watched the sun sink, her anticipation rising as it got closer and closer to the horizon. Her smile began an outright grin as it disappeared.

A moment later a deep voice rumbled from the darkness overhead. "Would you like some company?"

Lark craned her neck back. "What do you think?"

A naked body cleared the balcony railing in a long, graceful dive and plummeted downward. He hit so cleanly there was scarcely a splash as he disappeared.

Lark smiled in anticipation and drew in a breath.

Just as she expected, strong arms pulled her underwater against the long, muscular strength of his body. She wrapped her arms and legs around him as he drew her into a kiss. Lazily, they dueled with tongue and lips as they floated slowly to the surface, the water slipping along their skin in a warm caress.

Their heads broke the surface, but they went right on kissing, enjoying the slow rise of passion through their Truebond. Gawain's erect shaft lay against her belly, heavy and taut with need, just as Lark's nipples pressed against his strong chest.

She'd felt his pain. Now she could feel his urgent desire growing hotter and hotter as each second passed. In his mind, she could see everything he wanted to do to her, everything he wanted to feel with her.

And she couldn't wait.

Legs twining together, they kicked lazily, just barely treading water. Even the sensation of his skin sliding against hers was breathtaking, echoing as it did from his mind to hers.

Experimenting, Gawain cupped her breast in a big, warm palm. They both moaned at the sensation. He bent his head and covered one stiff nipple with his mouth, his tongue lazily circling, his teeth gently biting. Lark let her head fall back with a groan.

A wicked thought flashed through his mind. "Let's . . ."

She grinned. "Oh, yeah."

They swam to the edge of the pool. He levered himself out, then eagerly pulled her into his arms. Kissing with sweet, burning greed, they tumbled to the grass together. He left her lips, biting his way gently along the jut of her chin and down her throat. Even as he played, her fingers traced their own luscious patterns over his skin, teasing trails of heat through him. He groaned and began kissing his way slowly downward to the eager thrust of her breasts.

There, Gawain paused, sipping at first one nipple, then the other. Sighing in delight, Lark worked her fingers through his wet hair and held on as he slowly feasted. Experimenting with the sensations, he used tongue and teeth and even the tips of his fangs until she squirmed, gasping at his rising hunger and her own increasingly desperate need.

Now, she managed through the Truebond.

But I want to play, he purred.

You're driving me insane.

Gawain laughed. *Oh, I know.*

And it's my turn. Quick as the thought, she rolled him over on his back and straddled his chest, her head over his groin as she caught the smooth, delicious jut of his cock in her hand.

With a mock growl, he dragged her up and spread her legs over his face until he could reach her sex. As he gave it that first wicked swipe of his tongue, she engulfed the head of his cock in her mouth.

They both groaned at the storm of sensation. His. Hers. It was hard to tell where one went left off and the other began. Entranced, Lark lowered her head still more, taking Gawain's big shaft deeper and deeper.

It felt a little as if she'd suddenly acquired a giant clit. The sensations when he suckled her were more concentrated, but it was delicious either way.

Eagerly, they pleasured one another, each lick and stroke building their shared arousal into a blazing, almost unbearable pleasure.

When he finally slid two fingers into her slick and juicy depths, they almost came on the spot in a shared detonation of pleasure.

I'm not going to be able to last, Gawain thought.

Try. She swirled her tongue over the aching head of his cock.

Teasing wench. Two can play that game. He suckled her fiercely and thrust his fingers deep.

She yowled around his meaty cock, shivering at the delicious, blazing heat. *They certainly can.*

The muscles of her thighs were jerking, and his toes were twitching. *We'd better . . .*

Oh, yeah.

Lark had no idea who had thought what.

He rolled over with her and reared just long enough to rearrange them.

Then, his body braced over her on muscular arms, he started working his cock into her. The sensation was so stunning, they both cried out at the sweet, sliding friction of skin on skin, hard into slick.

She wrapped both legs around him as he sank deeper and deeper. All the way to her heart.

At last he could go no farther. Panting, they clung together, his body hard and sweat-slicked against her small, soft one.

Knowing they'd both come if they moved, they froze like that, staring breathlessly into each other's eyes.

Lowering his head, Gawain kissed Lark slowly, lingering

over the taste of her mouth. She swirled her tongue between his lips in a teasing little caress.

It felt so damn good to hold him. To be held by him.

I could stay like this forever, she breathed in his mind.

I can't. His grin flashed. *My dick won't let me.*

Slowly he began to thrust, keeping it gentle though his body wanted nothing more than a hard, plunging ride. She stood it as long as she could before she had to start thrusting her hips, wanting more of him, faster.

Obeying her need, he lengthened his strokes, working deeper, harder. Lark curled her legs around his muscular backside and held on as the storm began to whirl again.

It seized them again in a delicious rush—the feeling of his cock in her core. Slick and hard, soft and tight, sensation volleying back and forth between them, each adding to the next.

His vampire appetite suddenly escaped his ruthless hold, and he dropped his head to her throat. Knowing what he needed, Lark threw her head back with a soft cry.

His fangs sank deep, deliciously stinging and hot. Gawain began to drink even as his hips worked.

She came, her entire body ringing with it like a bell, triggering his. Climax fed climax into a whipping firestorm. Distantly she felt herself scream, saw him lift his head to bellow.

It seemed they melted in the heat, fusing in a single great red pulse that went on and on.

Lark lay sprawled under his delicious weight, unable to move. Even thinking seemed too much effort in the slowly cooling aftermath of all that pleasure.

Finally, sensing that he was a little heavy for her, Gawain rolled over with a groan and pulled her on top of him. She sighed and collapsed, boneless as a dishrag.

She heard his lazy thought. *Looks like it's time for another Round Table wedding. Those are always fun.*

Lark's lips curled into a grin. "Why, Gawain, was that a proposal?"

He lifted his blond head and grinned at her. "Would you say yes if it was?"

"I think you know the answer to that."

"Yeah." His grin broadened. "As a matter of fact, I do." Suddenly the smile faded, and he searched her eyes with his. "I love you, you know."

"Yeah." She brushed back a lock of his hair. "As a matter of fact, I do."

"And?"

"And what?"

"You know."

"Know what?"

His green eyes began to glitter. "Do I have to tickle it out of you?"

Lark started to jerk away, but his powerful arms tightened. "Oh, no you don't!"

"Oh, yes I do." Long fingers found her ribs and dug in, forcing a shriek of laughter from her lips.

"I'm going to turn you into a frog!" she panted between giggles as he tickled her ruthlessly.

"Ribbet. Come on, Lark, say it out loud."

"I love you!"

His hands froze on her ribs, and the merry laughter in his eyes. "Yeah," he said, his voice hoarse. "That's what I thought. Say it again."

She twined her arms around his strong neck. "I love you. Love you, love you . . ."

He dragged her close.

Love you.

A week later, John McGuin gave the bride away before a delighted Magekind assembly. It was impossible for even Lark to tell whether he or Tristan was more shamelessly proud.

Kel, meanwhile, lost the ring and had to conjure a new one.

The moment Arthur pronounced Gawain and Lark husband and wife, the gathered Majae filled the air with a blinding display of magical fireworks.

Deep in their kiss, neither noticed.

Turn the page for a special preview of
Angela Knight's next novel

MASTER OF DRAGONS

Coming soon from Berkley Sensation!

It had been eight months since Diana London Galatyn had last turned into a werewolf, and she was getting grumpy. Her back ached constantly and she hadn't seen her own feet in three months, though she'd been told her ankles were swollen. Meanwhile, Prince Dearg Andrew Galatyn was bouncing up and down on her bladder, suggesting a serious case of ADD. She could almost hear the psychic *"Wheee!"*

Diana splayed her hands over her huge belly and tried to think happy thoughts at her womb. *Three weeks. Just three more weeks, Dearg, honey. Then you get to come out into the big, wide world where there's lots of room for you and your bony little elbows. And everybody will adore you as the first Sidhe prince born in a hundred years.* She smiled to herself a little grimly. *Best of all, Uncle Ansgar won't be trying to have you killed, because Uncle Ansgar is worm chow.*

Ansgar, her husband's vicious brother, had hated Llyr from the moment he was born. On his deathbed, their father, King Dearg, had made Ansgar king of the Morven Sidhe, and Llyr the king of the Cachamwri. Unfortunately, that hadn't been good enough for Ansgar, who wanted both kingdoms. Over the next sixteen hundred years, he engineered the assassination of Llyr's ten children and all four of his previous wives, but all his attempts on Llyr had missed.

Diana and Llyr had finally slain Ansgar during the last assassination attempt eight months ago. Now Llyr, like his father before him, was king of both the Morven and Cachawmwri Sidhe, and everybody in both kingdoms was a hell of a lot happier.

And Diana, werewolf and former city administrator of Verdaville, South Carolina, was trying to adjust to life as Queen of the Sidhe. Becoming immortal was cool, and God knew marriage to a gorgeous fairy had its perks, but the workload was killer.

The royal couple had spent the first six months of their reign in the Morven kingdom, trying to repair the damage Ansgar had done over the centuries of his rule. This morning, after a two-month visit to Cachamwri, Llyr had embarked on a surprise inspection of the Morven palace.

Diana and her ginormous baby belly had gone along, though at the moment, all she was really interested in was a place to sit. The scarlet court gown she wore was lovely with its gold embroidery and gems, but it weighed a ton. And God knew Prince Dearg was no lightweight. No wonder the small of her back felt like a rabid wolverine was chewing on a particularly tasty knot of muscles.

Unfortunately, there didn't seem to be a single chair in the armory. All the vast chamber did hold was an astonishing number of weird-looking swords, not to mention spears, armor, shields, and whatever the thing with all the spikes was. All of it was arranged on gleaming wooden racks or hung on the marble walls between elaborate carvings of battle scenes.

Diana's attention focused on one particular bas relief. Were those fairies killing a *dragon*?

Before she could waddle over for a closer look, her tall,

handsome husband turned his head to look at his Morven
Sidhe chief advisor. A snarl curled his regal lips. "Trivag,
where's my sword?"

Lord Trivag took a step back, his mouth rounding in an
O of dismay as he scanned the armory, apparently hoping
the offending weapon would magically appear. A lean, dis-
tinguished man with waist-length cobalt hair shot with
gray, he looked about sixty, which probably made him six
thousand or so. "My king, I know not! I inspected the armory myself just two days ago. It was here then."

Llyr flicked his opalescent gaze to the three Sidhe cur-
rently assigned to guard the armory. "So, did *you* notice
anyone strolling out with the Ghostsword?"

All three armory guards fell belly-down on the marble
floor with a clatter of malachite armor. "No, Your
Majesty!"

"It was here when I inspected yesterday," one dared in a
strained voice. He was probably the leader of the three,
judging by the long, blue horsehair tail thrusting from his
helm.

"Oh, for Cachawmri's sake, get up. I'm not Ansgar. I'm
not going to have you executed," Llyr snapped, so thoroughly annoyed he raked a big hand roughly through his
hip-length blond hair. Well over six feet tall, the king had
the lean, powerful build of a marathon runner. Even
dressed in a faintly Elizabethan black velvet doublet en-
crusted with jewels, with thick hose and tall boots, he was
the most thoroughly masculine man Diana had ever met.
He glowered at the three men as they scrambled to their
feet. "Organize a search party and find that dragon-cursed
sword before it possesses somebody."

Diana's eyebrows flew skyward as she turned to look at
her husband. "*Possesses* somebody?"

The girl was no older than fourteen or fifteen, with thin,
coltish blue jean–clad legs and a jaunty pink T-shirt that

read *Princess*. Her mascara had run down her cheeks, and her lipstick was smeared across her chin, probably from scrubbing her hand across her running nose. She made no sound as she cried, but her body shook so hard with sobs, she vibrated the auditorium seat she occupied. Every few minutes, she stole a frightened look up at the nasty piece of work who held her life in one hairy paw.

Gary Dover stood a few feet away in the front of the auditorium, talking to a police hostage negotiator on a cell phone. He was a big guy with a top-heavy prison gym–build whose gleaming bald head was tattooed with a swastika. As he ranted, he gestured wildly with the small stereo remote he held. Each time the remote came up, the six hundred students around him cringed visibly. "I want my fuckin' cocaine, man!" he snarled. "And if I don't get it back, every one of these little assholes is dead! We are gonna blow this whole fuckin' school!"

Kel looked up at him and thought, *I'm really looking forward to killing you.*

Wrapped in an invisibility spell, the newest Knight of the Round Table crawled down the auditorium aisle on his belly, following the oily scent of C-4. For the past hour, he'd been checking under every seat in the huge room, methodically disabling pipe bombs. It was nerve-wracking work, because if any of the kids felt his invisible body and jumped, they would all be blown to hell.

Dover and his ten cronies had seized control of J.R. Rollings High just before the final bell. The smaller of the four high schools in the rural county, it had evidently looked like an easy target.

The thugs had herded all the students and their teachers into the auditorium. They must have been in the building some time before then, though, since they'd managed to wire fifteen seats with explosives.

After sitting down, the hostages were told that if they moved, the motion-controlled bombs would go off. What's more, Dover's stereo remote would also trigger the devices, and he was threatening to use it if the sheriff's department didn't return his cocaine.

Apparently, Dover's gang had been in the process of smuggling several hundred kilos through town in an eighteen-wheeler when somebody's drug dog had caught a whiff during a traffic stop.

Dover had not been pleased at this disruption of his plans. Evidently, he had a customer waiting on the drugs who scared him a lot more than the death sentence he could face over this stunt.

Not that he was ever going to see trial. Kel fully intended to kill his ass.

Taking another testing sniff, Kel followed the scent of C-4 to the girl in the pink T-shirt. Craning his head to look past her skinny little legs, he peered up at the underside of her seat.

Sure enough, a length of plastic PVC pipe was duct-taped to the bottom. Brushing it with his magical senses, he realized there was enough C-4 in that pipe to kill the girl, Kel himself, Dover, and ten or fifteen of the surrounding kids. That was besides the crater it would blow in the floor.

Apparently, the gang had been stealing military ordinance on top of trafficking cocaine.

Kel shot Dover a savage look over his shoulder. *I'm going to take my time with you, jerkwad.* Setting his teeth, he returned his attention to the pipe bomb and concentrated, sending a wave of magic through it. In a heartbeat, the C-4 transformed into a hunk of inert polycarbons, as safe as a stick of butter.

How are we doing with the rest of the gang? Kel asked Gawain through the temporary psychic link they'd created for this mission.

Taking out the last one now, his friend replied. Through the link, Kel felt the sensation of a sword sliding into flesh, heard a muffled grunt and the sudden weight as Gawain caught the dying gunman and eased him to the ground.

But when Kel glanced up, there was no sign of any movement among Dover's thugs. They all seemed to be standing at their posts around the room, watching their hostages with flat eyes.

In reality, all ten were dead on the floor, victims of the knight's silent skill. Gawain's wife, Lark, had created the magical illusion that they all still stood in their places.

After seeing a live report about the standoff on CNN four hours into the crisis, Gawain, Kel, and Lark had magically transported themselves into the school. A frontal attack would have been a lot more satisfying than creeping around like this, but they couldn't risk it until each and every pipe bomb had been located and disarmed. If they missed even one, kids would die.

How about the bombs? Lark asked.

Kel sniffed, but the smell of C-4 was gone. *All done.* He'd been the logical candidate to disarm them because his nose was even more sensitive than his vampire friend's.

Good. We ready to take Dover down now? Gawain's mental voice dropped to a growl. *I'm getting really tired of that bastard.*

Kel glanced up at the thug, who was still in full rant.

"If I don't get my drugs, you gonna be scraping these kids into body bags!" Dover lifted his voice to a bellow. "And if you think I'm scared to die, you just try me! I got nothing to lose, asshole."

Above Kel's head, the girl in the pink shirt sobbed again.

Kel bared his teeth. *Oh, yeah, I'm more than ready. This jerk's ass is mine.*

Gawain laughed softly, echoed by his wife's rich chuckle. *He's all yours.*

Go get 'em, tiger, Lark purred.

Kel rose to his feet, simultaneously killing the lights with a spell. As the auditorium plunged into darkness and the hostages screamed, he lunged forward, grabbed Dover, and spun, hauling the man with him. The gang member cursed in shock and swung at him, fists thudding against his face and chest. Kel ignored the blows as he cast a dimensional gate and leaped through, dragging Dover after him.

As Kel disappeared, Lark switched the lights on again. She'd dropped the invisibility spell around herself and Gawain, as well as the illusions around the dead thugs. Now she and her husband stood on the auditorium stage dressed in hopefully official-looking black body armor.

Though students and teachers alike had screamed when the lights went out, none of them had dared move, too afraid of the threatened bombs. Now they stared at their rescuers, some crying, all white-faced with fear.

"Okay, kids, it's over," Gawain announced. "We've taken care of the bad guys. You can go home now."

Voices raised in astonishment. "What? What about the bombs?"

"Who the hell are you?" That demand came from the high school principal, a heavyset man in a wilted, wrinkled suit whose round face gleamed with sweat.

Lark hopped down from the stage, walked over to one of the seats and knelt to pull out a pipe bomb. She tossed it aside as she returned to her husband. "The bombs are fakes."

For a moment nobody moved or spoke. Then the students and teachers broke into a babbling roar of joyous relief. In the confusion, no one noticed Gawain and Lark step behind the dusty stage curtains and disappear again.

Kel felt magic rush over his skin in a tingling wave as the gate transported him and Dover to the Mageverse Earth. Located in a parallel universe where magic was a law of physics, it was a world inhabited by unicorns, magic-using Sidhe—and dragons.

Fist locked firmly in Dover's collar, Kel shot through the gateway's other side . . .

And into empty air.

Instantly, both men plunged downward toward the ground a long way below, wind whipping their faces. Kel heard Dover shriek, his voice high with panic-stricken terror.

With a grim smile, Kel transformed. In the blink of an eye, his body shook off its human appearance and returned to its true form, muscle and bone shifting and growing, great wings snapping wide and catching the air.

In dragon form, Kel turned their headlong fall into a swoop, beating his wings to carry them effortlessly skyward.

Dover looked up. Catching sight of Kel's inhuman muzzle silhouetted against the sky, the thug howled like a damned soul.

"Shut up!" Kel snarled, dragging the yowling gang boss up by the scruff. A puff of magical breath stole Dover's voice, rendering him instantly mute. "Listen to you, screaming like a little girl. Didn't you tell that cop you weren't afraid to die?"

Dover struggled in his hold, batting at his clawed hand, mindless with fear. Kel curled his lip and gave him a hard shake. "I saw the look on your face when you were strutting around in front of those terrorized kids, waving that damned remote. Made you feel like a real man, didn't it?" As he beat his wings, flying higher, he thrust his fanged muzzle close to Dover's. "How does it feel to be helpless in the grip of something a hell of a lot bigger and meaner? You like it, asshole?" Exhaling a breath of magic, he broke the spell keeping Dover silent. "Well?"

"Let me go!" Dover howled.

"You did what?" Gawain stopped in his tracks and stared at him in astonishment. In human form again, Kel had met

them back at Avalon, the magical city the Knights of the Round Table used as their base.

In human form again, Kel shrugged. "I let him go."

Lark gaped at him. She was a lovely woman, as petite and dark as her husband was big and blond. "Just like that?"

"Well, yeah." Kel smiled slightly. "Of course, we were a thousand feet up at the time . . ."

"*You dropped him?*" Lark's brown eyes widened in horror.

"Yeah." He remembered the terrified tears of the girl in pink. "I figure he made about as big a crater as one of his pipe bombs would have."

Lark winced. "You are not a nice man, Kel."

He shot her a look. "Sweetheart, I'm not a man at all."